Praise for
laura anne gilman

PARANORMAL SCENE INVESTIGATIONS

Hard Magic

"Gilman's deft plotting and first-class characters complement her agile blend of science and spell craft, and readers will love the *Mythbusters*-style fun of smart, sassy people solving mysteries through experimentation, failure, and blowing stuff up."
—*Publishers Weekly,* starred review

RETRIEVERS

Staying Dead

"An entertaining, fast-paced thriller set in a world where cell phones and computers exist uneasily with magic and a couple of engaging and highly talented rogues solve crimes while trying not to commit too many of their own."
—*Locus*

Curse the Dark

"Features fast-paced action, wisecracking dialogue, and a pair of strong, appealing heroes."
—*Library Journal*

Bring It On

"Ripping good urban fantasy, fast-paced and filled with an exciting blend of mystery and magic... this is a paranormal romance for those who normally avoid romance, and the entire series is worth checking out."
—*SF Site*

Burning Bridges

"Wren and Sergei's relationship, as usual, is wonderfully written. As their relationship moves in an unexpected direction, it makes perfect sense— and leaves the reader on the edge of her seat for the next book."
—*RT Book Reviews* [4 stars]

Free Fall

"An intelligent and utterly gripping fantasy thriller, by far the best of the Retrievers series to date."
—*Publishers Weekly,* starred review

Also available from

laura anne gilman

and LUNA Books:

Paranormal Scene Investigations

Hard Magic

Retrievers

Staying Dead
Curse the Dark
Bring It On
Burning Bridges
Free Fall
Blood from Stone

And later in 2011,
PSI
returns with

Tricks of the Trade

laura anne gilman

PACK OF LIES

LUNA™

www.LUNA-Books.com

LUNA™

PACK OF LIES

ISBN-13: 978-0-373-80324-8

Recycling programs for this product may not exist in your area.

www.LUNA-Books.com

Printed in U.S.A.

FEB 10 2011

Lisa: pour le voyage entre lectrice et amie

prologue

My name is Bonita Torres. I am an investigator with the Private Unaffiliated Paranormal Investigations team of New York. And I love saying that.

Funny, how life can change really fast. Eight months ago, I was an unemployed college graduate without a clue what I was going to do with my life. Seven months ago, PUPI was created out of the wild inspiration of Ian Stosser and his best friend, Benjamin Venec, and we—a team of five twentysomething Talent—were hired, green as grass and still wet behind the ears. Six months ago we solved a double murder, and earned the chance to show the rest of the Cosa Nostradamus, the magical community, what we could do.

A chance isn't acceptance, though. The Cosa is naturally suspicious, and there were still a lot of folk out there who didn't want us around, either because they didn't trust us, or they were afraid we'd find out what they'd been up to. And in New York City, believe me, there are a lot of people who are up to something. Magic's been *around forever, but mostly on the honor system for how you used it. And some Talent? Not the nicest people around, always.*

So we busted our tails, and learned as fast as we could, perfecting the spells we'd already created and crafting new ones to fit our training scenarios, wondering if we'd ever get a chance to use them. In the months since the Reybeorn murders, we'd gotten one missing person case that ended well, and an organ-stealing case that didn't, so we're going fifty-fifty. Not great, but the bills—and our paychecks—were getting paid. Barely. Maybe more to the point, I had a job that meant something to me, coworkers I liked, and I got to live in the Electric Apple, New York City, where I could work twelve hours and then play for seven, sleep five and do it all over again. Life was pretty good.

All we needed were a few more jobs to really get going, establish ourselves. The only problem was that even now that we'd showed the Cosa what we could do, nobody ever called us until it got ugly....

one

We were surrounded, outnumbered, and out of luck. I risked a glance at my partner, and saw the same desperation on his face. We needed to think of something, something brilliant, something *fast*.

Too late. There was a crack like thunder, lightning filling the entire room, and we both fell to the ground like someone slammed a two-by-four over our heads.

A deep male voice pronounced our doom. "You're dead. Also, stupid."

There really wasn't much to say to that. Of the four PUPIs in the room, Nick probably would have milked the death scene. Sharon would have argued her way into a second chance. Nifty wouldn't have been dead *or* stupid, probably.

Pietr and I lay on the floor and were dead. Also, stupid.

The deep voice continued. "Now. Can one of you surviving idiots tell me where your cohorts fucked up?"

The voice belonged to Benjamin Venec. Top-notch magical Talent, experienced private investigator, owner of a pair of gorgeously intense brown-black eyes, and, along with Ian Stosser, one half of the leadership of Private Unaffiliated Paranormal Investigations, also known as PUPI. Yeah, Puppy. The jokes just write themselves, and we'd already made most of them.

If we were PUPIs, though, Venec was Big Dog, and obedience school was in session. I loved my job, but this seriously was not my idea of how to start out a Monday morning, especially the Monday after my old college roommate's annual April Fool's Bacchanalia. My eyes felt like sandpaper, and I was cranky over more than getting killed. Even on a good day, I was emphatically not a morning person.

Since Venec had moved on to his next victims, I risked raising my face from the carpet to see who of the remaining three PUPIs was going to chime in first. What, as Venec was always asking, did the available evidence tell me? Nick's shoes needed polishing, and the way he was rocking back into his heels suggested he wasn't going to volunteer. Sharon had toed off her two-inch heels, and there was a run in her left hose. That was unlike her, and I wondered briefly what epic catastrophe had hit her wardrobe that morning. Also, she was humming under her breath. She only did that when she was stumped, and was trying to scramble for an answer.

That left only one person, but he was out of my line of sight.

"Mister Lawrence?"

His voice amused, our former college linebacker made the call. "They zigged when they should have zagged."

Pietr, his face still down on the carpet, made a rude noise. Venec kicked him in the ribs, gently, and he subsided. Dead puppies weren't supposed to talk back.

"Right," Venec said, his voice thick with disgust. "I stand corrected, you're all stupid. Dead bodies, off to the side. Sharon and Nick, you're up. Don't expect the attack to come in the same pattern. I'm not going to make it that easy for you."

Easy. Hah.

Pietr rolled over and jumped to his feet with annoying agility. Show-off. I sat up slowly, feeling my back crack in protest. Venec reached down and hauled me to my feet without taking his attention off the rest of the team, like he had some kind of sonar that told him where I was. Maybe he did: Venec was occasionally scary like that.

Benjamin Venec. Not much scared me, but I was willing to admit that this particular Big Dog could unnerve me occasionally. His hand was dry and strong, his fingers wrapping around my wrist with a casual familiarity. I was so tired, I guess my control wasn't as strong as it usually was, and the touch sent sparks—of the purely incendiary, nonmagical sort—through my veins. Hoo-cha.

I took the lift, and ignored the sparks with the strength of months of self-denial and fierce rationalization. Unnerving, in the sexually charged way. We'd been doing a weird sort of dance since the first day on the job, me and the boss man—well, me anyway. Venec played everything close to the vest, and I had no idea if he felt it, too.

From across the room, Nick caught my eye, and gave me a slight but unmistakable smirk.

Yeah, Venec was undeniably hot, if you liked the brilliant, dark-eyed, moody, remote sort, and I knew damn well that he felt some of those sparks, too. I'd been around that block a time or two before, and I could tell when someone was reacting. He was also the boss, and that was more important than any fireworks show. I might be dead and stupid, but I wasn't dumb. A bed partner was easy enough to find. A good job? Lots tougher. Especially for someone with our... call them *specialized* skills. I wasn't going to risk that, not for anything.

"Move the chairs over here. Lawrence, shove the chest into the middle of the room. No, more to the left." Venec was barking orders like a B-grade movie director, resetting the stage for the next test. Nifty and Pietr lifted and toted, while Sharon paced around the edges, checking the layout as it emerged and trying to get one step ahead of whatever Venec was going to throw at them.

I snorted. Good luck with that. We were all damned good, but we were damned good because Venec taught us to be. He still knew shitloads more than we did all put together, with a decade more experience, and there was no way to predict the way his brain was going to jump.

Ian Stosser, Venec's business partner and the public face for PUPI, was widely acclaimed to be brilliant. For my money, though, I'd place the bet on Benjamin Venec. Ian was a flashy thinker, but my mentor always told me to watch the quiet ones.

"Pay attention," Venec said sharply, and I jerked a little,

sure he was scolding me. But no, he was glaring at Nifty. Good. Nifty could use the occasional slap down to remind him he was only two-thirds as smart as he thought he was.

Everything was finally rearranged to the Big Dog's satisfaction. Out of the game, Pietr and I sat on the chairs now shoved against the far wall of the office conference room, while Nifty leaned against the wall like a bouncer on break, and we watched Venec put Sharon and Nick through their test.

Venec was re-creating a scenario we'd run into last week: lung-runners, illegal organ-leggers, working out of a warehouse on Staten Island. They'd been a mixed group, Null and Talent, operating off the grid—literally—so that law enforcement was having trouble finding them. The pirates used current to keep the tissue fresh until they found buyers, which was a particularly nasty bit of work, and exactly the kind of thing PUPI had been founded to track down: magic used in the commission of a crime.

The hospital the tissue had been stolen from had hired us on the recommendation of a Board member who was also a Talent—our first "corporate" client.

We'd followed the traces of current they left behind, and confirmed the site, catching them with a half-dozen coolers filled with stolen human tissue. We had meant to alert the cops to come in and arrest them, but things got a little messy, and then they'd been tacky enough to try to kill us, rather than surrendering or running away. Venec took it personally when someone tried to kill us. Especially since the bastards got away. The fact that we'd recovered the coolers and gotten enough information to put the lung-runners on the radar for more traditional investigations was enough to get us paid—but not enough to avoid one of Venec's lecture/training sessions. "Fail better" was probably tattooed on his ass somewhere.

The good thing was that we were just as fanatical about learning as he was about drilling this stuff into our heads and reflexes. That had been one of the requirements to become a PUPI—the desire to learn how to do something new, and do it *better,* instead of following the worn track.

Sharon had put her shoes back on, and was kneeling by the foam chest that was standing in for the medical cooler of tissue. Nick had her back, the way he should—good boy. Nicky-boy was really good at his specialization, but sometimes a little flaky outside that, and I'd had to remind him more than once to keep his eye on the game.

Venec stepped forward and raised his left hand, indicating the show was about to start.

I wished deeply for a bucket of popcorn, because once you're dead, and not worrying about what's going to hit you next or how you're about to screw up, Venec's fun to watch. He has what my mentor calls an economy of motion that tells anyone paying attention just how damn good he is at manipulating current. No muss, no fuss, no showboaty waste of energy, just results. You can learn a lot by watching carefully.

The fact that he was hot like a hot thing was just a distracting plus. I'm a red-blooded twentysomething female who hadn't had a date, much less sex with another person, in three months thanks to the demands of this new job and all it was throwing at us. I might only be able to look, in Venec's case, but look I would, and appreciate.

The subject of my ruminations dropped his hand, and a wall of current-fire rose around Sharon and Nick, pushing them away from the cooler. They shifted fast, standing back-to-back. There was no heat, but the sparks were sharp and bright, crackling in the air as Venec directed them with just a flicker of a glance. I almost lost track of what he was saying, watching the neon-bright strands weave through the air.

Current—magic—had one aspect that people always seemed to forget: it was *pretty*.

It was also dangerous, and Sharon and Nick were giving the strands their full and complete attention. Just because Venec was controlling it didn't mean it couldn't hurt them, as per our prime example a few minutes before. My skin still itched from the bolt that had taken us out.

"All right," Venec said, his deep voice patient, but still rock-hard. "You're in the middle of a warehouse, the perps have outsmarted you and backed you against the wall, and your evidence is across the room. What are you going to do?"

The wall of fire was new—Pietr and I'd gotten hit from above, suddenly, in a literal rain of energy—but it was the same question. What are you going to do? I leaned forward, waiting to see what bit of brilliance they came up with that had escaped us. I am, unabashedly, a geek about this sort of thing. We were inventing procedures as we went—magic had been around forever, but paranormal investigations as a formal, scientific, proof-oriented gig was something new—and I totally got off on it.

"Come on, people," Venec said, still patient. "Time's passing. Suspect's gonna flit on you."

"Let them flit," a new voice said.

The current-wall faded and flickered out, Venec's hand closing shut and pulling it back in a graceful movement, like a conductor halting the symphony, and we all turned to the door where the other Big Dog, our founder and public leader, leaned in the doorway. Where Venec was square-shouldered and dark, Ian Stosser looked like a beeswax candle—tall, skinny, and pale, topped with a long ponytail of orange-red hair that was too healthy-looking not to be natural. Today he was wearing a dark gray suit, tie still tied, which meant he'd been in a meeting and just gotten back.

"This had better be good, Ian," Venec said, but he wasn't even half as cranky as he sounded. Stosser wouldn't have interrupted unless it was important.

"We have a case."

That was important.

Our office was on the seventh floor of a seven-story building far enough uptown in Manhattan to be decidedly untrendy in a neighborhood nobody was going to mistake for Park Avenue. We didn't get so many visitors that we had to worry about appearances, and not being in midtown suited me just fine, although it was a hell of a commute for Sharon, coming up from Brooklyn. The Guys had used the correlating savings in rent to rent a second suite, once they knew we were going to stick around, and restructured our half of the floor into a warren of workrooms and meeting spaces that gave the illusion of privacy.

Location and privacy were important.

PUPI had a problem that most small start-ups didn't face: We were routinely tossing around a lot of current during training. Current, the source of our magic, ran alongside electricity like horses in a herd, and sometimes they did the dominance thing. When that happened...well, you learned to be careful, and work as far away from delicate electronics as you could.

Going out into the forest for privacy the way they used to in the Bad Old Days wasn't really feasible, though—Central Park was just as wired as SoHo these days, anyway, and having a bunch of twentysomethings spellcasting in public might raise an eyebrow or two. Or maybe not; this was New York City, after all. Venec liked to keep our training in the office, though, so the Guys had modified the wiring when they did the other renovations to make sure that we didn't short out the entire building's electrical system, no matter what we threw at it.

But while we did most of our training in the largest workroom, and almost all the casual gatherings in the break room—where, not coincidentally, the coffeemaker lived— the briefings were held in the smallest office at the far end of the hall where Ian Stosser now held court.

We didn't have many meetings here—maybe one a month—but we'd already established a routine, doing a subtle push-and-shove to get at the three armchairs that fit in the space in front of Ian's desk. As usual, Nifty claimed the largest one, since he held on to the muscled bulk that had made him such a hot draft prospect in college. Sharon claimed the other on the basis of a short skirt not really suited for sitting on the floor, and Pietr ghosted into the third chair in that spooky way he had before anyone saw him moving.

Nick and I were relegated to sitting on the floor. Again. Thankfully I'd opted for black cargo pants and a black hip-length sweater today, in honor of the still-raw April weather outside. Spring in New York City was better than spring in Boston, but not by much. I tucked my legs up in front of me, elbows on my knees, and watched while Venec took his usual spot, holding up the wall behind Stosser's desk.

Ian Stosser and Benjamin Venec. The Big Dogs. The two men were an interesting contrast, and not just physically. Even after all these months, we didn't know much about Benjamin Venec, who was a closemouthed bastard when he wasn't tearing us new ones in the name of keeping us smart and alive, but Ian Stosser was—on the surface—an open book. High-placed in the Midwest Council once upon a time, he had made a very public break with them about a year ago. A few months after that, he came to the East Coast with the idea of holding Talent—both Council and the Unaffiliateds, or lonejacks—accountable for criminal misbehavior of magic. To do that, he created PUPI.

Why? What had happened in Chicago to send him here? That was where the book closed and not even my mentor, a man of considerable high-level connections himself, could get a read.

With Stosser's reputation, and the tendency of some Talent to misuse their skills, you'd think people would welcome us with open arms, glad that someone was there to ferret out wrongdoers...not exactly. The first few months we'd been open for business had been tough. Not everyone in the *Cosa Nostradamus* thought having us poking our noses into magical crimes was the best thing since sliced bread. Stosser's own sister was opposed to the very idea of PUPI, enough that she tried to get us shut down by any means possible.

Having the office rewired had saved us when one of those means, involving a current-strike against the building, coincided with the killer we were trying to take down deciding to take us on directly. Saved us—but not a teenage boy who had been in the elevator when the rest of the building went off-line.

I still occasionally had nightmares about that.

In the eight months since the boy died, and Little Sister had been disciplined, nobody had taken potshots at us—physical or magical. We'd even gotten a few jobs; a jewelry heist, the organ-legging gig, but that didn't mean we were wanted yet, or trusted. We had to do everything perfect just to be considered acceptable, and never mind that what we were doing—creating investigative tools that gave measured and quantified results out of a naturally chaotic and individualized power source—was totally made up as we went along. No pressure, right. I knew for a fact that Sharon was developing an ulcer, and I'd started chewing my fingernails again.

And all that got us here, waiting in Stosser's de facto office, hoping that this might be the job to finally break that last hesitation, and make us legitimate.

Venec closed the door behind us, for some reason—if

someone Translocated into the office, we'd have bigger problems than them overhearing us—and Stosser dropped the news.

"No time to give you a full briefing—this one's hot, and might get hotter. But for once, somebody with a bit of authority used their brains instead of their hair spray, and had us called in right away, so we have a chance to actually pull something off the scene." Ian paused, his gaze meeting each of us in turn, assessing us the way he always did, like he was ready to demand the impossible. "It's hot, and it's ugly. A girl was attacked early this morning, downtown, an attempted rape. Her companion murdered one of the assailants and partially disemboweled the other."

I could feel Nick, who was sitting beside me, shudder a little, although I wasn't sure which of the events caused him to react that way. I wasn't exactly cackling with glee at this assignment, either. Murder was… I wasn't jaded, but I'd seen a lot of death already. Rape? Okay, that was a trigger-point for any female, no matter how tough you were, but he'd said *attempted* rape. The disembowelment…that was, um, new. And carried a nasty visual I wanted very badly to get rid of. Thanks, boss.

Behind Stosser, Venec's heavy gaze held steady, but there was a twitch over his left eye that gave it away. Big Dog was a hard-ass, but I knew from personal experience that there was actual give-a-damn under that bastardized exterior.

"So why'd we get called in? I mean, if they caught the guy, and it was obviously self-defense or near enough…" Nifty was asking the practical question, beating Sharon to the punch. We were, in theory, all equal to each other, but like any pack there were alphas and omegas, and those two competed for lead the same way they fought for the chairs, using every angle they had short of stomping over each other. Sometimes I thought it was just Venec's glare that kept the stomping from happening. It wasn't that they didn't like each other—they did. We all got along fine. They were just fierce competitors; stomping was what they did for fun.

"You're right," Stosser said. "It should have been an open-and-shut case, none of our business, except for two things." He paused, as though he was trying to choose his words carefully. Anything that made Ian Stosser hesitate was not going to be pretty. I braced myself, mentally.

"One, both the victim and the perps are Talent—" someone snorted, Talent being no proof against being a scumbag "—and two, the accused killer is a ki-rin."

That made the room go quiet. I felt something catch in my chest: not pain, but something fierce and hot. A ki-rin. Dear god and a merciful universe, a ki-rin, here, in the city. A ki-rin, accused of murder.

I suddenly understood why things moved so fast on this one—and why we were called in. If anything went wrong, we were going to take the fall.

"This needs to be as clean and as tight as a waterproof drum," the boss man said, standing up, his words confirming my fears. "I want everyone on this, right now. So let's move, people."

We moved.

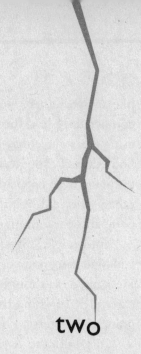

two

Normally we didn't all haul ass to a site—we didn't really have a normal yet, even after eight months—but Stosser had indicated all of us, and so all of us went.

Well, all but one. "You take them," Venec said to Ian as we grabbed coats and kits out of the closet and headed for the door. "I'll see what I can drag out of the unusual suspects."

Overhearing that made me feel better about this case. Based on the rather interesting individuals he brought in to lecture us on lock picking, surveillance, scams, and other things your mother wouldn't want you to know, Venec had collected an assortment of contacts in various low places. When we got back, I'd lay money that he'd have a full dossier on anything and everything there was to know about the people involved, even better than the official files.

Stosser looked like he was going to argue, then nodded

instead. He wasn't happy about it, though, and shoved us into the elevator with a look on his face that made us all hush our usual chatter. Not that anyone was feeling much in the way of wisecracks. Organ-leggers lent themselves to the bad jokes, the more disgusting or punny the better. Attempted rape and actual disembowelment, not so much. Add in a ki-rin… We were all quiet, locked in our own thoughts, in the time it took to get to the lobby and out to the avenue.

There was an SUV with TLC plates already waiting out-side our building. Obviously the boss had made some calls before he brought us in. Stosser got shotgun, the rest of us were in back, elbow-to-rib and knee-to-knee. The car came with a manic driver who swung through the morning traffic like he'd been a Shanghai cabbie in another life, shoving us around even as packed-in as we were. Nobody complained. The subway might have had more room, but it would have taken too long. Since we opened our doors for business, the main problem had been that we weren't called in until after everyone else had tromped all over the scene and made things harder for us to sort out. Today, we'd been given time to get in and take a look while things were clean…but the clock was ticking and the twenty minutes it took us was nineteen minutes too long.

I sat back in the seat, stuck in the middle, trying to ignore Nifty's elbow hitting my ribs, and Nick's cheap, toxic cologne in my nose, while Sharon and Pietr got the very back seat with all our kits. Four basic black hardcases and one bright red one: Pietr's, as though to make up for his unwanted but useful ability to disappear when you were looking straight at him. Sharon had added a discreetly stylin' silver tag to hers, and mine had a glittering 3-D ice-spider decal on the side, just where anyone looking to steal it would see it and be freaked out. Nifty and Nick didn't bother with anything, far as I could tell.

I stared up at the ceiling as we zoomed through lights that were yellow-turning-red, trying not to guess at what we were going to find on the scene. The trick to scene investigations was to look without expecting to find anything, examine without assumption. Current was directed by what we desired; even without the words of a spell, you could possibly create something just by assuming strongly enough that it was there.

Or so Venec warned us, at least twice a week.

The driver let us out on the corner, and zoomed off like he had to be in Queens three seconds later. The minute we got out, I was shivering inside my coat, but it wasn't because of the sharp wind coming off the river. Something had walked over my spine, and that was never a good thing. I had a slight touch of precog, what my mentor J called "the kenning," and it told me this was a bad place to be. Bad things happened here.

No choice, though. This was the job: investigating bad things.

The others were already walking toward the scene, and I had to stretch my legs to catch up. We weren't the only ones interested; there was a small crowd already gathered around the scene of the attack, maybe twenty people, and even from the street you could tell that the mood was not good. Sometimes there was a weird party atmosphere when people rubbernecked a crime scene. Not here. I could practically smell the current on them, crackling like ozone, and I knew the rest of the team was getting the same vibe: Talent, wanting to know why another Talent was dead, and a second wounded, at the hands—horn—of a fatae.

Normally interactions between fatae and humans in the *Cosa Nostradamus* were cautious but healthy, but something like this… I didn't need Stosser's warning still ringing in my ears to know that things would get a lot worse, and fast, if we didn't get the evidence sorted and delivered, soon.

I wondered, suddenly, why so many Talented bystanders were here. Coincidence? Or had someone put the word out, in the time it took for us to get called in? And if so…why, and who?

Questions I didn't have answers for, yet.

Someone in the crowd noticed our arrival, and a low mutter went up, like the first roll of thunder. Hot and ugly. Ian had it on the nose.

Stosser had already given the crowd a once-over, and was issuing orders. "Cholis. Run the tape. Lawrence, crowd-watch."

"On it, boss," Nifty said, and he and Pietr moved toward the crowd, walking like men with purpose. The tape wasn't the yellow crime-scene tape so beloved of Null cops, but a thin red extrusion of current that flickered and snapped in the cold air as they spun it out, walking a circuit around the scene. The tape was invisible to Nulls, but warned Talent and fatae alike away from the investigation. If they trespassed, Pietr, our rope-man, would know.

"Hey!" Pietr scowled at a lanky figure that brushed against the wire leaning in to get a better look. "Back off!"

"Or what, little man?" The intruder—your basic suburban white-boy macho wannabe in clothing too expensive to be tough—loomed over Pietr, who seemed to almost fade from sight, the way he did when stressed. There was an instinctive urge to go to Pietr's defense, but I checked it. We would all be given our particular assignments, and that wasn't mine. Nicholas James Lawrence wasn't all that big, for an ex-college linebacker, but he presented like a big-ass mofo when he wanted to. Nobody threatened a coworker when Nifty was around.

Satisfied that the guys had things in-hand, I turned my attention back to the boss. Ian's long orange-red hair was covered by a black wool watch cap, making him tougher to identify at a distance. I wasn't sure if that was intentional or not, since he was normally a flamboyant publicity-magnet. Oh, hell, Ian never did anything unintentionally. He was letting us go public, and playing it close and quiet himself. Interesting. Not useful, right now, but interesting.

"How virgin is the scene?" I heard the word come out of my mouth and winced. I'm not normally big on tact, but that had been particularly ill-chosen even for me.

Stosser didn't even seem to notice, although Sharon's cheek twitched a little in response. "Thankfully, one of ours was with the first responders, and was quicker on the draw than most of his peers. Paramedics took the human bodies, but the cops haven't gone over the scene yet." A grim smile touched his face. "New York's finest decided to wait for someone to come down and take care of the ki-rin before they approached the scene itself, so the area's about as untouched as we're going to get."

I couldn't blame the cops—I wouldn't want to deal with a ki-rin in a bad mood, either.

"Not that there's any doubt of who did what," Stosser went on, "but I am informed that the fatae community's already screaming for blood—more blood, I mean. They don't like that a ki-rin's been shown disrespect, disrespect being anything other than kissing its hooves in abject adoration."

Wow. That was the bitterest I'd ever head the boss man get. Normally he left the snide comments to Venec.

"What kind of blood do they want?" Nick asked.

"Who the hell knows." He seemed to remember he was talking to staff, not himself, and I saw the usual cool exterior go back up. "Our contact thinks the fact that there was any investigation by Nulls at all set them off. They're already demanding that the ki-rin be released, and nobody's even questioned it yet.

"The one thing everyone agrees on is that this needs to be cleared up and closed down as soon as possible, if not sooner. That means we have to determine exactly what happened, who did what, and in what order."

"That's what you built us to do," I said. And then, since he hadn't really answered me before, I prompted him again. "The scene?"

Stosser looked up at the sky, checking the thickness of the clouds. Normally we—Talent—like storms, since electrical storms are natural generators of current, but rain right now would seriously screw things up by compromising the scene. Magical trace washed away the same as physical, especially if there's lightning involved—current from the electric bolts could wipe the slate clean in one flash—and being wet made me look like a drowned albino rat.

"Like I said, reasonably untouched, for NYPD values of reasonable. Ground's been trampled by a couple-three cops, one of whom is our first-responder lonejack."

Poor guy must have shit a brick when he saw the ki-rin, and realized what he'd gotten. Ki-rin were not only rare, they were *ancient,* as a breed. Like dryads and greater dragons, they were given respect by every other fatae breed, and any Talent with a lick of sense or tradition. We were lucky our first responder didn't panic, and luckier still that he called the Council, and not one of the lonejack elders. The *Cosa Nostradamus*'s relationship with the NYPD is a long and fragmented one, but something like this was going to get every alarm jangling everywhere, and the Council—much as a lonejack would hate to admit it—was the best way to handle things. Council had the protocol.

"We have a signature on the cop?" Signature was the way we identified Talent, the way their current "felt." It was individual, like a fingerprint—but you had to know what it looked like, first. Problem was there wasn't a database for us to check, which mostly made identifying a particular signature near-impossible unless we had access to everyone on the scene, to tag them for comparison, and rule them out of any evidence we collected.

"Not yet. Nick, go find and fetch."

Nick rolled his eyes, then saluted crisply, and turned on his heel and headed out into the crowd. That left me and Sharon.

"The deceased has been carted off to the morgue, while

his companion is on his way to the hospital, presumably doped to the gills." That was standard for Talent in those situations—current is only under our control by conscious effort: when stressed, we can go haywire. Pietr was unusual in that he faded from view as a protective measure—most of us just shorted out sensitive electronics like, oh, life-support systems and finely calibrated medical apparatuses. Emergency-room staff hated to see us coming.

Ian went back to issuing orders. "Mendelssohn, I want you working the crowd. Listen, don't talk. If there's anyone out there with more than a prurient interest, or says any-thing—anything—that gives you a twitch, I want to know, immediately." While the Guys had us stretch in training, or on low-intensity cases, when we were on a sticky job they preferred to match people up with their native skills, and Sharon had a seventh sense about if people were lying or not. My teammate, characteristically stylish in a long black suede coat and a black wool beret over her blond hair, nodded and went off to do our master's bidding

And that left me. And the scene. No surprise. I didn't need to hear the band playing to know what my marching orders were.

"You okay with this?" Ian generally played the compas-sionate soul to Venec's hard-ass, but he really wasn't much on the touchy-feely when it came to us, more likely to toss us in without a by-your-leave. I blinked at his concern, wondering what triggered that, and then shrugged it off. No way I was going to make him think I couldn't handle it.

"Yeah. I'm okay."

He lifted the wire, the spell recognizing his signature and not sending an alarm, and we entered the crime scene.

Like I said, everyone on the team had their strength. If Sharon was a truth-scryer, I was a gleaner. I figured that my recall, both visual and factual, was one of the reasons I'd been recruited. Venec had run me through endless tests and scenarios, honing that ability and tying it into a cantrip we used to capture the scene intact. They'd tried, first, to teach everyone the spell—that hadn't worked out well. So unless it was an emergency, it was just me. My job here was to walk the scene, gathering as much information as I could, both physical and magical, and re-create it later for the rest of the team to study.

Since joining PUPI, I'd gleaned murder scenes, dipped into the minds of pathological abusers, and—Venec's idea of training—skimmed the hot emotions of a rabid Salamander. Reading the scene of a self-defense killing where we knew the identity of all the players should have been a piece of proverbial.

Except the guy'd been killed because he'd tried to rape a ki-rin companion. Scum, *and* stupid, and I was not looking forward to getting my mental fingers into what that left behind.

That thought drew my attention to what Stosser had said, about the NYPD not wanting to touch the scene until the ki-rin had been dealt with. What sort of trace did a ki-rin leave behind? I let my gaze pass over the scene, looking and yet not looking, and found myself noticing a shadowed corner near one of the riverside buildings about a hundred yards from the scene where two men—older, suited, officious-looking, and couldn't be more obviously Council if they'd had it branded on their left buttocks—had the accused killer contained.

My breath caught in my throat, despite my determination not to be impressed. I'm hardly a country bumpkin, but a ki-rin…my god. One of the most exotic and magnificent of the fatae, the nonhumans. They're sometimes called Asian unicorns, but that was so far off the mark to be useless. A unicorn was a horse with a horn and an attitude. The ki-rin were… It was too far away to see details, but I knew the description, same as any halfway-trained Talent. Body of a stag, mane of a lion, head of a dragon—and yeah, a single slender horn growing from the center of the dragonlike head. Wise, fierce, compassionate, truth-seeking…and, like European unicorns, associating only with women of untouched virtue.

Okay, obviously I wasn't going to get close-up and personal with one anytime soon. Considering the sole example present was currently pacing back and forth, making the suits with him display some seriously cautious body language, that was fine by me. Some glorious legends could remain legend.

It did make me wonder about the sexual experience of the guys talking to it, though, and—more to the investigation— why they were keeping it there instead of whisking it off… somewhere. Especially if the fatae community already had their knickers in a twist about anyone questioning it. Oh. Oh, no…

"We don't have to…" I asked Stosser, with a twitch of my fingers in the ki-rin's direction.

He followed my fingers, and shook his head. "No."

"Good." Because if the local looky-loos were upset about it being asked to step aside while the scene was cleared, I didn't want to think about what they'd do to the person who actually interrogated it.

That left one unpleasant bit still to be done. "You going to…interview the woman?"

She'd been taken to the local hospital—the same one her accused assailant was currently being treated in—and released. But we needed her statement, before things got even more muddled in her head.

"I thought that would be best," he said.

Understatement. Ian Stosser was the public face of PUPI not only because he was the founder, but also because he was a PR schmoozer par excellence. He looked you in the eye and every bit of his compassion and empathy and intelligence was focused on you, your problem, and he existed only to solve that problem for you. It was not entirely a sham—he did care, and he did want to solve the problem, otherwise he would never have gotten into this line of work. But Ian could and would kick it up a notch or seven. In a word: charisma. Natural, and magical. But he was also a bulldog when he was after something, as we knew to our own bruises.

"Yeah. Boss?"

He paused, one narrow red eyebrow cocked under that stupid watch cap.

"The girl…" I wasn't quite sure what I wanted to say. Actually, I knew exactly what I wanted to say, I just wasn't sure how to do it without getting fired.

He showed his teeth in a reassuring smile, a Stosser specialty. "I'll be gentle, Torres. Get to work."

With that, Stosser headed off for, I presume, the hospital. I watched him disappear into the crowd, then turned back to look over the scene. He was right: Time for me to do what I did, before anyone muddied the scene, or the cops came back and kicked us out, or anything else came along to make the job tougher.

I hesitated a moment, looking over the ground. We were down in what had once been the meatpacking district, alongside the Hudson River. It'd been prettied up over the past few years, and the city had put in walkways and greenery so during the summer it was a nice enough place to skateboard or bike, or walk your dog, but on an overcast, blustery almost-but-not-quite-yet spring day? Not so nice. Why had they been out here before dawn? A ki-rin wasn't the sort to club it up…but he wouldn't be able to say no to his companion, I bet. She might not be having sex, but that didn't mean she couldn't like to dance.

So. Run through the probable scene, capture the details, gather the pieces. I turned slowly, letting my gaze take in the entire area. The woman and her companion, maybe flushed and tired after a night out, had been walking along the path, there. It's not quite dawn, the visibility's crap, maybe some of the streetlamps flickered or went out. They're talking, maybe laughing, maybe arguing. Had she been drinking, drugging? Ki-rin companions were virgins, but I never heard they had to be pure every other way, too. And who knew what a ki-rin did for entertainment. So. Maybe not too steady on all six legs, maybe not seeing so well, and they came up to the building there, where the shrubs were planted, and...two men had...approached them? Jumped out at them?

I cast another glance over to where the two Council flunkies had been. As though they'd heard me wondering, they were now leading the ki-rin away, flanking it like a suited honor guard, to where a small trailer-van had pulled up to the curb. The ki-rin was smaller than they looked in pictures, with a pattern of marks on its linen-white neck that didn't look natural—bruises, maybe, or current-burns? A Null, someone who couldn't use current, didn't know about the fatae, might have been confused in the predawn light, might have thought that it was a really large dog, or maybe the girl was walking alongside a pony, or something. Or maybe not even seen it, if they were completely Null. That happened, sometimes: Something in a Null's brains just refused to acknowledge the presence of the supernatural, even when it was right in front of them, like not being able to see blue or green: current-blind.

A Null might not have seen it. The would-be rapists had been Talent, both of them. A Talent, ignoring the presence of a ki-rin? Impossible. Insane. Maybe they were high, or drunk, or...

Staring at the landscaping wasn't going to tell me anything, and we only had a small window before the NYPD came back to reclaim the scene. Time to stop avoiding, and do my job.

I took a deep breath, then let it out. "Ten. Nine. Eight. Seven..." In the exhale, I sank into myself, burrowing down into my core, gathering my magic to me.

During my mentoring period, J told me that everyone saw their core differently; for me, it was a tangle of threads and cables, neon-bright blues and greens and yellows. Personal magic, gathered from external sources and hoarded; like a tank of gas, if you ran out you were screwed.

For once, I had more than enough current gathered and stored; the trick was to control it, make it do what you wanted and only what you wanted. As I counted down from ten, I closed my eyes and pushed the soles of my boots firmly against the asphalt of the jogging track. My body was still, but my current was reaching down, finding the bedrock deep underneath, grounding in that solid base. That allowed me to use more current without worrying about affecting anyone around me—or, hopefully, their electronics.

When I opened my eyes again, deep in a working fugue-state, it was as though someone had dropped a scrim over the stage, and rolled back time to just before dawn. It wasn't real—but it was, too. Places hold memories, same as people. Not for long, and they're easily scattered and corrupted, but if you're fast and good, you can capture it. Like spirit pho-tography, Ian had said during training, only I was doing it with current instead of light-sensitive paper and chemicals. I could see, using mage-sight, the splatters of blood and other bodily fluids like Day-Glo paint on a gray background, and felt my stomach do a slow roll-and-turn. I didn't want to see this, I didn't want to see this, I didn't…

Enough. Everyone else was doing their thing; I wasn't going to go back to Stosser and tell him I couldn't hack it, after all. A hard shove set aside the whining inner voice, and a sort of Zen calm settled over my core. That was another thing that made me good at my job; like Pietr, I didn't get staticky and disruptive when my emotions were involved. I got very, very precise.

Ideally I'd let the scene play out in real time, getting it with my eyes as well as my senses. I could faintly hear the rumble of voices outside that suggested the guys in blue were back, and I needed to be gone. Just because we'd been called in didn't mean we had any actual authority, and pressure would come down soon enough to get all this dealt with.

I did a hard-and-fast scoop, pressing everything I could find into a strand of current, and sealing it away so the rest of my own personal memories or emotions couldn't tamper with it. Hopefully. We were still working out some of the kinks in that particular procedure.

"Miss?"

I opened my eyes to see a cop—maybe a few years older than me, clean-shaven and anxious-looking—staring down at me. Rookie, probably, sent over to get rid of the pretty little girl, while his partner did the real work. "I'm going to have to ask you to leave, miss. This..."

"Yeah, it's okay," I said. He had a faint telltale glint, seen with fugue-sight, that told me he was Talent, and so he probably-maybe knew who I was and what I was doing there. Or maybe not; just because you could didn't mean that you did. There were a lot of Talent who ignored anything magical. Lonejacks especially didn't care, if it didn't affect them directly and personally.

Either way, I wasn't going to give him cause to get annoyed. Our window had slammed shut. I gave my "packet" a mental touch, just to reassure myself it was there, and got lost.

★ ★ ★

There wasn't much point to waiting around for the others to finish up; they'd do their job and get back to the office when they were done. I walked over to the nearest 1 line stop and caught the next train uptown, keeping myself as still and focused as I could, the magical equivalent of walking with a glass of water on your head. Only if I "spilled," it would contaminate the entire gleaning and ruin our only record of the scene, and every minute I spent with it inside me, the greater the chance of contamination.

Not that anything I picked up was admissible in the court of law, even perfectly preserved, but we didn't exactly deal with the courts, or law, as most of the world knew it. We were of the *Cosa,* for the *Cosa,* and the *Cosa* determined what—if any—punishment would be handed out, based on what we reported. That was why the "Unaffiliated" part of "Private Unaffiliated Paranormal Investigations" was so important. The *Cosa* entire wasn't exactly filled with love and trust: Council looked down at lonejacks, lonejacks sneered at Council, and the fatae thought most humans were jumped-up Johnny-come-latelies, Talent only a little bit better. And what most Talent thought of the fatae could be summed up in two words: treacherous bastards. Have you read a fairy tale lately? Not the Disney kind; the real stuff. Even the good fairies are not the type you'd invite in for tea.

I no sooner had the thought than I looked up and had my attention caught by a good-looking guy sitting across the train from me, slouched in his seat, leather jacket nicely scruffed and jeans worn white in interesting places. While normally I'm all about the good-looking bad boy—or, occasionally, girl—I shook my head and smiled, to his obvious disappointment. The gills at the side of his neck were a dead giveaway, if you knew what you were looking for. Pickups were all well and fun, but I'd learned my lesson about playmates on office time. Anyway, mer-folk weren't my thing. Sardine-breath was a total turnoff.

Although it was reassuring to know that some human/fatae relations were still going strong.

The subway dumped me out at my stop, and I emerged into a distractingly normal scene: bright sunshine and busy traffic; people going in and out of the stores and buildings that lined our street. There were only two teenagers lounging on the stoop of the building next to ours—either the usual gang had decided to go to school today, or they'd gotten jobs. I gave the two a distracted wave, but didn't pause for our usual exchange of friendly catcalls.

I was buzzed into our lobby by the current-lock the Guys had put there to let team members in without needing to worry about a key, and took the stairs slowly, feeling the burn in my legs. We had an elevator, but I didn't like using it. It wasn't fear, or guilt, exactly. None of us used it anymore, unless Stosser herded us into it, like he had this morning. There were bad vibes in that shaft. And the exercise was good for me, anyway. Current burned calories, but it didn't build muscles.

"Anyone home?"

The office was quiet, and the coffeemaker was turned off; two signs that I was the first back. Where the hell was Venec? It was almost lunchtime; maybe he had run out to get a sandwich? If so, I hoped he brought back extras: I suddenly realized that I was starving. There was a bodega on the corner that made a fabulous meatball grinder, if he hadn't brought in food....

I dumped my coat in the front closet, and ran my fingers through my hair, trying to fluff it up. It was cut short again, curling around my ears, and was my normal wheat-blond color, for now. I had been contemplating going back to bright red, but the almost translucent whiteness of the kirin's mane stuck in my head, and I started to wonder if it was time to bleach it all out again....

"And spend half a year waiting for your hair to recover? Maybe not." I used to change my hair color the way Nick changed his socks—once every week or so—but bleaching wasn't one of my favorite pastimes.

Even as I was debating styles with myself, I was moving down the carpeted hallway, the weight of my gleanings a solid, unwelcome presence in my brain. Food, hair, everything my brain was churning over was just a distraction. I didn't want the gleanings in there any longer...but I wasn't exactly looking forward to the unloading, either. I loved my job, but I hated this part.

The room next to Ian's office was the best-warded one; the walls had been painted a soothing shade of off-white, and the pale green carpet everywhere else had been pulled up and bamboo flooring put down. There was a single wooden table and a single wooden chair in the room, and nothing else. I closed the door behind me, and leaned against it, trying to let my center settle itself.

"Seal and protect," I said, triggering the wards we had set

up to keep things inside the room inside the room. Once I felt the wards click into place, I pulled out the chair and sat down at the table.

Wood. Everything in our office was wood or plastic; no metal if it could be avoided. Wood didn't conduct current the way metal did, which meant we didn't have to be quite so careful all the damned time. I placed my hands down on the surface, my palms sweaty against the varnish, and exhaled.

"All right," I said to the packet inside me, reaching down with a gentle mental urge. "Come on out and show me what we've got."

We'd originally tried to create a virtual lockroom for things we pulled from scenes, both magical trace and physical debris. It worked great on the deposit, but got corrupted whenever someone tried to access it. We still hadn't licked that problem. This dump-and-display was something that Stosser and I had invented out of old spells and new needs. Some of the stuff the team came up with worked, and some didn't. We had to be flexible, adapt. Find better ways to fail, and then find a way not to fail.

Visuals were the easiest to process and share. Anyone could do it, theoretically. In practice, not so much. Nick and Sharon both made a total hash out of every try on their own, Pietr was around sixty-five percent, and even Nifty only got about eighty percent of each gleaning back in one piece.

I had a consistent ninety-three percent return rate on visuals, and a decent eighty-two percent on the other senses. That was why, no matter what happened in practice, it was me in the barrel, every time, and the hell with everyone taking turns.

Basically, the cantrip used current to create a permanent, three-dimensional display of the visual record I had garnered, sort of like what a computer would generate using pixels, only it was running off the electrical and magical impulses of my brain. The only problem was that, although the image would be here, in the room, I'd still be the one hosting it. The echo would still be in my brain until we dumped the gleaning entirely and I could detox, which generally required a full dose of current, a pitcher of margaritas, and a very hot shower.

I wasn't all that thrilled with my gray matter being used in that way, but Stosser swore it wasn't doing any permanent damage, and so far it seemed to be working. Whatever worked, we used.

It wasn't something I was going to tell my mentor about, though. J had let me hunt for the truth about my dad's murder when I was a teenager, had seen how much the simple fact of knowing what had happened to Zaki set me free. He was coming to terms with what I did, the physical and magical risks, but that didn't mean he liked it, and he'd like this bit of current-risk even less. J's always—some part of him—going to see me as the kid he took under his wing, someone he needs to protect. So, for the first time in my life, I wasn't telling him everything.

I sat back, relaxed as much as I could, and closed my eyes. The current-camera rolled, the virtual film unreeled, and the figures took form in front of me, one-third of the size but every bit as real. The shiver I'd had at the scene intensified, until it racked my entire body, a seemingly endless rolling wave of cold rippling along my skin. I'd known it was going to happen, it happened every time, even in training, which was why I was doing this alone. Unloading *sucked*.

The problem was, you couldn't disengage from what you gleaned, not after you took it inside. Visuals, sound, magical trace, it all carried emotional residue—a thousand tiny fish-hooks that caught at you. We'd learned that the hard way, going in to gather trace on murder victims during our first case. Then, we'd gotten caught up in the last moments of the victims' lives, almost been swamped by the experience. We'd refined the process since then, so it was an external view only that kept the hooks to a minimum. What we missed in information we avoided in agony and near-death. I was all about that.

Freaky shivers, I could live with.

The image flickered with the current I infused into it, and came to life. Girl, check, dressed in cute clubbing clothes totally unsuited for the weather, her coat open to the air. She was bubbly, bouncing. I could almost feel her adrenaline rush in the way she moved. I knew that rush, had been caught up in it myself over the years, when you're so tired and so energized you don't think you could sleep even if you were dead. Your brain's going a hundred miles an hour, and you know you're not making sense anymore, and you just don't care, because you feel so damn good.

I forced myself to look away from her. Where was…there was the ki-rin. For something so pale, it blended really well with the predawn shadows. She skipped ahead, and it fell back a couple of paces…and that was when it happened.

I made it about halfway through before I threw up, but my concentration stayed steady on the job, even while I was heaving the remains of coffee and bagels onto the floor.

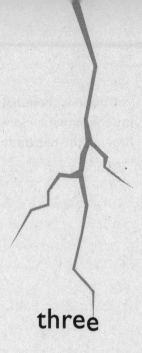

three

When I unsealed the wards and opened the door, Venec was standing there in the hallway. You know how some guys just make you feel better by looking at them? Not comforting or daddylike, just…"all right, you're here, the ground is solid" kind of way? Venec was like that. Well, sometimes, anyway. When he wasn't making you feel like an idiot.

He handed me a mug, and I took it automatically, my hand shaking more than I wanted. Venec took note, his gaze sharp, but he didn't say anything. Tea, not coffee. Not Pietr's green tea: herbal. My face screwed up in distaste even as I was drinking it. Heavy on the sugar, and I could feel my energy level starting to pick up again. Burning too many calories, using up too much current. I had to remember to watch that.

"You done in there?" he asked.

"Yeah."

Venec stood there and watched me drinking, his gaze on my face like a nanny—or a dark-feathered falcon, watching a rabbit to see which way it was going to hop. He didn't touch me, or try to offer any kind of comfort, which was good, because I didn't want any. I needed the rawness, the bitter taste in my mouth that not even sweet tea could erase, the acid burning in my gut. I needed to remember every detail of what I had seen, what I had felt. It wasn't even close to what any of the actual participants had felt, distanced by being third-person, but it would keep me going when we hit dead ends or inconsistent facts, give me the energy to push through and keep working.

The truth was I hadn't seen much of anything of the attempted assault, just a scuffle in the shadows. The flash of hooves and horn, after, had been far more clear. My brain was filling in more of those shadowed details than was healthy, but I didn't know how to stop it. Curse of an overactive empathy, one woman to another. If one of the guys on the team had been better at gleaning…

No. My instinctive reaction to that thought was, well, instinctive. As bad as it was that I had eavesdropped like this…even if the girl never knew we were poking around in her trauma, somehow I felt I had a responsibility to her now, to take care of that trauma. I couldn't protect her, but I could protect her memories.

The fact that I couldn't, really, that it was evidence now, preserved for anyone on the team to look at…well, they still had to go through me, in order to view it. That was a distinction without a difference but somehow, it helped

It did strike me as worrisome that while the initial attack

made me feel ill, the ki-rin's murder of the assailant didn't seem to affect me; it was as though I'd been watching a real—nonmagical—movie, like the blood and gore and dying wasn't real. Maybe because the ki-rin was fatae, I hadn't picked up its emotions from the gleaning, and I was reacting to that blank space? The dead guy had been a real human being, and he was dead. Why wasn't I feeling anything?

Because he'd assaulted her. Because I was glad he was dead. The thought bothered me, a lot. Justifiable, yeah, but we were supposed to see the facts, and I couldn't do that if I let my emotions cloud judgment, maybe make me overlook something. That was as bad as trying to protect the victim, in its own way.

The tea was doing its job, settling my stomach enough that I didn't feel like I was going to puke again. I finished the rest of the liquid, and held it upside down to show the boss I'd been a good little girl.

Venec looked like he was going to say something else, then stopped and tilted his head, looking at me like I was some new bit of evidence. That feeling that tiptoed into me whenever he did that came back, little muddy cat feet.

"What?" I heard the defensiveness in my voice, and reached down to touch my core, almost in reflex. But no, the current there was still and calm. Damn it, I would not let him get to me, not just by looking at me with that heavy gaze, like I was being weighed and judged, and the jury was still out. Nobody, not even J, not even my dad, had ever made me feel like that. I didn't like it, at all.

"Trigger the display for me, please," Venec said, and I got the feeling that wasn't what he had meant to say, but I was still unnerved enough that I didn't push. He could trigger it himself, with a little effort, and I was almost tempted to tell him to do so, but my mentor had taught me manners, and I had some natural smarts to go with it. The office mood was informal, but I never made the mistake of thinking that orders weren't meant to be obeyed, even if they weren't phrased as orders.

"There's soup in the ready-room," the Big Dog went on, still staring at me. "Go eat something before you fall over."

I stared back at him, not quite sure he was speaking in English. Soup. Soup…sounded okay. My stomach could handle soup.

And it hadn't been a suggestion. The sugar in the tea had helped, but it was going to drop me into a crash pretty damn soon, if I wasn't careful.

I went back into the room to reset and trigger the display, then pushed past him and headed for the kitchenette. Venec went into the room and I heard him sigh. Ah, give me a break, I thought; I'd cleaned up the worst of it. It was just going to smell a little musty in there for a while, was all.

The break room was still empty, and I found the soup in the fridge easily enough, tossing it into our small, battered microwave and letting it reheat, scrounging some crackers and a soda while I waited.

It was another half hour before the rest of the team started to straggle back from the scene. Nick was the first through the door. He stopped short when he saw me, and pasted on a snarky grin.

"Hey, Dandelion."

He loved calling me that, because of my hair being short and fluffy and naturally blond. I let him think it annoyed me, because it amused both of us. The things we did, the way the Guys pushed us, and we pushed ourselves, a lot of stress built up and there was only so much drinking you could do and still do your job. Teasing let us blow off some of that tension in reasonably healthy ways.

I'd been in some situations—high school being the prime example—where the allegedly friendly sniping could get nasty. Not here. Not to say we didn't occasionally do damage, especially Sharon's smart, sharp tongue, but it was never intentional.

From the very beginning, it had been like that, all the parts that didn't seem to fit somehow fitting anyway. Stosser and Venec had handpicked each of us, not just for our individual skills, but how we'd form a team. I don't know how they did it, but...it worked. God knows there was the normal tension you get when you throw high achievers into close contact, but there was more to it than just being coworkers, from that very first day. We counted on each other to be there—the job required us to work together, or fail.

The closest I could describe it to J had been that we were packmates. You didn't eat your own.

While all this skittered through my brain, Nick was waiting there, his body language expectant.

I sighed and gave in to ritual. "Bite me, Shune."

His put-on grin softened to a smile with real humor. "Am I the first one back?"

I was curled up on the couch in the ready-room, which had once been the lobby of the original office. I suppose there might have been better, more private places for us to hang out, but the kitchenette was there, and the comfortable chairs, and somehow we all just naturally gathered there when we were all in the office and not otherwise working. That meant that anyone walking in saw us immediately, but we didn't get many unannounced visitors. In fact, other than our first client and her son, I don't think anyone had come to the office except us.

"No," I said in response. "I was. You're second. As usual."

My heart really wasn't in banter today, though, and I guess he realized that, because he just nodded, letting the conversation die quietly. I spooned up some more of the soup—a decent tomato bisque—and watched him put his coat away.

"You get your shit from the cop?" I asked, I guess as a peace offering.

"Yeah."

He didn't sound like his usual puppy-dog enthusiastic self in that, and I sat up and looked more closely at him. Nick was slight, almost scrawny, with perpetually tousled brown hair that always looked like he'd just rolled out of bed, but he'd started out the morning looking if not dapper, then decently put-together. Now, he looked like crap, and his brown eyes had a cast to them that I was starting to get all too familiar with. "What?"

"Nothing. I don't know." He shrugged, a gesture that drove me crazy.

"What?" Unlike with Venec, I pushed Nick. Unlike Venec, Nick liked to confide.

"Nothing." He saw the look I was giving him, and smiled again, this time with the real sweet warmth I was used to seeing from him. "Seriously. I got the guy's signature, so we can rule him out of the evidence. I'm tired, that's all."

Uh-huh. We'd been working together long enough he couldn't bullshit me quite that easily. Smile or no, he was upset about something.

"Guy was scummy?" You couldn't always tell from a signature, but...sometimes it just oozed.

"No." Nick shrugged again, not finding the words he needed. "It's just...he's a cop."

Ah. I understood, the way I wouldn't have a couple of months ago. You work with crap, no matter how clean you are inside, a stink of it stays with you. It's like the smell inside the workroom—enough people throw up over time, and the smell won't ever go away, no matter how much lemon-scented cleanser we used. Cops stank. Even the good ones.

There wasn't really anything to say. Part of the job. Like carrying around the memory of an assault that didn't happen to you. I lifted my spoon. "You want some soup?"

Nick made a face, indicating his opinion of soup. "Nah. Nifty said he'd pick up a pizza on his way back."

I must have gone green or something, because he grabbed the container of soup and had the trash can under my face before I was halfway off the sofa. My boy's got good reflexes.

"Sorry, ah, hell, Bonnie, I'm sorry...here." He put the soup down and grabbed a paper towel from the counter, wetting it under the faucet and handing it to me.

I sat back and wiped my face with the back of my hand,

then realized what he'd given me the paper for and wiped my hands with it, instead. So much for that soup.

Nick got me back on the sofa, and dropped himself down next to me.

"You okay? You got a stomach bug?"

Easier to claim that, but...his concern was real, and we were honest with each other. You had to be, if you expected them to have your back. Nobody got to pretend to be a hero. "Scummy," I said, and tried to smile. He got it. He knew what my job on the scene had been, and what it meant.

He put his arm around my shoulders, his brown eyes puppy-sorrowful. "These things...nobody should have to go through it, and we shouldn't have to witness it, either."

I smiled a little and nodded, but there wasn't any comfort in his words. He didn't understand. He couldn't really. Oh, he got it intellectually. Intellectual understanding had shit to do with it.

You talk about rape, and every female over puberty understands, way more than a guy ever could, even the most sympathetic gay-or-straight male. Women know, instinctively; hammered into us by society, every single day of our lives, even before we know what sex really is. Even if you never talked about it, it was there, lurking behind your left shoulder, an awareness of risk, even if nobody ever touches you without your consent.

But that wasn't what was making me uneasy, why what I'd seen was bothering me so. Not exactly. Violence I could handle. I had never been a sheltered child, and I knew that people weren't angels—not that the angeli were all that nice, from what I'd heard. It was the entire concept of sex-as-violence that was… More than alien to me, it was supersize noncarbon-based life-form alien. J said I was a hedonist, I just believed that mutual pleasure was a noble goal. To me, sex was play: it was an expression of affection, of mutual satisfaction, and yeah, when time, of procreation. That someone could use it to *hurt* someone else? Being reminded that, in the wrong minds, it can also be a weapon? Scummy. Scary.

I struggled to hold on to my anger from before. Anger was better than fear. Anger I could use.

Nick rested his head on my shoulder, almost a cuddle, and even though it wasn't anything he hadn't done before, on tough days, my body shifted away from his. Then he sighed, and I felt a sudden urge to comfort him overriding my own discomfort. Unlike me, Nick *had* been sheltered. Dealing with scummy took more out of him than he wanted to admit.

Without thinking about it, my arm lifted, draping itself around his shoulders. Nick and I'd flirted—hell, we still flirted, because that was what we did—but I just didn't react to him that way, and Nicky'd adapted. Sometimes it was nice to have sex out of the picture and off the table, so you could offer comfort without wondering if anything else was being offered, too.

"Hey, guys. Whoops, did we interrupt something?"

Pietr had come in, unnoticed as usual, followed by Nifty, burdened with two pizza boxes, and Sharon, closing the door behind them. Still no sign of Stosser, unless he'd come in while I was in the workroom and Venec hadn't thought to mention it?

"Bonnie…"

"Bonnie is just fine," I interrupted, giving Nick a hard elbow in the ribs, and forcing him to move away a little. I'd let him coddle me, a little bit, because he was Nick and it made him feel better. But be damned if I'd announce it to the entire damned pack. He took the hint, and shut up.

"I put the gleanings on loop in the warded workroom," I told them, even as they were stuffing their coats in the closet, and heading for the coffee. "Venec's in there now. No idea where Stosser is—he went to interview the victim."

There were a few winces at that: I wasn't the only one assuming the worst. Ian Stosser might be smooth to the outside world, but we knew him a little better than most. Still, when he wanted something he could ooze compassion and caring. Just because he rarely used it on us anymore was no need to assume the worst…right? And he had agreed to be gentle with the girl. He wasn't going to screw it up.

Nifty put the pizzas down on the counter, and opened the lid of one. The smell filled the air, and while normally the combination of tomato, garlic and oregano would make me a happy girl, at this exact moment I didn't want to be anywhere near food.

"I'm…going to go get Venec," I said, uncurling from the sofa and making my escape into the hallway before anyone could say anything. I made a quick pit stop into the bathroom, to splash some water on my face and rinse my mouth out. It was your basic small-office restroom: two stalls, two sinks, wall-size mirror over the sinks, but about a month ago Sharon had made a big deal about putting new bulbs in overhead, so she could, as she said, apply makeup without looking like a corpse, and they cast a gentler, kinder light I suddenly really appreciated.

I leaned on the counter and stared at myself, taking inventory. Hair: still blond, still short, still almost-curly, like a palomino poodle. Eyes: a little bloodshot but nothing that couldn't be attributed to a lack of sleep. Skin: pale, but that was normal for me. Were there new lines around my mouth and eyes that hadn't been there last night? Probably. I was only twenty-two, but sometimes I felt like I was thirty, at least.

I loved my job. Ian had something else driving him, some figurative demon crowding his shoulder, but the rest of us... we just wanted to know why, who, what...and we liked to push ourselves. It wasn't an obsession: I could walk away, if it got too much—and I knew I never would. This was my passion, what I was driven to do.

I practiced a smile, something cheery and bright to reassure everyone I was fine, and shuddered at the result. Maybe not just yet.

I loved my job, but some days the fun level...wasn't.

Face splashed and mouth rinsed out, I wandered down the hallway and found Venec, as expected, in the room I'd left. The door was open, so I just stuck my head in enough to see him sitting at the table, back straight, elbows on the chair-arms, watching the display the way a meter maid watches a parking meter ticking down the last seconds.

I didn't say anything: He knew I was there.

One hand lifted, and the display stopped just as the ki-rin dropped behind his companion, a scarce minute before the attack. "The others are back?"

"Yeah."

"All right. Tell them to start writing up their reports, and I'll be with them in a minute."

I nodded, even though he wasn't looking at me. "Should they come here?"

"No." He stared at the frozen display. "No, I want them to come to the discussion with a blank slate. Time enough for them to watch this when we've looked at the rest of the picture."

In other words, nobody else needed to get their facts tangled by an emotional reaction. It made sense. Part of me was relieved that the girl wouldn't have her trauma spread around, and part of me was pissed that I got stuck with it... but Venec had gone there, too. I wasn't alone.

It didn't help as much as I'd hoped.

"And Torres?" His voice was quiet, a softer growl than usual.

I paused, but didn't look back. "Yeah, boss?"

"You did good."

That didn't help, either.

I walked down the hallway, feeling the walls press in around me. The others were still gathered in the break area. Sharon was writing up her notes already, slice of pizza in one hand, pen in the other, frowning intently, while the guys were bullshitting about baseball. Still no sign of Stosser. I leaned against the wall and watched them. Although my stomach gave another slow, queasy roll from the smell and sight of the pizza, I didn't feel the urge to throw up again. I didn't feel much of anything, in fact, the earlier unease drained from my body while I talked to Venec. While I was normally pretty calm—that was part of why I was so good at this job—that sudden loss of emotion didn't feel right. It was as though someone had siphoned the emotion out of me, and I knew enough psychology to know that probably wasn't a good thing.

I needed to get out of here, put some distance between myself and the display room, so when it all came slamming back, I could break in private.

I went to the closet, and pulled out my coat. They already had my report. If Venec or Stosser wanted me, they knew how to get in touch.

"Hey, where you going?" Nifty asked, wadding up his napkins and tossing them into the trash.

"Home," I said.

My apartment isn't much, by my mentor's standards, but it's better than what I'd been born into, and more importantly right then, it's all mine. My refuge. A cash payoff to the landlord, and I'd painted the walls of the main room a pale purple, and the kitchen dark gold. The furniture was a clash of expensive antiques and trash-day rescues that looked pretty damn fine, if I did say so myself.

I kicked my shoes off and dumped my coat and bag on the floor. There was a pitcher of sweet tea in the fridge, and I drank it straight, like I'd spent the past week being dehydrated in the Sahara, then grabbed an apple and went back into the main room. Most people who had studio apartments separated out their living and sleeping space—not me. My bed was on a loft platform in one corner, but my dining table was shoved underneath, and got pulled out whenever someone came over for dinner or stayed for breakfast. There were two love seats, reupholstered in gold velvet a shade lighter than the kitchen walls, and a black lacquered Chinese chest that held all my dishes and silverware. I'd had a coffee table at one point, but the glass chipped during a party when I first moved in, and I hadn't had time to find a replacement. Something sturdier this time…

Although…another party like the last one would get me kicked out of the building, payoff to the landlord or no. I'd been in such a rush to take the apartment before someone else could steal it from me, I hadn't thought to ask about the neighbors. They weren't bad, just mostly older and settled, and not really happy with parties, even quiet ones, that went on all night. Not that there had been all that many. Since moving to the city last summer, I'd tried to build up a net-work of friends, people who liked to go clubbing, to party not heavily but well, but the past few months the job had overrun all of that. If I hung out at all, it was mostly with the team, and when I did go out, it was weird…sometimes now even in the middle of a hot dance floor I'd feel this sudden urge to be home—alone.

I took a bite out of the apple, absently, and stared at the wall opposite me. Where most people would have a flat-screen television, I'd hung a mosaic made out of hundreds of colored glass tiles. The sunlight from the windows hit it just-so twice a day, and rainbows streamed all over the place. Magic. Right now, it was still, just bits of colored glass doing nothing special at all, except reflecting my image back to me, fractured and broken.

The apple tasted sour in my mouth, and my beloved,

comfortable space suddenly felt shabby and sad. I spit the apple into my hand, tossed the entire thing into the garbage can, and without a ping of warning—or asking permission—I Translocated my sorry ass to J's place.

When a teenager starts showing signs of magical ability, they're assigned a mentor, someone who will take them through the stages, teach them what they need to know and help them figure out their strengths and weaknesses. Sometimes it's a parent or cousin, but more often it's someone not related, a friend of the family with a skill level close to yours, or a particularly good rapport with kids.

Ideally everyone mentors, at some point, but the reality is that not everyone's good at it. And it's important to be good at it—you've got another person's life depending on your ability to teach them properly. We're taught one-on-one, not in classrooms, and the mentor-student relationship trumps almost every other bond we have, even after the mentorship ends.

In my case, Joseph Cetala was more than a mentor— he'd been standing *in loco parentis* since I was eleven. Long story-short version was I went from being the only child of a ne'er-do-well lonejack carpenter to the live-in student of a Boston lawyer/Council muckety-muck with contacts in the White House…and maybe even the Kremlin, for all I knew. By the time I came along he'd retired from all that, and just did some very quiet and occasional consulting of the sort you don't talk about. J hadn't been real happy with my going to work for Stosser and Venec—he wanted me somewhere safer, like a paralegal for a cushy law firm, or teaching in an inner-city school—but he was experienced enough and honest enough to admit that PUPI was needed, and that I was good at what I did.

That didn't mean he didn't worry. I might not tell him the shit that went down when we were on a case, but I wasn't stupid enough to think that he didn't hear about it, eventually. We'd reached a compromise. There was a lurking fatae with the inappropriate name of Bobo who occasionally showed up late at night to walk me home when things got rough—or Bobo thought they might get rough—that soothed J's discomfort, and we never talked about the dangers of my job.

Translocation only takes a few seconds, but it's a major power drain for most of us, messing with natural physics in ways that supported the whole "indistinguishable from magic" thing Zaki—my dad—used to quote. Nifty, who was our best practical theorist, had tried more than once to explain it, but all I cared about tonight was that it took me home.

"Bonita." J was in his early 70s, with fine patrician features and a shock of immaculately groomed white hair, and you'd think he'd greet you in the library of his ten-room apartment wearing a tuxedo and carrying a brandy snifter. Reality wore a pair of ratty jeans and a Harvard sweatshirt, and carried a bottle of Stella. He didn't look at all surprised to see me. He never did. "Would you like a beer?"

I would.

I dumped my shoes on the outrageously expensive carpet, curled up in the security of a leather club chair, and cradled my bottle in both hands, letting the condensation soak into my skin. The antiques in my apartment all came from J's collection, but he'd never had a hands-off attitude; to him, furniture was what you sat on, and a sofa was for naps as well as tête-à-tête. I knew better than to put my bottle down without a coaster, though.

We did the quiet chitchat for a while; he'd been down to NYC to take me out to dinner just last week, so there really wasn't much new to share, unless I wanted to talk about the non-thing that kept showing up between me and Venec, which I didn't, or the cold empty echoing thing where my emotions should be, which I really didn't.

"Hey," I said suddenly, realizing that something was missing. "Where's Rupert?" Rupert was J's dog, an aged sheepdog who had as much to do with raising me as J did.

"Vet. His stomach decided to disagree with him. I'm having them do a full checkup, just in case. He'll be home tomorrow morning, don't worry."

Rupe was almost fifteen. Anything that required an overnight stay at the vet worried me. And I knew it was worrying J, but if he didn't want to talk about it, we weren't going to talk about it. Time to change the subject. I thought about regaling him with the story of Jennie's party last night, or the way the hot doctor across the way from my apartment threw her most recent lover out wearing only his boxers and one sock—but finally had to accept the fact that I hadn't come here for distraction, but after-the-fact mentoring.

"We have a new job." He'd heard already; I knew he'd heard from the way his expression didn't change at all. J was a damned good listener, though; he just sat back and let me talk, or not, as I wanted.

I didn't want. It came out anyway.

"Girl, a Talent, barely out of mentorship, probably. Companion to a ki-rin." J was one of the most traveled, most experienced Talent I'd ever met. He knew how rare they are, here and in their native country. It's not like griffons, breeding two kits at a time, or the damned piskies, who populate like squirrels. Ki-rin are magical, even to us. If the perps had hurt it...I shuddered at the thought. If the ki-rin had been hurt, those rubberneckers would have been an angry mob of fatae, not human looky-loos. "They were out for a night clubbing, or she was, and he's keeping her company. Two guys, Talent, jump them on the way home. Jump her. The ki-rin had fallen behind a little. It was late, his mane is pure white so he isn't a youngster anymore, I guess." I paused, suddenly struck by the thought. "How old do ki-rin get, anyway?"

J hadn't moved while all this was pouring out of me, sitting in his usual armchair, legs crossed at the ankle. "I don't know. It's considered quite rude to ask."

"Huh. Well, it...didn't get to her in time. Killed the first attacker, wounded the second, I guess it didn't kill him because he didn't get the chance to do anything?" My hands were colder than the bottle I was holding. "The story seems straightforward, you know? Bad guys do bad thing, are killed—or maimed—by the good guy, survivor gets jail time. We've been asked to investigate only to make sure everything's clean, that it was self-defense, I guess. Stosser didn't say outright, but the only one who'd hire us for something like this, where there's no money involved, or a revenge motive, would either be family or Council, and I got the feeling it wasn't family. Don't know why Council would be taking such a hard-line interest, though."

Council was for Council members, which meant human, not fatae; even if a ki-rin was involved, their instinct would be to sweep it under the rug as fast as possible to protect their people. Had the dead guy been Council? It wasn't impossible—Council was the country club association of Talent, and there were as many ass-wipes in country clubs as there were hanging on street corners. But then they'd be trying to cast blame away from their man, not hire us to find out the actual facts.

No, something didn't feel right. I wondered what Venec thought of this case, and in that thought I could almost feel his hand on mine again, the smooth, firm touch sending another round of current-shock through my system, then flowing back out again, leaving me with a hitch in my breath.

"PR concerns, I suspect," J said. "There has been some… unpleasantness toward the fatae recently." He shifted, leaning forward from the hips. It was a tell he had, a giveaway sign when he was thinking hard about something. "In New York, and in Philly. Nothing here in Boston that I've heard. Minor annoyances, mostly, although some have become physical. Bigotry picking up a stick. I can imagine that the Council is concerned that this incident of yours not spark a greater conflagration. As it might, with a ki-rin involved."

I forced myself to focus on his words, not the echo of tingling on my skin. "Yeah. I can see why they'd want this handled without a hint of impropriety on their part." And that would explain the crowd that had gathered—they weren't there for the ki-rin, not to support or gawk at it, anyway. And the Council boys had been there to protect it, not confine it. "Nice to know the Council thinks we can be of some use, even if it's only to use us."

All right, so I was bitter. The Council was split into regional areas, and half of them had refused to authorize their members to hire us...but the leadership was willing to use us when it suited their needs, to protect their privileged asses.

"Bonita..." J's tone of voice was the same he'd used when I was missing the point during a lesson.

"Yeah, I know. It's going to take time to win them over. I know." My stomach wasn't queasy anymore, and my skin didn't tingle, but now my entire body was so very cold, so cold I couldn't even shiver. It didn't feel like shock or trauma, though—I knew those. It wasn't even the emptiness of waiting to break, from before. It felt more like...like something had been cut out of me, where the outrage and fear should have been.

Weird. Very weird, discomforting, and I did not like. But if I said anything at all about it, J would freak.

I took a hit off my beer, and tried to wash the feeling away. "Well, we're on the job now, and first look says this probably won't take more than a day or two to wrap up and write a report. Yay us. What do you think will happen to the ki-rin?"

"For killing his companion's attacker? A slap on the hooves, maybe. He would be within rights to demand reparation from the dead man's kin, on the girl's behalf. Every Council from here to Beijing would back him on that, if he did, and lonejacks…" He made a palms-up gesture. "Well, who knows how lonejacks will react to anything."

I shook my head, rolling my beer bottle back and forth between my hands. I love J, but he's a bigot in his own liberal way. Council and lonejack and fatae: the carefully delineated, political world that J lived in. I'd never had to worry about any of this before I became a Pup.

"And the girl?" I asked him, instead. "What rights does she have in all this?"

"She can take the survivor to court, if she…" J's voice trailed off.

The bitterness surged to the fore again, and I grabbed onto it; anything other than that cold empty feeling. "Yeah. Take him to court, and not only does she have to relive the attack, but she has to explain what happened to the other guy, the one who actually attacked her. Oh, my oversize, horned intelligent magical companion killed him. With his horn. Yeah, a single slender horn, right in the middle of his forehead…"

I hiccupped, and took a long pull of the beer to cover the crack in my voice. "J?"

"Yes, Bonita?"

"Why?"

He didn't pretend not to know what I was asking; he'd known me too long. "I don't know, Bonita." J had been a great mentor; still was, in a lot of ways. He'd always been straight with me, never lied, not even when I almost wished he would. "There are theories, and psychological jingo, but I've never understood how it translates into the human mind, thank god. I've just always been thankful that you grew up without encountering that sort of male, firsthand." His voice was quiet, but I could hear the sorrow in it, for that girl, for me, for every girl who had something beautiful and joyful and honest taken from them for nothing more than selfish cruelty.

The cold forming under my skin cracked a little under the touch of his voice, and the itchy heat in my eyes promised a buildup of tears, but they didn't come. We just sat there, and breathed in the quiet security of the library, of civilized behavior, until the daylight faded, leaving us in the shadows.

J reached out and turned on a lamp, bringing an amber glow into the room. "You'll stay for dinner."

It wasn't a question, but I nodded anyway. "Please."

A few hundred miles south in Manhattan, the same dusk was settling over the skyscrapers and brownstones, the sunset reflecting off the water and flashing last spears of light against the glass walls and windows of the financial district. Uptown, traffic was at rush-hour peak, but in the halls outside the PUPI offices, it was quiet. The seven-story building housed a dentist, a handful of CPAs, two lawyers, and a few offices whose signs didn't give away their contents or purpose. On the bottom floor, there was a photographer who was rarely there, and a literary agency. Neither office had many visitors outside of UPS and FedEx deliveries, although those seemed to come every day.

By contrast, the office across the hall had a steady stream of people going in and out, the same seven people, usually in a group and often, as now, in the middle of a seemingly continuous conversation.

"We could…"

"No."

"But…"

"No." Venec's growl warned the speaker not to push further. He had been itchy all day, morose and snappish, as though someone had shoved unbalanced current into his core, and he was in no mood to deal with the carping of overtired puppies.

There was a moving tangle of arms being thrust into coat sleeves and bags and backpacks being swung carelessly, and then they exited the office, Venec closing and locking the office door behind them.

"I don't see why you don't let us," Nifty said, his voice calm and reasonable in a way that set Venec's teeth on edge. "It's not like—"

He cut the overeager PUPI off midsentence. "Because I said no and how many times will it take for me to say that until at least one of you listens?"

"Seven." Sharon was positive.

"Four," Nifty contradicted her.

"Eleven?" That was Nick, looking thoughtful.

Venec shook his head, feeling the exasperation simmer just under his skin. He really should know better by now, he really should. He'd scouted each of them, chosen them, trained them. The talkback came with the other traits he'd selected them for, no way around it. Mouthy and Talented, the pack of them.

On that thought, he paused and looked around for Pietr, who was the only one who hadn't ventured a guess. "Where the hell is Pietr? Did we leave him in the bathroom or something?"

"I'm here."

Sharon jumped, as the voice seemed to come from just at her left shoulder.

"I swear, I'm going to bell you," she muttered. "Can't you cough on a regular basis, or something?"

"I would, but you wouldn't hear me."

Venec frowned, listening in, this time intentionally. That had to be getting to be a sore point—Pietr swore he didn't intentionally disappear when he got stressed, it just happened. God knew, there was enough stress in the office right now, after the day they'd had.

The usual reaction to having a stressful problem was to chew at it until it was solved. That was good, if they were on a hot trail. But they didn't have enough information yet to solve it, so they'd start chewing on each other, instead. Part of his job was to prevent that. Bonnie's need to get the hell out had been one he supported, even though he wished she'd said something to him beforehand. Now he needed to get the rest of them to go home as well, before he had to put a boot under their tails.

"Children, enough." He put extra exasperation into his tone, not difficult to do right then. "Everyone go home. Or go to a bar, or a strip club or whatever it is that you do to blow off steam. You just can't stay here."

That was the rule he had invoked to get them to leave: nobody stayed late, not when neither of the Big Dogs—and yes, he knew what the team called them—were around. He had made that rule after their first investigation. His partner believed that, with his sister scolded and publicly shamed for her part in the death of the Null boy, her posse of anti-PUPI protesters wouldn't do anything more against them. Ben was less certain of that, and not willing to trust any of his team on that chance. Besides, it gave him a good excuse to make sure they got a decent night's sleep. His pups thought they were tough and tougher, and they were, but it wasn't a much-older couple this time, or disembodied bits packed neatly in a cooler. It was a young girl, their own age. He might only be ten years older, but he had seen more than all of them put together. The case was shaking them, even if they didn't realize it. Better they take a step away now, get a breath, do something normal.

"We go to Bonnie's," Nick said in response. "But she's not home. I called and got her answering service, and she's not responding to a ping."

"Oh, god, she's not still dating what's-his-name, is she?" Nifty asked, distracted. "The doink with the goofy smile?"

Nick threw up his hands in a dramatic gesture of disgust. "What, you think she tells me everything?"

"Yeah." Sharon, Pietr and Nifty all responded in the same instant. Venec just closed the door quietly behind him while they were all preoccupied. He had no interest in their personal lives beyond how it affected their professional behavior, not even their sharp young technician, had no interest in her at all beyond her skills in the office.

"Right. No, she's not," Nick said. "I think we scared him off."

"We did no such thing."

"Of course we did," Sharon said. "He took one look at us and ran for the hills. No great loss, he wasn't right for her anyway. Too…"

"Stable? Sturdy? Much a productive member of society?" Nifty asked.

"Boring. Bonnie should not be with someone boring."

"Right." Nick rolled his eyes, still being dramatic. "And we're all having such good luck on the dating front, we can give her advice."

It seemed that nobody wanted to touch that comment, from the brief silence that fell.

"So if she's not home where are we going to go?" Nifty asked.

"We might try our own homes?" Sharon suggested caustically. "Since Big Bad Dad here won't let us work any longer, 'cause he's got a hot date or something…."

There was a flyer stuck to the nameplate on the door. Annoyed, Venec plucked it off, telling himself that his annoyance had to do with the solicitation, and not the way Bonnie's love life was being batted around. Too young, too much an employee. Too much trouble, damn it.

"We've done everything we can right now," he said to them. "Ian will be back in the morning with the girl's testimony and the ki-rin's deposition—" he hoped; his partner hadn't pinged to say he'd be late, but Ian was not what you'd call a steady-goer "—and then we'll be able to start putting the pieces together for our report. Right now, you're just chewing on your tails, and that's starting to chafe mine. So. Go. Home."

He shooed them down the hall, noting with concern

that they didn't even stop at the elevator, but headed for the stairs at the end of the hallway. He understood their aversion—none of them were going to forget the boy who had died anytime soon—but it wasn't good that they were now so conditioned to avoid it. He was going to have to do something about that, as well as the situation with Pietr.

He stopped to push the button for the elevator, meaning to set an example, and realized that he still had the flyer in his hand. Curious, he unfolded the salmon-colored paper and scanned the text, and then stopped and read it again, more carefully. On the surface it was an advertisement for a fumigation service. On the surface…

He had seen the wording before, on a different flyer, on his own door.

Do you have problems with unwanted creatures in your space? Looking for a way to evict them forever without chemicals or fuss? Call us.

He hadn't thought anything about it then, piled with the other flyers and junk mail that seemed to accumulate every week; current use was one of the best natural cockroach repellents, and his building didn't have a rat problem that he was aware of. Now, on its own, the wording seemed somehow more…something. He didn't know what, but it made him uncomfortable.

He was a cautious, suspicious sort by training as well as natural inclination, and he didn't believe in ignoring his instincts when they said something was wrong.

It was probably nothing; he might simply be overreacting. Or it could be important. That was his job, too; to scout things that might be important, and keep Ian informed.

More, he didn't like something about the wording of these flyers—or the fact that there was no company name on it, no website or email, only a phone number. That sort of thing raised a definite red flag—it meant someone was trying not to leave a trace. Pay-as-you-go cell phones were easier to dump than websites these days.

It wasn't all current, this gig. Sometimes you had to use Null methods, too.

"Sharon," he called, stopping her before she went into the stairwell. "Hang on a minute. You still in contact with the legal types you used to work with?"

She had come to them via a Talent-heavy law firm, specializing in discrimination cases and medical malpractice.

The blonde stepped back into the hallway, letting the others go on down the stairs without her, and looked at him inquiringly, switching easily from off-duty grousing to professional competence. "Yeah, why?"

He uncrumpled the paper, and handed it to her. "I need you to do some digging for me. Quietly."

It had been a long day filled with not much of anything, and Aden was tired. She heard the door open, the sound of Carl's steps in the hallway, but felt no urge to get up and meet him. The divan she was sitting on was comfortable, and he would come to her if there was anything to say. There was a skitter of claws as the dog was released from its leash and went into the kitchen to see if there was anything in its bowl.

His footsteps moved along the tiled hallway, down into the sunken living room, then stopped. She could feel the change in the air, but kept her back to him, looking out the floor-to-ceiling windows that ran the length of the wall. The beach was empty save for a single jogger coming down the sand toward then. The high season was still months away, and she would be gone by then, the lease on this house expired. She didn't know where she would go, then. Maybe Miami. Maybe Canada. Not home, not yet. She was not yet ready to deal with them. Not while they still slunk about like whipped dogs, too hesitant to do what was needed.

Carl cleared his throat. "They've hired your brother."

The bile swirling in her throat at his words was an old, not-unwelcome friend. There was only one "they" in this house. The Mage Council. Specifically to her, the Midwest Council, her home and kin, but she knew he meant the Eastern Council, the region her brother lived in now. They were all the same in the end, even if they claimed autonomy and embraced geographic limitations. The elite of the elite; the decision-makers, the voice of reason and control against the human tendency to excess. She had spent her entire life living up to their standards, hoping to one day be strong enough, respected enough to be asked to join the seated members, to be a decision-maker herself.

Her childhood idols had feet of clay.

She sighed, hugging her knees more tightly to her, still watching the blue-gray waves rolling up onto the shore. "And what should I do about that, rush in to protest? Try to save them from their folly? Because that ended so well, last time."

"The boy's death was not your fault." His reaction was automatic, but heartfelt.

"Of course it wasn't." She had not attacked with lethal force, only attempted to warn her brother, to force him to acknowledge the wrongness of his path. It was pure sad chance that the killer they had been chasing attempted to take them out at the same time, and that the elevator had failed in the resulting current cross fire and fallen, with the boy inside. Regrettable of course, but responsibility had to go to the owners of the building, who had not maintained their power grid properly. It merely reinforced her belief that Ian's foolhardy quest would bring only grief and disaster to their people, no matter his good intentions. "But the Council needed someone to blame, and my brother was once again golden. He challenges their decisions, denies their authority, abandons everything that we were raised to believe…and they not only do not slap him down, they *hire* him. It would make me laugh, if it wasn't so horrifying."

Carl came farther into the room, but did not sit down, instead standing behind her. She could see him reflected faintly in the glass; hands behind his back, silver hair uncovered, like a soldier reporting to his general. The thought pleased her.

"And so he is allowed to spread his theory further…."

Aden looked at the reflection as she spoke. "And there is nothing that I can do to stop him. I am still banned from going within two miles of his precious puppies, forbidden to speak against them for another year." The injustice of it made her want to spit. Never mind that within a year they would inevitably be out of business, their methods reviled, and her brother doubtless disgraced and discredited again. Who knew what damage they could do to the fabric of the

Cosa Nostradamus in a year? "There is nothing I can do," she said again, this time more softly, and her fingers unclenched, smoothing the nubby fabric of the divan underneath her as though petting a cat.

"Not directly, perhaps."

She didn't move, didn't stop stroking the fabric, or watching the waves rise and unroll. Both soothed her, kept her from dwelling on the injustices of the world. "And... indirectly?"

He didn't respond, his glass-shadow not moving, waiting at relaxed attention, and eventually curiosity forced her to turn around on the divan and look directly at him.

"Indirectly? And don't give me that 'the enemy of my enemy is my friend' crap. I have no desire to align myself with some radical group or lunatic antimagic front." Her voice was sharp, and she was pleased to see him flinch. Aden was a Stosser: she had objections to her brother's actions, yes, but she would be damned if she would lend her legitimacy to some nutcase who wanted them to deny their heritage and abandon current, or something equally insane.

"What about 'the enemy that can be used is a useful tool'?"

He looked entirely too poker-faced— there was something he was pleased about. She studied him a moment, putting her thoughts in order. She disliked speaking before she knew exactly what she was going to say, especially on matters of such importance. Carl was far too good a planner to bring her smoke and mirrors; something was up. Something that pleased him, and thought it would also please her.

"All right," she allowed, leaning back and nodding. "You have my attention."

four

By the time we reached the pecan tart, I'd gotten the ground under me, again, and was feeling kind of silly for overre-acting. "Dinner was, as always, delightful." It was—J was a fabulous cook, and an even better conversationalist. "But I should scoot—they're going to expect us in the office at Oh-god-Early again."

J smiled briefly, honestly amused. "The thought of you being a nine-to-fiver..."

"More like eight-to-eight," I said, and like that was a trigger, a yawn almost cracked my jaw open, loud enough that I was embarrassed. "It's not the company, I promise."

"You used to run three days without sleep," he observed, standing to gather plates from the table. "You're getting old, Bonita."

"And you're getting younger," I said, standing to help

him clear the table. A wave of exhaustion hit me, almost knocking me back into my chair.

"Bonita?" J moved pretty fast for an old guy. "Are you all right?"

"Yeah, just…" I had to double-check to make sure what the problem was. "Wow. My tank sprang a leak somewhere." I wasn't about to tell J how much our work took out of me—it would just be another thing for him to worry about.

There is no sigh like a mentor's sigh. "When was the last time you sourced, Bonnie? Not merely a hit here or there, either."

I couldn't remember, so I just shrugged, a bit of body language that I knew would drive him crazy. Even as a kid I'd forgotten to recharge regularly…back then, it hadn't really mattered. I could go months, sometimes, without hitting empty. Now? Two days seemed to be the max.

There were different ways to recharge, but mostly it came down to choosing between wild current, or man-made. Wild current was exactly that—magic that formed from a natural charge. Current ran alongside electricity, in ways we still didn't quite understand but were more than happy to use. So thunderstorms, ley lines, any focused electrons we can lay magical hands on, that was how we sourced wild current. Nick claimed he knew someone who could pull current directly from the atmosphere, but I think he was full of shit, because you'd either get so little it would be useless, or overrush your brains out and leave you a twitching, grinning wreck. No thanks.

Fortunately for us, anything that carried electricity also

carried some amount of current. That was where man-made current came from—modern generators. The old stories were a crock—modern technology didn't kill magic, it enhanced it, gave it another burst of always-accessible power in the form of generated electricity. Thank god, because I really hated sourcing wild. A portable computer or phone: that was a small hit. An apartment building's electrical system: more. A power plant? Smorgasbord. That's why so many of us lived in cities: 24-hour access where something was always turned on and working.

And why, every now and again, the entire power grid went dark, because some nitwit Talent had pulled too much, too hard. Bad enough to short out your own electronics. Taking down the grid got you Idiot Hall of Fame status.

"Bonnie..."

I smiled up at him, as innocent a look as I could manage, and he gave up. "I'll send you home, but you have to promise to recharge, all right?"

I held up my hand in solemn oath, and he believed me.

J was a master craftsman: he dropped me neatly into the middle of my living space, with only a slight wooziness that passed with a blink and refocusing. I sat down on the nearest love seat and did another quick check of my core. Mmm. All right, yeah. There wasn't anything nearby that would give me a full soak, but I could fix the immediate damage, at least.

I sank into a half fugue, and siphoned off a thin trickle, not from my own building, but the newer, nicer one across the street. They had cleaner wiring, so I was less likely to cause a burp in their service, or fry someone's computer. I'd do better this week, when I had time to hunt down a stronger source.

The recharge took care of the wobblies, enough that I could have gone through my normal bedtime routine. Instead, I stayed where I was. Talking to J had helped, the way it always did—that was what a mentor did, once they finished kicking you into shape—but I still felt worn down. Was it just this case hitting me hard? Or was it the job itself? Was I not hacking it? The thought scared me more than anything else ever had.

I loved this job. I couldn't, I *wouldn't* wash out.

At that moment I wished that I had a dog. Or a cat, or even a gerbil. Something I could pet when I came home, and cuddle, and know that it loved me. Okay, maybe not a gerbil. Rodents were nasty. But a cat, maybe. A cat would be good.

I'd never had a pet before; there was only room for one animal in J's apartment and Rupert was it, in no uncertain terms.

"Worry about a cat later," I told myself, leaning back and staring at the ceiling. "If one is meant to come, it'll come. Isn't that how cats worked?" I yawned, aware that, even recharged, my brain was getting fuzzy. I should go to bed. Should. Yeah. Right.

Even though I love my loft bed—it's big enough for two, comfortable enough to live in, and sturdy enough for a pillow fight, or any other kind of energetic activity—the thought of climbing up there right now was too much effort. It wasn't just the current-drain, or even the emotional seesaw I'd been riding. We'd been pushing hard, the organ-leggers case and now this, with no real downtime between. Was this what it was going to be like once we convinced the naysayers, and cases came on a regular basis?

The thought both thrilled and horrified me.

I ended up dozing on and off, curled up on the sofa, instead. I woke up a few times during the night, once from a dream of a large black cat sleeping on my chest, and then again when a truck rumbling by set off a series of car alarms down on the street, and then finally overslept, waking up only when the sound of kids on the street outside wormed their way into my consciousness.

Oh, fuck. I wasn't late—yet. But there was no time for my usual putter-around-the-apartment wake-up routine. A fast shower got me clean, and a rummage in my closet resulted in an easy-to-manage outfit of long black skirt, leggings, and black cotton sweater over my lace-up stompy boots. I managed to make it out the door by ten after seven, feeling like crap, but still on time. Thank god we didn't have a particular dress code.

Manhattan in the morning is a living stream of purpose; everyone's got a place to be and a problem on their mind. That doesn't mean it's an unfriendly place—just busy and preoccupied. Personally, I love it. I'm a social creature but there are times and places you just don't want to do more than grunt at your fellow human being.

This morning, though, my usual comfort level was replaced by something a lot less…comfortable. Walking to the station, and standing on the platform waiting for my train, I was acutely aware of everyone around me, not in the usual "get your elbow/cell phone/coffee away from me" sense but judging distances, evaluating body language, watching anyone who got too close…specifically anyone *male.*

Huh. It wasn't that I didn't do this sort of thing all the time. You have to, wherever you are. It's just basic common sense and security, and when you're being trained to observe and detect, that goes into overdrive. But normally it was background processing, something I did without being really aware, unless a warning signal pinged my forebrain. Today…it was all front-and-center consciousness, and very much focused on gender. The difference was like between healthy skin and abraded flesh. Every whisper of touch, every possible glance from a stranger, made me shudder in almost physical discomfort.

It wasn't worse than the cold numbness of yesterday, but it sure as hell wasn't better, either. What the fuck was going on?

I managed to clamp down on it long enough to get on the arriving train without screaming or snarling at anyone. Once on, I slipped and slid my way into an empty seat at the far end of the car, between a young Asian woman in a suit, eyes closed as though she were sleeping, and a large, middle-aged black woman with a bundle of knitting in her hands. She radiated a don't-mess-with-me-this-morning attitude that was soothing.

I exhaled, forcing myself to calm down. The car was full but not packed, and there was actually enough room that people weren't in each other's personal space, which always made for a more relaxed atmosphere. I had a book in my kit, but it didn't feel like a reading morning. I looked down, and only then noticed that in my rush I'd put on mismatched socks. Great. My fashion style was a little on the fashion-risk side sometimes, but that was going to be tough to carry off as intentional. I pushed the brown one down into the ankle of my boots and closed my eyes instead, trying to get into work mindset.

Usually it wasn't a problem. While I'm not a morning person, the hum of the subway's electrical power and the jolting of the train typically eased me into the day, while the promise of a puzzle—either a training session exercise or, as now, an actual job—to chew on got my brain to agree to function.

But this case… Damn it, I was the one who stayed cool. But my brain wasn't cooperating, even after a night's sleep and a recharging hit, so I couldn't blame it entirely on exhaustion.

It couldn't be the job itself: we had all the answers already. All we had to do was organize and present the evidence. But I needed to be in a nicely grounded state of mind to do that kind of sorting and organizing, and it wasn't happening, even after spending time with J. The sleeplessness, the raw nerves, and the lack of ability to dress myself decently were all warning signs that I was off-kilter, still. The unease, the cold numbness, the discomfort within my own skin…not good.

When I forced myself to look at the emotional side, rather than the facts, it was—*duh*—obvious. The girl, what had happened to her. It was tough for me to see what happened to her as a puzzle to be solved, a question to be answered, and nothing more.

I tried to focus again on the hum of current in the third

rail, letting it trickle into me like bittersweet honey. That helped, but the tinny crap music pumping out way too loud through the ear-buds of the guy standing in front of me was seriously annoying, and I almost wished that I had a cup of coffee just so I could accidentally-on-purpose slosh some over his expensive sneakers. When the sound suddenly spluttered and died—I suspected that another Talent in the car had taken offense and sporked him—it cheered me significantly.

Small revenge is large comfort, some days.

Between that and the hum of current, by the time the train dumped me out at my stop, my mood was better and my nerves under control. I tromped up the stairs, enjoying the ringing noise my boots made in the stairwell because some days I really am seven, pushed open the office door, and headed directly for the coffeemaker, shedding my coat as I went.

"Hey, girl."

"'Morning." I poured myself a cup of coffee and leaned over to see what Nifty was doing with the bits of paper he had laid out on the coffee table. It was a casual move, nothing I hadn't done dozens of times in the past six months, but this time I hung back just an inch or two more distant than I normally did, not resting my hand on his shoulder for balance. It took me a minute to realize it, and another one to realize why.

Damn it, this was Nifty. He was a good guy. He was on our side.

He was a *guy*.

I guess my nerves weren't quite as under control as I thought.

Whatever calm I'd gotten went sizzle like water on a griddle, my core shifting from its usual cool loops of neon to something more jagged and hot. Bad. Very bad normally, and even worse here, in the office. Be calm, Bonnie, I told myself. Be still and controlled, that's what you do, remember? You're the one who has the most excellent control.

Knowing why I was reacting this way, and that logic wasn't going to work, not right now, didn't help. All I could do was deal with it, and try not to let it get in the way of the work. With that in mind, I consciously leaned forward to get a better look at what he was doing, even as I smoothed the jagged spikes back down into cool loops through sheer force of will. I would not let nerves show. Would *not*.

"I really wish I had a camera right now."

I twitched, and looked up at Pietr, who had been his usual silent self until now, meaning I hadn't even realized that he was in the room. He had an amused look in his gray eyes, so I looked down to see what the hell he was talking about, and started to laugh. Me, my white-blond hair, pale skin, and black outfit, and Nifty's dark skin and white sweater— yeah, I could see where we'd make an irresistible target.

The tension broke, a little, and I could function again, control slipping back into place naturally.

"You try bringing a camera in here," Nifty said, mock-scowling, "I give it a week, tops, before it goes snap, fizzle, pop." Warding could only do so much; the moment current was free of either core or spell, it looked for an electrical stream to hook up with, the more powerful the better. That was why we'd trashed the original expensive coffeemaker for a simpler, if still wicked, brewmaster, and why there was only one phone and one computer, and both were down in Stosser's office, where nobody did any workings by order of the Big Dogs.

"So what're you doing?" I asked Nifty, leaning in a little more easily now.

"Girl had a bunch of scraps in her pocket, got 'em in this morning, courtesy of one of Venec's contacts. Looks like they were napkins or something, but there's writing on them."

I took a closer look. They were smudged and incomplete, but I recognized them. "Oh. She was collecting numbers."

"Numbers?"

"Phone numbers." I looked at him in astonishment. "Dear god, Nift, for a jock you sure are innocent…."

He stared down at the bits of paper, trying to see what I saw. "That's a lot of numbers for a virgin to be collecting."

I resisted the urge to pat him on the top of his buzz-cut head. "It's not about calling them, it's about getting them." He looked at me and I raised my hands palm-up in a don't-ask-me gesture. "Not my kind of game, but some do it. So our girlfriend was playing the game but not paying the pot."

"Looks like."

Quiet fell in the room as we both stared at the pieces of paper. Magic was all sorts of fun and splashy, but this was how we did most of the grunt work: Everyone put some elbow grease and some brain sweat into the mix, and we stirred it with a big stick until it smelled right. Another Venec quote.

Pietr put down the file he'd been reading and looked over the table at the napkins, too. "There are three different bars there, at least."

Nifty looked up at him, then down again at the table. "How can you tell that?"

"Different paper. Look at the textures."

"We supposed to go check each bar, see who she might have chatted up?" He sounded discouraged.

"We should," Pietr said.

"Why?" I tilted my head and looked at my coworker, playing devil's advocate. "You going to claim that she asked for it, somehow? That maybe she blew one of these guys off, before, and that's why they attacked her? Doesn't matter, to our job. We're not here for the why, just the who and the how. We know who did it. One guy's dead, the other's in custody, and the cops will get the story out of him. All we have to do is make sure the ki-rin's skewing was clean, or whatever the cop terminology is, and the case is closed. No need to poke around anything that happened before, right?"

"Right." But he didn't sound convinced.

I looked at Nifty, who looked back at me and shrugged. He didn't know what was up with ghost-boy, either.

"It's not about poking into her personal life or accusing her of being a tease, Bonnie. I just have a bad feeling about this. Like there's something under the surface, and it's going to bite us if we're not careful." Pietr was too mellow, as a rule, to be defensive, but he was skirting awfully close. Considering my own twitchiness, I wasn't going to rag on him for it.

"You got precog?" Nifty asked, interested. If so, he'd been holding out on us. Precog wasn't a common skill set, but it did happen, and would be amazingly useful in this job. My own kenning worked mostly on people I already knew and cared about, so it didn't quite qualify.

"No. I don't think so. I just…" He exhaled hard. "How would I know?"

That, I could tell him. "It feels bizarre, like a goose walking over your grave, only in your brain."

Pietr considered that a moment, rubbing his fingers along the front of his shirt. "No. It's more like an itch somewhere I can't reach."

"There's probably something you're seeing, but haven't identified. Did you…" I hesitated. "Did you look at the gleaning?"

He shook his head, a little stiffly. "Venec said no."

"So it has to be something you saw on the site, maybe, or talking to people?"

"Yeah, I guess. But what? And how the hell would I know, if it didn't strike me enough to consciously remember?"

Good point. I had no answer.

"Did anyone say anything that gave you a wiggy feeling," Nifty asked. "Was there anything in your report that you hesitated over, or rethought?"

I looked at Nifty in surprise. That sounded like something J would have asked me. Mr. Lawrence had better think about mentoring at some point, because he had the knack for it.

Pietr was considering the question. "I don't know. No." He shrugged. "This whole thing, it's making me feel…urgh. Uncomfortable. Dirty."

Huh. It might not have been something he saw, but something he was feeling. Like me. Of all the guys, it wouldn't surprise me if Pietr reacted that way. Nick got it on an intellectual level, but all those years of being overlooked and near-invisible because of a quirk he had no control over had given Pietr a level of empathy you didn't normally find in the average twentysomething male.

"Hey, guys." Speak of the devil and he pops in. Nick wandered over to the coffee station and refilled his mug. Sharon had bought us all individual—and individualized—mugs a month ago, after one too many "wrong coffee" incidents. Nick's was a bright blue, with a yellow happy face with a bullet in the forehead. It had an odd sort of fascination for me, in a way that my own—a beautifully appropriate black one with a colorful but dead parrot on the side—didn't. "You hear the news?" he went on. "Girl's not going to press charges."

"What?"

Pietr's yelp was outraged. I discovered that I wasn't even slightly surprised by the revelation. Depressed, but not surprised. Like I'd said to J last night, it's hard enough even today to come forward with sexual-assault charges. Having to explain how your attacker died? How about doing that without mentioning the ki-rin, Talent, the *Cosa Nostradamus* or anything else that would get you locked in the psych ward for evaluation? The very best scenario involved a *Cosa*-sympathetic cop and judge, where she'd still have to relive every minute of the attack; worst case brought up the possibility that they'd think she had killed the guy and nail her for manslaughter, provoked or not. And it's not like they could punish the guy who died, or bring back her relationship with the ki-rin....

Nifty didn't look surprised, either. I bet he'd seen a lot of that kind of scared-silent, all the years he spent playing high school and college football. The bitterness in my own brain surprised me again. I knew, with the rational portion, that I was being unfair, tarring Nifty just 'cause he'd been a jock. But the rational part wasn't leading in this dance.

Nick was nodding sagely. "Stosser told Venec, who just told me. I think she thought the ki-rin was going to pretend it didn't happen, or something. She went totally hysterical in the emergency room."

"Nicky, you're an insensitive asshole," I said. Nick must have realized how his words sounded, because he blushed. "I didn't..."

"The ki-rin is refusing to acknowledge her now, isn't it?" Pietr asked

The bitterness in my brain escaped into my voice. "You expected anything different? That's how ki-rin are—it's like asking a dryad not to put down roots, or a griffon not to fly. It's what they are—she had to know that before she agreed to the terms, and evidence is that she'd adhered to her part of it all the way up to that night. Being a ki-rin's companion isn't something you pull out of a Cracker Jack box. There's no greater honor, by fatae standards, a human can aspire to, and one asshole with more brawn than humanity took that away from her, for his own jollies. You think you'd be calm and rational right now, if it was you in that emergency room?"

That pretty much put a damper on the entire conversation,

and Nick took his coffee and his mug out with enough speed that I almost felt sorry for snapping at him. Almost.

"So if we can't do anything for her, and the guy who did the attacking is dead…are we still on the job?" Nifty wondered, giving up on his napkin-puzzle. "I mean, what does it matter? Christ, I'm sorry for the girl, but I can't see our client paying for our time if the girl is going to sweep it under the rug her ownself. It's over and done with, nothing to see here, move along, thanks for your time. Right?"

He probably wasn't wrong, and I'd wondered the same thing myself. Except… "J says—" it wasn't really a secret in the office that my mentor had Connections into all the best gossip lines, or that I tapped into them as needed "—that there's been a bunch of fatae-related incidents in town already. Folk are tetchy, rumbly—like the crowd we saw at the scene." I saw the guys process that, then nod. "He thinks the Eastern Council thought that if they did some proactive digging into this, or had us do it…"

"They'd be off the hook for whatever happened after," Pietr finished for me. "Nice."

"Council." The disgust in that single word dripped from Nifty's mouth and splashed into a thick puddle. "So that's who we were working for—again?"

Other than Stosser, I was the only Council-side member of the pack, and even my connection was only through J. Lonejacks didn't have much use for the Council, either the actual seated members who made the rules or the general members who followed those rules. Lonejacks didn't have much use for anyone who followed rules, period, which made for interesting group interactions—and probably why

Stosser and Venec kept us on such a loose rein most of the time, when we weren't in training.

"You didn't guess that?" Pietr sounded surprised. "Most of our work's going to come through Council contacts, at the very least, not lonejacks. Lonejacks settle their own scores. They're not going to suddenly step back and let us determine who's at fault—not until we have a lot more street cred, anyway."

I had a feeling Pietr's family was Gypsy—they tended to be more clannish than the independent lonejacks, but just as regulation-scorning, hence the nickname—but he had a strong pragmatic streak that put even Venec to shame.

"Council leads may be callous bastards," he went on, "but they're the callous bastards with a checkbook. And their checks clear faster than most. Get used to it."

Nifty looked like he wanted to argue the point, but couldn't.

"Doesn't matter, anyway," I reminded them. "Until we're told otherwise, we're still on the job."

"Here…" Pietr held out the file he'd been reading, offering it to me. "The dossier Ben put together, plus what we were able to add in the follow-up."

"Give me the highlights," I said, not taking the file. I thought better hearing information than I did reading it.

"Right. Dead would-be rapist was a local boy—lonejack, but his mentor's long dead and his only remaining family's crossed the river down in Ohio." Crossing the river meant going from lonejack to Council, or vice versa. It happened, but not all that often. "Not very well-liked, from what the people who were willing to talk about him said."

"Nasty? Or did he owe everyone money?"

"Had a less than savory reputation with women. No criminal charges, but a restraining order against an ex, and rumors he didn't always take no for an answer. Nobody's surprised he moved up—or down—to assault."

Nifty made a note in his pad. "Someone should have taken him out before this. Ten minutes in the alley would've done it."

Nifty had two little sisters still living back home, I suddenly remembered. I wasn't going to argue the pros and cons of presumptive justice, though, not right now. Especially when I pretty much agreed with him.

"His friend, on the other hand, the guy who landed in the recovery ward, is fourth gen lonejack, and a first-time offender. Hangs out with a stupid crowd, reportedly, but stupid isn't a crime, more's the pity. The two of them don't have any connections before about a month ago, when they reportedly met in a bar, and hit it off. So we've got bad seed leading bent sapling astray…."

"Or giving him the courage to do what he wanted to, anyway," I said. The fact that the guy was there in the first place made him just as responsible for what happened as the dead guy. The ki-rin might only be interested in actions. Me, I thought about intent, too.

Sharon came in from the outside hallway, her hair for once not in the sleek coif I coveted, but rather loose down to her shoulders, and her china-blue eyes were tired-looking. There was a lot of that going around today. She took off her coat and handed it to Pietr, who automatically hung it in the closet for her. I don't think either of them realized they'd done it; Sharon just had that aura around her—alpha female—and Pietr was our omega. "Is Venec around?"

"In back," Pietr said. "Why, what's up?"

"You finally quitting?" Nifty asked.

She shot him a glare, but you could tell that her heart wasn't in it. Considering that the two of them usually wrassled for alpha spot in the team with gleeful ferocity, that set off all sorts of alarms in my head. In Nifty's, too, because he actually sat up straight. "You're not, are you?"

"No. I'm not. You don't win that easily." She suddenly realized we were still on alert, and waved her hand. "It's nothing. I'm fine, it's nothing to do with the case. Just something Venec asked me to look into last night, is all."

Huh. I was going to make a crack about being teacher's pet, but whatever it was, it must have been grim, and she obviously didn't want to talk about it—or couldn't, if it was on Venec's orders—so we let her go in search of the Big Dog without further comment.

"So if we're all here, cheer, cheer, where's Stosser?" I asked, curious, after she'd gone.

None of the guys had an answer for that. "Haven't seen him since the scene," Nifty admitted. He sank back into the sofa, and put his feet up on the table, dislodging the napkin bits. "You think something's up?"

"With Stosser? You think I have a clue what's in Stosser's mind?" I paused, and gave a delicately staged little shudder. "You think I want to go there?" Genius minds were scary places.

I sat down on the other end of the sofa, not so meh-depressed that I didn't notice I was still keeping an unusual distance between the guys and myself…but I hadn't twitched when Sharon came in, and the women on either side of me on the subway hadn't triggered it, either. My brain gratefully seized on something concrete to analyze. Gender, definitely, and not mitigated by the size of a guy, since Nifty was all bulk and Pietr was slender. Raw nerves again, survival sense kicking in overtime when a male someone, known or otherwise, got into my personal space.

If you weren't used to noticing things, it probably wasn't, well, noticeable. Problem was that PUPI training was to *be* investigators, to notice things, and look for their causes. I saw it. I had to believe that the guys saw it, too. And nobody commented on it, which meant they were treating me as damaged, or at least delicate goods. Damn it.

I could feel my teeth grind, and had to consciously relax my jaw. Damn it; I was not going to let an atavistic fear make me change my behavior in useless and unhelpful ways. That would piss me off more than anything else, and it would cramp my ability to do my job, which was unacceptable.

I started to move forward, sliding along the sofa cushion, when the sound of the door being slammed open made all three of us jump. The boss man stalked in looking like seven years of bad luck, his long orange-red hair loose and charged with energy that might have been static but wasn't.

When a high-res Talent gets angry in your immediate vicinity, it's time to ground and duck.

"Boss?" Nifty got to his feet fast, blocking Stosser's progress without actually touching him. "Boss, dampen it down or you're going to short the entire building out. Again."

Stosser stopped hard and stared down at Nifty. The air

practically crackled, and my skin twitched. A little voice in my head told me to get down, under the sofa, away from the rush of current being raised in front of me—and another part was fascinated, like a little kid watching fireworks, or a pyromaniac in front of a roaring blaze.

"Boss." Nifty's voice was soft, but firm, the way you'd handle a scared dog. I didn't think that was going to work, not the way the boss was radiating current. My heart was pounding, my bp way up in the stratosphere.

ben! trouble!

I never called Venec by his first name. Ever. It was... too personal. But the emotion of that mental ping came out without conscious thought. By the time I realized what I'd done, there was the faint inrush of air and current that indicated someone had Translocated into the room.

"Ian!"

Anyone who thought that Benjamin Venec was the secondary force in PUPI, a mere sidekick to Ian Stosser's star turn, would've had that notion knocked right out of their head. Stosser's head snapped up and his entire body turned toward Venec like he was pulled on strings.

"Stand down, Ian. Whatever it is, stand *down*. I will not have another Chicago here."

Like that, like someone turned a switch off, the current dancing around Stosser's core went silent, his hair falling flat around his shoulders, and his skin flushed, then went back to his normal pallor. As Stosser's presence faded from the ether, I could feel Nifty's current curved around us like a protective barrier, and wasn't sure if I should kick him for thinking he was stronger than we were, or kiss him for being such a damned nanny.

"Lawrence." Venec's voice was still hard, and Nifty reacted with the same speed that Ian had, dropping his barrier and pulling the current back into his core.

Man, oh, man, oh, Man o' War. I started to breathe again, a little irregularly, and felt my heartbeat go back to almost normal.

Stosser had calmed down enough to talk, his voice clipped and red-hot. "I just heard from the head of the Eastern Council. Our vic in the hospital—the survivor—is now claiming it was a setup. That the girl lured them in, and the ki-rin attacked them, unprovoked. That it was a bias attack, fatae against Talent, and the girl was bait."

"Oh, fuck," Venec said, with feeling.

I echoed that, mentally. Our open-and-shut case? No longer open or shut. And I noted Stosser's word-use—from alleged assailant to potential victim. We now had to think about everyone as both possible wrongdoer and potentially wrong-done. Shit.

Sharon and Nick both reappeared at the doorway from the inner office, although I don't know if they followed the noise, or if one of the Guys had called them. Ian looked around, his eyes still cold and mad, and nodded curtly. "This is worst-case scenario. We need to look at everything again. New eyes, new brains, absolutely no damned assumptions or notions. If this was anything other than what it seemed at first, we need to know, and we need to know *now,* before anybody gets any stupid ideas about retribution."

He'd obviously heard the same stories J had told me about.

Not surprising—they were plugged into a lot of the same sources.

"We still working for the Council?" Nifty asked, fishing for details.

"We're working for the answers, Lawrence."

As answers went, that was totally true, and totally not useful. But if Ian wasn't worried about where the paycheck was coming from, I wasn't going to, either. We were on the scent of a more interesting puzzle than I'd thought at first, and I could *feel* the anticipation in the room. As everyone adjusted their thinking and processed the shit that had just been thrown our way. The hounds were on a new scent... or we would be, soon enough.

"All right." If I'd thought he was charged before, when he stormed into the office, I didn't know shit. Under control, Stosser was even scarier, practically shimmering like a heat vibration, and his voice was molten lava, sliding fast. "Pietr, fill Sharon and Nick in on the details, then you two start tracking down possible witnesses. Half the damn city's nocturnal, someone had to have been out there, and not just gawked after the fact! Bonnie, you, Pietr and Ben run through the gleaning again, maybe they can see something you missed. Nifty, have you gotten anything from those scraps yet? Now, people! Move!"

We moved.

The workroom still smelled like musty vomit and citrus cleaner, as expected. Next time we reorganized the office I was going to suggest that we use one of the offices with a window, instead. It might be harder to ward, but the fresh air would be welcome. Not that every gleaning caused people to toss their cookies…but I had a bad feeling going forward it might be more common than not.

The shudder I'd described to Pietr rippled through me, even as I thought that. Not the depression that had been dogging me since the day before, but something more familiar—and more unnerving.

"Oh, fuck," I said to myself, barely a whisper, heavy on the *k* sound.

"What?" Venec had come in behind me, and was in the process of pulling a chair out to sit down. Bad timing and worse luck he looked up in time to see me react. "Torres?"

I couldn't not answer. "Something just tagged the current. Something kenning."

"About the case?" The Guys knew about my kenning, but they also knew it was something that happened in its own time, not an on-demand party trick.

"I…don't know. It came and went so fast…whatever it is it's going to involve me. Maybe everyone. But…maybe not." Not every kenning came true. Just most of them. I wished I were home, to follow through—I had scry-crystals that helped me focus, but I didn't keep them in the office anymore. Too many people made woo-woo jokes.

"Triggered by the case?" One of the things that made Venec good to work for; he knew how to ask for something rather than demanding it. It was easier to think things through, that way.

I tried to hold on to the feeling, analyzing it as best I could. "I don't know."

"By the conditions around the case?"

"I...yeah. That felt right." It was like being brushed by a tornado when it hit the house next door. Something in all this was going to affect me...no, *us,* directly. I just didn't know what, or when, or why. Yay for the damned impreciseness of the future.

"Something we need to react to immediately?"

"No." That I was definite on. Whatever I had felt, it was down the road a bit. A mile or a hundred miles, I didn't know, but it wasn't going to hit us in the next couple of days.

"All right, then." That was the other thing that made Venec good to work for. He didn't do Drama. "Where's Pietr?"

I made an effort to look around the room before answering. My coworker had shared a few sparse details of his life with me, back during our first case, that made me determined never to crack a joke about his chameleonlike ability to disappear, but that didn't make him any easier to spot. But no slender form revealed itself, leaning nonchalantly against the wall.

"Not here yet. Should I start the reel anyway?"

"No. We need to see it from start to finish." Left unsaid, but evident in his voice if you were listening, was the fact that he wasn't looking forward to seeing it again, either. That made me feel...not better, exactly. Less bad, maybe.

"Hey."

As usual, Pietr appeared as though he'd been there for ten minutes. If he'd gone to the other side of the force, he'd have been a hell of a Retriever.

"Got the others caught up to speed." He slid into the chair next to me, boneless as a snake. Venec sat in the other chair, and the lights came down. "How much did you manage to pick up in your gleaning? I don't think I could have gotten anything, not after all the looky-loos muddled up the scene."

A major drawback to doing something as brand-new as investigative magic was that there wasn't a tradition for our group to fall back on—and the *Cosa Nostradamus* was all about tradition. If Talent or fatae wanted to gawk, we didn't have the oomph to stop them. Yet.

Another reason for us to slam-dunk this job, so we could hold it up as an example and justification for "get the hell out of my way."

Pietr was still waiting for me to respond. I really didn't want to talk about what I'd done, so I just toggled the mental image of a switch, and the display appeared in front of us.

"Oh."

Even smaller-than-life, a gleaning representation packs a wallop. Like watching a movie where you know what's going to happen, and the director knows you know what's going to happen, so rather than mess it up with soundtrack and fancy camerawork, just lets it play out straightforward, in absolute silence. I could feel my skin tighten on my arms, and a knot of tension form in my chest, somewhere inside my lungs.

no preconceived perceptions

The warning ping felt private, but Pietr nodded his head once, slightly, so he heard it, too. I focused my attention on the display, trying to let it run in front of my eyes as though it hadn't already been seared into my brain. Look as though it's all new, everything a shiny dispassionate fact....

The scene, still and dark, the lamps casting just enough light to create deep shadows. A flicker of movement...down there, off-camera. Then two figures; the girl, slight and cute in her club clothes: short skirt, jacket carelessly open to the night wind. She had legs like a colt's, and hair that was long and tangled from dancing. The ki-rin came to her shoulder, its head slightly above hers when it was lifted, even-level when it ducked down as though to say something. I don't know why anyone ever described them as horselike. Seeing it now, with distance, it was built more like a deer than a horse, and the dragon's head should have seemed odd on top of that muscled neck, but didn't. The horn, about the length of a forearm and twisted the way you traditionally see it in pictures, seemed too ethereal to do anything like gore a man to death.

"They're walking really slowly." Pietr's voice, out of the room's darkness.

"They're tired," I said.

"It's cold. You'd think they'd move it along?" Venec, to my left.

"If she's been dancing, the cold air probably feels pretty good, if she's even aware of it. The clubs can get really close and hot."

They took my word for it. I guess neither of them was much for clubbing.

The two were walking forward, fully in view now, within the range I'd gleaned from. The wind tossed bare branches on the trees along the path, and even if the girl didn't shiver, I did, imagining how cold it must have been, that hour before sunrise. She leaned in against the ki-rin, put her arm over its neck, ruffling the white lion's mane the way you would a beloved friend's hair. Such total, thoughtless comfort made what was about to happen even harder to watch. If the vic was right, if the ki-rin had set her up as bait, used her trust... the thought just—

"Did you see that?"

"What?"

"Over there. To the left."

Where the attack happened. I brought the display back a few seconds, and looked where Pietr had indicated.

Two deeper shadows in the shadows. That I'd seen before. The brief red glint of something...I'd missed that. A cigarette butt? Yes, the flick of ash about hip-height: someone pausing to have a cigarette. Two shadows: two figures. Two men, waiting in the shadows...smoking?

No preconceptions. I let the display roll.

The ki-rin fell back, the way I'd noted before. I let my brain just take it in, as dispassionately as I could. In a human, you would have expected it to kneel down and tie its shoe, perhaps. The girl, so affectionate a moment before, went on her way, seemingly not noticing that her companion had dropped away. Was she still talking? No way to tell. She was walking with a distinct kick to her step. If she was sober, she was floating on the endorphins of the night.

One figure stepped out of the shadows. The cigarette smoker. The girl stopped, her body language... I'd said at first that it was patient, the way you are when a stranger approaches you when you're in a good mood, and you're going to give them real directions, or whatever spare change is in your pocket. But looking now, she seemed…expectant. Flirty? She leaned in and put a hand on the stranger's arm. Damn, how had I missed that before? Could the second man's claim that they were set up be right?

What happened next was fast and brutal. The second figure came out, grabbed her, dragged her back into the bushes. My stomach rose up again in protest but this time I held it down, forcing my eyes to stay on the display. Next to me I heard Pietr swear in a language I didn't recognize, his body convulsing as though forcibly keeping himself from getting up to help the three-quarter-size figure in need. On the other side of me, Venec was perfectly still and quiet. The current in the room sparked and sizzled with their agitation, and I had to focus to keep my own current steady and unaffected, to keep the display from shorting out in response.

control I heard, a whisper of a ping, and the current in the room cooled, still unsettled, but not dangerous.

The ki-rin raced forward, after a pause that seemed to take forever, but couldn't have. Just long enough for her to be thrown to the ground, her clothing torn, her skin bruised and mauled…

stop Venec's voice in my head, layers of reminder in that one-word sense. Stop projecting. Stop assuming. Stop. I stopped, and let the visual evidence unfold.

Five minutes, maybe, from the first grab to the ki-rin's arrival. Why had it been so slow? Then the dragon's-head jaw opened in what must have been a roar, and a shadow jerked away. The second vic? The ki-rin ignored it, that graceful body rearing back and hooves and head coming down in attack mode, the horn angled down, and the darkness was suddenly the brighter for blood splattered across that pale body…

"Stop it." Pietr's voice, hard.

I managed to pause the display. It was getting easier to control it, although I still had to concentrate. Pietr leaned forward. "That second figure. He was the one who approached, but he never did anything. His cigarette stayed lit the entire time, I didn't see it move at all. He was just standing there."

"He wasn't part of the actual attack," Venec said, confirming my initial theory. "That's why the ki-rin let him live."

"He was the hook," I said, seeing where Pietr was heading, looking with my brain instead of my emotions. "He brought her close enough to grab. But he wasn't acting as the lookout. Otherwise he would have seen the ki-rin coming, and warned his buddy. He didn't."

"And he wasn't expecting trouble, either," Venec said, rolling off our thoughts the way we did when we hit stride. "The positioning was all wrong. He was…more like he was waiting while his buddy had a go, but not expecting to have to restrain her, or help. As though she approached them, hot off the club scene, looking for some action. Just like our perp claimed."

"But the guy did grab her. It wasn't the other way around." I looked at the others, and they nodded. However she approached them, she hadn't gone to the ground willingly. "Hang on…." I let the display go, and we watched as the ki-rin pulled back, then turned on its back hooves and lashed out at the second figure. He didn't escape unscathed.

"Punishment to fit the crime," I said. "But he didn't run. Why didn't he run? He should have, at that point."

"Unless he was in shock," Venec said thoughtfully, trying the idea out.

"Like he wasn't expecting a ki-rin?" Pietr wasn't buying it. "If I had been part of that, and saw my buddy get gored, I'd be running like hell, especially if I originally thought the girl had been alone."

"Not expecting it…or he wasn't expecting it to attack him?"

The guys both turned to look at me. I leaned back and stared at the frozen display, a weird coldness stroking my spine, the way it did when my mood went from dark to pitch-black. The emptiness and the depression were both gone, and anger filled the space, but I wasn't sure where to direct it…not yet. "He stood there…not part of it, but part of it. He approached her…but never touched her, didn't seem to be part of the attempt…the ki-rin ignored him until well after the fact…. You were right, Pietr, earlier. I've got a really hinky feeling about this, too."

We were done—for now, anyway. I shut down the display and tucked it back into the carefully constructed nonspace it was stored in. There was already some degradation occurring. No matter how good my memory, eventually it would fade, especially if we kept watching it over and over. Nothing lasted forever. The thought was comforting, actually.

When I'd finished closing up, we went not to the break room, but to the largest of our workspaces, with a large conference table, and eight chairs. There were only seven of us, but I guess the eighth chair came with the set, and nobody ever moved it to another room.

Nifty was already there, drumming his fingers on the arm of his chair impatiently, a notebook open on the conference table in front of him. "Four different clubs, all in the same area," he said to Venec when we came in. "I pinged Nick with the names, and he and Sharon are checking them out."

"What clubs?" I asked.

"Daylight, Roseroom, the Woogie, and Mei-Chan's."

"I know them."

"Of course you do," Venec said dryly, and Pietr snickered. Hey, I never made any bones about being a club kid, and I wasn't going to apologize, especially if it gave us information we needed.

"Roseroom and the Woogie are fatae-friendly, so it makes sense they'd go there. Daylight's new, I went there once and wasn't impressed. Retro-trance, wasn't my thing. Mei-Chan's, that's classy. Very expensive. Was our girl in the money?"

"Not particularly, no. But she might have been hoping to meet someone who was?"

"A sugar daddy who wasn't looking for a bed-toy? Unlikely."

"A sugar mommy?" Nifty asked.

I snorted. "Virginity isn't dependent on a penis, Nift."

He blinked, and then blushed a little, like his brain had never gone there before. Yeah, right.

"Well, until the others get back, that's all I got. You?"

Venec filled Nifty in on our revised evaluation, while I looked over the notepad he'd been working on. A penciled map, linking the four clubs, trying to figure out the possible routes that would land them on the park walkway at that hour. No direct lines anywhere.

"So, someone's lying," Nifty said.

"We knew that already." Venec, tired-sounding. "You don't get two wildly dissenting stories without someone being full of shit. The hell with the client—they just wanted to cover their asses. Well, we were on the scene, so now no matter what happens, it's our reputation that's on the line. We can't back off, not without looking incompetent."

There was a brief silence as everyone digested that fact. Had we been set up, more than just the Council using us as a splatter-sheild? We'd screwed ourselves by taking the case so fast, without knowing more detail, but we'd been so hyped to actually be on scene first, not last-called...

Oh, hell, I would have made the same decision Ian did. We knew that we were being used, but we were in the business to *be* used, when it all boiled down to bones. Eventually, people would learn that we didn't give a damn what their games and goals were: we were after the facts.

"We need to get answers, and we need to prove what happened, without any room for doubt. If we don't, this will never be settled to anyone's satisfaction, and that doubt's going to come back and bite us on the ass hard enough to take a chunk out right when we can least afford it."

In other words, it was not only this case that was on the line, but also our ability to function down the road. But no pressure, puppies.

"So, obviously, the first thought is it's the second attacker who is lying." Pietr was thinking out loud. "His buddy's dead, he's laid up with serious medical bills piling up, so he's trying to blame the girl, saying she was a willing partner so the cops have no reason to get involved, and the ki-rin... did what? Overreacted? Got jealous?"

Stosser came in as we were talking. He looked calmer, but his body language still sang tension, and it hit a note in me, too. I could feel myself tense up. The others seemed oblivious, focusing on their own notebooks.

"Would a ki-rin's companion give that up for a quick lay, suddenly?" Venec asked, testing the theory. "Or maybe there wasn't as much respect between the two of them as we'd been assuming...trouble in paradise?"

"No." I was definite about that. "They had been physically affectionate, just minutes before, really comfortable with each other. If she was going to break ties there are ways to do that, formally, so both can go their way with honor. This... that sort of thing would be a slap to the ki-rin." I thought. My knowledge of ki-rin was pretty much what J had told me over dinner, and even that was mostly hearsay and legend. None of the fatae were open with their lives—except the piskies who shared too damn much—and unlike some of the older European breeds, who made their living off their reputations. The Asiatic breeds weren't exactly inking tell-alls for TV.

"What about the girl," Pietr said. "What reason would she have to lie? She didn't shy away from the first guy, our survivor, at first. Could his story be true, that she went willingly—or changed her mind at the last minute? Could the cry of attempted rape be a way to protect herself, so nobody would know about her betrayal of the ki-rin, and that's why she won't press charges? Because she doesn't want anyone actively investigating her story?"

It was a fair, if ugly, question. The *Cosa* reaction would be exactly what we were seeing—a willingness to shove it under the table, and allow the ki-rin historical rights to revenge, not rock any boats. But it didn't say nice things about the girl if she flip-flopped like that. My immediate response was to leap to her defense, but Venec's injunction made me keep it in check. Was it possible?

"She was attacked, and injured, even though the bastard was interrupted before he managed penetration," Ian said. He had been the one to see her in person, so he'd know. "She's shaken and scared, physically and emotionally damaged… no. I think the refusal to press charges has more to do with shame than fear of being revealed as a liar."

Stosser was a pretty good judge of character when he wanted to be, so we were willing to accept his take on the situation. The fact that she had injuries also supported her version of the story…unless she liked that sort of thing. I didn't want to bring that up, but…

"Also, she's Talent, although so lo-res as to be practically Null, and being a companion was serious status uptick to her," he said, echoing my earlier point. "I can't see her letting that go, and certainly not in such an insulting manner. The news that this guy is countering her claims made her—"

"You told her?"

"Boss! You said you'd be gentle!"

Stosser looked taken aback when Pietr and I both jumped on him for that. "Well, yes. I went back while you were working, after I got the news. I wanted to see her reaction."

Oh. My. Dog. I'd known Stosser was a cold bastard, but that…wow. Even Venec looked a little sick.

"Shame or fear, the counterclaim raised the possibility that she might not be an innocent victim." I guess everyone's expression was the same, because this was the first time ever I'd heard Stosser be defensive. "It was our best chance to gauge her response to the news, before anyone had a chance to warn her."

Might not being the operative term. I could understand why he'd done it, I guess; fast and brutal was sometimes the best attack, and we were fighting for our professional lives, but damn.

"Damage done," Nifty said, shaking his head like he still couldn't believe Ian had done that. "What was her reaction, as though we don't already know?"

Stosser looked way from us, admitting just a sliver of guilt with that action. "She burst into tears and refused to speak to me any longer."

I would have thrown something at him, myself. And that something would have hit him, too.

Venec touched my arm, like he knew how close I was to saying something that might get me fired, and I felt annoyance settle down, my temper going back to its normal even tone.

"So we have a he-said/she-said situation," Venec said, with a look at his partner that didn't bode well for later out-of-office discussions about tact and human kindness. Good. Although the thought of Venec lecturing anyone about tact was kind of funny.

"If the actual attacker is dead," Venec went on, "and the

ki-rin will say only that he was retaliating within his rights for his former companion's dishonoring...what does that leave us with? I know the myths about this breed, but most of the fatae have a historical association with...twisting the truth, in order to get their way. Could the ki-rin be lying?"

"No." Stosser answered that one. "You can't judge them by the standards of the rest of the fatae, Ben. I'm not sure a ki-rin is even capable of lying. The unicorn mythos is right about that as well as the virginity obsession. Pure and true, loyal and loving, et cetera, et cetera. Fierce bastards, too. I saw what was left of the dead guy. I'm not sure there's enough left to do an autopsy, although the ki-rin thoughtfully left the face intact for identification."

"Kind of it, I'm sure," Pietr said.

"I don't think kindness was in its plans," Nifty said. "Maybe the girl is scared of the ki-rin, now that she's not protected? It may choose human companions, for whatever reason, but I've yet to meet a fatae that wouldn't choose the nonhuman side in a heartbeat. They're just as happy to stamp us into the ground, most of them, given the chance."

"Wow, fataephobic a bit, aren't you?" Pietr asked, echoing my own reluctant thought.

"I like most of 'em fine," Nifty said, scowling at Pietr. "I just don't trust 'em. Not with my life and not with yours, either. I read my histories. For every good fairy godmother or kindly elf, you get a dozen bog-spirits and water-sprites just cackling about the chance to put us down."

I wanted to argue, but he was right. On the other hand, we'd written those stories, we humans. I wondered what the fatae had to say about us?

"Y'know," Pietr said, breaking into my thoughts, "I'd have expected a black man to be a little less bigo—"

"Hey! Watch it!"

Pietr held his ground, even when Nifty stood up, leaning across the table, and I tensed, not sure if I would get between them or dive under the table, if it came to that.

"Down!" Stosser didn't have the deep voice Venec did, but he could do a command as well as any dog trainer I'd ever seen. Nifty sat down, if reluctantly, and Pietr leaned back, nonverbally letting go of the argument.

Stosser wasn't appeased. "Do I have to assign you two scutwork until you learn to play well with each other?"

"No, sir," Nifty said quickly. Too quickly for the Big Dog's satisfaction, because he glared at Nifty. It should have been funny, stick-skinny Stosser trying to physically cow the former football player, but it wasn't. It was scary. Nifty blinked and looked down, and Ian turned to the other culprit, waiting for his response.

"No, boss." Pietr shook his head, looking much more rebuked than Nifty had managed. I wasn't sure I trusted his response any more, but it came across better.

For some reason Stosser looked at me, and I looked back, as wide-eyed and quiet as I could manage.

"Right now," Venec said, and he was talking to Stosser, not us; you could tell when he put on his Big Dog-to-Big Dog voice, "we have a record of events that could be used to support either claim—there's just enough leeway to allow reasonable doubt on anyone, especially without anything more than torn clothing and bruising that could have been consensual roughhousing."

Oh, good. I didn't have to be the one to bring that up. Wasn't my thing, but I knew plenty of people who were in the Life, and being thrown down on the ground and restrained with force was their idea of a cozy Tuesday-night date.

"Damn it." Stosser was still pissed, but I was right, it wasn't that cold fury anymore. Thankfully. I much preferred calculating Stosser to furious Stosser. "It's going to come down to the weight, not the quality. That puts the onus on us to collect everything, and I do mean everything, I don't care how small or insignificant or duplicated the effort."

Yeah, we'd already gotten that, boss. But I kept my mouth shut, and so did Nifty and Pietr, for once. When the Big Dogs went at it, you didn't get involved. We all stayed very still and quiet, and listened really hard.

"Are Sharon and Nick still out?"

Venec nodded. "They're checking on the clubs the girl hit that night."

"Right. Pietr, Bonnie, I want you talking to the fatae, any one you can lay fingers on. See what they're chattering about. Ben, you and I will deal with the Null aspects. Nifty—" He looked consideringly at the big guy, and I could see Nifty bracing himself for some kind of punishment detail.

"There was a cop first on-scene, one of ours." Talent, he meant. "The guy who called the Council in. I need you to find him, talk to him. See if you can jog anything loose from his memory, anything that seemed out of place, or didn't jibe with protocol."

Nifty nodded, trying not to show his relief. It's not a job

I'd have wanted, but he could do guys-together-shooting-shit better than anyone else on the crew.

Ian nodded at us all, his gaze steady as a basilisk's, and just as unnerving. "We're still on the job, even if the parameters have changed. A crime was committed—we just don't know what crime anymore. That's what we need to determine. It's important to get this one right, the first time, and have it locked down solid—you know what's riding on this."

A girl's reputation. A man's death. A *Cosa* shitstorm. Our professional survival. Yeah, we knew.

"No mistakes, no slipups or oversights. Take all day, all night if you have to. Be back here in the morning with something to give us. I don't want theories or hypothetical situations. Facts only. Everything else is useless."

five

The four of us were heading out on our fatae—and fact-finding—missions, Stosser on our heels heading who knows where, when Sharon and Nick came into the lobby.

"Changing of the guard?" Nick asked, but his face didn't match the lighthearted tone, and I could tell he was making an effort.

"Any success?" Stosser asked them, before either of us could make a response.

"They all have a CCTV setup, but the recording's wiped after twenty-four hours if nobody files a complaint," Sharon said. "All legal by current laws, if incredibly skanky." Sharon sounded disgusted; she might have been a great legal researcher but she'd have been lousy in court. "And if anyone knew or remembered anything, they weren't talking. We should have sent Bonnie—she'd have been able to get something out of somebody there, turning on her trashy charm."

I made a shallow, mocking bow. Sharon wasn't being obnoxious, much; her country club-style lush blondeness might turn some heads, including mine, but when it came to ferreting my way into the good graces of Goth-club bartenders and hyped-up bouncers, I'd perfected the art by the time I was sixteen. Like I said, I never made any secret of being a club kid.

Stosser didn't like being second-guessed, and we'd already gotten the lecture months ago about learning to adapt, and not to rely on another teammate's strengths to get the job done. Thankfully, he spared us another sounding of it. "Go upstairs and put together a report of everything you saw, everything you heard, even if it doesn't seem useful. Total brain-dump, down to the faintest flicker. Then go get something to eat and take a nap. You both look like shit."

"Thanks, boss," Sharon said, but Nick looked relieved. Knowing Sharon, I'd bet good money she'd been running them both ragged all day.

Down on street level, we split up to go our separate ways, Nifty downtown to the 6th precinct to hunt down his cop, Venec hailing a cab to go god knew where to talk to god knew who, and me and Pietr left standing on the street corner, looking at each other.

"So."

"So, I said." It wasn't funny, at all, but I felt the urge to start laughing, mainly because the depression and weird vibes off Stosser were gone, leaving me feeling suddenly light-headed. Stress was seriously whomping my ass. "Where the hell do you find fatae when they're not asking to be found?"

"A Gather," a familiar voice said from over my left shoulder.

Seeing Pietr jump and yelp was fair payback for all the times he'd managed to scare a month off my life with his random disappearing/reappearing act, but I had sympathy. The first time I'd met Bobo, he'd done the same to me.

I turned to deal with the newcomer. "Damn it, aren't you only supposed to lurk nights? No, don't tell me, your employer broadened the terms of your contract?"

Bobo looked moderately sheepish, which on him was a good trick, considering he was a brown-furred, black-eyed fireplug that could have been the inspiration for Wookies, only shorter and sweeter-tempered. Proof that Manhattan was home of the terminally jaded; people passed right by us and didn't even blink.

"Ahem?" My companion coughed gently, but pointedly.

"Oh, sorry. This is my coworker, Pietr Cholis. Pietr, this is Bobo. He's…" How do you explain having a Mesheadam bodyguard? "He's under obligation to my mentor to keep me—" I almost said "unmolested," but changed words between throat and tongue "—out of trouble."

"That's full-time work" was all Pietr said. "What's a gather?"

A Gather—capital G—was, apparently, exactly what it sounded like. A bunch of fatae in a local area gathering together to eat, talk, eat some more, and generally make nice and reform alliances—or smooth over harsh words before they caused real trouble. Sort of like a neighborhood cocktail party, except without the alcohol. Most of the fatae never developed a taste for the stuff, which was lucky for them. And lucky for us, too. Some of the breeds were nerve-wracking enough without having to worry about them being drunk.

Normally, we'd never even know about a Gather, much less be allowed to attend. Bobo figured he'd be our ticket in.

"Thank you," Pietr said.

Bobo shrugged, which on his bulk was a particularly impressive thing. Pietr and I looked like skinny kids next to him. Skinny, furless kids, specifically. "Hireman says watch out for her, keep her safe. You two go wandering around looking to stick your noses in fatae business…. Not so safe. Better we keep it in a controlled situation, where folk are already in a good mood."

We hailed a cab that was willing to stop for us, Bobo barely fitting into the yellow sedan, and directed the driver to drop us off on 72nd and Central Park West, where Bobo said a Gather was happening today. I didn't know if they were regular things, or we just got lucky, but I'd take it, either way.

The local fatae had chosen the Pintum, a small section of Central Park next to the Great Lawn specially planted with pine trees, for their meeting place. It was nice: There were swings, and a circular walking path, and a bunch of wooden picnic tables, and signs that forbade any kind of sports or unleashed dogs. A place specifically set up for lazy lounging, according to the signs posted everywhere. I approved.

A quick glance around as we walked down the path showed about twenty fatae, half a dozen different breeds ranging from small, winged creatures clinging to posts like large bats, to a griffon and her cub playing catch with a soccer ball. Years ago, before I'd met more than a handful of piskies, I'd gotten my hands on a DVD of *Labyrinth,* that movie with David Bowie as the Goblin King. Singing, dancing, insane giggling, the whole works. It built up certain expectations. This Gather was…nothing at all like that. I think Pietr was disappointed. I know I was.

"You expected a bonfire and roasting oxen?" Bobo asked, I guess sensing our mood.

I glared up at him. "Thanks. Now I'm hungry."

"Oi! And…oi!"

A man strode up to us, his cowboy hat askew on his head, a glass bottle of Coke in his hand and stuck a warning finger up in Bobo's face. Wow, that was ballsy. "You're new in town so maybe you don't know the rules, but no humans here, pal!"

Funny, he looked human enough to me. But a closer look showed that his ruggedly good-looking face was a little too symmetrical, his ears a little too pointed, and his hat, when removed for emphasis, showed small nubby horns peeking through the curly brown hair.

A faun. A taller, bulkier, more human-looking faun than I'd ever heard of before, but seeing the ki-rin had been a reminder that pictures and descriptions could and often did lie. First-person observation. No preconceptions.

Fauns were just as cute as they were alleged to be. That I observed firsthand.

"They with me. I bring."

Bobo, despite his name, spoke excellent English. Gerunds and everything. He was playing dumb-big-brute for a purpose. I was put on alert.

"I don't care if they're king and queen of the prom." The faun gave us a once-over, then stopped and gave me a once-over again. I smiled at him the way I would one of J's business contacts: not quite showing teeth but letting him know they were there. Polite, but promising nothing. He smiled in return, but showed his own teeth, white and even and too perfect to be real, except they probably were.

"You're puppies," he said.

"We are." I wasn't sure if that was a good thing or a bad thing, from his tone.

"You're here about the incident yesterday morning? The one down in the meatpacking district?"

There were enough incidents he felt the need to be specific? "We might be. We might want to talk to anyone who was there, if they want to talk to us."

"And if they don't?"

I tilted my head, working the little girl cute for every dollar it was worth. "Then I'll talk to you."

Pietr had totally disappeared from the faun's sights. So had Bobo, probably. The thing about fauns is that they could be serious sons of bitches, until you got their...ears pricked up. Then they could only think with their pants.

"Are you trying to seduce me, girly?"

Bastard had the startled "Mrs. Robinson" inflection down perfectly, and I started to laugh. All right, honors about even. If we'd met outside of work situations, I might have tried to seduce him, in fact. Not that it would have taken much doing. I'd never had sex with a fatae before, but fauns were historically polyamorous and not all that shy about species lines. They were also supposed to be impressively inventive, and gloriously hedonistic.

And he wasn't tripping any of my "caution-male" alarms, the ones that had been going subvocal-but-strong since this damn case started. Interesting. Was I recovering, or was it a nonhuman thing, like the mer's come-on?

"We're trying to find out what happened," I said, switching over to a more professional manner, lechery off the table for the moment. "If you know about PUPI, then you know we're not here to take sides or run an agenda. We're here for the facts."

The faun looked cautiously scornful. "Not the truth?"

Ow. What do you say in response to that? I took the fallback position. "Truth is subjective."

His eyes narrowed, but there was suddenly a spark of humor in his expression. "Kierkegaard wanted to eat his cake and have it, too."

Smart and horny, and he got the cake quote right. I really might be able to love this guy.

"I'm Bonnie," I said, extending my hand.

"Danny." He shook my hand, the palm-to-palm contact showing me a guy with a firm grip and well-manicured nails—maybe his feet were hoofed? Hmmm.

Pietr gave me a quick shove in the back with his elbow. Oops, had I said that last bit out loud? From the twinkle in Danny's eyes, I had. As J often lamented, I didn't have an ounce of shame, and just smiled cheerfully at my companions. Pietr was used to it; Danny recovered quickly, as I'd suspected he would.

"Let me introduce you around, introduce you to a few people. No offense, pal," he said over his shoulder to Bobo, "but like I said, you're new. They're not going to trust your vouching for her…or her Retriever friend. Is he here to work, or…?"

"I'm not a Retriever," Pietr said wearily. He got that a lot, along with the jokes. Retrievers were Talent who were supposed to be able to use current to disappear even when you were looking right at them, making them natural-born thieves. Pietr was too damn stand-up for that, though.

"No?" Danny looked mildly surprised at Pietr's denial. "Man, you should be. Okay, come on, both of you. And try not to rile anyone, okay? Things are a little jumpy these days, and even vouched-for humans might not get a nice reception from everyone."

Danny hadn't been kidding. The fatae were mostly social—nobody hissed at us, or turned their backs, or brought out poisoned claws or quills—but there were a few conversations that dropped dead as we approached, and nobody really seemed to know anything at all about what happened except as how the ki-rin really couldn't be blamed, could it?

"No, sir," I said for the tenth or thirteenth time to a grizzled lizard-fatae wrapped up in sweaters against the raw spring air. I wondered if it was related to a salamander, and what it was doing out and about before the temperature got above 70. "I don't see as how any blame could be assigned. A ki-rin has honor to consider."

It nodded, and Danny took my arm like we were strolling through the park…which, actually we were. The thought almost made me laugh. Thankfully, Danny either didn't notice or didn't want to know what made me grin this time, and we moved on through the crowd. The pattern was the same with every fatae; Danny would introduce us, and then one of us—Danny, Pietr or myself, Bobo having stayed off to the side—would slide the conversation along to where we wanted it. It wasn't subtle, and I don't think anyone didn't know what was up, but they were talking to us. I prided myself on the fact that Council-sent investigators—even the diplomatic types like J—wouldn't have been able to get so far. They were talking to us, not because they were scared, or needed something, but because of who—and what—we were. For the first time, being a pup *meant* something. But was it enough?

"It's really a matter between humans," the griffon said, when Pietr asked her if she'd heard anything about the incident. "You are all so…difficult to understand. I can barely tell you apart, half the time, it amazed me you find so much to disagree about."

"They're not investigating a political dispute, Hrana," Danny said. "A girl was attacked."

"Oh. Well, the ki-rin took care of it?"

And that was it, as far as she was concerned. Honor had been satisfied.

"You PUPI should stay on your side of the fence," a schiera said suddenly, looking at me from its upside-down perch with oversized, almost liquid-black eyes. Its claws flexed nervously, and I shoved Pietr a few inches back, away from the implied threat. This breed was one J had made me read up on. Schiera were not only obnoxious, but they were also deeply poisonous, and I had my doubts anyone was carrying antitoxin—or that they would share any with us, if they decided we'd deserved to be scratched. "We don't need you, and we don't want you. We don't want any humans."

A few of the fatae around him looked amused or wearily patient, as though they'd heard that rant before, but some others nodded their heads in agreement. So much for goodwill....

"Yeah, you schiera'd do really well without humans to mooch off of." A foxlike kitsune snickered, but I noticed that it kept its distance from the schiera's claws, too. The fact that the bat-winged fatae were garbage-eaters was definitely not the sort of thing that you brought up at a polite gathering— or Gather.

"Are you saying we're parasites?" the schiera asked, its screech making my ears ring and my head ache. Obnoxious, poisonous, and *loud,* I amended my earlier description.

The kitsune fluffed its three tails slightly in what might have been amusement. I got the feeling it wasn't so much defending us as settling an old score—or just causing trouble. "If the shoe fits, as our human cousins say..."

"They're no *Cosa*-cousins of mine," bat-wing screeched, and my headache went up a notch. Next to me, I could feel Pietr wince. "No cousin at all!"

Oh, shit. I tensed, not sure what was going to happen next.

"Am I a cousin, Ardo?" Danny asked the schiera abruptly, and the kitsune's tails went still, his eyes brightening with interest as his gaze flicked between the two. Uh-oh… What was about to go down?

The schiera glared at the faun from its upside-down perch. "You are fatae."

Wow, that was grudging.

"Am I?" Danny demanded again, stepping forward into the schiera's personal space, and making a big deal about exposing himself, arms spread, to a 360-degree view. "Am I a cousin?"

There was a short silence after that, and my new friend's appearance suddenly made sense to me. Cross-breed. Wow. That was…unusual didn't begin to cover it.

"Am I a cousin, Ardo?" he demanded again, waiting.

"You are *Cosa*-cousin," Ardo said, finally, its liquid-black eyes rimming a little with red. It wasn't happy, no, but it wasn't going to deny the faun. Interesting. My new friend might be more important than he was letting on.

"Then these humans are my cousins," Danny said, maintaining eye contact. "And therefore they are your cousins, as well. You will treat them with at least a smidge of your usual gracious and delightful courtesy—" there was a smothered laugh from someone at a safe distance "—or I will be deeply annoyed with you."

The two locked stares, one upside down and one right side up, like cats measuring up who was boss-tom. It reminded me a lot of Stosser and Nifty's dance earlier, except that there wasn't the accompanying buildup of current, since fatae didn't use it that way. And this one felt nastier.

"Do you understand me, Ardo?"

Hitting his breaking point, the schiera launched itself off

the perch, claws out, a shrill noise that nearly shattered my eardrums coming from its throat like a miniaturized war cry. Danny managed to jump aside and push me out of the way, all one almost-smooth gesture. Pietr, of course, had already disappeared, although he could have been right beside me for all I knew.

Bobo was standing over me before I could do more than blink, growling deep in his furry chest, a seriously scary noise. His thick fur was ruffled, making an impressive barrier against claw or fang, and while his own teeth were canines, not fangs, they were capable of biting through the schiera's wing with one hard munch.

The schiera, being mean and bigoted but not stupid, got the hell out of Dodge, straight up and away.

"You all right?" Bobo didn't look down at me, but scanned the crowd, waiting to see if anyone else was going to be stupid. The kitsune snickered, but everyone else suddenly needed to Be Elsewhere in the crowd.

"Yeah." I did a quick self-check. Bruised and out of breath, but okay. "Danny?"

The faun was already back on his feet, and I noticed, from my vantage point on the ground, that he was wearing seriously scuffed but gorgeously tooled brown cowboy boots.

"You little fucker!" he yelled, slamming his hat down on the ground and yelling into the now-empty sky. "You come back here and try that again! I'll turn you into schiera jerky with your own damn venom, you little ass-wipe excuse for a flying rat!"

All of a sudden, it was all too much. The stress of repeat-edly viewings the attack, the chasing after news, the sudden reversals and the sniping...and now a half-faun cowboy wannabe having a hissy fit in the middle of Central Park.

I lay back on the cold, pine-needle-coated ground, and howled with laughter until my eyes started to water and my ribs hurt, and Pietr reappeared next to me, looking worried, like I'd finally gone around the bend.

"Bonnie?"

I was laughing too hard to answer, and finally he just left me alone until I calmed down and could hoist myself up to a sitting position, still giggling a little. It wasn't funny, but I felt a lot better. Most of the remaining fatae had moved off to another area of the Pintum, and the party went on, although it looked and sounded a lot more subdued.

"Better?" Danny was sitting on a nearby bench, watching me.

"Yeah. Thanks." I didn't hold a lot of emotion pent-up inside me, normally; this blowout had been unnerving, but useful. "You?"

"I'm used to it."

Ouch. Yeah, I could imagine being a half-breed wasn't fun at the best of times.

Danny stared at a nearby pine tree with that thousand-yard stare that meant he wasn't really looking at anything in the park, and then turned back to us, his good-looking features composed, like he was about to recite a speech someone else wrote for him.

"Look—" he seemed hesitant, which I already knew was *not* normal for the man "—shit's going to go down, there's no avoiding it. We need to share information, so nobody gets caught with their britches down and no paper on the roll."

"Elegantly put," Pietr said, and Danny's facade almost cracked.

"But not here," I said, asking a question—not about the location, but about the wisdom of talking in the middle of so many already-overcautious fatae.

"No. Not here." The facade melted, and his face softened into more relaxed lines, once he knew that we understood what he was offering. "There's a place in midtown where the steaks are fine and the martinis beyond compare."

And there was proof, if I needed it, that his human half was dominant, since the fatae rarely drink, and even more rarely with that kind of connoisseurship. Also, that he was quite possibly as interested in me as I was in him. He wasn't playing coy, but we were both on company manners, so it was tough to determine his ulterior motivation.

Not that it mattered. I wasn't going to Mata Hari, but I was totally not adverse to flirting to get what I needed. I had a feeling Danny would respect that.

Bobo begged off—steaks and silverware weren't his thing, and I wasn't sure even the most accepting of restaurants was ready for him. Pietr and I accepted with pleasure; a half-fatae favorably inclined to our doings could be a damned useful ally to have, especially if he was making the offer unsolicited. Venec would kick our asses if we didn't pump him for all he was worth. Lunch was going to be all business. Totally all business. Really. I nodded firmly to myself even as Danny led us out of the park, and we caught the B/D train down to the restaurant. Business, yeah. I think Pietr might actually have believed that.

The Tavern had heavy red drapes and cute young waitstaff and Danny was right, they made killer steaks and devilish martinis. I sipped one, and put it down on the table firmly. I'd be back here, some time when I wasn't on the job.

"You don't like it?"

"My body mass, one of these might kill me."

Danny laughed, and passed me the basket of breadsticks. He'd taken off his cowboy hat, and fluffed up his curls enough that the nubs of his horns were mostly covered, but the staff didn't even look twice. At least one of them had casually identified as Talent when we came in—we made up a lot of the professional waitstaff in the city, because it was a steady, relatively low-tech job—and that meant this place was probably fatae-friendly.

Or so I would have said, before today. Now—I wasn't sure how much being a *Cosa*-cousin meant. But if Danny came here, it was probably going to be okay.

"So how much do you know about what we do at PUPI?" Pietr asked. "You looking for a job?"

"Hah. You are looking at former Patrolman Daniel Hendricks. Before the physical exams got so, erm, invasive. Went into the private sector, after that. Investigations for hire. So it's my job to know when there are new players in town."

Oh, that was interesting. Danny's value as an informant just skyrocketed—which, sadly, also meant that his potential as a playmate went down. Drat. "I thought we were the only ones doing what we do" was all I said.

Danny downed half his drink in one smooth swallow.

"You are. I've got an unapologetic bias—I'm working for my client's interests, whatever they may be, and will do what's required to get them forwarded, within legal limits. You're…you're more like cops."

"Now you're getting nasty," Pietr said, only half joking.

"Hah. You don't know half of it." Danny got serious. "What I do, there's a call for it, but it is what it is, and sometimes it doesn't come out clean. Like I said, I have a bias. The city needs you guys, hell of a lot more than they need me." He finished off his drink, and lifted it so the bartender would know he needed a refill. "Used to be maybe a fifth of the force was *Cosa,* or knew their partner was *Cosa,* and we could actually do something about a current-based or fatae-specific incident, even if not officially. Now? Not so much. And forget about a Talent moving up in the ranks, especially if he's lonejack. So stuff that we used to be able to slap hands over gets out of control, because the lonejacks can't get their shit together and Council doesn't see anything that's not served upon china platters."

Harsh, but I couldn't say it was untrue. Council—and therefore us—were involved here only because of the ki-rin, and the potential for political fallout.

"I'm not going to ask you anything about the case 'cause I don't want to know. I'm only snoopy when I've got a paycheck on it. But I will tell you what you need to know, if you don't already, no charge for the telling. City's on edge. Your reception this afternoon? I'm seeing it, more and more. And you guys're Talent. Nulls?" Danny shook his head, and forked a bunch of green beans into his mouth.

"I wouldn't want to be a Null in a dark alley if that schiera

was in a pissy mood. I'm not saying he'd attack unprovoked…
but I'm not confident he wouldn't, either. Not anymore. And
nobody's paying any attention. It's just…simmering."

"This is recent," I said. "I mean, really recent. When I
came to New York this past summer it…it was off, a little,
but not this bad." There had been that fatae in Central Park,
the one I'd pointed out to Nick our first month here, but he
hadn't menaced us, just…not been friendly, not even in the
Cosa-passing-on-the-street way I'd been used to, in Boston.
There hadn't been active dislike—or fear.

"Yeah." Danny thought about it. "Yeah, it started around
then. Whispers and rumors, mostly."

Beside me, Pietr was taking notes in the little spiral books
we all carried for exactly that, while I kept Danny talking.
For all the cantrips and current-tricks we were learning, in
the end it all came down to information.

"When something simmers," I said, keeping Danny focused on me so that he wouldn't get self-conscious about
Pietr writing down his words, not that I didn't think he
didn't know exactly what we were doing, "it means that the
heat's being kept on it, at a steady pace. Coincidence—or is
someone monitoring the heat?"

Danny didn't have an answer for me, not that I'd really
been expecting one. "I've been hearing about a friend of a
friend, a guy he knew, or her cousin's lover…but the stories
were all the same. Fatae, roughed up by a human."

"Talent?" It wasn't impossible—piskies were pranksters
just asking for a beating, and other fatae like redcaps and
the angeli didn't always play nice, and some grudges were
species-wide and went back generations. A Talent looking

for payback wouldn't be unusual, although mostly they knew better. A Null, on the other hand, could be unpredictable as hell, if they suddenly found themselves confronted with something out of a fairy tale—or a bad acid trip.

Danny actually laughed at that, a dry, husky chuckle. "You think most fatae can tell the difference? You've got two legs, no wings, no horns, no fur. Hrana was right about that much. You all look the same."

Ow. The feeling of depression and self-doubt that had fled earlier returned, settling against the back of my neck like the push of a ten-pound weight.

"Fatae don't trust Council," he went on, "and everyone knows lonejacks won't do shit about other lonejacks unless there's profit in it for them. That leaves you guys. Maybe."

There really wasn't much you could do with the topic, after that. The rest of the meal we tried to talk about other things: Danny was a fabulous storyteller, in addition to being good-looking, and more than once I got the feeling he, at least, would be interested in something off-the-clock. He might be more subtle than his full-blood kin, but not by a hell of a lot.

But I wasn't going there. Partially because I'd learned my lesson the hard way about playing with anyone who might be relevant to the case, even remotely, and partially because I had the feeling that, unlike his fatae kin, Danny was looking for a One True Love. Me? Not so much. So when the meal was over, and we'd argued over who was picking up the tab—we won, since it was a business expense—I shook his hand, got his card, and went home. Alone.

I had just come up out of the subway when someone knocked politely at my awareness.

busy?

My visitor was pretty much the last person I expected to have ping me after hours: Sharon.

wassup?

The ping came back not in words, but an image—of the local art-house theater halfway between her place and mine—and a time. She was inviting me to the movies.

I totally had not been expecting that. Sharon and I worked well together, and the entire team socialized off-hours, but she and I weren't buddy-friends, not the way Nick and I were.

Thinking about what waited for me back at my apartment; an empty space, a cold bed, I made my decision.

be there in thirty

And so the night I'd planned to spend following my mentor's directive to rest and recharge, I instead spent at a moth-eaten movie house with my coworker, eating overly buttered popcorn and watching a Cary Grant movie. Her idea, not mine, but I have to admit, the acting was great, the plot— even as silly as it was—didn't make me wince, and the eye candy, although stylized, was quality. And watching it gave me a little unexpected insight into my coworker. Plus, getting outside my head for a while made the self-doubt and depression take a powder. All good.

After, neither of us seemed to want to go home, and so we ended up in a 24-hour restaurant the size of a shoebox, and drank too much bad coffee and didn't talk about anything other than the movie. It was...nice.

"Y'know, if you think Irene Dunne was cute, I have a friend I should introduce you to."

I was weirdly touched. "Shar. You fixing me up with your friends?"

"Friend, singular. If you're interested. She's about a year out of a bad breakup, so the worst of the psychotic behavior should be over, and the rest would probably just amuse you."

I wasn't sure if it was a good thing or not that she had such an accurate read on me. But then, that was what Sharon did. I read scenes; she read people.

"It doesn't bother you? That I double-up my dating pool?" I'd wondered that; she and Nifty were both such straight arrows, pun intended.

Sharon arched one of those neatly shaped blond eyebrows at me. "You're bi. Big deal. I'm more worried that you'll go through the available dating pool here and we'll have to import people from the left coast to keep you occupied."

I made a ha-ha noise. "Not likely. Y'know, thanks for the offer but…not right now. I'm not really in the dating mood right now."

Sharon paused before taking a sip of her coffee and looked at me over the top of her mug. "Who are you and what have you done with Bonita Torres?"

"Very funny." Okay, it was. I had a definite reputation, and normally I didn't mind it at all. But it was more reputation than fact, these days, and not just because of this case.

A sudden flash of dark eyes and the memory of a touch,

skin-to-skin, shivered through me, and I shut it down, hard. "I just...I'm tired, Sharon. Aren't you?"

"Yes. Of course I am. You're the Energizer Bunny, not me."

Sharon was the oldest of the pack by six years, but we'd mostly broken her of reminding us of that fact. Mostly.

Now that we'd gotten on the topic, sort of, I wanted to ask her about the case, to find out if anything about it was bothering her, if she was finding her reactions to people slightly off-kilter or unusual, if she was feeling the same depression and doubts that I could feel hovering, just waiting for a way back in. But the nonwork atmosphere we'd established over popcorn and bad coffee was like a mist around us, keeping the words from getting said. I wanted to know, but I didn't know how to ask, and the moment passed.

Around 2:00 a.m. I finally staggered back to my apartment for the second time that night. My sheets were cold, and even a quick hit of current to warm them up didn't replace the feel of another body next to me. I could've had a warm companion for the asking. Hell, I had a little black book with names I could have called, even now, if I didn't want to be alone.

"There was a time," I told the dark blue ceiling, "when my bed had hot-and-hotter running company. I was young and energetic and... And god, now I just want to come home and sleep."

All right, that was just a smidge of exaggeration. But I had told Sharon the truth—I was tired. And right now, the way I was feeling, it was probably better I not have anyone in my space who wasn't me. My nerves were shot and my sense of the universe needed adjusting.

The world wasn't any colder or darker than it had been a week before. I hadn't discovered any terrible truth about males of any species I didn't already know before. I hadn't learned anything about my own gender that I didn't know.

Intellectually.

Emotionally, that was another issue entirely.

I pulled the covers over my head, snuggled into my pillows, and searched for a happy place to take into my dreams. It was a long time coming.

Benjamin Venec wanted to be in bed. It was almost dawn, and good, law-abiding, reasonable adults were snuggled in comfortable beds, or just waking up to face the day, not shaking down dubious characters in even more dubious back offices.

"Man, I don't know nothing!"

Venec let a sigh escape him, not entirely feigned. "That? I find very easy to believe."

Lizard was a skinny skank of a human, skin like the underside of a rock and the morals of a squid. He ran a massage parlor—legit, not a skin house or gambling cover—down in Chinatown that was gossip central for a certain type of Talent, "certain" meaning criminally minded. That was why Venec had decided to pay him a little social visit.

Well, that, and the need to actually *do* something more than just sit around and worry. Let Ian ride the desk and deal with the theory and the politics and the make-nice with clients. He was more the hands-on sort, and sometimes hands-on was exactly what was needed. For the situation— and his own sanity. Being the boss was starting to make him a little crazy, like someone was pushing on his chest and the back of his neck at the same time, trying to squeeze him thin, and not even the training sessions with his pups were really scratching the itch to *do*.

Not that he was down here on PUPI business, tonight. Not officially. Tonight he was conducting his own investigation, for his own peace of mind. The two "exterminator" flyers he had found had sent him out into the street, talking and listening, and the gossip he got back was making him uneasy. While he didn't have Bonnie's kenning, or Ian's skill of reading the moment, or even Sharon's ability to truth-sense, uneasy feelings usually meant problems coming down the road, things you sensed, even if you couldn't quite see them yet. Maybe not now…but eventually. Benjamin Venec was a firm believer in being prepared for problems.

"Liz, if I find out that you've been withholding information, I'm going to be deeply disappointed in you."

The speech, and his pose, was right out of a diet of too many mafia movies as a teenager. It seemed to work, though, because the Lizard turned an even nastier shade of pale, and his stubby little nose twitched like a rabbit's.

"I swear." He made a production out of shuffling paper on his desk, but never let his hands go anywhere near the intercom, or the panic button set on the side of the desk. Not when Ben was watching. Lizard wasn't Talent, but he knew enough to predict what a pissed-off Talent could do. "We got some hotheads come in here after a day of work, talking trash, but that's it. Nothing like what you're talking about. No violence, not even a shove. The supernaturals, they're good folk, mostly. Everybody gets along down here, so long as they're not the IRS."

Cash-and-carry industry; rake in the dollars and don't worry about anything except not getting caught. Ben felt a sneer curl at his lips. He'd brought in coked-up bikers and current-wizzed Talent, and they'd all been good folk—when they weren't trying to take his limbs off or fry his brain.

"All right." He leaned back, giving Lizard some breathing room. "If you do happen to hear something, anything, from anyone, you'll let me know, right?"

"Of course." Lizard, deciding that the danger had passed, plastered on an ingratiating smile. "So, why don't you stay a while, relax, now that business is done? I have a new masseuse working, hands like silk over steel, she'd work those tension-knots out of you like something indecent I'm too much of a gentleman to mention."

The offer was tempting, Christ knew. Two years ago, before Chicago and the fallout from there, he'd been a single operator chasing down bail jumpers and errant spouses, hiring himself out for short-term security gigs on the side. Not much glamour, and damn few thanks, but only himself to ride herd on, and the money was good. But when Ian had called him, out of the blue and ten years after they'd last said goodbye, he'd dropped everything and gone up to the Midwest. And then…and then Chicago, and everything After. That was how he judged time these days: before, and After.

But After had PUPI. Ian wanted perfection, and Ben had

to ride herd on the kids every minute, make sure they were as good as they thought they were, and then build them back up when they realized that they weren't. Keep them focused on the job, and not their hormones or...

Especially not their hormones. Or his own, for that matter.

His brain served him a flash of impossibly fluffed hair, and laughing eyes, perfume like warm peaches, and the whisper of an impossible blend of Boston upper crust and New York Latina in her voice, and he felt himself grow hard at even that memory.

Bonnie Torres. The moment he had first sensed her, searching the ether for her father's killer, he had known there was something about her, something they would be able to tap for the still-nascent PUPI team. He'd been intrigued by the feel of her thoughts, at first, the way she balanced passion and logic so cleanly. He hadn't expected the impact her physical presence would have on him. His own personal hell every day, the way she could flick his switches without even trying. And at night...

At night, when he didn't have to be Big Dog, didn't have to be the boss, the teacher...in the privacy of his own over-heated imagination, sometimes her face overrode his current partner's appearance, and he let himself pretend, just for a moment.

"Thanks, but no," he told Lizard, not without some regret. "I kind of like my knots where they are."

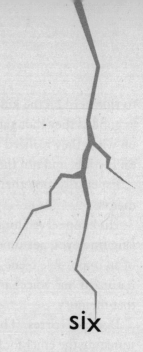

six

What happened in New York City didn't always stay in New York City. In this case, what happened there was of great interest to a man in a quiet office building in Corpus Christi, Texas.

Two men, actually, although Ray West was more concerned with his brother's interest than his own.

William West did not, at first glance, appear particularly important or imposing, despite the luxurious corner suite he occupied. Seen on the street a bystander would notice that his hair was brown and slightly shaggy, his suit was nice but not particularly stylish, and that he had the attitude of a man who had somewhere to be, right now, and get out of his way. And that bystander would, if he or she were a smart human, get out of his way.

Ray had worked for his brother for twenty years now, and not even the memory of the scrawny kid with a lisp

Bill used to be kept him from feeling a sense of awe and menace hanging around his brother as an adult. Something had changed in Bill during college, or maybe it had just come to the fore once he had enough power to not worry what others thought, but Ray didn't question it. Not when that hard, cold willingness to use people made them all a great deal of money.

As his right-hand man, Ray worked very hard to keep Bill from getting upset. Some days it wasn't possible—there seemed to be so many things that annoyed his brother. Today, though, would be different. He had just gotten in from the airport, barely stopping to drop his bags off before coming to report on the results of his trip. "She agreed to your proposal. Things are already in motion."

Ray had brought their pet Talent—a young man with the ability to do what they called the Push—with him, ready to start work, assuming that his negotiation would be successful. You assumed success, you got it; that was the West way.

The fact that their target was Talent as well was no barrier: human or fatae, Talent or not, they were all tools to be used.

Bill nodded, placing the dossier he had been reading down on his desk, and getting up from behind his desk and going to the oversize sideboard that ran the length of his office. He lifted the hinged door and took two wineglasses down, holding one up in question. Ray nodded. It was first thing in the morning, but they had both clearly been up all night—he on the plane, his brother doing whatever his brother did in this chilly office, all alone.

"Of course she has," Bill said in response to his brother's

comment. "It's an obsession with her, to stop her brother from successfully establishing his plan to keep Talent accountable for their actions. She will snap at any straw, and we offered her a very tempting one." He poured a measure of ruby-red liquid from a decanter into the glasses and offered one to Ray, who took it with pleasure. They clinked glasses lightly, toasting to their new venture.

Oskar, their Talent, wasn't good for much else—he was a straw of a human, jumping and starting at every noise, but he could convince a nun to do a striptease, if that's what you wanted from him. Their Talent, augmented by Aden Stosser's knowledge of her brother's personality and thought process, and especially his weaknesses…it was a perfect match. With her directing their Pusher, they could undermine not only her brother, but also his partner. With both of them incapacitated by doubt and uncertainty, their cadre of half-trained investigators would be ineffective at best, and ideally fall apart completely. Even if anything were traced back… Aden was the one with the known grudge, and the black mark already attached to her name. Oskar would claim that she hired him, and nobody would doubt it for a moment.

Neither Ray nor Bill were Talent. Ray never felt the lack; he couldn't say if his brother did or not. Certainly they had enough Talent working for them, one way or another. West Enterprises, Inc. was a consulting firm with specialized clientele worldwide, ranging from media to military, with fingers in both the Null and Talent communities.

You could work with Talent, but you didn't have to like them. Ray felt that Talent were…not quite normal, not quite predictable, like cats. Dangerous cats. Having met with the woman, unlike his brother, Ray had a hesitation—not to the plan itself, but the possible consequences. He thought about phrasing it delicately, or not mentioning it at all, then shrugged. Bill was in a good mood; it was probably safe to say something.

"You know she's nuts, right? We can't trust her a step without our hand on the back of her neck, because god knows what she'll hare off to do, and take our Talent with her." Not that he was worried Oskar would implicate them in any way; he was well-paid to behave, and his heirs would be even better-paid if he died loyal.

"She is not crazy," his brother said in correction as he returned to his desk and sat down in the chair, motioning for Ray to sit down as well. Bill's voice was calm, almost amused, and deeply confident, as though the universe would not dare order itself any way other than he planned. "She is obsessed. Much the same way her brother is, ironically, if toward a conflicting goal. A family characteristic I am quite pleased to make use of, for my own purposes."

Ray sat down and looked into his glass, neither agreeing nor disagreeing.

Bill had read the dossier; he knew how Aden Stosser thought, and how she would react—that was his skill, in judging people's basest instincts, and then making use of them to accomplish his goals. That, he always said, was the secret to his success. Aden Stosser was just another such tool.

But Ray remembered the look in the woman's eyes, the way she had practically quivered at the thought of getting another chance at her brother's organization, and a faint unease settled in his mind. Tools could break, or slip, even under the most cautious hand. No. He was tired from the flight, that was all. Aden Stosser was crazy, and powerful, and that made her dangerous, yes. But his brother was just as powerful and, Ray admitted to himself, just as crazy in his own way.

Bill didn't seem to notice his brother's unease. "I have to go to Cincy tomorrow, for a meeting. You'll be able to keep an eye on things here?" He didn't look up to see his brother's reaction: of course Ray would cover things. That was his job.

"You'll be back on Thursday?" Ray leaned back in his chair, a heavy mahogany piece older than he was, and forced himself to appear unconcerned and in control of things, taking another sip of his wine. Aden was the last piece they had needed, and now she was theirs. Nothing would go wrong. Nothing would *dare* go wrong.

"Friday at the latest. I'm not expecting any difficulties."

"Difficulties. No, I can't imagine they would give you any at all." The two brothers smiled at each other, for once in perfect accord. The project Bill would be closing—the acquisition of a particular piece of legislative support—had been in the works for a year, and the final deal was a foregone conclusion.

But the word plucked at the unease, again. Difficulties. Humans were always the variable, the thing you couldn't be sure of, and when you brought magic into the equation.... Ray chewed at the inside of his mouth, thinking, then brought the subject up again, despite his better judgment.

"This Aden, why does her brother's little project bother her so much?"

Bill looked at him, and Ray wished he'd kept his mouth shut and his hesitations hidden. But it was too late now— falling back was worse than stumbling forward. "Much as I don't want Stosser's eye turned on me, personally," he went on, "you'd think these Talents would want everyone in compliance with their own laws, not breaking them." It didn't make sense, and he wasn't comfortable with things that didn't make sense. Human reactions weren't always logical or practical, but they made sense, once you understood the players and their desires. Aden Stosser...her desires were contradictory, confusing, making an already unpredictable situation even more difficult to gauge. "So what's her game?"

"I don't know and I don't care," Bill said. He took a sip of his wine, looking deep into the glass, following some thought of his own. Ray got the feeling that he was barely in the same room anymore. "I know what she wants, though, and it's what I want, too. If she can stop him, then we won't have to worry about his brats causing trouble, later."

West Enterprises was legal...but their clients weren't always. And for that reason, it was in the interests of West Enterprises, Inc., et al to ensure that the so-called Private Unaffiliated Private Investigators never became any sort of player. Bill West believed in taking care of potential problems before they became actual ones. That was how his business had thrived over the years.

"I won't have one of our projects derailed because they were sniffing around."

Ray let himself chuckle, considering the expensive wine

in his glass. "Careful, you're one step away from sounding like the foiled villain in a Scooby-Doo cartoon."

Bill stared at his brother, his gaze even and cold, making Ray immediately regret his moment of levity. "I have no intention of being either foiled, or a villain. Merely successful."

And what Bill West wanted, he got. No matter how many bodies it took.

Dreams stalked me though the night, some of them in black and white, like the movie Sharon and I had watched, and some so saturated with color it made my eyes hurt. And there were faint mutterings, like someone in the room next door speaking my name over and over, so I couldn't hear details but couldn't tune it out, either. Kenning while you slept was a one-way ticket to headacheville.

Despite the dreams, I somehow managed to sleep through the usual garbage trucks and car alarms my neighborhood was heir to, but a sharp noise inside my own apartment finally woke me up. I lay in bed, tangled in my sheets and still groggy from crap sleep, and tried to figure out what the hell that noise was. I didn't own an alarm clock—hadn't since my freshman-year roommate's alarm had shorted out the third time. So what the hell…

The third ring gave it away. The phone. Right. Half the time I forget I even have a phone, because nobody ever uses it. If the team wants to reach me, they pinged, and…there wasn't really anyone else these days who needed to talk to me.

Except one.

A glance out the window showed me it was still early, although well past dawn. He would have been up and had breakfast already, counting down the minutes until he could risk calling without me snarling in his ear. Sometimes having someone who knew you that well was…

Well, it was nice. Even if he was a morning person with a morning person's impatience to get things started.

I slid down off the loft bed and padded naked across the space to pick up the phone. "Heya, J."

"Bonita."

Uh-oh. J only used my full name when he's in formal mode. Well, two could play that game. "Yes, Joseph?"

He chuckled, letting me know that there wasn't a catastrophe waiting to leap, just him yanking my chain. "Will you be joining me for dinner this weekend?"

This wee…ah, shit.

"Of course I will," I said with an assurance that I don't think even he could tell was faked. I hadn't ever missed J's birthday dinner, not even when I was doing my semester in Madrid. And this year I'd totally, completely forgotten about it.

Damn it, I was total crap. I bet Bobby—J's first mentoree, now a high-powered lawyer out in California—had not only remembered, but already booked his flight home.

I reached across the desk and grabbed a pen, and scribbled *dnr J Sat* on the back of an envelope that came in yesterday's mail. "The usual for gifties?"

"What, I should suddenly change my stripes now?"

I laughed at that, despite feeling that I was a disappointment, a loosah, all that crap. I rubbed the back of my neck, trying to work out the kink there that was making my head ache. "Just figured I'd ask...."

We made some more small talk, and then hung up, leaving me feeling not quite out of sorts, but moderately fey and feckless. *Loosah,* the voice muttered in the back of my brain. *Disappointment. Failure.*

I hated not being the perfect student for J. On top of being an overachiever, I loved him as much as I'd loved my dad—maybe more, part of me admitted—and it hurt to think I might have missed his annual birthday dinner. Especially since he wasn't a young man, and each one, god forbid, could be the last.

I sat at the desk, and stared down at my phone. It was a battered relic of the pre-cell phone age, and wasn't safe-wired—because my core ran cool, it didn't usually interfere with the phone lines—but I'd grown up in a household that had everything grounded to a fare-thee-well, and it still bothered me, a little, that I didn't need to take those same precautions. J had reassured me, over and over, that my running cool didn't mean I was any less powerful than anyone else, but it was true, I wasn't high-res the way Nick was, or Pietr. Even Sharon and Nifty could generate more buzz than I could, and the Big Dogs? They could take us all in a blackout, and not raise a sweat, I suspected.

Yeah, I had the recall, and the kenning, and a fair hand at crafting useful spells but...in the *Cosa* you weren't judged by how much money you had or how good-looking you were, but by how much power you could channel. Current was currency. At least if you were a Talent. The fatae had other ways of counting, but they did count.

I frowned, two fingers drumming the top of the receiver as the thoughts sparked and jumped in my brain, driving the doubts to the sideline. Counting. Who counted?

The scene at the Gather emphasized that there was politics everywhere. Lonejack, Council, even the fatae had their levels, from the piskies at the bottom and the greater dragons at the top, second only to the old ones nobody ever talked about anymore. It was all about how much power you could contain and control.

Power. Power and prestige. It was starting to come together in my brain, although I wasn't quite sure what "it" was, yet. Status. That girl had been—was—lo-res. The dossier Venec had put together said she was blue collar through and through, the first in her family to go to college, probably at the ki-rin's urging. Her mentor had disappeared from the picture when she was seventeen, not unusual, but... The ki-rin had shown up the year after, and had seen something in her, something special. I got the feeling that she'd hung her entire sense of self, her well-being, on that, on being a chosen companion, and now that was gone, or at least damaged, broken.

If you suddenly weren't special anymore, couldn't stand out in the crowd, what chance did you have?

I shook my head violently, trying to knock the thought out of my head. Enough self-pity, Bonnie-girl, I told myself sternly. That was her. That wasn't me. My self-esteem was and always had been perfectly fine and not hung on any one thing, thank you very much.

I stood up and headed for the shower, hoping that hot water would soak this mood off me. I'd been living with shortcomings, current-wise, my entire life. I had achieved more than my dad had, and less than J, and that was all right with me.

Look where wanting to be special had gotten our victim.

That shower, and the unexpected gift of a subway car sliding into the station the moment I passed through the turnstile, didn't quite banish my fey and gloomy mood, and I climbed the stairs at my destination still distracted.

It was a block from my subway stop to the office, taking me past a row of brownstones that had seen better decades. The weather was dry and reasonably warm, so some of the boyos were there, hanging out.

"Hey, mama!"

I shot a dirty glare at the one who had shouted, all of fourteen, wearing a pair of jeans so new they squeaked, and a battered Rangers jersey.

"*Ai mama,* pretty lady," he said, staggering back with his hands to his chest like I'd actually wounded him, "who done you wrong this morning?"

I reined in my mood and slapped it soundly. No need to take it out on someone just trying to say good morning.

"Do yourself a favor, Jack-O," I said to him. "Don't ever miss church. God gets you. Maybe not that Sunday, but eventually."

I don't think Jack or his buddies had been inside a church since the last time their mothers dragged them in by the ears. That was okay: it had been at least that long for me, too. But

the comeback amused them enough that I was forgiven for
not playing our usual flirting game.

They were good kids, mostly. Bored and restless, but good
kids.

"Kids, hah. They're all of maybe six years younger than
you," I reminded myself as I went into the lobby, the current-
lock on the door buzzing me through without a pause. When
we started, that buzz-in had been a puzzle, a challenge. Once
I'd figured out how Venec set it up, it was just another useful
bit of current-tech.

Those six years might as well be a lifetime; I felt at least a
decade older than my street-corner homeboys. I was being
too good a girl, that was all. Upstanding Citizen Blues. All
work and no play was making Bonita a very sober girl. This
weekend? I was dying my hair again. Definitely. Magenta.
Or maybe a nice dark purple. Give Nick something new to
rag me about. Hell, maybe I'd get him to dye his hair, too.
Strawberry-blond would look good on him. And then we'd
go clubbing all damn night.

I stopped in front of the elevator, intending to brave my
inner turmoil there, too.

*A spark of life, suddenly gone out, even as we heard the clang
and crash of the metal box hitting the basement floor.*

I chickened out before the doors opened, and took the
stairs instead, justifying it as exercise. There wasn't anyone
in the break room, but the coffeepot was hot and half-full,
so I wasn't the first one in. I grabbed my mug and poured
a shot, then tested the milk for consistency. Still liquid, still
safe to drink. All it took was one solid mass glopping into
your morning coffee to make you forever suspicious.

My movie-watching buddy came in from the inner office. "Hey."

"Hey yourself." I saluted Sharon with my mug, and took a sip. The brain cells stirred, then shook off the last of the morning's unease and resettled themselves into something closer to work-mode. I probably could just make coffee at home, but had never gotten around to buying a coffeemaker. Why bother, when by the time I got into the office someone had almost always prepped a fresh pot?

"You sleep last night?" Sharon asked.

"A little." Like a rock, hard but uncomfortable, thanks to the dreams.

"I didn't," Sharon said, her voice glum.

That made me give her a long hard look. Last night she'd been in black wool slacks and a dark blue blouse, over loafers, her hair in a French braid—about as casual as she got. Today, a dark blue suit, subtle check pattern, skirt at regulation-knee, plain stockings, black low heels, lilac silk blouse, blond hair in its usual chignon and her curves still as kill-a-trucker lush as ever. Like her 1940s movie heroines, Sharon was cool class all the way. But the woman I'd met back in August would never have admitted to the slightest hint of weakness, even if she'd had a week of insomnia.

I wasn't sure if the change made me feel better or not.

"Bad dreams?" If I could blame it on the popcorn we'd shared, or the coffee, I'd feel a lot better.

"No, I just couldn't sleep. I couldn't stop thinking. There's something wrong about this entire case. You feel it." She wasn't asking a question.

"You mean other than the he said/she said, the potential

fatae-versus-human crap, and the overall ickiness of rape that makes me want to scrub my skin?"

"Yeah. Other than that."

I considered my teammate more closely. She didn't flinch under the scrutiny, maybe understanding that I wasn't looking at her, exactly. Sharon could tell if people were lying. Or maybe she could tell if they were telling the truth. I wasn't sure which, or if there was even a difference. It wasn't precog or kenning, but the fact that she was feeling hinky about this case, too... Just like Pietr.

The Big Dogs hired us for our instincts, not our looks.

"You've done the most interviewing—what are you getting off the people you talked to? What did you put in your report?"

She pursed her lips, then her face twisted like she didn't know what to say, and she looked away. "I don't know. I... The humans are all so filled with emotion, so that confuses the issue. And fatae are tough to read. Their vibes aren't the same, not to us, and not even to each other, so I can't get a baseline. And some of them...their inherent magic just screws with me."

Fatae didn't use magic, not the way we did. They *were* magic, living breathing current. For Sharon, it must have been like trying to ground and center in the middle of a lightning storm. Possible, but really damned difficult with all the distractions.

I felt Venec come in, even with my back to the door, and I held up a hand to keep him from saying anything, not even thinking about how the boss might take it. "So what did you get from the humans, other than emotions?"

The words came more easily this time, as though she'd been thinking about it, subconsciously, just waiting for the right question to be asked. "Everyone feels the same. I can't... The eyewitness stories don't add up, they contradict and cross each other, but they all feel the same. There's none of the disruption I get when someone's breaking from the truth. They're all totally and absolutely convinced that they're telling the truth, even when they can't be. It's making me uncomfortable." She stopped, tapped her fingers on the counter, her polished nails clicking. "This...this whole case is making me uncomfortable, and I haven't even had to talk to the victim," she said thoughtfully.

No, she hadn't. Stosser should have brought her with him—but who knew that we'd have to question two different stories? The evidence we had should have been enough to settle what happened. Next time, we'd know better. Even if the Boss Dog insisted he would do it himself; he was the boss, but *we* were the investigators.

"There's too much belief," Sharon went on, her expression changing slightly, like a shift of light. You only saw it if you were watching for it. "Too much certainty for it to be real."

I almost understood what she was saying. Almost. "Didn't someone feel more certain, more...whatever truth feels like? I mean, everyone can't be lying."

"No?" She sounded like she was up against the ropes, emotionally, and something Danny had said tickled something in my brain, about truth and subjectivity.

"Sharon...can everyone be telling the truth?"

Her head jerked up like I'd yanked a cord, and there was

a sparkle back in those lovely eyes. "Oh. Huh. Okay, that's trickier."

The thought was a wicked nasty one, and I was talking it through even as she processed the suggestion. "Is that even possible? I mean, if one person's telling the truth, and the other has a story that contradicts it... I know truth is subjective but that's... Someone has to be lying!"

I listened to my words a second, and then added, "Or at least...they have to be not telling the truth. Right? I mean, even through a filter, there's truth and then there's not-truth. Right?"

Oh, god, my head hurt. Behind me, I heard Venec start to say something, then check it. I wasn't sure Sharon even noticed that he was there, as she sank into the sofa with a graceful movement that I envied madly. "There's an old joke one of the partners used to tell," she said, indirectly responding to my question. "I don't remember the setup but the punch line was 'the truth, the other truth, and the legal interpretation.' I never worried about the legal side, because that's not...it's not truth so much as it is best-supported-belief. But what I'm getting now...maybe if two people believe something with equal ferocity, they're both true? I mean, isn't that all religion is, anyway—strongly held beliefs claimed as The Truth? And maybe if the perps, being Talent, believed it strongly enough, it affected people who were there, watching?"

Venec made a louder noise that could have been either a cough or a laugh, and Sharon stopped, as though she suddenly realized he was there, but I ignored him. We were not going to get into another religious "discussion" like happened last week. Not without referees handy, anyway.

"Yeah but…the difference between sexual assault and a girl coming on to you isn't like arguing over whose burning branch or dust-devil spoke louder," I asserted, not looking at Venec, even though I could feel him coming closer.

Sharon focused on me again. "I don't know about then, but now—the guy got beat up pretty bad, saw his buddy smashed into dead pulp in front of him. There could be brain injuries they haven't found yet. Maybe he really does believe what he's saying? Or maybe he can't tell the difference anymore between what he did and how he justified it?"

"Could you tell, if you spoke to him?" Venec asked, finally joining into our confab directly.

Sharon considered the question, hard, humming under her breath. Finally she said, "I don't know. I've taken depositions from people in injury cases before, but… Hell, Ben, it would be easier to talk to the ki-rin. I could get a baseline from it.…"

"Not possible," Venec said, moving all the way into the office to stand between us. His dark curls were slicked down as usual, and he looked rested, but deeply annoyed. Not at us, though, I was pretty sure about that. "We have been informed that the ki-rin, overset by recent events and in mourning for the loss of its companion in such a brutal manner, has decided to return home, and will speak with no one while it undergoes a period of reflection and preparation prior to its travel. End quote."

Not unexpected, really, but the news still settled like doom on the two of us.

"It's ducking us," I said. Ki-rin didn't lie, so anything it said would be taken as a hundredweight of gold—like Sharon said, the baseline we could measure everyone else by—and the Council would accept it. Hell, everyone would accept words as gospel, from a ki-rin. So if the girl's story was true, why wasn't it talking?

"Or, equally possible," Venec said, "all of the above claim is also true. It is in mourning and reacting perfectly within character. So far, every player in this scene has acted exactly to character."

In character, telling contradicting truths... "You know what we need? We need a way to talk to the dead guy."

"Bonnie!" Sharon, for the first time since I'd known her, looked seriously horrified. "That's...!"

"A joke, Shar. Okay? A joke."

Mostly a joke. It was possible. Theoretically, technically possible. Current was akin to electricity, and electricity was what the body ran on, and for someone, as the saying goes, "only mostly dead" you could... But it wasn't done. In fact it Wasn't Done At All. Necromancy was one of the really old magics, the stuff that got left behind when Founder Ben—that's Ben Franklin to Nulls—codified the rules of current, and moved us away from superstition and into rational usage.

You might still find people practicing hedge magics; sympathetic magic, or charm-making, stuff like that. If you were Talent, they'd work, mostly. If you weren't...well, you might believe that they worked.

Messing with the not quite dead? No thanks. I'd let some-one crazier and more high-res than me play in that minefield. Like the old ones, that was stuff best left uncalled. Venec just looked at us and didn't say anything, which made me wonder, a little uneasily, what his stance on necromancy was.

Nifty and Pietr showed up then, breaking the mood with a rather heated discussion about baseball that had obviously been going on for a while. While they were hanging up jackets, bitching to each other about stats of some incompre-hensible function or another, Nick staggered in, and Venec kicked us into the main conference room.

Just walking into the room and sitting down, I felt the last lingering shreds of doubt and mental fuzziness fade. The break room was more comfortable to hang out in, but the moment I sat down at the conference table, I felt... energized? Maybe. More confident, less distracted. I guess J was right, and your surroundings really do make a differ-ence: sofas were for schmoozing; straight-back chairs were for strategizing.

Or maybe it was just being surrounded by my pack that made me ready to get back on the hunt. I wasn't going to question it, right now.

Once we were all settled, Stosser came in from whatever back corner he'd been hiding in, and joined the party. Unlike Venec, Stosser looked surprisingly unkempt, wearing the dress-down crunchy granola jeans and flannel that never quite looked right on his tall frame, like a CEO playing woodsman. His face was the normal deadpan, but there were shadows under his eyes that suggested that Sharon and I weren't the only ones who didn't sleep well last night.

Venec was in the process of filling the others in on what Sharon and I had been discussing earlier, so I zoned a little, slipping almost without thought into a light fugue-state where I was almost hyperaware of my surroundings, and studied my coworkers.

Sharon had already surprised me once today, but I knew that her Perfect Princess attitude was backed by a sharp mind, so even being surprised by her wasn't all that much of a surprise. If we'd met in a bar somewhere I'd have been angling for her phone number by the second drink—and she would have shot me down with style and élan.

I watched her for a minute, just for the pleasure of it, then turned my attention to the boys of our group.

Boys. No, men. The tinge of unease that had been dogging me since the gleaning tried to stage a comeback, but I pushed it away. They were my coworkers. My friends, damn it. My pack.

Nick was still the slightly built kid I'd first tagged him as, although the past few months he'd bulked up a little to slender rather than scrawny. You'd think there couldn't be a strand of guile in that entire body...until you discovered that he was a current-hacker, one of the rarest of Talent who could actually interact with computers, using current to get what they needed. Every government organization willing to admit we existed had wanted their paws on him—and a few illegal organizations, as well. But PUPI had gotten him. He said it was because they'd promised nobody would shoot at him...but since in the past months we'd gotten shot at, psi-bombed, tied up, and threatened with loss of bodily organs, I think he might have made a mistake, myself. Why-ever, I was glad he was with us.

Nifty…was still an enigma. On the surface, he seemed an obvious choice for the corporate world: college football superstar; middle-class black kid who made good, then took a look at his odds and decided not to go pro. He claimed that he was planning on going to grad school, and yet he ended up here, with us. Ambitious, aggressive, and loyal; I still had no idea how his brain worked, or what drove him. He was listening intently to Stosser, jotting comments in his spiral notebook without looking down, even though I was pretty sure he was memorizing it all, too, the way he used to memorize game plays.

And Pietr, our ghost. By not looking for him, I could find him easily: in his usual spot at the corner of the table, chair tipped back slightly, gray eyes watching everyone the same way I was. Not a buddy, the way Nick was, but we worked really well together, quietly and without a fuss. He reminded me of J, which was funny because if there were two people more opposite than my upper-crust, high-profile mentor and Gypsy-bred, invisible-under-stress Pietr, I hadn't met them.

The PUPI team. My packmates. They were all good guys. Complicated, yeah. Moody, occasionally. Violent…maybe. If provoked. But not one of them would ever, ever hurt me. I knew that like I knew the layout of my apartment: 3:00 a.m. and pissed out of my mind, I could still walk it without bumping into anything. There was no reason that each and every one of them, today, sent a faint unease through my blood, like a distant alarm.

Disturbed, I moved my attention to Stosser. At least with him, I knew to be uneasy. High-res, high-powered, high-energy, and would do whatever it took to achieve his goals, including moving us around a board of his own creating. J had warned me about Ian Stosser, but the threat was all up-front and obvious, and we'd accepted the risks when we took the job. He would use us…but for something we'd signed on for, and believed in. That made a difference, didn't it?

"I want results today, come hell or high water and I mean that literally. This guy's going to be released from the hospital and if there're no charges pressed he may just disappear, and then we are screwed." Ian's long, orange-red hair was moving as though a breeze was stirring it, a sign that he was seriously upset, even though his current-core was under tight control—there was no repeat of his heat-shimmer from earlier. "We are going to comb the damn site, yes, again. Somewhere there's a piece of evidence that will tell us what really happened out there. Because if those bastards really did attack that girl, and destroy her innocence enough that the ki-rin had no choice but to repudiate her, then the survivor has to be punished. Otherwise, he'll think he can get away with it again. And if he didn't, if…something else happened, then a man is dead at the ki-rin's hooves, and I want to know why."

There was a sort of collective sigh within the room, although nobody made a sound. This wasn't about the Council's mandate anymore. It wasn't even about our reputation. This was about Ian Stosser's rather overdeveloped and manic need for justice. Right now, I was good with that. I got the feeling everyone else was, too.

Stosser leaned back, and Venec took over the briefing. "Sharon, what you were saying earlier about levels of truth? I want you to follow up on that. Do you think that you could create a spell that would sort out degrees of truth?"

"Truthiness?" Pietr asked.

"That's not a word," Nifty retorted.

"Yeah, it is."

"Children, hush. Sharon, can you do it?"

Sharon thought it over. A lot of what we did was using old spells in a new way, a very specific, repeatable, consistent way. Magic as science. That was part of why Council was so uneasy about us: they weren't real big fans of innovation unless they controlled it, and you can't control something that's designed to give the same result no matter who uses it. Especially in the hands of someone using it to find answers, not prove a point.

While Sharon was thinking, I turned my gaze on Venec, the only member of the team I hadn't done a quick-check on, and at that exact instant he looked up from his notes and looked right at me. I mean, right *at* me, like he had mage-sight on in full force. There was an instant of disorientation, his familiar, exhaustion-lined face somehow becoming the mask of a stranger, and something hit me in the gut, stirring my core like a lightning bolt.

Benjamin Venec. The first time I saw him he was playing a dead body, to test us—our job interview, to see if we had what it took to be pups. Even then, I'd been drawn to him, physically. But this…this was different. I surfaced out of my own fugue-state and back to normal space with a gasp, feeling like I'd gone two rounds with a zero-gravity roller coaster. What the *hell* was that?

When I looked at him again, cautiously, his attention was back at his notes, like nothing had ever happened. My skin was sizzling, and he didn't think anything had happened?

I stared at him, and there was just the tiniest twitch in the muscle next to his eye, above his ear, and a drop of sweat at the hairline.

It could have been from anything, but it wasn't. He was as damned-full aware of what had just happened—whatever had happened—as I was. But he wasn't going to acknowledge it. I knew that, the way I knew…

Hell. I just knew. The spark during the training session, this… I couldn't analyze it, not the way my nerves were singing at me, but this was new. This was…

Was going to have to wait, whatever it was. I took a deep breath, found my core, and grounded and centered quickly, forcing myself to focus on the briefing, and only the briefing.

"There are truth-scrying spells," Sharon was saying. "But mostly they're useless, the same way polygraph tests are. Once someone's aware that you're testing them, they can cheat the system. It would have to be indirect, something they couldn't sense and respond to…."

Sharon's voice trailed off and she tilted her head back, and her "let me think, let me think" humming started again.

"Right." Stosser took over the discussion when Venec didn't say anything, still too busy studying his notes. "Lawrence, you work with her on that."

Sharon and Nifty were constantly warring for alpha spot, but they were also both really good at brainstorming. It made sense to put them both on it.

"The rest of you—"

"And Nick," Sharon said, breaking off her humming to lay claim.

Stosser looked surprised: we didn't often interrupt him.

"I think what I'm going to do…it's going to need his specialization."

Nobody ever actually said "hacker" out loud. You didn't even think about it too much. It was an amazing, rare skill… but it was also one of the ones that could go most spectacularly blooey, so it was like not mentioning certain breeds of the fatae—if you don't name them, they won't come by and screw things up.

"All right. Shune, you get to stay inside. Torres, take Pietr back to the scene and don't come back without something useful."

Well. That was nicely non-directed and open-ended. And completely unhelpful.

how the hell are we supposed to know if it's useful or not?

Pings didn't actually use words, but emotions and intents that our brains transcribed into something comprehensible. This one came on an arrow of frustration wrapped with a hint of amusement, shaded with Pietr's unmistakable mental flavor, and I ducked my head to hide the smile I could feel rising. Ian Stosser thought we were all nearly as capable, competent, and borderline-brilliant as he was…and expected us to perform to those standards.

We did our best, and our best was pretty damn good, but our brains weren't Stosser-level.

"I'll follow up on that other matter," Venec said. Stosser looked surprised, and I *knew* some ping went back and forth between them, but Ian just nodded and that was that. Whatever the other matter was, it was need-to-know, and we didn't need to know.

The others filed out, talking animatedly about ideas for a spell. Part of me really, really wanted to be going with them. I was good at crafting spells, and seeing where we could improvise—the Guys had said that I was their best tech, hands down. I should have been working with them.

Instead, I got to go back to the site. Again. Like I wasn't going to see it in my dreams for the rest of the year, already?

"Bonnie."

I didn't jump when Venec came up behind me, despite my general unease. Like before, in the common room, like all the time, he had the ability to slip into my personal space without me reacting—even now, when every other human male other than my mentor set my nerves jangling. Freaky. Although considering the first time we'd met he'd already been in my head, scouting me while I hunted Zaki's killer, maybe I'd gotten so used to second-guessing his motives and intentions that it felt normal to have him in my personal space.

And, after what had just happened, whatever had just happened, him being able to do anything didn't surprise me, although it was starting to really piss me off.

Venec glared at me. "None of that made any sense."

My brain hit a brick wall, and I blinked, gaping at him. What the hell? I knew damn well I hadn't said anything, and that wasn't the kind of thing you say out of the blue, so he had to have heard my thoughts without me knowing, which was impossible, so therefore he hadn't done it. But he had.

Even as I was chasing that logic tangle, I was answering him. "I know it doesn't make sense, but you have a better explanation?"

He'd gotten into my brain before, during that scouting expedition. That's why I knew how damn strong he was; that sort of eavesdropping took immense control and power, as well as the particular skill set called the Push. But even then I'd known someone was lurking, and I'd been strong enough to shove him out.

All right. He knew the feel of my brain, we worked together closely, and right now I was so wound up, it was probably inevitable that I'd leak something. Venec was already always monitoring us, so…

No. That still didn't explain it, or the weird dizzying zing I'd felt earlier from him just looking at me, or… It was weird and disturbing, and I really wanted it to not happen again. I didn't like things I couldn't track down and nail to the wall and break down into basic, comprehensible facts. I especially didn't like things that disturbed and distracted me during a job. The only thing that made me feel better was that I was pretty sure Venec felt the same way about not liking it.

He hesitated, like he was going to say something, and then his hand came down on mine, just a brief contact, palm to the back of my hand. It wasn't anything special: we'd knocked into each other more than once, walking in the office, and there'd been taps on the shoulder, a hand up from the floor…but this one felt different. This wasn't the correction of a teacher, or the help of a coworker. This was a *touch*.

Everything that had been happening until then, the past eight months of building tension, suddenly hit flash point, and I barely had time to think *holy shit and Shinola* before everything exploded.

Not physical, not emotional, not even metaphorical. *Magical*. More than what I'd felt before, more and worse and totally not anything I'd ever felt before. For a second I swore I could feel the thump of his brain working *inside* mine, and then current slipped from his core into mine, or maybe the other way around, or maybe both, and it was like an entire storm's worth of lightning inside your underwear. Literally, because in addition to the current-shock, I got a sexual jolt like I hadn't had since the first time a guy went down on me.

My control tightened and my walls went up like they hadn't since my first high-school dance, and we stared at each other, my pulse racing like I'd just realized I'd missed a flight I was supposed to be on.

What the *hell?*

I wasn't sure if it was his thought or mine. It felt like mine but it sounded like his, and—

"Hey." Pietr stuck his head back into the conference room, his expression a little annoyed. "You coming, Torres, or do I carry this solo?"

"Yeah." Venec sounded dazed, like he'd just seen—or

felt—something he wasn't expecting. That made two of us, Big Dog. "Bonnie, go."

I didn't just go—I fled.

seven

Pietr must have sniffed something in the current, because he hustled me out of the office like he was afraid the place was about to explode. I was so taken aback by what had happened that I let him, barely even noticing his presence as he handed me my coat and we went down the stairs and out through the lobby.

I pride myself, with some justification, on being more analytical than impulsive, on staying focused and calm. Even when I was diving into some new hedonistic impulse, I never lost control. And yet right now I felt like every single inch of me was fizzing and spazzing like a ten-year-old on her first current-rush. What the hell had just happened? Yeah, okay, Venec and I had sparks. We had chemistry. We had ha-cha-cha, like Zaki used to say. None of that explained the weirdness when we looked at each other in fugue-state, or my thoughts landing in his head without intent or effort.

That last…it just wasn't possible. There wasn't any such thing as telepathy, just fine-tuned pings, and pings didn't happen without intent. Not once you got past the wild years of prepuberty, at least, and the two of us were damn-well past that sort of idiocy.

And that…oh, my god that current-shock between us, just then? My legs went wobbly just thinking about it, and not just because it had been too long since I'd had a play-partner who was also Talent. That had been…wow. It made my earlier jumpiness feel like nothing, like an unpleasant hiccup knocked away by an orgasm. And okay, maybe not the best choice of analogies, even if it was probably pretty accurate.

Even once I recovered myself a little, my skin and synapses settling down, there were so many unanswered, probably unaskable questions filling my head and wondering what the hell? that I let Pietr, for once, do all the heavy lifting in the conversation.

It was a very quiet subway ride down.

We stopped on the way over to the scene, and picked up coffee and a bagel with cream cheese from one of the corner carts. The harsh caffeine did the job, burning my throat and making me focus on the here and now. Pietr kept sliding looks at me, the way guys do when they think they're being subtle. I ignored him, eating the bagel as we walked even though I wasn't really hungry. We burned calories fast, when we were working, and even with J's scolding I hadn't had a chance to recharge properly.

Finally I reached out and slapped my partner on the shoulder, letting him know I knew he was hovering.

"You okay?" he asked.

"Yeah," I said. I didn't know if it was true, but we were going to make like it was.

We crossed the street at the crossing, ducking around the cabs waiting for the traffic light to change, and turned left, surveying the site. The difference a few days made in an otherwise unremarkable site was...scary. Where, in the early morning of the attack, the ground had been bare and cold, reflecting nothing but blood and mud, it was now...

"Sick."

"Huh?" I looked at Pietr, almost surprised that he was still next to me.

"All that. It's...sick," he repeated.

"All that" was the piles of offerings: flowers and stuffed animals, saints' candles in their tall glass pillars, and countless notes, folded and already yellowing. One pile had built near the site of the actual attack, and the other located on the other side of the walkway. Literally opposed; one facing off against the other, vying to be the more impressive, more important statement.

"You've never seen memorials before?" They sprouted anywhere there had been a violent crime—hit-and-run, a deadly mugging, a drive-by shooting...some grew, some didn't. It all depended on how much publicity they got, how much word of mouth.

Pietr put his kit on the ground, and bent to pick up one of the notes from the second memorial. He opened it, and then dropped it almost immediately in disgust. "Never ones dedicated to a dead would-be rapist."

That's what the second group of notes and candles were: an homage to the dead man. I picked up the note Pietr had dropped, and smoothed the paper out so I could read it.

We know the truth. That animal will get what's coming to it.

It was handwritten, in black ink, in a scratchy script that looked like a woman's, or a man with a penmanship class somewhere in his past, dripping with hatred for the ki-rin.

"Are they all like that?" Pietr reached to pick up another one, but I grabbed his elbow roughly, stopping him midreach. "Don't touch anything else. Wait."

Pietr stood, and watched me, his gaze cool and patient. In the hierarchy of our pack, I wasn't alpha, but Pietr was omega. If I said wait, he waited.

"How many notes, would you guess?"

He looked the collection over carefully, walking around but careful not to step inside an invisible but obvious boundary. "Twenty? Maybe twenty-five? A bunch are weighted with stones, but not all of them. It hasn't rained or been particularly windy overnight, but some of them might have been blown away."

"Seven candles. None of them have burned all the way down—one was never lit. Do you know what saints they're to?"

Pietr gave me a Look. "You think I'm a good Catholic boy? You're the one with the Latina last name."

"Believe me, I'm not a good Catholic boy, either." My dad might have been, but by the time I'd come along and my mom had walked out, he'd given up on the Church of Anything except his work. He'd been a carpenter, a damned good one. J said the only way I took after him was my attention to detail and a certain fondness for things that weren't good for me. J went to church but never made a deal about me joining him or not, and anyway he went Protestant.

And none of that had any bearing to the case, so I shut that line of thought down, and brought my attention back to the notes.

Pietr got down on his knees and pulled a small notebook and ballpoint pen out of his coat pocket, squinting at the labels on the sides of the candles and writing something down for each one. Was there a patron saint for accused rapists? I was betting there was. Probably the same one pedophiles and abusers prayed to.

"Count the visible notes, too," I told Pietr. "But don't touch any of them, not even to get a better count. Not yet, anyway."

"And the stuffed animals?"

There were only three in this pile. One teddy bear with a broken heart sewn to its front, and two snowy-white and sparkly unicorns with their horns cut off. Despite my attempt to be cool and calm, a shudder went through me at the casual promise of violence implied by that.

"Just make note of 'em. Unless you brought a camera?"

Pietr gave me a Look.

"We really need to start. Even if it goes on the fritz half the time. One of those cheap disposable ones that use actual film, maybe." I made a note to myself to buy a few and throw them into my kit. It couldn't hurt. Especially if it meant I didn't have to glean every damn detail at every damn crime scene, going forward. Relying on magic for everything was just stupid. And I'd tell Stosser that, too, if he bitched.

My partner shrugged and opened his kit, pulling out a vial of metal shavings and a natural-bristle paintbrush. The current-charged shavings, brushed around an object, would help us determine if anything had been magically booby-trapped, without us actually triggering it. Nifty and I had run that up, after one of Venec's nastier tricks during training. "You think someone left an unpleasant surprise?" I asked.

"Maybe. I'm not going to take any chances with people who leave offerings to an accused rapist."

Accused, attempted rapist, technically. But since I shared the sentiments, I left Pietr to his job, and stepped across the paved jogging path to look at the other pile of offerings.

More stuffed animals here—a lot of unicorns with their horns intact and blue ribbons tied around their necks. Blue, for...right. The Virgin Mary. Purity and loyalty. Between that and the candles...had any of the victims been religious? I hadn't even thought to ask, or wonder if it might be important. Something deep inside said it wasn't a factor, but Stosser would give me hell if I thought of something and dismissed it on a gut feeling, especially if it turned out to be relevant, later. I pulled my own notebook out of my coat pocket, and jotted the thought down for later.

So. There were fewer notes on this side, but more candles, almost all of which had guttered out. Interesting. Had they been left here earlier, and the others placed later, or were they better protected from the wind on this side, and so didn't blow out?

I pulled a strand of current from my core and played with it absently, passing the energy from gold to green and then back again as I thought. It wasn't as good as holding one of my scrying crystals, but it helped. "Is there a spell to determine when something was placed in a location, and if not, can we fake it?"

"What?" Pietr called from where he was crouched, his head turned to look over at me.

"Nothing. Thinking out loud. Damn bat-ears on your head, boy."

My partner made a rude gesture, and went back to his own job.

About ten stuffed animals, a bunch of roses, now dead and brown, so they'd probably been put there right after the attack, and a hand-tied bouquet of early wildflowers, wilted but still pretty. Did florists sell wildflowers, or had someone actually gone out and picked them? A scattering of notes, mostly on note cards rather than the sheets of paper in the other shrine. I wasn't going to touch them until Pietr had tested this pile, too, but one of them was faceup and still legible:

You did not deserve this. We will hold you in our prayers.

Nice thought. Useless, in my opinion, but nice. Nobody deserved any of this—even the dead guy hadn't deserved to be gored like that, not without a trial and conviction.

I paused, and considered. Yeah, even though I hadn't felt anything watching him die, I really did believe that.

Good. Okay. A little of my balance came back, and with it, my focus. Let the anonymous mourners pray. I'd take a more proactive route.

I took out my notepad again, and did a quick sketch of the display from a couple of sides. I should have gleaned it, but the thought of having to regurgitate it all up again… This way everyone could see it, and leave me out of it after the fact. Distance. The Big Dogs were always on us about keeping distance, and I'd proven already I needed more of that. Besides, J had spent good money giving me art lessons. I should use it every now and again.

The scratch of the pencil on rough-coated paper was soothing, and the lines quickly resolved into something recognizable. I was no great shakes as an artist even after those lessons, but I'd become a reasonably competent draftsperson.

When I had everything sorted to my satisfaction, I put the notepad away and chewed on the end of the pencil, looking at the display without really seeing it. No preconceptions, Stosser said. Facts only. Find clues. Clues to what?

In my hyperaware state, I actually heard and felt Pietr come up behind me.

"Everything's clean on that side. No signature flares, no nasty surprises…just paper and plastic and baby-safe fabric."

"Great. Check these?"

He knelt to do so, while I kept staring out across the site, my eyes half-focused. "What are we looking for?" I asked, as much for my own benefit as hoping he'd be able to tell me.

"Something that shouldn't be here."

"Very helpful."

Thankfully, expectedly, he didn't take offense at my sarcasm, but finished the testing.

"All clear here, too. When you did the gleaning...what were you picking up? I mean, I know what I saw, but...was that everything? If this was a crime of passion, do you think if we went in together..."

"Yeah. Oh. No. No no no." I saw what he was leading to, and I wanted no part of it. "That ended really badly last time, remember?"

Last time we had gone in to get a full gleaning, and gotten trapped in the backlash of the emotions of a Talent as he died. We'd all been linked together, pooling current, and still the overrush had been so powerful we almost died, too. Stosser and Venec had laid down the law after that: physical gleanings only.

But Pietr had a point, damn him. The physical detail told us who was there, and what the end result was, but an emotional reading of the attack would tell us more about the *why*. I hadn't done it before, in my first gleaning, because it was dangerous—and unneeded. But now, with doubt about the attack itself, if I could glean the girl's emotions, maybe get a better idea of what she had been feeling...

Did not want to go there. Did not even think about going there. Losing objectivity was a really bad idea, and I wasn't sure it would count as a "fact" in Stosser's eyes. But if it let us nail down the case, then it was good, right? But I wasn't going to do it linked. I was better than Pietr at gleaning and—

And if it had been rape—even attempted rape—then I owed it to the girl to keep her feelings on this side of the gender fence. That went back to my feelings about the first gleaning: there was no need for her to be violated like that twice.

"I go in alone. And if this doesn't work," I warned him, "we never ever mention it to anyone, and the Big Dogs never know."

"Naturally."

Hah. Good to be on the same page with that.

"You—"

"I've got your back," he said calmly, and I could hear him settling down on the grass behind me. I could visualize him without even looking: slender and dark, his face still but his gray eyes watchful, probably making a face at how cold the ground was even through his long wool coat, but not saying a word of complaint; resolved and ready. If anyone came along while I was otherwise occupied, or if anything happened, he'd be there to take care of it. That was why we worked in pairs, whenever possible.

I could let go of the physical now.

It took me a few minutes longer than usual to slide into a working fugue-state. I was too aware of where I was, of what had happened here, to let myself relax, even with Pietr watching out for me. He was my partner, my friend…but he was also male, and right now that awareness was influencing everything else. No way to avoid it. This was a place where violence had been done; violence and sex wrapped up in each other and fueled by male aggression. Being female, in this place, had been dangerous.

Face your fear. That had always been J's mantra. Face it, own it, and then get on with it. I took a deep breath and accepted my unease, and then tried to let it go. Some of it clung, like ice on a window, but enough slid away that I was able to center myself and move down into my core.

Seen with mage-sight, Pietr was only slightly more visible than he was normally: a calm soothing flow of current, like one of the deep and still lochs J and I saw when we went to Scotland. Nessie might well be under there, and you'd never know until she took half your boat for a snack.

Pietr and I worked so well together because we were so much alike: the others on the team had jangly, sparky, high-movement cores, especially Nifty, who never seemed to settle enough to be properly grounded. Pietr and I, we were the calm ones.

That was why Stosser had sent us. He knew that we were going to try this. Damn him. I still wasn't quick enough to pick up on his reasons until they were shoved in my face.

When you're in full fugue-state, though, it's tough to really worry about anything outside, anything nonmagical. You're too grounded, too totally focused. That's the point of grounding; nothing can knock you over, magically or physically, if you're doing it right.

I opened my eyes, and looked out at the shrine for the girl.

Almost every offering carried the faint, barely visible echo of current that inanimate objects acquired when they were held for a long time, or with great emotion, by a Talent. Not unexpected. She had been—was—one of us, and news was spreading fast. Most of the current-traces I saw were the normal blues, greens and golds, pale and dark, coating the objects like refracted light. An occasional burst of red and purple, agitated even after all this time away from the person who had handled them. A faint hint of... I leaned forward, trying to trace the shadow I saw. Something neon and not-neon all at once, sliding away when I tried to connect with it. If I'd been on my own time I might have followed, made contact, but interfering with the evidence was very much not standard operating procedure as hammered into us by one Benjamin Venec, and I really didn't want him reading me a lecture this week.

Besides, I'd never even heard of black current before, and I wasn't going to go poking my fingers into something I didn't know. I gleaned the memory of what it had looked and felt like into a safe place in my brain, and moved on, diving deeper into the ether, moving beyond the current and into the emotional undertow.

The offerings all came up muted and mingled; the only thing I could pick up for certain was anger and sadness and a tinge of something I couldn't quite identify, but thought might have been applied to the black current. Figuring I'd taken as much off that as I could, I moved my awareness back up and beyond...toward the site of the actual assault.

I don't know if someone had directed people to put their offerings here, or if it just happened, but neither pile was at the exact spot. It took me a few seconds, in mage-sight, to identify the bushes I'd seen in my gleaning, but the moment I touched it, there was no doubt. I'm not an empath—I've never met an actual, functional empath, although there are some who claim they can read strong emotions, even in

Nulls. But there are some emotions so strong that they take on an actual solid presence in the current, without having to go into the undertow. Fear. Pain. Anger.

Really strong emotions, almost strong enough to create an echo of who had been projecting them.

Almost, but not quite. It was enough, though, to confirm that the strongest of those weren't the emotions of the participants, but rather the offering-makers. I wasn't getting fear or lust or even anger, but a sense of greed, worry, anticipation—and a tricky, twisty thread of something I couldn't quite recognize.

This was useless. The people who left their offerings might have had the wrong place...but they'd walked all over the actual site, knowingly or not. And they'd been projecting just enough to contaminate anything that had been there, to draw tendrils off, and plant feelers of their own in, until untangling it was well beyond my abilities.

But what about the girl? Where was she, in all of this? I tried again to find her, searching for older, stronger emotions underneath, but came up empty.

Normally that would be, well, normal. We're taught control as our very first lesson in mentorship. Control is what allows us to use current, and not get brain-fried by overrush, when current overpowers the meat. Still, she had to have tried to defend herself, to call for help, and emotion-driven signatures etch themselves deeper. Panic or fear or any kind of heightened excitement—good or bad—should still have resonated in the ether. Instead, I got the magical equivalent of dead air.

I was good, but not good enough.

"We need to get Stosser out here," I said. My voice sounded odd to my ears, as though I was listening from underwater, and Pietr's acknowledgement was even more distant and watery, but I didn't pause to consider it. Standing up, I walked across the pathway, absently slowing down to avoid a middle-aged Rollerblader who seemed equally oblivious to me, and went back to the other pile of offerings, the ones Pietr had cleared first. Pietr followed me, keeping a few careful paces between us, to make sure his signature didn't interfere with whatever I was reading.

"Holy shit."

I can, when the need calls for it, swear like a seasick sailor. But this…it blew everything more explicit out of my mind.

"Bonnie?"

torres? A sudden ping in my head: concern and alarm wrapped in a silver bullet.

"Hang on," I said to my partner, patting the air to indicate the need for quiet, and dealt with the surprise visitor.

what are you doing? My ping in response was formed of definite annoyance, like that silver bullet sent back to the source. If he was going to take up lurking in my head again, shadowing me like some damned untrained amateur, we were going to have words, me and Mister Venec were, oh, hell yes.

heard yelp The pingback was still alarmed, although it was muted now that I'd responded. Normally pings just carried the sense of words, but maybe because I'd been so attuned to emotions, or working in deep fugue, I could practically taste his concern, like the bittersweet of fresh blackberries on my tongue.

Oh, for... *am okay*

sure?

go away, venec!

He took the brush-off, and any sense of him slipped from my awareness. Left alone, I was able to concentrate on what had shocked me. The tinges of black in the current I'd seen across the way were nothing compared to what was roiling over the other shrine-offerings. Not everywhere—there was a lot of clean blues and an interesting shimmering brown, plus a lot of red, faded around the edges: all colors I'd learned to expect off an emotionally charged item, although nobody really knew why, yet. The black, though...

My first instinct had been right, I decided. There was no way that black gunk was safe to touch. I didn't even want to *look* at it.

"Pietr. C'mere." I waggled my fingers, hoping he would understand what I meant. Sure enough, a few seconds later I felt his fugue-state slide up next to mine, like two soap bubbles floating next to each other. A gentle brush and the bubbles touched just enough to connect; still two distinct bubbles but with a shared wall between them. Another new trick we'd been working up; it took a lot of teamwork— and a lot of trust. I was pleased to feel it working without a hitch.

see that?

The shared spot made our pings turn into actual words, more than merely emotions or impressions, but it took a lot of energy to hold steady, and I could already feel my reserves starting to ebb.

★what is that?★

★don't know. there was some on the other side but not as much. none at the actual attack site★

Pietr muttered under his breath. ★it looks…almost familiar. like I've seen it somewhere before★

I got a sense of him stretching out, trying to touch it, and mentally slapped that idea.

★don't★

★why not?★

★you're kidding me★

A sense of unknown danger, and Venec busting my ass if Pietr got himself killed.

A sense of amused reluctance flowed into me, then agreement, a suggestion that we were done, and the soap bubble popped.

I followed suit, rising out of fugue-state and getting back my awareness of the outside world, wobbling a little as I did so. The pile of offerings looked exactly as they had before. I turned and looked back at the site of the actual attack. It looked the same, too. But it *felt* different now.

"So?"

We'd barely gotten into the office and shucked our coats before Stosser pounced, dragging us into the main conference room to make our report. Everyone else was already there, looking pretty beat-down. I was guessing the morning had gone about as well for them as it had for us. At least there was food—I'd been using too damn much current again, and I was starving like that bagel had been two days ago. Nick leaned over and shoved a white cardboard carton in my direction.

"So, nothing." I pulled out a chair and grabbed the carton, opening it as I spoke. If I focused on the food, I could ignore Venec sitting across the table from me. I was still freaked over the incident earlier that morning, and pissed that he was bopping into my head like he owned it, and a hundred other things that I didn't have time or energy to deal with right now. "I couldn't get a fix on anything dating back to the actual incident. Too damn many Talent tromping all over the site, making it into a damned shrine, contaminating it. Like someone walking through blood splatter with muddy shoes."

Mmm, grilled tofu and mushrooms in some dark brown sauce that smelled wonderful. They'd hit the Thai place, yay. I reached for a fork, and caught Sharon giving me a speculative look. I felt the immediate urge to see if my long-sleeved T-shirt had a stain on it, or if I had mud on my face, or something, but refused to give in.

"I was afraid of that," Stosser said. "Damn."

It took me a minute to realize he was responding to what I'd said.

"Shrine?" Venec tilted his head in query. "Was that what you were reacting so strongly to?"

Nifty leaned forward, clearly expecting some new revelation to chew on. I declined to enlighten him. Whatever was happening between me and Venec was going to stay between me and Venec. Or, hopefully, just between me and me. I so did not need or want complications in my life right now, and shit like that was totally a complication.

Even though I really wanted to know why and how it happened. And my id was screaming for more, please, of that sexy stuff.

Outwardly, I shook it off. "Sort of. Sorry about that, boss, didn't know I was projecting." I meant it to come across as snarky, but Venec refused to take the bait.

"Don't take it personally, Torres. I keep tabs on all of you, in case…"

In case we needed an immediate bailout, was what he wasn't saying. Did I believe him? No reason not to…I'd known he was keeping tabs, if not how closely, but it felt like he was throwing up smoke, somehow. That was job-related. The connection between us… I was suddenly aware of Nifty still watching me, and I moved the conversation on.

"Anyway, yeah. Two piles of offerings, one for the girl, one for the dead guy. You were right, people are choosing up he-said/she-said sides. And…" I hadn't answered Venec directly, but the cause of my yelp needed to be shared, if not the aftermath. "There was something there, on the site," I said slowly. "I don't know if it's connected or not, or if it's important."

I had the boss's attention now, and everyone else's, too. Even Nick put down his fork.

"Everything, Torres," Stosser ordered.

Right. "There was… When I looked at the items, there was an undercurrent around some of them, like if you were looking at a stream, nice and clear, and then suddenly you saw an oil slick running along the bottom."

"Oil slicks float," Sharon pointed out.

"Fine. God, you're annoying sometimes. Sludge. Sewage. Something thick and nasty."

"Could it have been from the ki-rin?" Stosser asked. "We don't know much about the fatae, if they have their own significant signature..."

I shook my head. "No. Emphatically no. Not unless every damned thing ever said about ki-rin was totally wrong."

"But you're sure it was current?" Nick asked.

"I... Yes." I wasn't sure why I was suddenly so certain, but I was. It hadn't looked or felt like any current I'd ever encountered; I'd never hesitated touching current before, in any form, tame or wild, but... "Yes, it was current."

Pietr picked up the report. "Bonnie's right. It was nasty. I only caught a glimpse of it, working backup, but you did not want that anywhere near your core."

Hah. That from the man who had wanted to stick his fingers in it, magically speaking.

"But you don't think it's related to the crime itself?"

I looked at Pietr, who was, as usual, holding up the wall with his backside. He shrugged. I looked back at Stosser. "It might be. The fact that it's all over the site can't be overlooked. I'd suggest either you or Ben go take a sample. It's out of our league."

"Hey!"

Nifty was the one who protested, but Sharon looked ruffled, too. Nick just picked up his fork again and went back to eating,

"No, she's right," Venec said. "I heard her reaction when she saw it. Anything that makes Bonnie jump like that—"

"Hey," I protested, which he ignored.

"—is not something that we want you guys poking around in. I'll go down tonight and investigate." There was something in his voice that made me look sharply at him, but he was unreadable. I had the feeling that if I dug a little I could pick up whatever he was hiding but...no. If I wanted him out of my head, I had to stay out of his, too. Fair was fair.

"So the scene is basically a wash?" Sharon asked, clearly disappointed.

"Pretty much, yeah," I told her. "Except the amount of attention it's getting. That was unnerving. Is that sort of thing normal?"

"You're asking about normal in this city?" Venec was amused, I could tell that much without even trying, although his voice was dry, as usual. The Big Dog had a dark sense of humor.

"You know what I mean—Talent-specific attention. My mentor says that there's tension growing everywhere—are we looking at a potential flash point?" I was really proud of myself for using that term. I just hoped I'd used it right.

"I don't think so," Stosser said, but he didn't sound as confident as I expected from him. From the looks on the faces of my coworkers, though, they were all reassured. "There's something building," the boss went on, "but the players have pretty much gone to ground on this particular instance, and not letting themselves get co-opted, so... But that doesn't mean we can slack off. We close the case this week, before anyone gets any bright ideas."

Pietr moved the spotlight over to Sharon. "Any luck with the truth spell?"

Sharon looked uncomfortable, which was damned unusual for her: she had a fabulous poker face. "Not...exactly. Maybe."

"Maybe?" Stosser didn't sound too happy. I guess they hadn't had a chance to give their report before we came back?

"It doesn't exactly go truth-lie...more like...shades of gray," Sharon explained. Her hands stayed steady on the table, not moving at all. She may not have been confident, but she wasn't going to apologize or temporize, either.

"What, a white lie versus a Really Bad Lie?"

Sharon visibly bit back an instinctive riposte—even she didn't snark back to Stosser during business hours.

Nifty started to say something, but someone must have kiboshed him, because Sharon went on uninterrupted. "More like it tells us how strongly the person being tested believes what they're saying, or if they have doubts."

"Less truth and more veracity? Conveying truth, rather than absolute truth?" Venec leaned forward, like he'd just scented something particularly juicy. That was what we'd been discussing, in the break room: *believed* truths. What was he seeing that I wasn't?

Sharon nodded. "Yeah. Exactly. And before you ask, yes, I'm pretty sure I can fine-tune it so we can tell the difference between fact and faith, but first I need to figure out exactly how accurate that fine-tuning can get."

"What, you didn't test it?" I asked, surprised. Sharon was methodical and Nifty was thorough. For them to let it go without a test...

"We did, but…well, in order to really test it we need an accurate benchmark, and…"

Suddenly the looks I'd been getting from my coworkers since I got back made sense. "And you needed somebody who is besettingly open, not to say distressingly honest, to get that benchmark, huh?"

Sharon looked at Nifty, who looked at Nick, who looked up at the ceiling as though disavowing any and all knowledge of any such conversation. "Well. Yeah."

I sighed. "All right," and I offered up my hands as though expecting to be cuffed. "Do your worst."

We set up in the second-smallest conference room, since the main "experimental" one was still housing my gleaning, and nobody wanted to try to run two different spells at the same time, especially when one was still experimental. Like the movie said, "Don't cross the streams." Just because you don't think anything bad will happen doesn't mean nothing will.

We shoved the table off to the side of the room, and I got to sit in the armchair, with Sharon sitting across from me, about a foot away. The rest of the crew hung back, lining the wall on the other side of the room: they weren't needed, but nobody wanted to miss the show.

Having a spell cast on you is an interesting experience. Despite the popular media-driven opinion of magic-users— thanks so much, J. K. Rowling—most of the time we don't actually use formal spellwork; hell, most Talent didn't use current knowingly, day-to-day. Maybe a flick of it to reheat coffee, or make the homeless person go to the other end of the subway car, or keep from getting wet if it rains and you don't have an umbrella. Small things; mostly directed at inanimate objects, or other people—Nulls, who wouldn't know magic if it hit them in the face.

Having someone knowingly cast a spell on you, sitting there and letting it happen, was a lot like getting a shot. The technician might tell you it wouldn't hurt, and you might know it wouldn't hurt, but you braced yourself anyway.

Sharon smiled at me, amused. "Relax, Bonnie."

"This is relaxed as you're going to get from me. Do it already."

She nodded, and I could almost see her ground herself, slipping into fugue-state. Her face went still, almost slack, and her personality went Elsewhere, deep inside her core. Weird to watch...

"As I ask, so must you answer, truth inherent, not subjective."

Wisps of current prickled on my skin, and I shivered.

"Nice touch, that, the 'not subjective' part."

Her eyes opened, and she looked at me, personality back front and center. "Thanks."

"Of course, it's bullshit, since all truth is subjective. It's all your point of view. Like someone's definition of sexy. I think you're hot, Nifty doesn't. Which one of us is wrong?"

I said it so conversationally, so casually, I think it took everyone a minute to realize what I'd actually said, myself included.

I'm not sure who blushed harder, Sharon or Nick. Nifty just laughed; he didn't give a damn if Sharon knew what he thought of her, one way or the other. Neither did I, really, but I'd prefer to have made the comment under my own steam, not a spell.

Now that I was aware of it, the current shimmered around me, like the haze you see over a campfire, only iridescent. It wrapped around my hands, and up to my chest and throat.

I held my hands up, examining them. "Pretty. Can the rest of you see it?"

"Nope."

"Nuh-uh."

Even Ian was shaking his head no, so it wasn't a question of skill or power. The caster and the castee were the only ones who would be aware of it. "That intentional, to make it visible to the speaker, sort of full disclosure, or did you screw up?"

"It was intentional," Sharon said stiffly. I'd figured it would be; Sharon might have worked with lawyers, and held her cards close to her lovely chest, but when it came to current she was about as unsneaky as they came. If she was going to spellcast you, she'd let you know.

"So. Test me. Or have we already established that it works?"

"Can you tell a lie?" the boss asked.

"I can lie like a professional when I need to," I told Stosser. "Otherwise you'd have fired me already." Oops.

"Can you lie *now*, Bonnie?" Sharon asked, redirecting my attention to her. "We need to test if someone can shade the truth while the spell is on them."

"Oh, right." I tried to think about something I could say that would be a half-truth. I blinked, and then blinked again, unable to come up with a single thing. All right, so I was a blunt, honest sort as a rule, but I had been telling Stosser the truth—I *could* lie, when needed.

Only not now.

All right, Sharon had wanted to test for half-truths and gray areas, too, right? How about something that wasn't quite a lie?

"I've never slept with anyone I didn't know their name."

There was a snicker I barely heard. Damn it, I'd meant to say anyone that I didn't love—which was a sort-of lie, because I'd never slept with anyone I didn't like a great deal, but love...that was a little trickier to pin down. I wasn't sure I'd ever actually been in love, honestly.

"First name, or last?"

I seized on Nifty's question, meaning to have a little fun with him. "First, of course."

Except what I said was "First and last, of course."

"Damn it!" I put my face in my hands, willing myself not to say anything more. I had no problem with being honest, but even I had some things I had no desire to share—and the knowledge that the decision wasn't mine anymore was making me feel distinctly uncomfortable.

Nobody should have their volition taken from them, not even if they agreed to it beforehand. The right to not incriminate yourself, right? Even if you were not guilty.

Sharon nodded at my outburst. "Not what you meant to say?"

"No. Forget about it, get this thing off me. I don't want to be your lab rat anymore." Especially with recent events. I wasn't even willing to think about what had happened between Venec and myself, not even inside my own head right now: if someone asked me the wrong question, unknowingly...

Sharon hesitated, shooting a glance sideways at Stosser.

"I mean it, Sharon. Break the spell or I'll do it myself." I didn't know if I could, actually, but the panic I could feel start to bubble up inside wasn't something I wanted to mess with. And if I, without any real things to hide, felt that way... what would an actual suspect feel like? If panic hit, and they tried to throw off the spell...

Sharon needed to recalibrate this thing to be less obvious, and fast, before she tried it on anyone else. Otherwise she could get hurt.

"Shar..."

Stosser nodded, and Sharon released the strands of current, letting the spell disperse.

The result was almost immediate, and my panic faded. I took a deep breath, calming my nerves and letting my core settle back into its usual cool coil. "Well. That was a truly delightful experience. We'll have to do that again sometime real soon."

Venec, damn him, laughed.

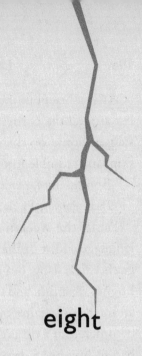

eight

Much to my surprise, what had felt like a half hour, max, in the hot seat had actually eaten away what was left of the afternoon. Stosser and Sharon's debriefing—making me relive every detail, every feeling and frustration, so they could figure out how to modify the spell—took us into the evening. The late lunch kept me going, but when I staggered out to find the rest of the team hanging around like vultures, I demanded someone buy me dinner and a drink. Possibly lots of drinks.

My coworkers, bless 'em, are usually up for a challenge like that. Sharon was understandably wiped out from controlling the spell and just wanted to go home, and Nifty claimed a previous engagement, but Pietr and Nick took on the obligation.

Venec and Stosser were pointedly not invited. I don't think they even noticed.

After a brief but intense negotiation, we ended up in the bar around the corner from my apartment. The guys could stagger home on the subway: I wanted to be able to hop, skip, and stumble into my own lobby.

"Bonita, *chica, cómo está?*"

"*Bien, gracias,* Paula."

Paula, the weeknight bartender, spoke seven different languages, four of them fluently and three well enough to get her face slapped. I only spoke three with any comfort— English, Spanish, and German—but that was enough to play an interesting game of Russian roulette: each drink had to be ordered in a different language, and if I screwed it up, I had to buy her a drink, too. Things always got expensive late at night.

"Hey, Paula," Nick said, sliding onto a barstool, even as she was pulling a Stella for him, then sliding it onto the counter with a smooth motion. My drink changes with my moods and how crappy a day it's been; Nick was born with Stella at the teat, and never looked back.

"*Labvakar,* Paula. Bourbon, *lūdzu.*"

"*Labs vakars, mans labs draugs.*" Whatever language they were speaking, from the way Paula was careful with her pronunciation, I was betting it wasn't one of her seven. Good for Pietr. Keep the barkeep on her toes.

"I'll have whatever you're giving him." I was tempted for a shot of tequila, but that was for really, really bad days. This was just bad and cranky. Bourbon would do for that.

Paula leaned on the bar, her forearms threaded with lean muscle I could only dream of managing. "Uh-huh. You want to talk about it, or just sit and throw peanuts at each other?"

Paula's not Talent, but I don't think there's a professional bartender in town who doesn't know about the *Cosa*. Fatae may not drink, but a lot of drunks see them. She knew who we were, and what we did for a living.

"Peanuts," Nick said.

"Right you are."

Dermody's was the kind of place you'd take a first date—and probably back again for the third date, if things went well. There were intimate tables with comfortable chairs, and a long granite bar with stools that encouraged long-term loitering, all under lighting that let you see your companion, but not so bright that it showed imperfections. Overall, the bar was comfortable without being cute, friendly but not loud, and you could strike up a conversation or sulk over your drink, and either choice got equal respect. And it was a five-minute walk from my apartment. If only it weren't so damned expensive, I might live here.

"So, do you think Sharon—"

"Nuh-uh." Pietr cut Nick off before I could. "No shop talk. It's well after office hours even for the workaholic, and we are relaxing, not stressing."

"But..."

"Do you want to turn into Sharon?" I asked.

Pietr winced appreciatively. "Ouch. That was cold. Funny, but cold."

Nick took the top off his drink, wiping away the foam from his mouth. "You guys can really just turn it off? Just..."

end of day, not talking about it anymore, not thinking about it anymore?"

"No." I had to be honest—maybe some remnant of the spellwork? No, just my natural bluntness again. "No, I can't just turn it off. But the first thing I learned, on our first case, was that there comes a time you have to just…let go. For a little while."

Our first case, when I'd almost fallen hard for a suspect. Will Arcazy, of the dark red hair and easy smile. He'd been a person of interest in the murders we were investigating, a couple killed over a real estate deal gone bad. Will had turned out to be…well, not guilty of murder, if not exactly innocent of responsibility, but the damage had been done. Once the case was over, he wanted nothing to do with me for the sin of having investigated him. I hadn't loved him—but I had liked him a lot, and being given the cold shoulder had hurt.

I'd been sitting in this bar, in fact, nursing that hurt, when Venec had found me, poured me into my apartment, and given me a piece of good advice. "This is a tough job. You're going to be asked to pick up a lot. Carry it on your skin, not your spine."

I didn't share that with the guys, though, just repeated my own advice. "Let it go. At least until tomorrow morning. It will wait."

"Right." Nick didn't sound too certain, and I didn't have anything to add, so we sat there, drinking our drinks, in quiet reflection for a while. Paula refilled the peanut dish, and set us up with a pitcher of water and three tumblers.

I guess she knew a long drinking night when she saw one coming in.

"So," Nick said finally, proving my suspicion that he was purely incapable of going ten minutes without talking. "When're you going to throw another party?"

"When my neighbors forgive me for the last one, probably." It hadn't been particularly loud, or run all that late, but someone on the floor below had taken offense and left a nasty note on my door. I guess it was all adding up. "Anyway, isn't it time someone else hosted a party, for once?"

"Pietr won't let us near his place because it's too nice, Sharon lives too far away—" Translocation when drunk was usually a really bad idea, and the subway ride home from Brooklyn where Sharon lived was a pain in the ass after midnight "—and you can barely turn around in my apartment."

Nobody volunteered Nifty's place; we'd all been there. Once.

"I'll tell you what. I'll host—if you let me dye your hair."

"What?" His hands went, protectively, to the brown mop on his head.

"Seriously. I'll even let you choose the color." I figured we could talk him out of anything seriously objectionable. Unlike Pietr, Nick's taste was…dubious.

"Dye my hair?" He was still stuck on that thought.

"Why not? Chicks dig it."

"They do?" He looked to Pietr, who spread his hands in a "why you asking me?" expression, then to Paula, who had been listening with a third of an ear. She winked, but left what that wink meant open to interpretation.

"A guy who dyes his hair?" I nodded seriously. "Open to new things, experiences...maybe wild things..." I waggled my eyebrows like a cartoon lech.

"All right. Deal." We shook on it, Pietr and Paula our witnesses.

A few more drinks and a plate of chicken nachos, and the guys started acting like guys, rating the other women in the bar. Normally I'd join in—give the female point of view, maybe undercut a few sexist observations with the cold claws of feminism—but I wasn't in the mood tonight.

Drunk and annoyed, the things I'd been trying not to think about came out.

"Why do guys do that? Use violence, I mean?"

Nick stopped, mid-rating of a redhead with too much shelf showing. "I thought we weren't going to talk about the case."

"We're not. This isn't about the case. It's just...wondering."

Pietr didn't seem surprised. "If it weren't for the case, you wouldn't be asking. But I get where you're coming from, I think," he said, putting his drink on the bar with a definite clink. "It's not about sex, those guys. It's about power. Control."

"Yeah. I know. And I even understand the whole S&M thing, kind of. I mean, the role-playing aspects of it, the pain-for-pleasure stuff, it's not my game but I know enough people who play it. That's different. It's mutual, agreed upon...it's *play*. But how does forcing someone to have sex give you power...my brain just doesn't go there. Is it because I'm female?"

"No." Pietr was definite on that. "It's because you're gentle."

"Oh." I wasn't sure I understood that, or that I bought it, entirely, but when nothing makes sense anyway...

"I mean, not gentle like soft, gentle like considerate," he tried to clarify. "You *like* people. You want to help them, make things better. And what those guys did, or tried to do...that kind of mentality, the personality that can do that, it's not just about forcing women, or even forcing sex. It's about making someone do something they don't want to do. It's about seeing them as tools, or pets, not people." He frowned, picked up his drink again, and then frowned down into it, too.

"So what is it? A need for power? Anger?" I knew hatred—I hated the man who had killed my father, even now, years later—but the kind of anger that made you hurt someone...maybe Pietr was right; I'd never thought of myself as particularly gentle, but that kind of anger just wasn't in me. Maybe that was why I couldn't understand what I'd gleaned from the scene.

"I think that they're bullies, mostly. The studies I've read say the weak are the ones who need violence to get off, not the strong ones."

Okay. That, I understood. It was as good a theory as any, anyway. And it was interesting, that Pietr had read up on that. I raised my glass in toast. "To taking down the bullies."

"To taking down the bullies," Pietr echoed, and Nick

raised his glass in silent agreement, tipping the rims gently—or as gently as we could, after half a dozen drinks.

"Hey, Bonnie, you were working the main scene—did you get to see the ki-rin, up close?" Nick asked me, obviously wanting to change the subject.

"Not up close, no. I didn't want to, honestly. It scared me a little."

"What, because you're not lily-pure virginal?" From someone else that would've been insulting. From Nick, it was an invitation to whap him upside the head. So I did.

"No, you moron. Because it had blood dripping from its horn and hooves and even if I'd been a vestal virgin I'd have been careful about going near anyone who'd just been through that kind of trauma."

Pietr caught the tail end of that statement. "You think it was traumatized?"

I rolled my eyes in exasperation. "No, it was perfectly mellow and unfussed. Give me a break, of course it was traumatized. Or at least seriously upset and angry. It saw its companion attacked, and killed another being, a *Cosa*-cousin, even if he didn't know it at the time, and I suspect it did—"

Memory of my earlier thought came back, and I stopped. "Damn. Pietr, we looked for emotional resonance, and then we were distracted by the crap we found in the memorial piles, and I think we screwed up. Did anyone think to check for trace of actual current-use at the scene?"

"We looked for emotional trace…." he began, not sure where I was going.

"Yeah, but not actual current-trace. Damn it!"

Nick scowled at me. "It was a physical attack, not a current-blast. The guy died of horn-and-hoof disease."

"Think, Nick," I said, feeling a surge of energy run through my legs, making me want to swing around on my stool. That meant I was on the right track, somehow, even if I didn't know what it was, yet. "It was physical, yeah, but all three of them were Talent. Something like this, even a lo-res player like our girl should give off sparks. A guy fighting for his life against a ki-rin?"

"We looked for emotional trace carried on current, but not the current-trace itself. Damn." Pietr got a sort of hazy look in his eyes. "I pinged Sharon, gave her a sense of what we're worried about. She'll check it out in the morning."

Sharon's train passed by the site, coming in, so that made sense. My brain raced on ahead, trying to figure out how to use that new evidence, if there was any. Odds were, there wasn't anything left to find, but if there was, Nifty had been talking a couple of weeks ago about sifting current-trace into a time-graph. If he could manage that, we'd be able to tell who shot first, as it were. That would be a huge piece of the puzzle, especially if we could prove that the girl tried to defend herself after the attack, but before the ki-rin waded in, supporting her version of the story.

And if we didn't find anything, or Nifty couldn't make the time-sift work, well then, no need to mention to the Big Dogs that we'd overlooked it in the first go-round.

"Do you think it can be trusted?"

My thoughts were on the bosses, so it took me a minute to figure out what Nick was saying, and about whom. The ki-rin. The creature everyone's original assumptions rested on, because ki-rin could not lie.

"As much as anyone or anything with their own reasons for doing things can be trusted, yeah," I said, finally. "You used to be a total fanboy about the fatae. Why the doubts now?"

Nick got a little puffed about that. "I'm not...most of the fatae we've met so far have been okay, if a little standoffish. But this—ki-rin are supposed to be perfect. Everyone says the ki-rin can't lie, don't lie, paragons and champions of virtue, et cetera. But can it really be trusted? I mean, it doesn't seem to have much use for humans overall, except its companion, and look at how fast it dumped her."

He had a point. I didn't pretend to understand the fatae, but would it have killed the ki-rin to go with the girl to the hospital, or visit after, or something? Hell, maybe it would. We didn't know enough. Nobody knew enough, thanks to the ki-rin's fetish about privacy.

The burst of energy ran out, and I stopped swiveling in my seat, suddenly exhausted again.

Nick went on, oblivious to my mood change, building up steam. "And why virgins, anyway? Like not having had sex makes you a good person or something?"

Ooooo. I suddenly wondered if we'd hit a nerve...and if the ki-rin would have been willing to talk to Nicky-boy. The thought was...novel. Also slightly horrifying.

"It's not the virginity per se," Pietr said. "From what I've read, they're not looking for a lack of a sex life so much as lack of desire." He paused. "They're not real big on the passion or drama sex stirs up, the ki-rin. I guess virgins are restful."

"Hah. Here's to being unrestful," I said. We clinked glasses again, and called for a refill.

"You should sleep with Venec," Nick said suddenly, doing one of his wild topic-changes.

Next to me, Pietr made a noise I don't think I'd ever heard before, and I turned to see him gasping, tears in his eyes, and his glass held out from him as though protecting it.

"Oh, good job," I said to Nick, trying very hard not to think about what he had actually just said. "You made him snarf his bourbon. Man, that's gotta sting."

"Motherf— Yes," Pietr managed to reply. "It did."

"You totally should," Nick went on. "You think nobody noticed that little goo-up back in the office?"

I started—how the hell?

"*Au contraire,* my dear Dandelion. You held each other's gaze a bit too long and moved away a bit too fast for a room full of investigators not to notice."

Oh. He'd only seen the physical reaction, the first time. All right. That I could explain away. If I wanted to. I decided to just smirk, instead. That was more in character. Less likely to raise suspicions, or give either of them anything to chew over.

"Anyway, it will do you both good," Nick said, clearly not sensing that the conversation needed to end. "I'm your bestest buddy and I know what you need." He made a determined little nod that was disgustingly cute, and I had to bite back a giggle despite my annoyance. "Reduce stress, give you a lilt to your step…keep Venec from being such a hard-ass on the rest of us…"

"Good luck with that," Pietr muttered. I had to agree. Even assuming I ever went there, which I wasn't going to, I suspected he'd still be a hard-ass. I'm not sure I'd want him to be anything else, either. It would be…weird. Like…like seeing J in a dress, or something.

That image made me blanch, and I finished the rest of my drink in a rush, hoping the booze would burn it away.

"I'm not sleeping with the boss."

"So don't sleep with him during office hours," Nick said, with the air of a man solving all the world's problems, and Pietr choked on his booze again.

Paula came over then, and leaned against the bar like an old-timey barkeep from a Western. "Don't you kids have to go to work tomorrow?" It was almost last call—or maybe past it, I realized, looking around the almost-empty bar.

"Do we?" Pietr asked me. I gave him a wide-eyed stare back, my best "you're asking *me* this *why?*" look.

"We do," Nick decided. "'Cause there are still bullies out there to be put down, virgins to be rescued, and paychecks to be deposited. Not in that order, though."

"You're drunk," I told him.

"I am." Nick sounded proud of it, too.

Pietr snorted. "Don't worry, I'll make sure he gets home," he told Paula, hauling Nick off the stool with one hand while he slid his credit card across the bar to cover the tab. Pietr and I were the only members of the pack who could carry credit cards with us on a regular basis—like cell phones and laptops, the magnetic strip on credit cards reacted badly to constant exposure to a Talent's too-often unstable core.

We walked out into the cold night air, and I could feel myself sober up. "You guys go on...."

"Hell we will," Nick said. His voice was a little slurred, but he was standing and walking fine, and Pietr let go of him. "Two blocks out of our way isn't going to damage either of us, and I have ghost-boy here to take care of me on the way back to the subway."

"Don't call me that."

Unlike my acceptance of Nick's pet naming habits, Pietr let it get to him. Nick usually knew better—he really was drunk.

A shadow fell over us, noticeable even in the darkness, and I flinched, while Nick's body language went into tough-guy mode, and Pietr became a shadow within the shadow. If you didn't know what to look for, you'd swear he had disappeared.

"Bonnie. Pietr. And Other Human."

"Bobo." I relaxed. "I should have known."

"Yes, you should have." The pidgin English of before was gone, his normal conversational tones much more comforting.

"What the hell is..." Nick caught himself when I glared. "Sorry. *Who* the hell is this?"

"Bobo, this is Nick. You already know Pietr." I really didn't feel like explaining anything to Nick right now— friend or no friend, drunk or not, he'd just insulted both Pietr and Bobo in the space of three minutes, and I was annoyed at him.

"You'll take our girl from here?" Pietr asked.

"That is the plan," the fatae said.

"Good. 'Cause I'm knackered. 'Night, Bonnie. See ya tomorrow. Come on, Shune. Walk, or I'll leave your drunk ass on a street corner somewhere."

The two of them strolled down the almost-empty street, bumping shoulders and insulting each other loudly. Men. I swear, I loved 'em, but I completely did not understand them, and did not, most of the time *want* to.

Next to me, Bobo coughed gently, a reminder that we were standing outside on a cold street corner, and offered me his very large, very hairy arm. "Home?"

"Home," I agreed, suddenly very, very tired.

Of course, lying in bed, every inch of my body whimpering for Morpheus to put me out of my exhausted misery, I couldn't actually fall asleep. My brain was too wound up to stop, but too tired to do anything useful. Thoughts about the case, about the weirdness with Venec, about how much we were drinking these days, about the fact that I really needed to recharge before my core collapsed, they all chased around my brain and kept me awake but without any results.

I considered pinging J, thinking maybe the old man would still be awake and willing to chat, but squelched the urge. I'd made it clear to him—and he had, however grudgingly, accepted the fact—that I'd made my career choice and he had to respect it. Touching base with him mentor-to-mentee was well within our ground rules, and I could always call on him professionally if needed, but turning to him every time I had a bad day...not so much.

Normally this wouldn't be a problem. The best way to get out of your head, when it got too messy in there, was to focus on your body. Good clean healthy distraction. Going for a long hike, or dancing up a storm, or…yeah, sex would have been nice, but doing it alone was getting depressing, and while I had that little black book of people I could call—new friends and old, and even a number of exes, since I liked to end things on a positive note—the thought of calling any of them left me feeling surprisingly…uninterested. Not just because of the unease brought on by the case, either. The moment my brain went there, my body remembered that hot, intensely sexual charge I had gotten from Venec earlier. It wanted more of that, please.

It wasn't going to get more of that, damn it. I might be casual about my relationships, but they were always relationships, and I was not going to fall into bed—or against the wall, or any other place—with my boss. Either of my bosses, although the thought of having sex with Stosser was enough to cool my libido down considerably. Ew, and also, no thanks.

I sighed again, and punched up the pillow under my head, as though that would make me able to sleep, suddenly. Times like this, I really resented not having a television, even if I would have to replace it on a regular basis.

Why was I suddenly insomniac? I'd gotten a handle, I thought, on the fear—hanging out tonight with the guys had restored most of my natural equilibrium. So why was I still feeling this discomfort, this doubt, deep in my bones, stirring my current uneasily? It wasn't natural for me, at all.

I followed the thought back to the source: it wasn't natural. Therefore, it was external, the weight pressing on me from outside, not in. All right. It's not as though I couldn't identify the stress, easy enough: I'd seen what should have been pleasurable physical release turned into a crime. The thought wasn't new, but it sunk into a new spot this time, a slow glide through my brain that set up a tingle of disturbance. Crime. Assault. The mutation, the mutilation of affection into violence. My own feelings about casual intimacy, turned into something terrible. I was doubting myself, because if she could have been wrong, so could I.

Okay, that made sense.

I frowned up at the ceiling, just a few feet over my head. It made sense, but it didn't fit. Something like that would explain my skittishness, maybe, and I'd taken steps to deal with that, facing it down and dissecting it to harmless bits. But the self-doubt…that felt different.

I just couldn't think of anything else that might have triggered it.

Easier to turn the searchlight on our victim. Why had she been so casual about meeting the two men at first? Why hadn't the ki-rin been with her, to protect her? Had she trusted them? Why? The shadowy images flickered inside my lids, the gleaning echoing inside me, and wouldn't shut down, even when the skittery panic and uncertainty flared again, and I tried to slam that door shut.

My core flared in distress, and a responding flicker of current touched it, as though it had been waiting for a summons.

Venec. I knew even before the signature identified itself.

all right?

A sparse thought, touched with a glimmer of worry, and a sharp tingle that ran from the top of my spine all the way down my arms to my fingertips, sharp enough that I lifted my hands above the covers, expecting to see current sparking above the skin.

I was used to feeling sparks between us, but this was different; way more intense, if not quite on the same groin-searing level of that earlier connection. And just like that the burn was gone, instead becoming a soothing coolness, easing my tumbled and troubled thoughts. It was invasive, the touch on a level with that first recruitment a year ago, but for some reason this time it didn't bother me. It should have…but it didn't.

all right? he repeated, more urgent this time.

yes. no

His touch soundlessly asked permission to go even deeper, and I granted it without asking what, or why. A cool touch, like menthol on the skin, only inside me. It should have freaked me out; I knew, intellectually, that I should be freaked out and objecting, but I had let him in, and it felt…good. Not orgasmic. But like the time after, when you're soothed and sated and too comfortable to move to clean up.

sleep he whispered. *for this moment, forget, and sleep*

My eyes closed, and I slept.

In a prewar apartment building across the Hudson River in New Jersey, with a very expensive half-view of the Statue of Liberty, Benjamin Venec folded his newspaper in two, carefully, and placed it on the desk in front of him. His gaze was distant, as he looked at something far beyond the walls of his home, and his expression was troubled.

"Is there a problem?" his companion asked, stretching lazily on the sofa where she had been paging through a book.

"No," he said. "No problem." And there wasn't. Bonnie was sleeping peacefully, now. His mentor would have had him doing laps with a twenty-pound backpack if she'd known what he'd done: there were rules for those who had the Push, rules and ethics drummed into your bones from the first flash of current in your core. He wasn't a stickler for rules—for himself, anyway—but that one stuck and held. You didn't Push casually or without consent, and never mind he told himself it was within the job description, that he had her tacit, if sleepy, permission.

He'd gone too far, though; he had only intended to make sure Bonnie got a good night's sleep. But once there, the lure of her psychic scent had almost overwhelmed him, the ease of contact drawing him far deeper than he'd intended, and what started as a gentle Push to soothe her restless thoughts, to direct them toward something peaceful so that she could sleep, had...

Had what? What had happened between them, in the space of those few seconds of contact? He didn't know, and that made him uneasy as hell. His lips twisted into a rueful almost-smile, and he shoved his fingers through his hair, pulling at his scalp gently as though that would make the headache he could feel building go away. Hell, the entire situation with Bonnie had started with uneasiness, and with yesterday's fireworks it was rapidly escalating into... What? He didn't know, but it wasn't anything good.

He was very used to being in control—demanded it, in fact. Of himself, if not the situation, and this...

Had not been under his control. Not the attraction, not the spark, not the way he had known that she was startled and upset—and certainly not how he had responded instinctively, current gathered as though he himself were under attack.

"Ben?" Malia was looking at him, her lovely eyes narrowed as though she knew that his thoughts were on someone else entirely. If she really knew, she'd cut his throat.

"I'm fine. Just thinking."

All the events of the past few days—it was too much for coincidence, too intense to brush off as part of the physical attraction they'd been dealing with since day one. It was also obvious that their current-spark wasn't Bonnie's doing, as he'd thought at first; her emotions tonight had been almost painfully innocent of guile.

And it wasn't him; he'd checked on the others before without anything like that ever happening, nudging and corralling as needed, just as he'd done since he'd started recruiting, back when PUPI was just a glint in his partner's eye. Ian was brilliant, no doubt, and burned with the desire to put things to rights, but it was a cold fire, at heart. He saw people, even his own people, as extensions of himself, and assumed they reacted the way he did. It would never occur to Ian Stosser to check on how a case was affecting the team, because it wouldn't affect *him*.

Ben didn't mind, really. Let Ian handle the publicity, the schmoozing, the bright light and glare of the Council's scrutiny. He'd take care of the people side of things, make sure the team was working well, no jars or cracks, no exhaustion or doubts keeping them from doing what needed to be done. For the most part, it was a matter of nudging them one way or other, of making sure that their teammates were aware of something, and letting them handle it from there.

Trouble was, what had happened tonight went well beyond that, beyond anything he could justify as work-related. The fact that Bonnie had allowed him in, the fact that she had… hell, they both had enjoyed it, he admitted to himself, remembering the cinnamon-sweet taste of her in his mind, the warm feel of her current twining against his; none of that mattered. Combined with the current-spark they'd shared, that he would swear neither of them had intended, the situation was dangerous as hell on several levels.

So he wouldn't do it again. He'd stick to purely physical interactions—and there was irony in that that he wasn't willing to examine. Work only. Nothing personal. It wasn't as though there wasn't enough on his plate already to keep him occupied.

Like the situation he was looking into, off-hours, with these alleged "exterminators." The thought made him frown, distracting him from the memory of Bonnie, warm and restless in her loft bed. The advertisement had seemed simple enough at first—a basic sheet of paper, white with black print, offering an office extermination service. He had seen

four now, all with slightly different ads. Tonight's, stuck in
the poster-frame in the PATH car on his way home, had
been more overt:

> *Tired of your clients encountering unwanted visitations? Con-*
> *cerned about the infestation of your building? Your neighbor-*
> *hood? Call us. We can clean things up for you.*

On the surface, it read like a hundred and ten other flyers
that circulated regularly around any decent-size city, fly-by-
night companies feeding on the city-dwellers' eternal infesta-
tions. But Benjamin Venec had years of listening to Ian and
his Council cronies speaking the fine art of doublespeak, and
he knew propaganda when he heard it, especially when it
was escalating like that. The malice practically oozed off the
page of the most recent flyer, if you were sensitive. Malice
and hatred, and a particular scent that came from fear. These
exterminators might be out to rid the world of something,
but Ben would bet every bill in his wallet it wasn't bedbugs
and cockroaches.

The moment he thought that, he was surprised by an odd
twinge of doubt. It touched on his call on this, then spread
to his ability to handle all the things pressing for his attention, the idea that he was capable of keeping so many things
in the air and under control at the same time. It felt like the
whisper of rot in his ear, and he frowned, forcing himself
to stillness.

That wasn't him. Those weren't his thoughts. When he
doubted himself—which he often did, although he would

never admit it to anyone other than Ian—it came loud and harsh, not sickly sweet and slithering.

Outwardly, he was still contemplating the wall, to all observances a man deep in thought. Inside, a single spider silk–thin filament of current, shivering with energy, reached up from his core, slinking like a cat in the grass, intent on its prey. Keeping a steady, grounded control, barely daring to breathe, Ben let the hunter flow over his skin, and then snapped it forward, lashing out at the sensation of that whisper, trying to trace it back to its source. It disappeared, half a second ahead of his attack, and Ben clenched his molars together, forcing himself to show no reaction, even as the current dissipated into the air. If there had been someone there, trying to Push him, they'd gotten away clean. But if they tried again, he'd know.

Pushers were rare, but not unknown. It wasn't the first time someone had taken a shot at him, and it wouldn't be the last; he had pissed off too many people in his career, and he would doubtless piss off many more. He noted the attack, filed it under "problem; later," and went back to his real concern: the rising sentiment against the fatae, the violence that was seething under the melting-pot veneer of New York City. The "tributes" at the attack site. These flyers. The general mood: something was up. Something ugly.

Lizard had sworn he didn't know anything, nobody knew anything about any violence, but other sources had been more forthcoming, about things whispered in dark corners and private cafés where humans weren't invited, of violence committed against the weakest of the fatae, the defenseless. Of piskie nests being destroyed, and nets thrown where selkies slept, drowning them in the night. What Bonnie and Pietr had learned from their faun contact had just confirmed the things he had already heard.

And Sharon's investigations tied these flyers to it; no Talent was willing to admit hiring the service, but at least one person had commented to her on how much better, how much cleaner their neighborhood was, for *someone else* having that service in. Fatae were in danger—and starting to react with violence to that danger.

There was nothing in anything he'd learned to tie that into an attack on a young girl, companion to a ki-rin...but nothing to say they weren't connected, either.

If the angeli, those human-hating sociopaths, got involved...

"Damn it." He got up and stalked across the apartment, stopping in front of an oversize photograph of a lightning storm at sea, and frowned again, this time letting his irritation and frustration rise to the surface.

"Ben? Seriously, what is it?" Malia had abandoned her practiced kitten-pose, and was looking at him with real worry now.

He started, having completely forgotten that she was there. "It's nothing. I'm sorry. I'm just not very good company tonight. You probably should just go home."

A look of hurt flashed across her face, and he felt like a shit, but he suddenly needed his own space back; space and quiet to think.

Malia picked up her things and left, noisily, without her usual kiss goodbye. He noted it and then forgot it, already back in his somber thoughts.

Something was happening in the city; something that involved the fatae. He couldn't run the risk of it involving PUPI, too. Not without knowing what "it" was, anyway. There was already too much pressing at them, too many people eager to see them fail, and they couldn't afford the distraction of violence breaking the surface. And that meant, if nobody else was going to do something about it...they had to. Ian had to take these problems seriously, now, before they erupted.

Convincing his partner to do anything outside of his narrow, if diamond-focused, vision...that would take some doing. And yelling. But that was part of his job, too.

The visual, of Bonnie now sound asleep in her bed, came back to him, and he smiled a little. She slept like a little girl, sprawled and careless. As though drawn by the thought, a tendril of her dream reached out and enfolded him. It didn't negate the concern or urgency, but in that one instant, he was somewhere far more peaceful, far more sweet.

So sweet and peaceful and natural, he didn't wonder how that tendril had escaped her sleeping mind and touched his wakeful one without conscious thought or intent—a thing he had always been taught was impossible.

nine

I'd thought, with the exhaustion of everything that was going on—not to mention the alcohol in my system—I'd wake up feeling shaky and starved. Instead, the first ray of sunlight coming through the windows found me coming awake naturally, feeling as though I'd slept for ten hours—almost disgustingly bright-eyed and proverbially bushy-tailed, like someone had slammed the door shut on the doubts and worries that had been nipping at my heels. Because of Ben's late-night virtual tuck-in? Maybe. Embarrassing, if so, but maybe. Whatever the reason, I'd take it.

I slid down from the loft bed and zipped through my morning routine with a cheerful hum in my throat, and came out of the stairwell bright if not early at nine-fifteen, thanks to the subway. The weather had finally, grudgingly, agreed that it was spring, and the air had a softness to it that hinted at green grass and lazy afternoons to come.

Two of my boys were already on their stoop, drinking coffee and reading the newspaper.

"*Ai*, you're going to stunt your growth drinking that stuff!" I warned them as I walked by, waggling a finger in mock-instruction.

"My growth's jus' fine, momma," the younger of the two catcalled back, making a rude gesture with his free hand, while the older boy—Dee, his name was, I thought, or DJ— whapped him over the head with the newspaper. Even after months of back-and-forth, they weren't quite sure if I was one of them or not—I didn't look barrio, but I could talk it—and we walked a line between casual teasing and disrespect. I guess Dee thought that had gone over. I let myself grin a little. I might have spent years twelve to twenty-one living in an upper-crust Back Bay apartment, but I'd spent enough summer afternoons as a preteen hanging out on stoops a lot like theirs, down off 4th Avenue, where I'd lived with Zaki.

"You just keep eating your Wheaties," I told them, "and I'm sure some day you'll make a nice little girl very happy."

They whooped at that, and I chalked up a point for my side. Girls are much tougher than guys when it comes to trash-talking, really.

I buzzed myself into the building, took the stairs double-time—not even out of breath, go me!—and heard…something. A low rumbling growl, was my first thought, or a drill being used somewhere in the building. Walking into the office itself, the growl resolved itself into two voices… male, angry.

"Ben, we don't have time for this." Stosser.

"Then we have to make time."

I felt a shiver run through me that had nothing to do with the change in temperatures from raw spring rain to the still-overheated offices at the raw unhappiness in Ben's voice. This wasn't argument, this was out-and-out disagreement.

Stosser again, firm and determined like the knees of god. "No. We don't. It's not our concern, and we're not going to make it our concern."

"Damn it, Ian, stop being such an arrogant shit and listen to me."

"Wow." It wasn't the noise—although the voices were carrying clear through the walls—as much as the harsh static in the air that made me wince. The pleasant float I'd been carrying crashed and burned away, leaving me with an ache between my eyes and a sense of foreboding. "Do I want to know what's going on?"

Nifty shrugged. "Don't know myself. Came in, heard them going at it, decided to stay right here until someone sent out the all-clear. Told shadow-boy to do the same."

Nifty was occasionally arrogant and obnoxious, and always opinionated, but he was also nobody's fool.

Pietr, curled on the other end of the sofa, looked like hell. I was guessing he'd not had as good a night's sleep and the atmosphere in the office wasn't helping: harsh current and hangovers did not mix. I was just as glad that Nick hadn't staggered in yet; he'd be hurting, based on how trashed he'd been the night before.

"Anyone thinking an out-of-office breakfast meeting might be a good idea?" I asked, fighting down the urge to find out what exactly was making Ben—Venec—so unhappy. It might have been happening in the office, but Nifty was right, I didn't think it was our business, and we had no business messing with anything else. You did not get between the Big Dogs when they rumbled.

Nifty raised one thick-fingered hand in agreement. Pietr was already off the sofa and grabbing his coat by the time I finished the question.

By the time we came back, filled with greasy hash browns, crisp bacon, and runny eggs, it was almost 10:00 a.m., and the office was quiet.

"Too quiet," Nifty said. Funny, he wasn't usually the one who could pick up my moods. There seemed to be an awful lot of it going around, though.

"Anybody else in?" I asked Pietr, who was hanging up our coats.

"Yeah, Sharon's coat is here. Not Nick's though. Lightweight may still be sleeping it off."

"You hurt him last night, didn't you? Bonnie, you've got to stop being so hard on the kid," Nifty said. "He wants to keep up with you, and he can't."

"Not yet," I said, playing along, trying to lighten the mood. "Give him another year. But nobody can drink you under the table, big man, so you're safe."

"Hah."

Nifty outmassed us all by a considerable margin, but he drank on par with Pietr—steady but not impressive in terms of consumption. None of us were heavy drinkers, actually, despite the previous night's activities. I had a feeling that might change, though, if the jobs kept going like this.

Suddenly I had a lot more sympathy with all the noir detectives in the old movies, who always had a bottle stashed somewhere nearby. I might take up smoking, too, if it weren't impossibly expensive. And if J wouldn't put me over his knee the first time he smelled tobacco on me.

I looked at the door that led into the main office, and smothered a sigh. We had two choices: wait for one of the Big Dogs to come find us, or dig them out. The former was more appealing but the clock was ticking and the urge to get working outweighed everything else.

"Come on, guys," I said, and led them through the door, in search of boss-shaped objects.

Ian and Sharon were in the midsize workroom. The boss looked up when I stuck my head in, and looked pleased to see me. I so didn't trust that pleasure, not after the last go-round with Sharon's latest concoction.

"We think we have the hiccups in the truth spell worked out," he said, confirming my fears. "Come in, come in."

"Do I have to?" I asked, even as Pietr elbowed me through the doorway.

"Relax," Sharon said. She had her hair pulled back in a sleek ponytail, was wearing a gorgeous—and seriously expensive—dark red cashmere sweater that should not have looked that good against her pale coloring, and looked like she'd gotten ten hours of sleep, too. I didn't think it was for the same reasons, though—or if it was, it was because she'd had someone actual flesh and blood in her bed, not ghosting through in her head.

"I figured out what went wrong, before," she went on, resting her hand on a pile of papers; the documentation of her work, I was guessing.

"That's reassuring." I sat down next to her anyway, mainly because I knew I wasn't getting out of there short of fighting my way out, and putting the table between me and the boss man felt like a good idea. There was a vibe coming off Stosser that I didn't quite trust. His eyes were too bright, his smile too wide, and it wasn't the usual glamour he threw on whenever he had to be charming in public, either.

He didn't like fighting with Venec, a little voice told me. I was pretty sure it was my own voice, but it could have been a nudge from Sharon, too. Being on the outs with Venec made him uncomfortable...he relied on his partner to be his mirror, his conscience. When they argued, it made him question his own decisions. He, like me, wasn't used to doubting himself.

Definitely my own voice. I don't know how I suddenly knew that about Ian, but I did. It was like looking out a fogged-up window and then having someone clear it away and everything was sharper, brighter.

"Where's Venec?" Nifty asked, fitting himself into one of the chairs at the other side of the table. The look Stosser gave him made even Nifty's cocoa-dark skin turn a few shades paler, and Pietr faded out of view a little.

"Walking off his snit," Stosser said, and I was right, his voice wasn't so much angry as worried. I wasn't sure anyone else could tell, though, and when I tried to focus on it, the sharp awareness faded back to the usual softer edges.

I think I liked it better that way. Even in our job, there

were some things you didn't want to know, and Stosser's
thoughts were high up on that list. Like I'd said before,
genius brains were scary things, and my own smart-but-
not-scary brains were overworked enough right now.

"The problem was," Sharon said in the bright tone that she
used when she thought she'd been dumb about something
before and was by-god going to do better now, "I was projecting too much, trying to draw the truth out. So it went
deeper than it should have, and, well…"

"Yeah. And well," I mimicked. Sharon flushed, and I
relented. Wasn't like I had room to mock, the way I might
have screwed up the scene read. Had Sharon been able to
stop this morning, to read the scene for us? No way to ask,
not right now.

"It's okay," I said to her, instead. "Thankfully for all concerned, I don't actually have any secrets." Which was a lie.
Especially now. For the first time in my life I had something
serious that I didn't want anyone else to know.

"You're young yet," Stosser said, absently. "I'm sure you'll
collect some as you go. But I've been working with Sharon
on her ideas, and I think that we've modified the spell enough
that it will now focus on the thing we're asking about, rather
than…being a blanket all-truth spell. Specifically, it won't
trigger the anxiety Bonnie reported."

Oh, good. So glad my trauma was useful. I knew better
than to say that out loud, though.

"And if the person is resisting?" Nifty asked, his brain
already leaping ahead to problems.

"Then I'll know," Sharon said. "Not what they're lying

about, but the fact that they're resisting telling the truth, yeah."

"But we won't be able to isolate *what* they're resisting, specifically?" That was Pietr, picking up the subtleties, as usual.

"Fine-tuning the spell can wait until we have the leisure for that. All we are concerned about is the specific matter at hand," Stosser said, and his voice was crackling with current, enough that everyone dropped the side discussion then and there. "The Council, as expected, has indicated to me this morning that they are not going to pursue this matter any further, and would strongly prefer than we not, either."

That went over real well, especially since it seemed, for a minute, like Stosser, of all people, was going to tell us to drop the investigation.

"However," he went on, "Ben has uncovered some information that suggests the issue may be more involved than I had originally thought. If so, then it is even more important that we determine exactly what happened—and the Council be damned."

Since half the office would gladly damn the Council already, that didn't really raise any eyebrows, but I did note that he was taking whatever Venec had brought up earlier seriously, despite his annoyance. I wondered if Venec knew that.

All the others were focused on was that we would be allowed to investigate further.

"So what next, boss?" Nifty asked.

Stosser looked up at the ceiling while he gave us our orders. "Due to pressures within the fatae community, the

ki-rin is off-limits to us, and the suspect will have lawyers
on us the moment we start asking questions—and we have
no legal standing to counter a lawsuit. The girl is the weak
link."

I winced, but he was right.

"We need to talk to her again, to get some kind of response from her so that Sharon can gauge the veracity of her
claim. If she is telling the truth, then the ki-rin's actions are
vindicated. If not…"

"If not, there's a whole new mess of shit hitting the air
vents, yeah," Nifty said, nodding. "That will not go down
well at all, not with nobody."

"Anybody," I corrected automatically. He glared at me,
and I made a moue of apology.

"Shit you cannot imagine," Stosser said, his voice hard.
"Sharon, you and Bonnie will go talk to her."

"You think, after the last time you talked to her, she's
going to talk to us, boss?" I didn't want to be the one
to point that out, but seriously—did Ian really think… I
sighed. Of course he did. She was, as he said, the weak link.
Therefore…

"You'll find a way to get in to talk to her."

Yeah. We were still on the job, and tact and sympathy and
respecting a victim's wishes had nothing to do with that,
from Stosser's point of view. Not when we needed answers.
At least he was sending us, and not the guys, although that
might just have been luck of the draw.

"He's not a cold bastard, exactly," Sharon said five minutes
later, once we'd escaped from Stosser's hearing. "He's just…
focused."

"Obsessive," I corrected.

"Well, yeah. But we knew that from the start."

We had. The very first day, during our job interview. Ian and Venec had set us up to discover a dead body in the office—Venec, playacting—to test our dedication and initiative. We'd been hired because the Guys thought we matched their dedication to the truth.

And we did. That didn't make what we were going to do suck any less, though.

"I wasn't able to get to the scene," she said, before I could find a way to ask without making it sound like I thought she'd forgotten. "I stopped, but there were a bunch of fatae there, poking and sniffing—literally. I didn't think it would be a good time to look for current…."

"No, you were right." The last thing we needed was feeding the fatae fear of Talent, and no matter how Sharon tried to explain, it would have fed that fear. "Damn it. Not knowing is going to bite us on the ass, I know it."

Sharon shrugged, as though to say there was nothing to be done about it right now, which was the truth, and we caught the M-120 crosstown to the N line. The girl—whose name, I finally learned from the sheet of paper Stosser handed us, was Mercy, and the irony of that almost broke me—had been released from the hospital, and could be reached at her apartment, way out in Astoria.

Sharon and I didn't get seats next to each other on the train, so I spent the trip out dozing, listening to the contented hum of current riding the third rail. I loved subways: it was like listening to a cat purr. Right then, I needed the soothing, and kept letting little tendrils of current out to spark off the electrical system, pulling in the excess current like sips of champagne. Stupid—if I'd mistimed it, the entire train would go dead and we'd be stuck, along with a lot of other cranky travelers—but I never claimed to be smart all the time.

When this was all over, I was going to dive headfirst into the nearest power station, and totally restore my core, just so I'd remember what it felt like.

Mercy lived a few blocks away from the last stop, in a three-family brick house that had seen better days, but was still holding on to respectability. The postage-stamp yard was paved over with concrete, and there was a nice set of chairs and a glass-topped table waiting for warmer weather.

"She's on the third floor," Sharon said. I nodded, and rang the appropriate doorbell. Mercy's last name was Trin, printed in neat black ink on a waterproofed card. Someone had taken effort to do that right, and I suspected it hadn't been the landlord.

There wasn't an intercom, so we waited a few minutes, and then just before I was about to push the bell again, there was the sound of feet on the stairs, and a low voice asking from behind the door, "Yes?"

"Ms. Trin? My name is Sharon Mendelssohn. I'm here at the request of the Council."

Well. That wasn't…exactly untrue, and nicely bypassed the current status of our hire. If Mercy asked, would Sharon fess up? Probably. I'd be ready to duck.

There was a soft sigh, then the sound of a chain lock being undone, and the door opened.

Mercy Trin was definitely the girl I'd seen in the gleaning,

slight and seemingly frail, but now I was seeing her in color—
and part of that color was a nasty green-and-black bruise
across half of her face, where someone had obviously slapped
or punched her. I exhaled, hard, and her gaze swung from
Sharon to look at me. I guess we passed muster, because she
stepped back and let us in.

Luckily we were both in shape from taking the stairs at
work every day, because the three flights up were steeper
than normal. I was egotistically gratified not to be out of
breath when we got to the third-floor landing.

"I'm not Council," Mercy said in her quiet voice, as she
ushered us into her living room. It was pretty—not girly
like I'd half expected, but done in mint greens and soft
browns. Pastoral. I guess that made sense, considering she'd
been hanging with a fatae for the past few years. Not all of
them were forest-dwellers, but I didn't see a ki-rin being all
in-your-face techno, either. Or maybe it was. What the hell
did I know?

There were places on the wall where it looked like something had been hung, recently. Photos, or paintings? If I were
a betting girl, I'd lay odds they'd been of the ki-rin.

"Neither am I," Sharon said to the girl—Mercy. "Council,
that is. My coworker, Bonita, is."

That was stretching it a bit—J was Council, yeah. I'd
never really affiliated myself one way or the other, despite
J's totally unsubtle hopes in that direction. But Sharon was
running this show, so I just smiled and nodded, hoping to
pass along some of what Venec once snarkily but accurately
called the naturally annoying competence of a seated Mage
Council member.

"We're just following up on the terrible incident earlier this week…."

Mercy swayed a little, and I touched her shoulder as gently as I could, easing her down onto the sofa and sitting next to her, making sure to keep a good ten inches between us in case she needed space, but close enough if she suddenly keeled over.

"I'm all right," she said. "Thank you."

"If it were me, I'd still be in bed and having occasional hysterics," I said, moved by some unknown urge. I didn't know if that was the truth or not, but it was enough to make her laugh roughly.

"I wish I could," she said softly. "But…it doesn't work like that."

Odd choice of words. "What doesn't?"

I wanted to look at Sharon, to see when she was going to take control, but was afraid to lose Mercy's attention and maybe give the gig away before Sharon was ready to cast the spell.

"Trying to hide. Or run away. It's done, and I have to live with it. Doesn't matter, now. They find you anyway, and they're even worse then, because you've validated what they were saying anyway, because you wouldn't come out and deal with them…but dealing with them just makes it worse."

I was totally lost now. She was rambling, not meeting our eyes, twisting her delicate, fine-boned hands together like she was trying to rub the skin off them. I wanted to grab her hands and still them, but didn't.

Mercy was still talking, although I was pretty sure it wasn't to us. "Afterward, I just wanted…to be left alone. To…figure it all out. But then they showed up…."

That made me lean forward and put myself back into the dialog. "Mercy, is someone giving you grief? Because of the attack?" One of the perps' friends, maybe, trying to scare her? Was that why she decided not to press charges?

Off to the side I heard Sharon sit down in the armchair opposite us, the cloth of her skirt making a *srrssshing* noise against her stockings, and a whisper of something that might have been spell words, subvocalized. There was a slight rise in current-spark in the apartment, but I was aware of it only because I was looking. Mercy, being lo-res, probably wouldn't pick up on it.

"What happened, Mercy? Please tell me?"

I felt like a total shit. I really did. But the spell, and the sympathy in my voice, must have worked because rather than clamming up, Mercy started talking to me directly.

"Si-Ja was…was everything to me. I was seventeen when we bonded, and that's old—usually companions're chosen when they're seven or eight, but it couldn't find anyone, all those years alone, and then it found me, almost by accident, but he said there were never any accidents, and once we met it was all I ever wanted, to be its companion, to listen to its stories, and travel with it—it loves to travel but it's hard, you know, for a hoofed fatae to get around, all the doors and things…." Mercy seemed to realize she was running out of air, and stopped long enough to take a deep breath. When she started again, her voice was slower. "And it would sing me to sleep, when I had a headache, and carry me sometimes, when I was tired…. Si-Ja's a good soul, an old soul, and there's nothing it wouldn't do for me…."

Her voice, soft to begin with, faded into nothing. Shee-Jah. The ki-rin had a name now. I didn't know if that made things better, or worse.

"But that's all gone now," she said. "All gone. I didn't know how much it would hurt. Even worse than…" Her voice trailed off. I'd been right. She really had wrapped her entire sense of self into being the ki-rin's companion. Damn.

"Why didn't you press charges?" Sharon asked, finally.

The girl—Mercy—jerked as though someone had stuck her with a pin, and shook her head, not looking at Sharon. Her hair, longer than mine, straight and shiny and so black she had to have Amerindian blood in her background, fell into her face, covering the bruises and shielding her eyes. "No. No…no."

"If it was because of Si-Ja, because you didn't want to have to go in front of a Null court and talk about it…honey, there are lawyers and judges who know about the fatae. It wouldn't…"

"No!" She looked at Sharon then, her eyes wide and filled with panic. "No! They think I betrayed them! They told me…they threatened…"

"Who threatened?" Sharon sat up straight like the arrow of justice, but I was the one who asked. "Mercy, who told you that you betrayed them?"

The spell, or something, kept her talking. "When I was at the hospital. There was a note, on the bed when I was wait-ing for the doctor to come in…someone had known I'd be there, had left it for me. Someone in the hospital…a doctor, or a cop, or…someone with authority, who knew what had happened. They said that I was a disgrace, that by being Si-Ja's companion I'd been a disgrace to every Talent, and I'd caused that man's death, and if I said anything, they'd kill me and Si-Ja both. That I should just shut up and go home and be thankful nothing worse happened to me."

She swallowed hard, her throat practically convulsing to keep from saying anything more. Her hands now lay limply in her lap, palm up and fingers curled in. Passive, accepting, like an old woman's hands. I knew I should try to keep her talking, but somehow it felt too cruel. Pietr was right. I liked people too much to be good at this.

"Someone threatened you, if you reported the rape?" Sharon's voice was so cold and thin, it could've done stand-in for an icicle. Arrow of justice, yeah.

Mercy nodded, then shook her head as though denying it. "I didn't… I wasn't expecting that. I didn't…" She suddenly seemed to realize that she was spilling her guts to two strangers, however sympathetic, and clamped her lips shut. I noted, almost in passing, that she was wearing colored gloss on those lips, but no other makeup…like she had been trying to pretty herself up, when we came by, and interrupted it.

Or, she just naturally wore gloss on her lips to keep them from chapping. It didn't mean anything.

I filed it away anyway.

"Did you keep the note, Mercy?" I asked her, as gently as I could. "It might help us track down whoever it was, and make sure they leave you alone." If the bastard who had written it was Talent, we might be able to pick up usable trace.

"I burned it," she said flatly. "I don't want to talk about this anymore. What does it matter? It was all…it's all over."

The urge was to push a little more—I didn't want to go back to Stosser with nothing—but Sharon stood, and I followed suit.

"We're sorry for intruding, and about such an unpleasant matter," Sharon said, in the smooth, professionally sincere voice I bet she learned back in her legal beagle days.

"Unpleasant? That's one way to put it." Mercy looked out the single window in her sitting room, as though expecting someone to be lurking there, three stories off the ground, and shook her head again. "You need to go now."

Apparently, we really did need to be told twice.

We went back down the stairs, and I'd put my hand on the doorknob when Sharon made one last attempt to connect. "Don't be afraid of them," she said. "Whoever it was…we'll make sure they won't hurt you."

"Why?" Mercy was blunt, looking Sharon right in the eye now. "Why should Council worry about me? I'm nobody. Nobody, now that Si…" She lost her steel, and faltered.

"Council may not," Sharon said firmly, meeting her gaze. "But we do."

The front door closed firmly behind us, and we walked down the sidewalk back toward the subway station. I shivered, even though the afternoon air was actually pleasant, with the sun still lingering overhead. "You didn't take the spell off," I said, lifting a hand to stop Sharon.

"It will fade. Unless there was someone hiding in the back room waiting to interrogate her, she'll be fine by dinnertime. Back to normal."

Sharon's voice was odd; still cold, but dryer than usual.

"What's wrong? I mean, other than the fact that someone threatened her...."

"I don't know. I just... The entire time, I felt there was something wrong."

"You mean other than the whole being threatened, traumatized, not-wanting-to-deal-with-it vibe she was giving off?"

"Yes, more than that." The dryness in her voice ratcheted up a notch, and I regretted my flippancy. This was what Sharon was good at; I needed to listen to her.

"Was it something in the spell? Was she lying?"

"No. She was telling the truth. The spell worked, in that part. But I think that it was how she was telling it that made me feel weird." Sharon shook her head, walking faster. "The spell does something to my sense of people, something we hadn't anticipated. It's harder for me to see them clearly. I need to think about it, before I make my report."

That was a "shut up and leave me alone" if ever I got commanded. I moved faster to catch up, keeping quiet, and wondering, quietly, to myself, if the kind of person who left anonymous notes and candles to a murdered rapist would threaten the victim, too. And if they were, could we trace them down from the limited evidence we had left?

I was willing to give it a try. Right now I needed to do *something*.

She'd been wearing lip gloss. My mind went back to that...

why? There had been something off about it. I'd noticed it because it was smudged, smeared off her lip, just a little. Not the kind that happens when someone kisses you—the kind when your hand is jostled. Or your hand is shaking too hard to apply the wand properly.

Did that mean anything? Maybe, maybe not. But my heart ached, and I wished for the first time ever I wasn't on the job, so I could have gone back and cuddled her until she stopped shaking, stopped blaming herself. Nobody should be left alone feeling like that.

But I was on the job, and we were PUPI. The U stood for unaffiliated—and that meant we had to be impartial, too, otherwise it all fell apart.

Knowing that, knowing it was the only way to help her, didn't make it suck any less, just like I'd predicted.

We were almost to the subway when we both stopped, like somebody had nailed our shoes to the sidewalk.

feel that?

yeah My flesh was still prickling from the wash of current that had just shot through us; too strong to just be a stray tendril off someone's core.

Pinging each other was automatic by now: J might think it was slapdash and sloppy of the younger generation, but when you were in a situation where you didn't want anyone else to know a conversation was going on, it was damned useful. And the better we got to know each other, the easier it became.

hostile?

My feeling was that anything that made us freeze in our

tracks like that was not friendly, at best. I sent that, not in words, but a wash of "what do you think?" sarcasm.

us, or someone else? Someone else, by implication, Mercy. We'd been in close contact with her, used current on her; we'd feel an attack on her, at least for a little while after.

A fair question. I didn't know.

Then the current-wave came back, strong enough to make me stagger, and I knew. Us. Definitely us.

keep walking. don't stop

The sound of our heels on the pavement was way louder than they really could have been, but I could hear each step clearly over the traffic next to us, and the rattle of the elevated subway pulling in to the station overhead. I focused on it, letting my breathing match the *tap-tap* of our steps, until my entire body was focused on that noise, my awareness hyperalert to anything and everything around us in a way that wasn't fugue-state, but felt like it. The current-wave was gone, but I could still feel it on my skin, like piskie-size spears jabbing into my skin, looking for the lethal spot.

"Breathe, Bonnie. It's okay."

I nodded, but didn't let myself break the pattern, even as we climbed up the metal steps to the subway, and waited for a train. Not until we actually were in the car, and the doors shut, enveloping us in a comforting metal embrace, the sensation of being pricked to death fading, did I let go.

I took a near-normal breath, then another. "Who do you think that was? Was it related to Mercy?"

Sharon gave me a look that would have wilted a Mack truck. "Whoever threatened her doesn't want her talking to anyone else, either. We were being warned off."

"Yeah." That had been my take, too. "Didn't work, though."

A small, perfectly vicious smile curved Sharon's lips, the smile that made us forgive all the ways she occasionally drove us crazy. "No," she agreed. "It didn't."

"Will you sit down?"

Venec didn't sit down, but he did pause in his pacing. "They should have been back by now."

"The 1 train's been screwed seven ways from Sunday and twice more during rush hour, all week. Relax, Ben."

His partner snorted: you didn't get to hire a guy because of his obsessive-possessive paranoid tendencies and then get to tell him to relax. Ian's brain was clearly elsewhere. Or he wasn't taking their missing pups seriously.

"If they were in trouble they would have let us know." Ian gave his partner a long, assessing look. "Why are you worried? What aren't you telling me?"

He couldn't say. There was an itch, or a twitch, or something in his skin that made him jumpy, like live wires stroking his core, feeding him too much dirty current. He had been on edge for days now, and while he wanted to chalk it up to the uncomfortable convergence of events, case and his own research, he knew there was more to it. The under-his-skin feeling had all started with that snap-crackle-pop with Torres, with that damned exchange they'd had that he still didn't understand.

Be damned if he was going to say anything about that to Ian, though.

"I don't like this case. I didn't like it when you brought it in, and I like it even less now. Someone's playing us."

Ian stretched his legs out and clasped his arms behind his head, willing to be distracted onto this older argument. "God, you'd think you were a cloistered nun before you came here. Someone's always going to be playing us, Ben. Especially the Council, bless their overcomplicated souls. They think they can use us, for their own ends." He smiled, a smug little smile that annoyed the hell out of most people. "And we will let them…so long as it allows us to do what we need to do."

Ian had always been a cocky bastard. "What happens when their game and our needs don't coincide—or come into conflict?"

"Let me handle that, Ben."

Cocky bastard. "I hate it when you say that."

Ian didn't laugh—he never did—but that smile grew a little warmer.

Ben started to pace again, prowling the confines of the small office.

"Someone tried to Push me, last night."

That wiped the smile off Ian's face, but he looked thoughtful, not surprised. "Was last night the first you felt it?"

"Yes. Why?" He looked at his partner. "Did someone try you, too?"

Ian shrugged, a surprisingly graceless move, considering how elegant he could be when he wanted. "You know I can't tell things like that." It was a weakness in his skill set, and one that had to rankle, not that he ever let it show. "But now that you mention it…doubt, and annoyance?"

"Self-doubt, yes. Someone trying to make me feel insecure about my decisions."

Ian snorted, knowing how well that had probably gone over. "Then yes, about, mmm, two days ago, for me. Interesting. Good to know that it's external. Do you think it's related to this case?"

"No," Ben said, then added, "Maybe. Bonnie had a kenning, at the beginning of all this, something related to the case, but not directly, coming down the pike, not right away. If she was sensing this, then it will affect the team, too, so probably case-related."

"Kenning isn't precog, we can't make assumptions. She might have been sensing the fatae problem you're chasing, too. That connection would tie it into the case enough for her to feel the tremor."

Ben grunted, neither agreeing nor disagreeing, then went to the door, his hand lifting to the knob. "They're back. I'll round everyone up."

Ian held up a hand to stop him, his expression changing from mild consideration to active interest. "I thought you set the door downstairs to Automatic?"

He paused. "I did." Once the team had signed on, he'd set elementals, tiny creatures that lived in the current stream, to watch for each of them, and activate the electric lock when they approached. That way they didn't have to carry keys, or worry about someone in the office buzzing them in. It also gave them a little extra security, in case their hands were full...or they were being followed. No chance for someone to attack while they were waiting for the door to be opened.

"Then how did you know they were back?" Ian asked, reasonably enough.

Ben opened the door, willing himself not to turn and look back at his suddenly intently observant partner. "I don't know. But I did."

"Uh-huh."

"Boss!"

Anything else Ian might have been planning to say was drowned out by Nifty's yell down the hallway.

"Is he talking to you, or to me?" Ian wondered, distracted from his earlier question.

"I think it's a singular plural. Come on, let's see what our girls have come back with."

"Better not let them hear you call them that," Ian murmured, but got up and followed his partner down the hallway.

The team had already gathered in the main conference room, ranging themselves around the table. Mendelssohn and Lawrence anchored each end, left and right, with Shune and Torres separating them. Ben paused and focused, and saw Cholis sitting next to Shune.

Pietr noticed Ben looking directly at him, *seeing* him, and smiled; it was an almost shy grin that caused an involuntary smile in return, before Ben tamped it back down into his normal stoic expression. But Pietr saw it.

And so had Torres. He knew that even before he turned to look at her.

He knew she was there. Knew where she was, knew the moment she had come back into the building. The information hadn't been intrusive, and not at all disturbing, which bothered him more than if it had been disturbing. Awareness of her return had slid into the back of his brain without fanfare, the way you knew a lover lying next to you had woken up even when your eyes were still closed.

That wasn't normal; if he had wanted to be aware of someone coming in, he could have set the elementals to alert him. But he hadn't. And neither of the girls—hell, none of the pups—were good enough to slip under his guard like that. Nothing got into his brain except what he brought in. His control was better than that, even when he was distracted.

Ben let Ian stride past him to open the meeting, and took a seat at the far end of the table, where he could monitor everyone's reactions, as usual. Whatever had happened between them, whyever it had happened, it had opened a channel he didn't control, and he was going to figure out what it was, and shut it down.

Later. When they had time.

I felt Venec's gaze pass over me, and shivered; thankfully, he looked away, and I had time to get my nerve endings back under control. Stosser didn't waste any time with pleasantries, as usual, grabbing a chair and opening the meeting. "All right, people, it's been a busy morning, things to discuss."

Nick took advantage of everyone's attention being focused on the boss to lean in and whisper in my ear. "I see your fatae buddy got you home safe."

I snapped the pencil I'd been playing with in two in surprise. What the hell?

"What the hell is your problem, ferret-boy?"

For once the words didn't come out of my mouth, but

Sharon's, who had picked up his words, even though they were meant to be quiet.

"Didn't you hear? She's got her own personal fatae bodyguard to keep her safe."

Oh, we were not going there. Abso-damn-lutely not, and I didn't care how bad his hangover was or how annoyed Stosser got at a sideline conversation happening during his meeting. "Are you more pissed off at the fact that you didn't get to play drunken Sir Galahad last night, or the fact that Bobo isn't human?"

"A bodyguard?" Sharon looked at me, and I shrugged, refusing to listen to Nick's splutters, aware that we now had everyone's attention. Great.

"My mentor called in a favor or two. Bobo's large but sweet—sort of like Nifty with hair, and he's the one who got us in to see the Gather, so I'd say he's more than justified his presence, not that I have to justify a damned thing in my life to you, Shune. Or anyone." I glared around the table, daring anyone to say anything. I might be annoyed at J's presumption in arranging a bodyguard but I'd be damned if anyone else was going to say a word against him—or Bobo, for that matter, who was becoming a friend.

"Yeah, but a fatae? With everything that's going on in the city?" Nick made a face. "You're trusting yourself with—"

"With what?" I don't have a temper, but I was tired and frayed and between the interview with Mercy and the weirdness with Venec, and my general ickiness about this case, things were starting to get hot in my core. "With what, Nicky-boy?"

He leaned forward to respond, but anything he might have said was cut off before it left his throat.

"Enough!"

Stosser, using the Big Dog voice. "Nick, reconsider your words and then deal with your damn issues, whatever they are."

Nick winced, the bellow making his hangover come back to haunt him, and I almost felt sorry for him. Almost.

"And you, Torres." I cringed. "This Bobo. He's the one who took you to the Gather?"

"Yessir."

"And he's on your mentor's payroll?"

"Yessir. Only after-hours, when he doesn't think it's safe for me to be out alone." That was what J had said, anyway. I got the feeling Bobo was reinterpreting the guidelines, since he'd shown up not only during daylight, but also when I was with coworkers, and was taking an indirect but active interest in what we were doing.

"Useful," Ian said, and it was clear that we were done with the topic.

Venec was glaring at me like I'd done something wrong, but his mood swings—and my reaction to them—were the least of my problems right now. I sat back, still fuming over Nicky's behavior, and let Sharon give the report; she enjoyed getting up in front of everyone more than I did. As per her background, she was concise and precise, right up to where we were magically accosted on the street.

"You both felt this…malice?"

"Oh, yeah." I answered Ian before Sharon could take offense at having her word questioned. "Someone was definitely watching, and wanting us to know that they were watching."

"Who?" Venec asked, and I could feel how tense he was, even across the table.

Sharon looked at me once, as though to confirm her own impressions, then answered. "Talent, obviously. More than that, I don't think I could say. There wasn't enough flavor to the sensation to even tell male or female."

I raised an eyebrow. She could tell that? Color me humbled.

"They were pretty high-res, to make us both react so strongly without giving anything away, and definitely not friendly…although I didn't get a sense that we were in specific danger, just…being warned away."

"By whoever threatened the victim," Venec said.

Sharon looked at me, and I nodded.

"I want everyone to be careful," Venec said, giving everyone the two-second intense glare thing he did so well, each in turn. "If what Torres and Mendelssohn felt was from the same people who threatened the girl, any one of us could be their next target. If this is the same group that has been targeting the fatae, we know they don't hesitate at physical violence, so just watch yourselves."

"None of us have the kind of connection the girl did," Nifty objected.

"Mercy." Sharon glared at him. "Her name is Mercy."

"Fine. Whatever." Nifty leaned back in his chair, his body language showing he was raising a point, not picking a fight. "It doesn't change the fact that none of us have that kind of associations, none of us hang with the fatae—excepting Bonnie—"

"Don't you start," I muttered, but he was right. I was, as Nicky'd already pointed out, the one with the most connection with the fatae, and they didn't know the half of it. J had some friends who couldn't pass for human even on their best day.

"—so why would we be targets?" Nifty finished.

"Lawrence, you're asking me to explain the thought processes of bigots, people who generally say that if you're not one hundred percent in agreement with them, you're not only wrong but dangerous."

Stosser stirred at that, but Venec glared him down, too, and he subsided without saying anything. Interesting. The boot was on the other foot, today.

Ian took control of the meeting back. "At this point, all we have are unverified reports of attacks being made on fatae in this city, and others. Ben has been following up on this, and he thinks that it's a real problem. I am...not inclined to disagree at this point, although I will remind everyone that it is not our main point of concern, except as and if it impacts our case."

Venec lifted his chin slightly, and his mouth tightened slightly.

"However," Ian continued, "it would appear—verified by our own observations and experiences—that those who are targeting fatae have no hesitation threatening fellow Talent as well. As Ben said, watch yourselves."

Venec opened one of his folders and pulled out a flyer, sliding it onto the table. "I do believe that the two events are connected, yes. How many of you have seen these around?"

We all leaned forward to take a look. I shook my head, but Sharon and Nick both nodded.

"They had them up in the lobby of my building," Nifty said. "Super trashed 'em all, because we have an agreement with another exterminating company. What's the big deal?"

"You ever have a problem with roaches or silverfish in your apartment, Nifty?"

"Of course not. Current scares 'em away. So what? I think there's maybe one other Talent in my building, everyone else is supposed to suffer?"

"They're not exterminators," Sharon said. "I checked on their alleged company, which took some doing, since all they offer is a phone number. No license was ever granted, so far as the city's concerned, this company doesn't exist. The service they're selling isn't pest removal."

The side project Venec had asked her to look into? She had seemed disturbed by it, but not really concerned.

"Not the kind you find in the Yellow Pages, anyway," Venec said grimly, leaving the flyer on the table and leaning back in his chair

"Wait a minute...." I was picking up something from him—not satisfaction but a dark resignation, the kind you get when bits come together in the worst possible scenario.

Sharon beat me to the punch, though. "You think all this is connected. The attack on the girl...the claim that it was all a setup on the part of the ki-rin...you think it's connected to this antifatae sentiment...and that the extermination

advertisement is part of it, all one great big city-wide plot?"
She had the best poker voice of all the pups, but even she
was drawing close to incredulity.

Venec met her gaze with his very best Big Dog look: stern,
straightforward, and totally intense. "I think it's all deeply
coincidental. And I don't trust coincidences."

"Right now, it's only a theory," Ian said, for once the
calming voice of the two, and that freaked me out more than
anything Venec said. "It's not a theory I support, particularly—there's enough nasty in the world without it having
to be connected—but it's worth keeping in mind so long as
you don't let it distract you from the specific job…finding
out who did what to whom." He looked briefly at Venec, and
I felt an entire speech pass in that glance, although I wasn't
sure exactly what was being said. "I remind you again, we
are neither judge nor jury—just the investigators."

Ow. That was pointed, and I could tell that Sharon felt
it, too. But it was a good point to remember. The fact that
we'd never had enough evidence to do anything about the
guy who killed my dad…I could have acted on my own,
based on what I did know. But I hadn't. Zaki wouldn't
have wanted blood on my hands, not like that. Same way,
if there was some plot…our job was to find evidence, not
pass judgment.

"If the antifatae fever spreads, if we can link them to this…
the Council will have to do something about it, won't they?
If those people are threatening us, threatening members of
the *Cosa?*" I'd walked away from Zaki's killer, back then,
pretty sure that the guy would never hurt anyone again. But
this…I couldn't just look away, once we knew something

for certain. Not after hearing Danny's stories, listening to the fear in Mercy's voice.

"I stopped trying to predict what the Council might or might not do years ago," Stosser said. "You'd be advised to do the same. Not all of them are like your mentor."

"So what you're saying is that the Council, locally, if not as a whole—" and bless the San Diego Council for giving us a tentative thumbs-up last month, so their members could approach us, not that anyone had, yet "—while refusing to authorize us for their own people to hire directly and then hiring us on the side for their own benefit, will not act on information we uncover in the course of an investigation, even if it adversely affects their members, in order to avoid granting us legitimacy."

"That about sums it up," Nifty said.

"Hypocritical bastards." I didn't mean to say it out loud; it just slipped, and Sharon laughed. "Welcome to the lonejack mindset, Torres."

I was not amused. J had raised me to have some respect for the Council as a whole, even when he railed against individual members. But for them to sit quiet about this...

Maybe they wouldn't. J said people were already talking about this at his levels. If we brought them evidence, they could go after the bastards before it got out of hand. But we needed evidence, first.

It always came back to the evidence.

"Lawrence, lead us through the dance," Stosser said.

Nifty got up and walked to the far wall, which had been painted over with chalkboard paint so we could work things out without wasting reams of paper—one of Nick's occasionally brilliant ideas. He picked up chalk, and started to do his thing—diagramming the problem like it was one of his college games.

"Day one. Girl and fatae out clubbing, two human Talent out for an early-morning cigarette. Intersection."

Neatly swooping chalk lines, one white and one green, joined on the board.

"Result, one dead Talent, two injured Talent, one male and one female, and one fatae, unharmed but bloody."

So far, purely the facts, just the way Stosser liked it.

Nifty drew a dual-colored line down a few inches, then split them off again. "Day two. Stories diverge. He said, she said." A third chalk stick appeared in his hand, and he managed to draw a red line without dropping the first two chalks still between his fingers. "Day three. Third story appears—threat against injured female to force her to drop charges."

"Alleged threat," Sharon said. "I believed her, but they're not verified."

Nifty nodded. "Alleged threat. But you both were threatened by a force that appears connected." A fourth chalk appeared, and a blue line echoed the red one. At this point he had all four chalk sticks clutched in his hand, and I was totally distracted wondering how he managed that. My own hand flexed, and I remembered that Nifty was twice my size—he could probably handle an entire crayon box in one paw.

"Do we want to put in the antifatae group as a sideline, if we're going to include a threat that might have come from them, or as a main line, if they're an instigator?" Nick asked. We all looked at Stosser, who nodded—reluctantly, I thought. "Main line."

A fifth chalk, and a purple line appeared, parallel to our investigation. He was going to run out of colors, soon. "So that's—"

It was the magical equivalent of an air-raid siren going off next to your ear, and I fell off my chair from the blast— literally. Current was swirling up from my core, ready to be shaped into defensive or offensive charges as needed, by the time I scrambled to my feet. I scanned the room to see where the threat came from, and realized that nobody else had responded the same way—except Sharon, who was standing, her chair tipped over behind her, current haloing her like St. Elmo's fire.

Her gaze met mine, and realization flooded us both. Mercy.

There was a rush and a swirl, and before I could ready myself, Sharon had Translocated us both back to Astoria.

ten

Being Translocated by someone else is a different feeling from doing it yourself—the difference between launching yourself from a swing and being tossed from a well-aimed catapult. Sharon had the skills, and a good touch, but she didn't know me anywhere near as well as J did, so I landed dizzy and disoriented, which is exactly how you don't want to be when arriving in the middle of a fight.

I ducked under a roundhouse and came up with my head into the guy's rib cage, butting like a nanny goat. My dad's girlfriend taught me that one, when I was still a teenager, along with the "never be afraid to get your thumb into someone's eyeball" rule. I missed Claire. I wondered what happened to her, after my dad died....

"Bitch!"

"True," I said sweetly, instinctively blocking a sizzling lash of current with a wall of my own. God, was he kidding me? Fighting with current like that was kid stuff; normally you outgrew it by the time you were fourteen—at least for girls. Boys seemed to take a while longer to learn that an unspecified flailing, even with current, was neither macho nor particularly effective. I went down, hooking my arm around my attacker's knee, and used his body's own motion to yank him facedown onto the ground. His concentration shot, the current-lash sizzled and flared out. I rolled over and planted my elbow in the small of his back, then pulled a sharp splinter of current up through it, touching right at the base of his spine.

"One pinprick, and you're in a chair for the rest of your life," I told him. "And that's manual power for you, not electric."

I wanted him to fight back. I really did. I guess he heard that in my voice, because he went limp like a bearskin rug. Damn.

Keeping that point of current nailed to his spine, I risked looking around. Sharon and Mercy had squared off against three guys, all of whom looked like they could pass in a crowd at a society fund-raiser, if you dressed them up better. Not your average goon squad. Two of them looked like they'd been roughed up; the third, the one hanging back slightly, was unmussed. Either the coward of the bunch, or their ringleader. Or both.

The current in the apartment was dangerously over the top—and even as I thought that, the overhead lights shorted out with a magnificent fall of sparks, and the immediately recognizable sound of a computer giving up the final ugly ghost came from the other room. In seconds, the entire building went silent, the way only a Talent can hear. No electricity at all. We'd killed it.

Lack of an immediate power sourcing didn't seem to be stopping the trio of baddies, though, and my side seemed to be outnumbered, if not outgunned. I changed the point of current to a net, pinning my guy to the ground, and went to join the fray. He might be able to work free, but it would take him a few minutes. J taught me that trick—although it was supposed to be used on would-be muggers. Close enough.

Unlike my first guy, these three were making a very nasty attack. They were trying to pull current from Mercy—and now Sharon—so that their cores would be weakened, making them easy prey for a physical attack. Mercy was bleeding out of her nose—not a good sign; she was way overextended. Looked like she'd put up a damn good fight before calling for help, though, from the way the guys were sweating.

Draining someone was nasty but still basic. Using current as a true offensive weapon isn't something most Talent learn. Defensive, yeah—like the current-splinter I'd used on the first guy, and a few more tricks that would scare off a Null, but that was it.

Most Talent don't get trained by the Big Dogs.

"Get down," I said to Mercy, shoving her a little on the shoulder. She went to her knees without resisting—I got the feeling she was used to following orders. Or maybe she was just too drained to think straight.

I took her place standing next to Sharon. I bet I didn't look too imposing—skinny blonde chick in black, with too many silver hoops in her ear—next to Sharon's Corporate Woman skirt and hose, but they were in for a surprise.

Sharon didn't even look at me, busy holding off all three by herself. I could see the faint echoes of her current, straining to keep the others at bay. I was guessing that she was using a variant of the firewall we'd been working on in training...but that wasn't meant to be worked by one person alone.

ready? I asked her.

ready

These guys might be working together, but that didn't mean they were working in tandem. And that, thanks to Venec's endless drills, was where we had a kick-ass advantage.

The three guys facing us had expected one lo-res girl, already scared and traumatized. What they got was two women, full-power and trained to act. And *pissed*.

My current, cold and blue like a winter sky, met Sharon's hotter, more staticky flare, and twined like serpents on a caduceus. Only it wasn't in a healing mode.

tiger strike?

A wave of agreement flowed from me in response to Sharon's prompt, and our current struck like a gigantic cat's paw, starting to the left and sweeping across them, at exactly neck level—adjusted in motion, since they weren't the same height. We'd practiced on each other, though, for exactly that scenario.

Unlike practices, the claws here weren't sheathed. Current curved and sharpened, taking near-physical form, and the first goon on the left cried out and clutched at his throat in pain. His pull on Sharon and Mercy faltered, and I came with another swipe of my own, cutting through the pull and throwing it back on the source, the way a cat would bat at a mouse. Visualizing it that way made it stronger, more "real" in the physical world, and the shock of it knocked him out of the attack.

The third guy had figured out what was going on, and tried to form a defense, raising a wall of current of his own. It protected him—but also stopped his attack.

Second guy, a tall blond fellow, was either more determined or less smart than his companion, and kept pulling at Mercy. I heard her whimper and my mood, already sour, took another dive. She'd already been assaulted once; be damned if I'd let these bastards do it again.

Without waiting for Sharon to catch up, I shoved the claw back at him, this time not swiping across, but digging in... not at chest level, but lower. Considerably lower.

Let the punishment fit the crime.

He howled and dropped, and I gave him a purely physical kick in the gut for good measure, the tip of my boot making a satisfying *thwack* on impact.

At that point they realized they weren't going to be able to manage whatever they'd come here for, and must have called for help. There was an external surge of current, and all four intruders popped out with the usual rush of ozone-scented air.

I collapsed onto the floor next to Mercy, and let my current retreat from the caduceus. It didn't go all the way back into my core, though: my nerves were still twitching, and my current reacted to that, settling like a second skin around me, cool and soothing.

While I still had the stink of them, I gathered up our impressions of the guys, their signatures, their looks, even their smells, and did my best to transmit them directly to the office, reaching for whatever awareness was first available.

bonnie?

Venec, of course. He was startled—we'd never done a person-to-person translation like this, without warning or prep, and I wasn't even sure how I was managing it—but he opened to me without hesitation.

attackers I told him, pouring everything into that one thought, compressing as much as I dared, not sure how long I could hold the link open. A weight pushed against me, like a wave when I used to bodysurf as a kid; Venec, supporting me with his own current. I didn't have time or energy to wonder how he was doing that. With an odd clicking sensation the sense of them left my head and went into his. There was a brief mental touch, almost a hesitant caress, and then he was gone.

I leaned forward until my forehead touched the carpet, stomach-sick and dizzy.

"You okay?"

I wasn't sure if Sharon was asking me or Mercy. I just nodded, too tired all of a sudden to even speak. It was one thing to use offensive current in practice, when you were ready and prepared. Getting pulled out of a meeting on a second's notice, and facing off against four strangers, without the chance to load up beforehand, and then do whatever it was I'd just done...

I could have eaten an entire porterhouse, at that moment, and gone back for dessert. And then taken a two-day nap.

"Mercy? You okay? Who were those guys?" Even as I asked I knew the answer to both questions. They were the goons who had threatened us on the street earlier, or sent by the person who'd done it, and no, she wasn't okay at all.

Mercy curled on the floor like someone had just cut all her strings. She wrapped her arms around her knees, and wept silently, shuddering little-girl sobs that broke my heart and made me want to promise her that it would be okay, that it would all be okay. And I couldn't. Because it wasn't, and it wouldn't be.

"We need to take her somewhere," Sharon said. "Somewhere safe, where…"

Where someone could coddle her, was what Sharon wasn't saying. Where they could talk her out of whatever semicatatonic state we could already see creeping in. There had been too much, and she didn't have the outlet of laughter—only sadness, and pain.

I thought instinctively of J, but that didn't feel right. J was too brusque—perfect for my preteen wise-ass self, but not this damaged girl.

mash Distant, distracted, but still connected, somehow, enough to feel my quandary and come up with a solution.

"We'll take her to Mash's," I said.

Mash was a legend in New York City. He had retired years ago, like my own mentor, but unlike J, Mash couldn't say no…and didn't try to. If you were a Talent between the ages of ten and twenty, his three-story brownstone was a perpetual open house; no questions asked, advice and sympathy—and the occasional ass-kicking—always on offer. Mercy was a little old for that, but I suspected that Venec was right; it was the best and maybe the only place for her right now. Mash not only took no shit from adults, but he also had the current to back it up.

I suppose we could have asked for a Transloc from someone back in the office, but we'd both had enough being tossed around the city for one day. Personally, I'd had enough for a month: Translocation wasn't one of my better skills—I'd learned it late, and under protest—and it took way too much out of me, even as a passenger. The thought of bundling Mercy into a subway car wasn't appealing, either, even assuming she could have made it that far surrounded by strangers. Instead, we called for a hire-car, bundled her into the back, and settled in for the trip back to Manhattan.

on our way I told Venec, who returned a noncommittal grunt that meant he'd heard me, but was otherwise preoccupied, probably with the stuff I'd sent him, and catching the others up on what had happened. With luck, they had enough to track those bastards down.

It occurred to me suddenly that my pings to Venec were using actual words, not images or emotions. I didn't know if it was because of all the training we were getting, using our current more, or...

Or what. What the hell was going on between us, anyway, and why now, all of a sudden?

I was too tired to follow that thought anymore, right now. I closed my eyes and let the hum of the car around me lull me into a light doze until we hit the East Village, and Mash's brownstone.

My credit card, naturally, was shot to hell after that little firefight, so we had the driver call the office to get someone there to authorize the payment. I flipped the bit of plastic between my fingers thoughtfully. More current, more usage...yeah, I could see that my days of being able to carry magnetic cards were nearly over. Damn.

Mash met us at the door. He was ancient, and irascible, and scary as hell if you were an adult with bad intentions, but he took one look at Mercy and ushered us straight in, no questions asked, yelling to someone to bring chocolate and a cat, and a bottle of whiskey. Teenagers scattered to do his bidding, others quickly clearing a place at the huge wooden kitchen table, and setting up extra chairs.

"Here you go, dearling, sit here, that's right." Mash took a red stripy kitten from someone and handed it to Mercy, who uncurled enough to cuddle it in her arms. The kitten, rather than scratching or wiggling to get away, settled in calmly and started to purr. Mash poured two shots of the whiskey, and broke off a chunk of dark chocolate that smelled awesome, coaxing Mercy into opening her mouth so that he could place it on her tongue.

"She'll be all right now," Sharon said. "Come on, Bonnie. We've got to get back."

It took me a minute to remember what she was talking about. Back to the office. Right. Meeting. Roundup... That tickled something in my brain, and I took a second to chase it down.

"I'm going to take another look at the site," I said. "Tell the boss."

Sharon wasn't happy at being messenger girl, but she nodded, and while she went uptown, I took the crosstown bus to the meatpacking district, where the attack had taken place.

As much as I wanted to go after the goons who had threatened Mercy, and us, we had to keep focused on the original crime. Stosser, damn him, was right about that. I'd written off the lack of any residue from the girl to her being lo-res, and all the looky-loos muddling the scene. But Mercy had put up a pretty good fight for an amateur before we got there today. So why hadn't I found any trace of her on-site?

Part of it might have been not knowing exactly what I was looking for. She'd been a cipher, a shadow on the gleaning, "the girl," or "the victim." Distance and lack of bias were all well and good, but they weren't the only answer. But between the interview, the ping for help, and the trip to Mash's, I had a firm hold of her signature now. If Mercy had done anything, felt anything strongly, I should be able to pick it up from the site, no matter how faded.

And if there still wasn't anything there? If there wasn't any defensive current to find, from her, or the perps?

Then that would tell us something, too.

I got off the bus at 8th Avenue, and walked to the site. The sky was a clear blue, but the sun wasn't very strong today, and I wished I'd worn a sweater over my long-sleeved T-shirt, since Translocation didn't go via the coat closet to grab my jacket. Busy sidewalks, the usual weekday traffic, people in suits and jeans going to and from, intent on their business.

It was easy to be anonymous in New York City—it was hard to stand out, in fact. And yet, I could feel eyes on me, watching me, following me. The weight of their attention had a strange, almost stale feel to it; familiar and totally alien at the same time. Nonhuman eyes.

Fatae eyes.

They knew who I was—or, more to the point, *what* I was. Either from the Gather, or Danny, or the fatae gossip lines, they knew. They were still here from this morning, when Sharon saw them, only now they were just watching, judging, and it was freaking me the hell out.

And there wasn't a damn thing I could do about it. The U in PUPI stood for unaffiliated. That was Stosser's mantra, his impetus, and it was one we all agreed to, believed in. Repetition made habit. We had to be seen as impartial and unbiased to all sides. Not just client and suspect, but Talent and Null, human and fatae. If we weren't, if our findings were dismissed as being bought or biased, then everything we did would be completely useless. Worse than useless; they could be used against the people we were trying to help.

Before, I'd been frustrated at that: now I got a real sense for the tightrope we'd been shoved out on. If we did this wrong, if I did this wrong, it would be game over. The fatae, at least, would never trust us.

I couldn't afford to do it wrong.

There were only a few people around, once I made it across the wide expanse of West Street: an occasional jogger, rapt in their headphones, or a nanny pushing a stroller, trying to give kidlet some fresh air before returning to their high-rise apartment. The site itself was a little more worn than before, but the pile of offerings had been refreshed on both sides. New flowers, new saint's candles. None of the participants had been religious, according to the dossier, so it wasn't specific to them: someone else was bringing god into this. It might not mean anything—people called on random deities all the time, even if they didn't actually believe and would be horrified if someone answered. Religion was rote and empty ritual for a lot of people. Faith, though…

If you believed in something hard enough, a lie can become truth. Yeah.

Holding on to the memory of Mercy's signature, I sank into fugue-state, and let my mage-sight flicker over the area. I wasn't looking for anything specific, nor was I trying to glean everything from the site. This was more akin to scanning the ocean's surface, looking for sign of a humpbacked whale, or dolphin's leap, out of the whitecaps and swells.

Only, instead of a dolphin or whale, I caught a sea monster. There were things lurking around the edges: new things, gathering and waiting. Some a block away, some within reach if I were to stretch out my hand. Some human, and some not. The eyes I felt on me before, and more. Sharon had only said a few…this was more like dozens. Right now they were passive, merely watching. Was this rubbernecking, *Cosa*-style? Or did it have something to do with the larger events around us, the antifatae tension Venec was worried about? Everyone had their eyes on us, right now, waiting to see what we did, what we decided—what we reported.

"Need to ask Venec what he thinks," I said, the sound of my voice startling me, and sending several of the more alien observers skittering farther out of range.

thinks what?

I yelped, and fell onto my knees. Off in the distance I was damned sure I heard a snicker from one of my invisible observers, but ignored it, more intent on the sudden intrusion of a voice in my head.

how did you hear me? I demanded. That wasn't supposed to be possible. Screw that, it wasn't possible! I was tempted to throw up a total block, the kind you're only supposed to put up in case of emergencies—like blinding and deafening yourself while standing in the middle of traffic, it was more dangerous than it was useful—but my curiosity got the better of my outrage.

how do you do that?

There was a pause, as though Venec was as shocked to hear my voice as I had been to hear his, and then:

was afraid of this

As answers went, that wasn't. But Venec's mental voice lingered in my brain, more solid and specific than any ping I'd ever gotten, the same way it had been earlier that day, and I could feel him poking around, probing at the limits of that connection—not in his brain or in mine, but somewhere overlapping. It was like the current-bubble I'd formed with Pietr that allowed us to share a point of view, magically, only there hadn't been any spell, no intentional opening-up...

That weird current-spark, earlier in the week. That amazing, near-erotic feel of something transferring between us... No. Impossible. Current didn't work that way. There was no way to "accidentally" use current—you had to will it to do something, or it would turn back on the user, not go do something on its own, the same way a hammer would

come down on your finger, not go attack someone else if
you weren't paying attention to the downward strike.

But the answer felt right, if impossible, and I could feel
Venec's agreement as well, distant and right next to me at
the same time. That, and his late-night visit in my head,
and this... How, as J used to say over and over in lessons,
was subject to If. Once If was met, then How was merely a
matter of time and study. If we were connecting on some
level neither of us had ever encountered before, then something had happened. If neither of us had intentionally done
something, then either someone else had done it to us—and
we both thought of and rejected that idea at once; this thing
was locked between us, nobody else's signature anywhere to
be found—or we'd somehow done it unintentionally.

I could *feel* his awareness and uncertainty about all this,
tasting it the way a dog would taste the air for rabbit or
squirrel.

Impossible or not, when my walls and barriers had been
down during training, and his had been down, too, for whatever reason, then our usual current-brushes and attraction
had...done what? Done something, damn it.

Suddenly the insights I'd had into Ian earlier made sense,
too. They hadn't been mine, they'd been Ben's. It wasn't
just his thoughts that had access into my brain, it was his
knowledge, too.

My freaking earlier had been nothing compared to how
I felt right then.

get out I ordered him, and slammed up walls fast
and hard enough to dismember any mental fingers left in
the way.

Holy shit. The urge to hyperventilate came and went, but my hands were trembling and my pulse was too fast for comfort. Did not like, did not want. No. I might be casual about sex, I didn't have any of the usual hang-ups about body image or privacy or personal space, but there were certain things that were mine and mine alone and my brain was #1 on that list. Pings were all well and fine but I decided who I talked to, I decided what was in my brain.

Deep breath in.

Deep breath out.

Deep breath in.

Anyone watching me would have assumed a panic attack and they'd probably have been right. But slowly it came back under control. Whatever had happened, it was Venec. Venec, who had shadowed me before, when I was greener, but had shown respect for my privacy. Venec, who when I told him to leave, left. Venec, who didn't seem any happier about whatever was going on than I was.

Benjamin Venec, who guarded his privacy so closely that we didn't even know where in the city he lived, or if he was in a relationship or had a cat or a goldfish or if he'd hatched out of an egg in Stosser's backyard.

He was dark-eyed and broad-shouldered, with thick curls he tried to slick back but didn't have the patience to keep groomed, with strong square hands that were the hands of a workman, not an artist. Calloused fingers and strong muscled arms, and my pulse started to speed up again, if for more pleasant reasons, just thinking about those hands.

"Well, you're back to normal then, aren't you?" I asked

myself ruefully, relieved when there were only my own thoughts in my head in response.

I tried, after that, to slip back into a working fugue-state, but it was no use. I was too aware of every tremor around me, every shimmer of current, every twitch of movement. Going deeper would require me lowering the wall I'd erected, and be damned if I was going to do that right now. I was too off-kilter, too vulnerable. Any faint trace of the original players left here would have to stay hidden for now...and probably forever, after three days of wear and tear on the scene.

I came back to full normal awareness, still holding up my walls, and sighed. I was very much not good at failure, even if there were extenuating circumstances. Especially when there were extenuating circumstances: that felt too much like making excuses, and covering up the fact that we'd failed to gather everything in the first go.

Live and learn, J would say. But what if, someday, a screwup like that meant someone *didn't* live to learn?

The air felt colder than when I'd arrived, and I looked up to see that the sky—pale blue that morning—had clouded up to a thick gray. I was too tired to do more than sniff in ether, but there didn't seem to be any storm-hint in the air. Pity; I wasn't much for sourcing wild, but people—Talent— tended to relax more when the spring thunderstorm season started, and we were definitely, all of us, the pack and the entire damn city, in need of relaxing.

Venec was gone when I made it back to the office. I knew it even as I was climbing the stairs, even through my strengthened internal wall: he wasn't in the building.

"Coward," I muttered, letting my wall drop enough that he would hear me. At least, I assumed he could hear me. Odds were he had his own wall up, to keep me out. Reasonable enough. I didn't think he was enjoying this any more than I was—he'd sounded so annoyed when he realized he'd heard me that it was almost insulting, actually. Irrationally—and I knew it was irrational and I couldn't help it—that just made me pissier.

"Hey." Pietr greeted me when I stormed into the office, and picked up on my mood immediately. "Whatever it was, I'm pretty sure it wasn't my fault."

I had the instinctive urge to say something wise-ass and cutting, and bit down on it. He was right: it wasn't any of his fault.

"Venec booked out for the day?"

"Yeah. About ten minutes ago."

Hah. Just as I was getting out of the subway. "Coward," I muttered again, for good measure. "Stosser?"

"Disappeared about an hour ago."

"What are the others doing," I asked, and then realized that I didn't give a damn. I loved my job but right now I did not want to be anywhere near anything that had anything to do with Benjamin Venec.

"Gone home, Venec's orders. Twelve hours of sleep before we're supposed to come back." He seemed oblivious to the fact that he was disobeying that order.

Venec was right, damn him. I was wired with the need to *do* something, but we'd all had a hell of a week, and if I pushed it much further I really would fall over. I needed to get out of here, and ideally get out of my skin, if only for a little while.

I gave Pietr a long considering look that had been known to make some people nervous. He met it square, his gray eyes calm and knowing. Hrm.

"You want to go get dinner?"

Pietr suggested the place, a little red-meat joint down by the seaport that the tourists didn't know about, and was perfectly willing to not talk about a damn thing that had anything to do with work. And somewhere over the course of a bloody-rare steak and my second vodka tonic, I decided that I was going to break my "no coworkers" rule, and have sex with Pietr. Feel-good, no-promises, tension-easing, *playful* sex. I was pretty sure he knew what I'd decided and was fine with that.

We finished dinner and paid the tab, and found ourselves standing on the sidewalk in the dusk. It had started to rain while we were eating, the kind of rain that's like mist against your face.

"My place is closer" was all he said.

Pietr's place was like him: quiet, almost elegant in its simplicity. He had a one-bedroom on the ground floor of a prewar building, with wooden parquet floors and an upgraded kitchen with very nice stainless appliances I coveted, and a bathroom twice the size of my own, but there were security bars on the windows that would have driven me nuts in a week.

His bedroom was totally what I would have expected from him: Shaker-style maple furniture with clean lines and a definite solidity, the bed in the middle of the room, decent-size, two pillows, a golden-brown comforter and white sheets. Everything was clean and neatly organized, and there were black-and-white photographs on the wall, of scenes I thought I recognized. I walked over to look more closely.

"That's Budapest."

"Yeah."

I turned to look at him. "You took these?"

He shrugged and nodded, as though embarrassed.

"They're wonderful." They were. I didn't know much about photography, but these really gave you a feel for the place and the time of day.

"Old camera, not much electronics to fuck up. I used to love playing around in the darkroom. I haven't been able to do much lately, though. We're..."

"Changing?"

"Yeah." His embarrassment shifted to curiosity. "You've noticed it, too? Ever since we started really working out, using current more, it's harder to be around any kind of electronics, even the stuff that used to be safe. You think..."

"I just noticed it myself. I don't have a theory yet, but yeah, it's got to be tied into how much we're using, even when we're not using it. Is the core a muscle, the more you use it the bigger it gets? Or..." I realized how we sounded, like we were still in the office, and laughed. "Damn it. This is ridiculous."

"What is?"

"Me, babbling. I don't babble, ever. I'm scared. I...I haven't been scared...ever. I mean, yeah, scared about a lot of things, but never this. Never about sex."

Pietr sat down on the bed. "Are you really scared? Or just not quite so sure of yourself anymore?"

I had to stop and think about that, damn him. There had been so much today, dealing with Mercy, the attack, the deal with Venec…it was no wonder I was feeling wobbly and weirdly off-kilter. I'd known I was using sex to make myself feel better, but was I using it to hide from those wobblies, instead of dealing with them? And if I was, was that wrong, necessarily?

"I am not used to not being totally sure of myself," I admitted.

"I'd noticed that."

That made me laugh again, the way I think he'd meant it to, and suddenly I saw again the glint of mischief I'd noted in him, that first day in the office. It had been too subdued lately, buried under training and the weight of what we'd experienced. I was glad to see it back. I was glad to be part of what brought it back.

"I'm okay being a diversion," he said, his face serious, although the spark remained. "But I don't want to be an excuse, or a thing you hide behind. Yeah?"

"Yeah." I sat down on the bed next to him. It gave way under my weight, and I made a mental note not to stay the night. Soft beds gave me backaches.

"It's not just physical," I said suddenly. "I mean…the diversion. I…" I really did like him, and the urge to take comfort was matched by a very real appreciation of both his form and his brain.

"It's all right, Bonita. I understand."

And just like that, the awkwardness was gone, and I felt

like my old self again...well, sort of. There was still this weird space in my head where the wall was up, keeping me from being quite the same Bonnie as usual, and part of me that felt weird, getting down to it with a coworker after all my promises to myself and to J that I wouldn't mix business with pleasure, wouldn't screw the job up with my usual casual attitudes. But Pietr stripped down nicely to long lean muscle and just enough flesh to be comfortable, his hands were as strong and as soft as I'd suspected they might be, and he had a streak of wicked inventiveness that challenged my own. And he very definitely was not a virgin.

And he was excessively and pleasingly diverting.

After a while I propped myself up on my elbows, wriggling around the pillows, and grinned down at him. "You were a saxophone player in a previous life, weren't you?"

"Trombone," he said, looking up with that glint in his eye, adjusting the spread of his hands across my hips, coaxing me into a better position, even as he shoved one of the pillows off the bed and onto the floor. "High school band. I was horrible. But I practiced really, really...hard."

Laughing when you're about to slide into orgasm is possibly one of the best ways in the universe to get rid of any lingering depression. My wall held, but it seemed easier to maintain, somehow, in the sticky aftermath.

Pietr was very guylike in the ability to pass out right after orgasm—his second, my fourth—and he snored. I had meant to get up and get dressed afterward, leaving a note to ease any awkwardness, but it had been a very long day, and I was very tired. And the bed was surprisingly comfortable, even if it was too soft. I curled up against the warm body next to me, listened to the rain coming down outside, and slept.

eleven

I woke up to a warm but empty bed, and a note on the pillow that Pietr had gone out running. I lay there, staring at the ceiling, and did a quick check on my entire system. Core still low but otherwise...

Settled. Calm. It wasn't the sex, as such, but the intimate contact that did it for me; the sharing of pleasure. Now, if I could just hold on to that, when things got hinky again...

I collected my clothing from the pile on the floor, got dressed, and considered my next move for about ten seconds. I scrawled a note on his note—gone home to shower, see you later—and let myself out of the apartment.

It wasn't the same as leaving in the middle of the night, and I'd never had a real problem with the so-called Walk of Shame, dragging myself home after a night out, but I still felt sort of awkward. I'd broken the one rule I had, and while I wasn't sorry—rules that no longer made sense needed to be updated—leaving like that bothered me. Maybe I should have waited, or showered there, or…

No. We both knew what we'd been doing the night before; no promises had been made or asked for, and he hadn't told me to wait for him to get back or anything, just that he'd see me later. It was copacetic, right?

The rain had let up a little overnight, but it was still damp and miserable. The site of the attack would be washed clean; any chance we had of collecting any kind of evidence was over. What we had needed to be enough. Please god, it would be enough.

I made it uptown before the morning rush really kicked in, dunked myself under the shower, grabbed a PowerBar for breakfast, got dressed, and was back on the subway in plenty of time to not be late to the office, if the transit gods were kind.

"You're late." Nifty stood by the coffeemaker, impatiently waiting for it to finish brewing. He looked as dapper as always, but there were traces of dampness at the hem of his chinos that made me think he hadn't been there all that long, either.

I shook off my umbrella and shoved it into the closet with my jacket, running fingers through my hair to assess the damage done by the rain and wind. "I know. Sick-passenger delay. We got our marching orders?"

"Not yet. Stosser wanted everyone to show up before we started. Don't worry, you're not that late. Nick's last man in, today."

"We should start a pool." Actually, we shouldn't. I might not lose, but I'd never win, either.

"Is the coffee ready yet?" Pietr came in from the back offices, mug in hand. "Hey," he said to me, casual and calm as he ever was.

"Hey," I said back. "Not yet, based on the way the big man over there's lurking."

"Damn. My coffeemaker died last night—totally shorted out."

Current-flare during sex could do that, even low-vulnerability tech like coffeemakers and alarm clocks. If he was trying to make me blush, he was going to have to work harder than that. But he just dropped the comment into the conversation and went on, like there was no ulterior motive at all. A part of me I hadn't been aware was tense, relaxed. Copacetic.

Nick came in just as the coffeemaker made the all-clear beep. His hair was plastered wetly to his forehead, and his mood was thunderous even at a distance. Great. What now?

"Told you not to buy that cheap umbrella," Pietr said, and disappeared back into the office. Nick made a face, and I relaxed, making a note to buy him a decent rain hat, something really dorky. Coffee properly doctored, I followed Pietr's tracks, with Nifty and Nick bringing up the slightly damp rear, pun totally intended.

"Good morning, everyone," Stosser said. He was wearing another of his funky, trying-to-be-crunchy-granola outfits today. That always freaked me out, because flannel and denim so didn't work on him; he'd been born to the bespoke-suit brigade, same as J. Venec was standing by the single window, holding the blinds away with one hand to look out onto the street below. Or maybe he was checking to see if it was still raining. He looked over when Stosser spoke, and did a weird kind of almost-invisible double take that I felt more than saw.

Huh. And uh-oh.

I'd be lying if I didn't admit to a certain distinctly feminine pleasure at the fact that I knew that Venec knew something had changed, but at the same time part of me just wanted it all to get shoved under the table—or better yet, out the window. This was part of why I hadn't planned on fishing off the company pier, damn it. I'm an uncomplicated girl: work is work and sex is sex and the two shouldn't get tangled, ever. The fact that I had only myself to hold responsible didn't help, either.

Not that it was any of Benjamin Venec's business. He was my boss, not my keeper, no matter what kind of wonky current had sizzled between us.

I took the seat next to Sharon, who was busy jotting something in her notebook. I leaned over to read, trying to distract myself, and she raised her arm, warning me away. I took the hint and moved back, watching everyone else take their seats. Venec stayed by the window, exuding a sort of silent-brute brooding force that was only partially playacting. All right, he was going to be Tough Dog today, and Stosser was going to be Guide Dog.

"Mash informs me that the girl will be staying with him for the duration. She is traumatized and shaky, and he strongly suggests that we not approach her further." Ian's face twisted a little at that, and I suspected that Mash had used stronger words in his suggestion. From what I'd heard and seen, Mash didn't have much patience with things like tact or diplomacy, and probably hadn't given Ian more than three syllables before slamming the door in his face, physically and metaphorically.

"So that avenue of investigation's shut down," Sharon said. Her voice sounded resigned, making me think she'd been privy to that bit of news already.

"I don't think we were going to get much more from her anyway," I said. "Whatever else happened, she was seriously scared about those threats, and now? The only one who could get her to talk would be the ki-rin, and it won't associate with her anymore." Knowing why it was acting that way—that it didn't really have a choice—didn't make me any less angry.

"The ki-rin isn't associating with or talking to anyone," Ian said. "My source says that it's claimed the privilege of extreme age, and refused to speak to anyone save his own kind."

I'd been right, then: the ki-rin was old. The Asian cultures had more respect for that than we did, even now. Combine age and stress and grief, and the ki-rin might as well be on another planet, for all the access we'd get.

"Great," Nick said, echoing my own thoughts. "It would take an act of god to get near it, now, and not even Stosser's got god in his back pocket." He looked sideways at the boss. "Do you?"

"Unfortunately, no. Nor, despite Ben's best efforts, do we have access to the perp, who has been released from the hospital and will not be charged with anything, as the girl refuses to press charges and the ki-rin is legally incapable of doing so."

"And the site's dead," Sharon said, confirming my earlier thoughts. "I stopped by on the way in, and…" She shook her head. "Clean as washed slate."

"So what the hell are we supposed to do, just close the file and demand our payment?" Nifty sounded pissed off.

"We can't," I said. "Ian was right, earlier. This isn't about who hired us, or why. It's about the truth. It's about us being put on the job, and not stopping until we know, for certain, what happened."

"Something bad happened there," Sharon said, adding her vote to the tally. "A girl was attacked and a guy was killed and we still don't know who was telling the truth and who was lying about what happened. We can't just walk away and say it doesn't matter. I don't care if the check clears or not—I can't just leave it that way."

I cared a lot about if the check cleared or not, but Sharon was dead-on, otherwise. We'd been hired to determine what had happened—the Council might be willing to let things rest, but that wasn't the PUPI way. We closed the case, not just for our own peace of mind, but for the victims, too. Although I was starting to wonder just who the victims were, here….

"It's worse than that," Venec said, and I got the feeling he was responding to my thoughts as much as Sharon's words. "If it were just human against human we could maybe let it ride. But the fatae are involved, and now the antifatae movement is involved—or at least someone holding those views is threatening the victim. If we back off now, it will look as though the Council told us to—that the Council was hand-in-glove with whoever threatened the girl, and silenced us, too. We can't afford to let it go. This is a match, people, and the entire city is tinder."

That fell like it had a real, solid weight, and Stosser used the moment after to push his chair away from the table and stand up. "Things happen at a time for a purpose," he said, and I guessed that was as much of an apology for doubting him as Venec was ever going to get. "The convergence of this case and Ben's investigations, and our involvement in both, however glancingly, isn't coincidence. We are meant to be involved—and to act. So do so. Ben, get them moving, and keep me updated."

Nifty leaned back to say something to Pietr and Nick, while Sharon flipped open her notebook again and scribbled a new note in it, then looked at Nifty, her expression pure challenge. Fighting off Mercy's attackers had put the ginger back, and she wanted lead. The question was, did Nifty want it just as bad, or would he give way? It was always tough to tell with him.

"Where are you off to?" Venec asked, leaning forward across the table toward his partner. His voice lowered a bit, but if he'd really wanted to keep it private he'd have pinged, so I felt no shame in listening in.

Ian hesitated, only half a second, but Venec felt it, and therefore so did I. Boss man was avoiding something. "Oil on water," Ian said finally. "Some local wire-wits tried to make a fuss over our involvement, claiming we were interfering with the natural order of magic, get us shut down. The usual crap. I have to give our dog-and-pony show again, make nice with the villagers."

The same claim his sister had made. No wonder he didn't want to bring it up. "Better you than me" was all Venec said, and I could feel his desire to be nowhere near the political pow-wowing as though it were my own emotion. All right, that was going to get annoying, fast. I took a deep breath, grounded myself, and rebuilt the wall between us. At some point I'd have to figure out how to make it more pliable, to let him reach me in case of an emergency. But for now, in the same room, it would have to do.

"Okay, puppies," Venec said, clapping his hands once to get everyone's attention as Stosser slipped out the conference room door. "Be brilliant. Find a way to wring new facts from the evidence, and answer the million-dollar question—who is lying?"

"That's not the question," Sharon said. "Bonnie was right, when this all started. The question is…can everyone be telling the truth? Because they all are, as far as we can tell. That's the problem."

"So someone's lying well," Nick said.

Sharon shook her head, stubborn. "No. I don't think so."

"Truth's Sharon's gig," Nifty said, handing over the lead gracefully. "Let's go with that. Short of psychosis, which one of us probably would have picked up, how and why can you believe a lie is the truth?"

"Love and religion," Pietr said promptly.

"Wise-ass."

"No, he's right," I said. "Not religion, exactly, but faith."

My thoughts earlier, when I was on the site, attached themselves to Nifty's words, illuminating them in my brain so I
could find the edges of the puzzle and fit them together. I
thought about Mercy's expression, the desolation in her eyes,
and the fear in her voice not at what might happen to her,
but for what already had. Her life had been destroyed...but
she still loved the ki-rin. Still had faith in it. Why?

"For love and faith, people can convince themselves of
almost anything," Sharon said in agreement.

"And money," Venec said.

"And money. But the ki-rin's got money, and attacking
Mercy wouldn't bring any to our perps, so I can't see that
being a cause. So...love?"

"Mercy loves the ki-rin," I said. "Without a doubt. Not
human-to-human love, and not a girl-and-her-pony love,
either." I remembered the smeared lipstick, the attempt to
put herself back together, when everything inside was shattered. "Something different, but real."

Nifty asked the next question. "Did it love her? I mean,
it dumped her pretty fast...."

"It didn't have a choice," Sharon said. "She wasn't pure
anymore, by its rules; even though there was no actual rape,
she had been tainted." Her voice didn't show any emotion
but I could see what she thought of that in her face. "It has
to follow its nature. I'm betting there's something in its
makeup, genetic or magical, that requires it adhere to the
rules, the way mers are stuck in tidal waters, and brownies
are tied to specific buildings."

"It...was fond of her," I said, remembering the images I'd
seen, still putting them all together with what we'd learned,

even as my coworkers were doing the same. "I don't know if it feels love the way we do—love isn't restful—but...it was fond of her. It wouldn't have chosen her, otherwise."

"I think it's safe to say that she didn't love the guys who attacked her...she didn't know either one of them, far as the dossier says." Venec tapped the folder on the table in front of us. We all had copies, but the original stayed in the office at all times, to make sure you could check something at any time, and it was the most updated version. "No connection, no contact... Nothing to indicate they'd ever even been at the same party at the same time. No love, no faith, no money. Not even a way to claim hate as the opposite of love, since neither of our perps, for all their other flaws, had ever come up with antifatae reputations. Two separate pairs, meeting by purest coincidence."

"Huh."

We all looked at Nick.

"What?" Sharon asked.

"Nothing. No. I don't know." I could practically see his own pieces slotting together behind his eyes, and wondered if he had something I was missing. "Gimme a minute." He got up and left the room before anyone could ask him another question, like he was afraid one more word would ruin whatever he was building.

"Right." Sharon took point. "Recap." She stared at the chalkboard wall, where the colored lines mocked us, refusing to explain themselves at all. "All the physical evidence is inconclusive or unavailable, the eyewitness reports contradict, and we're running out of time before somebody does something stupid, according to Ben."

That sounded, depressingly, about right.

"Nifty, you're thinking everyone's got something to hide?" Sharon asked.

"Professional cynic, that's me. Yeah. I've never met anyone who wasn't hedging their bets, somehow. But you're pretty sure the people you talked to aren't lying?"

"Ninety percent sure. Maybe even ninety-five." She hummed a little in frustration, trying to explain it to us. "There's a feeling people have around them when they're telling the truth, this rock-steady grounding, but it's rare. Damned rare. Most people, if they were even slightly unsure of their truth, waver a little. Human self-doubt."

"So you think this certainty's unnatural?" Venec asked.

"I interviewed a pure-P psychotic once as part of a deposition, and he had that same grounding no matter what crap he was spouting. It's usually a warning sign."

"You could have made a fortune as a professional witness evaluator," I said in awe.

"I don't make money off my skills," Sharon said, all Miss Prim again suddenly, and then realized what she'd said, and laughed. "You know what I mean. Not that way. That would have been...unethical."

Straight shooter: that was our Sharon.

Nick came back in, carrying a case about the size of a notebook, and put it on the table at the far end from the rest of us.

"Are you sure that's smart?" Venec asked him, worried.

"Yeah, I'll be fine. We rigged this one special. The battery's warded seven ways from Sunday, and up and down, too."

"Holy shit, that's a computer?" I was distracted by the shiny, I admit it. Laptops fascinated me. Desktops you could ground and protect easier, but every Talent I'd heard of who used a laptop singed it within a week. Knowing I couldn't use one without killing it the first time I forgot and pulled current nearby didn't keep me from wanting one, though. It was so cute!

"Jesus, man," Nifty said. "I have paperbacks larger than that thing."

"Talent are always way behind the tech curve," Nick said, flipping the lid up and waiting for it to power up. "They're called netbooks, people. Cheaper, lower powered, fewer bits and pieces to get whacked by current, but just as useful as a larger machine. They're pretty damn durable, but try not to have a spike for the next half hour, okay, everyone?"

I could see why Venec was worried: mixing current and tech was, well, risky, even for someone like Nick. But if he wanted to work in here, with the risks… I guess I wouldn't have wanted to miss the brainstorming, either.

"All right, back to work," Venec said, herding us into a tighter group at the near end of the table. "Ignore Boy Wonder over there and focus on the problem. I think we're on the right track, what Sharon and Bonnie were saying. There was a lot of powerful belief on the site, enough to influence the bystanders. What depends on being believed to be true? Religion and politics…I think we can rule those out. Love seems to be an impasse right now. So we're back to money?"

"How? Seriously—unless you're going to claim that someone took out a sexual hit on Mercy, or hired Mercy to entrap those guys..." My voice trailed off. I couldn't imagine reasons to support either scenario, and from the expressions on the rest of the pack, neither could they.

"I still think hate's a pretty good reason. I mean, the two guys knew each other, maybe..." Nifty's voice trailed off the same way mine had. "But they didn't know each other more than a few weeks, and the survivor was, by all his friends' accounts, fascinated with his new badboy buddy."

"What if the wildest theory's right," I said, slowly. "What if it was all part of the antifatae group, I mean, from the start? And they jumped her for associating with a ki-rin, the way white girls used to get attacked for dating black guys?"

"They did?" Pietr looked bewildered.

Nifty nodded, although I wasn't sure if he was responding to my comment, or the question. "Yeah. Yeah, maybe. That could work. Damn. I hope not, because there won't be a chance of keeping a lid on this, then."

I had the passing thought that we could bury it, but no, Nifty was right. That wasn't what we did, and anyway, once you dug something up, it tended to stay up.

Sharon picked up the thread. "Bonnie, do you think that could account for the blackness you felt? Hatred? Something so nasty it can't be burned clear even by current?"

I thought about it, trying to remember the icky, sticky feel of what I'd sensed.

"No. Hatred's clearer than that, not sticky and...greasy. Grimy."

"Madness," Venec said, maybe catching one of the tendrils of my memories, because he shuddered a little, so slightly I was probably the only one to notice. "You felt madness."

"Yeah." The bits clicked into place once I had the word to identify them. "Yeah. Rage and fear and scared and funny, all at the same time. Ugh." I was the one to shudder then, and Venec's hand reached out to touch mine, almost like he wasn't aware of what he was doing. Flesh-to-flesh, and the shudder left me. Just like that: I was grounded and steady again.

His hand pulled back like I'd burned him, and my skin felt cold where he'd touched, and I wanted him to cover me again. Bad. Very bad. We really needed to do something about that. But not right now, not here. I curled my hands in my lap and tried not to look at him.

"Crazy-mad. Rabid-dog crazy. That would tie in to it being part of the antifatae crowd, right?"

"But the trace was on the sites after the fact," Nifty pointed out. "We didn't feel it immediately after, when we were at the site. Did you?"

The gleaning was starting to go fuzzy around the edges in my head, thankfully, but that much I knew without having to consider it. "No. We didn't pick up any current on the scene." I stopped, and considered that. "Think about it, guys. We couldn't find any current from any of them. Not enough to carry emotion, not anything."

"We didn't test…" Pietr looked sideways at Venec, our screwup out of the bag.

"We shouldn't have *had* to. Three Talent, a violent confrontation, and no current residue even a few hours later? Not from them and not from her—it was a purely physical defense. Any current they used, it was weak as hell—or it was wrapped tight around their core." The way it would be if, for example, they had a spell cast over them: to make them believe something.

Stosser had cast a similar spell to make us believe that Venec was dead, during our job interview. We'd felt the magic around *him,* not on the scene.

"Maybe Mercy learned, after the attack? She wasn't very good at it, clumsy as hell," Sharon said, playing devil's advocate. "But yeah—it would be instinctive to *try.* Unless she was so used to the ki-rin protecting her all the time…"

"Maybe." That had the depressing ring of truth to it. "And she was tiny, they wouldn't have felt the need to use current to subdue Mercy, especially once she was down on the ground. But it's still odd that the guys wouldn't use any to protect themselves, once the ki-rin showed up."

I'd barely gotten the last word out of my mouth when the table suddenly jumped straight up into the air, almost knocking us in the face. Five blasts of current hit the table, shoving it back down again and locking it into place even as hands slammed down to control it, physically.

"Damn it!" Nick said, more annoyed at the current-spike than the table actually moving, and a burst of chatter came from the rest of my coworkers as they tried to figure out what the hell had just happened, but I knew.

"That doesn't prove anything," I said to Ben. "You've trained us to react, to defend ourselves. She didn't have that advantage. Not sure the perps would, either." Like I'd said earlier, not everyone got trained by the Big Dogs.

Venec nodded an apology at Nick, then turned back to me. "You would have reacted differently, before?"

"I wouldn't have thought to lock it down," Pietr said. "But I would have shoved, instinctively."

"Yeah, me, too," I admitted, and Nifty nodded. Only Sharon didn't chime in, but sat there with an odd look on her face. Nick, at the other end of the table, had already gone back to working over the netbook. There were strange spirals of current circling around it, and I was suddenly very glad I couldn't actually see the screen. The one time I'd helped Nick with his tech-magic, even in a very secondary role, it had given me a serious headache.

"I wouldn't have done anything," Sharon said finally, in response to Venec's question. "Or, I might have, but I would have tried to pull it back in, immediately. My mentor was part of the Reasonable Limits school, and I guess I absorbed a lot of that. I tried to pass. As a Null, I mean."

"The what school?" Nifty asked, before I could.

"Reasonable Limits. It's…what it sounds like, I guess. That current isn't something to use instinctively, but only after deliberate thought and only if nothing else is appropriate to the task. It grew out of the Old Magic, during the burning years, when even the hint of magic could get you killed, and merged with emerging environmentalist philosophies in the 1900s, and…" Her voice trailed off, trying to explain it to us.

"That's insane." Nifty sounded horrified. "Not using current isn't the answer to people being scared of us."

"Different ways of approaching the problem," Venec said calmly, cutting off what might have become another argument. "The fear was real, generations of it, and I know you

all have enough education to know how quickly suspicion
can turn to fear can turn to violence.

"But I think we can agree that even if the girl had Sharon's kind of training during mentorship, some sort of instinctive current-use would have been a normal reaction to
violent physical threat, if there were any. And we sure as hell
would have found trace of a violent emotion in the original
site, especially if she then pulled it back into herself, rather
than letting it disperse naturally. I'm assuming that someone
checked on that, at least?"

Bastard. "Someone" meaning me, since I was the gleaner
of record. "Yeah, I did. I didn't find anything that could be
identified as from Mercy, who had the most reason to feel
emotion. Never met the dead guy, or the other perp, so had
no basis. But everything was pretty much overlaid by the
black goop by then. I'm not good enough to strip that away
without destroying the scene. Maybe you or Ian?"

Back in your lap, *boss,* I thought with justifiable vicious-
ness, still not meeting his gaze. I was pretty sure he heard
that, too.

"By the time I got there, too many people had been on-
site," he said. "And Ian…"

Ian Stosser was many things, including brilliant, persua-
sive, and charming, but he left the hands-on gruntwork to
us.

"So what little we have, the fact that she didn't feel a
strong emotion, and didn't use current to defend herself,
that points to the guy's claim being true, that they weren't
threatening her?" Pietr asked.

"No," Venec said, and I could hear the frustration in his voice, no weird linky-link needed.

I felt my brain fold over on itself, trying to figure out where he was going with that. "Why not?"

There was a hissing, staticky noise from the other end of the table. I forced myself not to look, and could tell everyone else was doing the same. The skin on my arms and neck was all goose-bumped, though. Nick was doing something at a level none of us could match; not better, not lesser, just using skills that we didn't have, and personally I didn't want. Hackers could and did overrush faster and harder than anyone else, and when they did, every network in the region went, to use the technical term, blooey.

Venec went on with the discussion, pretending there was nothing at all happening down there, nope, nothing at all. "Because they didn't use current to defend themselves, either. A Talent being attacked by another human, maybe they'll keep it on the down-low, try not to escalate things, especially if they don't know the others' power level."

Kids played at that, games like snap-dragon and push-tag, to see who was stronger. Adults played different games, more subtle, but we played them.

"Being attacked by a fatae? An obvious fatae?" Venec drummed his hand against the table, a gesture I hadn't seen him use before. Irritation? Anger? Frustration? Maybe all of the above. It made my fingers itch in sympathy, and I refolded them carefully in my lap. There was a time to mirror the boss, and a time not to. This was a not-time.

"Being attacked by a ki-rin, those toughs should have

been shitting themselves, and hauling out the hard power. They didn't. Is that damning enough, though?" I asked.

"They may not have had time to," Nifty said. "I saw the autopsy reports." He and Pietr got that job, mainly because I puked all over myself the first and only time they had me read medical stuff, and Sharon and Nick just out-and-out refused. "It was over so fast, I bet the guy never realized what was happening."

Pietr shook his head. "The first guy, maybe. But the other guy did. He saw the first attack happen, was far enough away that he had time to know what was happening, which, Bonnie's right, would have made me shit myself, no matter how much a hard-ass I was."

"He fought back—the ki-rin had bruises." I hadn't gotten close to the fatae, but even at that distance the dark marks on its chest and neck had stood out against the nearly luminescent skin, enough to be noticed, so at odds with its perfection otherwise. "A human wouldn't be able to hit that hard physically, especially once he was down, so they had to be current-strikes. But not enough to be fatal. And not enough to leave any lingering signature that we could pick up or, I guess, that the Council suits who took it away would have picked up?" I heard the question in my voice, but didn't think I'd get an answer. They might have, and they wouldn't think to tell us. Why should they? They were convinced it was a justified kill, whatever else had happened, and they had no further interest beyond that. God, I hated amateurs.

From the look on Venec's face, he was having the same bitter thought.

"We can ask, but I bet they didn't even notice," Nifty said. "I'm not sure it matters. The available evidence—the fact that there was no trace, and only limited bruising—suggests that the second perp wasn't strong enough to hurt the ki-rin significantly." He shrugged, his broad shoulders lifting in an almost operatic gesture, telegraphing both frustration and resignation. "This guy is not one of life's better results. Just because the average Talent could do it…well, half of everyone is below average, right?"

"Average or mean? Never mind." Pietr waved off his own question as irrelevant. "You're right, we made a logical assumption that current was not used in the attack or defense, because we didn't find any lingering traces at the site. And Bonnie says that there was no fear, not the kind he should have felt, fighting for his life—just the way there was no fear from Mercy. That's what we should be focusing on, not the defensive blows. Why weren't we picking up any emotion in the signatures, especially once we were specifically looking for it?"

"Bonnie's right, we may not be good enough to pick it up, especially with how many other people were on the scene so fast," Sharon said bluntly. "And yeah, Ian and Ben might have had better luck but…emotions? Come on, people, let's not give ourselves demigod status just yet."

Brutal, but true. Hell, the fact that we could identify signature so clearly was a major leap for most of us from what the general Talent could do. I could see everyone let themselves relax a little from the self-questioning that we were all doing, even—maybe especially—Venec.

"So is this a dead end," Pietr asked, "or evidence we have to look at differently?"

"Dead end," Sharon said. I had to agree. Magic, for once, wasn't helping us solve this case.

"So we have a lot of...nothing." Venec got up, stretching his hands over his head to the ceiling, and we all heard his back crack. My spine whimpered a little at the noise. He seemed to feel better, though. "Come on, people, we can do better than that. What are we overlooking?"

"Money."

It was almost a relief to let my head turn and finally look to the far end of the table. Nick was shutting down his netbook, closing the lid with the air of someone with a stupendously fantabulous secret. He got up from his chair, and staggered a little, putting a hand on the back of his chair to steady himself. Current-wear. He'd probably just burned five-six hundred calories, with that kind of tight-focus work.

"We already thought about that," Nifty objected. "We couldn't figure any way it would make sense."

"That's because we weren't thinking the right way," Nick said. "We've been going about it all totally the wrong way."

I blinked at him, feeling myself get pissed. What did he mean, the wrong way? I'd chased down every single damn avenue I could think of....

"What's the one assumption that we've been making about this case, all of us, from the very beginning?"

We stared at him, and he grinned; sweaty, ego-triumphant,

and perfectly willing to wait until we bowed down before his greatness and begged for the answer.

"If you don't spill, I'm going to hold you upside down by your scrawny ankles and shake it out of you," Nifty said, instead.

"Spoilsport." Nick sat down, folded his hands in front of him and leaned forward. "The assumption we've all been making was that this was a crime of passion—lust or hate or just sheer moment-of-opportunity violence. It wasn't."

"A calculated attack?" You could hear the gears turning in Venec's head, and Sharon was drawing lines and boxes in her notebook with quick strokes, muttering as she reworked whatever logic-equation she was using.

"Maybe. More to the point, calculated by someone *else*. See, I got to thinking…none of it made sense, right? Like Sharon said, usually you doubt even the stuff you're almost a hundred percent sure about. That's just natural. Everyone being so rock-hard in their truth, that's the kind of thing it takes a while to build up, and usually it needs, I don't know, a trigger or something. Something or someone reinforcing their belief that it's all hunky-dory, reassuring them. We're all much more likely to believe someone else, someone with authority or enthusiasm, when they say it's all golden, right?"

"Point?" Venec asked, but he was alert, not doubting. He knew Nicky-boy was on to something. I was barely able to breathe, I was listening so hard. Nick had it, I could feel it, like all the puzzle pieces clicking in, even if I couldn't see the final picture, yet.

"My point is, people aren't as smart as they like to think

they are—there's always trace when you try to meddle. Only we weren't finding any trace at all—no guilt, no anger, no residue. So I thought...we've been considering the things that matter to the *Cosa,* Talent and fatae, either one. Why? What if this had nothing to do with the *Cosa* at all—what if it was just a human thing?"

"None of the players were Null," Sharon objected.

"None that we knew about," Nick corrected her. "But that's not what I'm talking about."

He didn't stop to check our reactions this time, but lurched right into the explanation.

"I went looking in the most likely places where our players could have ulterior motives—health and wealth. No medical records beyond the basic for our girl, nothing at all for the others. So someone might have been slipping them something to make them violent, or whatever...or maybe not. Moving on, I just did a deep read into their financial records, what they've been spending, what they're investing, that kind of thing."

He paused, shaking his head. "Man, don't ever use Trade-World for your brokerage house, they're almost painfully easy to hack. Anyway, guess who got pretty little deposits into their bank accounts?"

"The attackers?" Sharon said.

"Our survivors," Nick corrected her triumphantly. "All three of them—ki-rin, girl, and alleged attacker who didn't get whacked."

"Ki-rin have bank accounts?" That surprised the hell out of me, although I don't know why.

"Ki-rin even have brokerage accounts, *chica.* It dabbles a

bit here and there, although nothing major. But I don't think that matters, although it's damn interesting, because we've got a smoking gun right here in their checking accounts. Whoever it was sending them the money staggered times and sources to make it look random, but it came to the same total amount for all three of them. What are the odds on that, huh? And a sum of money like that? Can support a whole lot of certainty, even without the added fillip of magic."

"And the source?" Venec asked, impatient.

"A little more digging, and I found the answer to all our questions."

He waited, trying to build suspense.

"Your ankles are looking grabable," Nifty warned, and while I usually had time for Nick's games, even I was getting twitchy. I didn't even look at Venec, knowing the thunderous expression that was probably glaring at Nick right now.

"All right, fine. Turns out the dead guy? Had a serious insurance policy for an underemployed loser, made out to his best friend from back home. A million dollars payable on certification of death. Nice, huh?"

"Fuck me," someone said softly, almost reverently, and suddenly all the parts started clicking together like prefab furniture. The colored chalk appeared again, and Nifty grabbed them off the table, wiping the old board clean and starting fresh.

"Gimme the starting play," he told Nick.

"Financial transactions, starting seven months ago. Sums from between $2,000 to $5,000, deposited on seemingly random days, several times a month, to each player's checking account, for a total of $25,000 each."

It seemed cheap to me, but I knew firsthand that people killed for less, without flinching or regret. $25,000 to some people was a year's salary, a way out of debt, the salvation of a dream—was that the price for a scum-of-the-earth's life?

"A few were electronic transfer, a few were cashier's checks, and a couple were cash, which must have been fun to process. Those were the smaller ones. I'm not a money guy, but it sounds like they were broken up to avoid any kind of pattern-trigger?"

"Likely," Venec said. "And that would suggest that whoever set this up knew what he was doing...or had watched enough television to think he knew what he was doing."

"Our best friend of the deceased is an MBA?"

"Sadly, no. Mr. Harrison, Null, is a schoolteacher. Not even a math teacher, either. World history, pounding dry facts into ninth graders' heads, out in Nashville."

"What the hell is a schoolteacher doing best friends forevering with a skeevy guy like our dead body?" Nifty asked.

"Went to high school together, managed to keep it going." Nick shrugged. "I'm not going to argue nature versus nurture with you. People hook up and stay friends for all sorts of weird reasons. All I know is this Steve Harrison and our very dead Paul Blake named each other in their life insurance policies about seven years ago, so it's likely he knew about the *Cosa,* and, it seems, the less savory parts of it."

"So how did they know about the ki-rin, how to lure it into this?"

"Don't know. Unless we can get it to talk, odds are we'll never know."

"'Scuse me," I said, and got up. Venec and Pietr both watched me leave the room, which weirded me out a little; the others kept going on the play-by-play.

I grabbed my bag from the closet, then walked down the hallway to Stosser's office. The door was open, so Ian had already left to do his political oil thing. I sat down at the desk, and pulled a card case out of my bag. Had I put it in there...I had! Picking up the phone, I dialed the number on the business card, and waited. Venec might have contacts in the police force, but I had friends in lower places than that.

"Sylvan Investigations. How can we help you?"

The voice was pleasant, mellow, and male.

"Can't afford a receptionist, huh?"

"Bonnie?" The voice made an instant switch from smooth to raspy. Raspy sounded better on him. "How you doing? Why are you calling? Who died?"

"Are you always that paranoid?"

Danny made a rude noise. "Bonnie, when a Talent calls me on the phone, it's never good news. Unless you're calling to invite me over for breakfast?"

"Not this time, sorry. I have a favor to ask you."

"I knew it. All right, Blondie, shoot."

"Can you dig up any dirt on a guy named Steven Harrison? He's a history teacher out in Nashville. Yes, Tennessee, you know of another Nashville? He's not a Talent, so my contacts would be useless. He doesn't have a police record, far as we know—" if he did, Nick would have found that

"—but I figure he's probably going to have something off-color in someone's file somewhere." You didn't be BFF with a loser like our dead guy without some trouble, somewhere. I trusted Nick's talents, but there were some things that needed magic…and some that needed old-fashioned snooping.

"This has to do with the case you're working on?"

"It could help us crack it."

"And you'll owe me?"

"PUPI will owe you."

There was a pause, the sound of papers being shuffled, and he laughed. "I'll settle for that. How can I reach you?"

I gave him the office number, and, after a second's thought, my home number, too.

"God, I wish you people could use email like the rest of us. At least you're not demanding it all be couriered, because P.B.'s rates are getting crazy. I'm assuming that these are landlines?"

"You betcha. I gotta get back into the fray. Let me know as soon as you've got something!"

The entire exchange had taken maybe ten minutes, but by the time I made it back down the hall, the chalkboard was already full of names, timelines, and exclamation points, and everyone was talking rapid-fire, bouncing ideas off each other.

"If he was just killed, yeah, there might be suspicion on the event," Sharon was saying. "But a known sexual predator who gets what's coming to him? Nobody would be surprised, and damn few would question the actions of the killer…. No, it could work."

"If he died while committing a crime, though," Pietr responded, "the insurance company might stop payment, right? What's the legal ruling on that?"

"If he's killed in the commission of, or in connection to the commission of a crime, all payments are off. It's more complicated than that, because if it was simple we wouldn't need lawyers, but if he was charged with a felony the insurance company would be able to refuse benefits." Sharon might not have my total recall, but she was damn reliable for legal stuff.

"Legal rulings are moot," Nick said irritably. "If the girl won't talk, then it's he said/she said and there's enough reasonable doubt to turn him into a possible victim. She doesn't press charges, there is no crime."

"And they can't use the ki-rin's involvement to prove the assault because that would require Nulls admitting to the ki-rin's existence," Nifty added, making a swooping red circle around the ki-rin on the board, and then crossing it, to make the international Do Not Have sign. "So the insurance company has no basis to not pay, even if they smell something off—an investigation would turn up nothing other than the surface report."

"So our antifatae activists are enabling the scam to go forward, by giving her a reason not to accuse her alleged attacker...." I was trying to catch up with where they'd gone while I was out of the room.

"That would be the end result, yeah," Nifty said. "I don't know if it was our perps' original plan, or just a happy-for-them secondary result of bigotry. But it sure as hell gives her legitimate motivation for keeping quiet, in case anyone—like us—starts sniffing around."

"Wait a minute," I said. "If we're going to propose that the guy was set up to get killed by the ki-rin, which it sounds like we are…?"

There were nods around the table.

"It all works," Nifty said, and gestured to the tangle of chalk marks that backed up their thought process. "If she doesn't file a claim and nobody's going to fess up that a crazy-ass unicorn skewered the guy, then the death will be listed as by unknown assailant for unknown reasons, case open and nobody expects it to ever get solved. The insurance company might or might not sic their own investigator on it, but they'll hit the same wall—the girl isn't talking, the ki-rin won't talk, and even if they have a Talent highly placed enough in the company to know what happened, I really doubt they're going to want to put down in writing the cause for refusal, especially if any kind of truth-spell shows what we got, that they were all telling the truth. So the company pays out, eventually, and this Harrison guy pockets the money and comes out nicely ahead, even after the payout he made to have his buddy set up and killed."

I didn't have any drama with their logic, just one small tangle in it. "There were three payout chains made. You're saying that Mercy was part of this. That she…"

There was a weird little silence. They'd been so caught up in figuring out the logic-chain, they'd forgotten that part of it. The fact that she'd been complicit in her own attack. And it had been an attack—if we were right, the dead guy had tried to rape her, therefore triggering the ki-rin's justifiable-to-the-*Cosa*'s actions. He hadn't known it was a setup, and his partner couldn't have stopped him, or he risked tipping the game. The violence had been real.

"People do a lot of things for money," Venec finally said, his voice dry. "I can't speak for the girl, but $25,000 tax-free can make people do things you'd swear they'd never do."

I thought about Mercy, how subdued and scared she'd been. Subdued, scared…but not traumatized. Not physically or, really, mentally. Not the way a sheltered girl whose first sexual experience had been against her will should have been.

You never want to know what people are capable of. Unfortunately, this job gave us a front-row ticket.

"Losing the ki-rin's companionship overrode everything else," I said out loud. "I'd thought she was in shock over that, so it was blotting out the physical aspects, but…"

"But she might have been bruised and battered, and sad but not scarred," Sharon said. "Damn it. She *played* us."

"And the ki-rin went along with this?" Venec wasn't questioning that, just making us consider all the elements.

Nick shrugged. I was starting to understand why my mentor trained that movement out of me—it really did give a passive-aggressive vibe. "Never assume a fatae isn't just as eager for filthy lucre as a human. It took a hit in the stock market, so maybe it thought this was an easy way to recoup its losses? If the girl was willing to exchange sex for money—there isn't anything immoral in that. Illegal, okay, but the ki-rin doesn't live by our laws. Not for sex and not for murder. So it hears this plan and his companion's okay with it, for whatever level of stupidity, and hey, it's just a trash human nobody was going to miss, anyway, right? No, Bonnie, I'm not being a bigot, just pragmatic. I mean, we're not exactly outraged on the dead guy's behalf, are we? And we're the only ones who seem to care what happened to him."

Ugly, but true. I felt more than a little sick.

There was a chime in the air, similar to the one Stosser used to call us in for a meeting, but with a different pitch. The phone was ringing.

"I'll get it," I said before anyone else responded, and dashed down the hallway before anyone could ask if I was expecting a call. There was no way it could be Danny already.... But it was.

"You're fast."

"Don't spread that around, I'll never get another date. You sitting down?"

I sat. "Talk to me."

He did. I started to take notes, and then stopped, and just listened.

"Holy... You rock. I'll get back to you later, k?"

Walking back through the hall, I was trying to figure out how to pass along what Danny had dug up, but in the end, I just walked in, and blurted it.

"The cop who called the Council? First guy on the scene, the one who spread his signature all over the site? The one who claimed he was just doing his civic duty, calling the Council? Drinking buddy to our schoolteacher heir back in college. What do you want to bet he's got a payoff hidden somewhere, too?"

"Motherf—" Nifty started to add that fact to the crowded board, and just stopped. "Too many connections. There's no way anyone could think there was reasonable doubt, not with all this. Not the way every single damned player ties back somehow to our presumptive heir. This was all a scam, start to finish."

"Not a scam," Sharon said, and her voice was tight with anger. "Conspiracy to commit murder, plus insurance fraud, and…god, I don't even know what else. The evidence…just the Null-admissible material would be enough, and it would hold up in court, I think, enough to convince a jury, yes. But…it'll never get there.

"They planned on that. They planned on all of this to cover their asses. The lure, the setup, the conflicting stories that raise reasonable doubt that couldn't be proven one way or the other because they believed their own truths. Even if someone got on her enough that she had no choice but to press charges, the case would probably be dismissed because she didn't agree to a rape kit. They even planned for the Council to be involved from the start, the cop calling them in, to ensure the situation was muddied by their tromping all over it. The bastards probably hoped the Council'd help sweep any investigation under the rug, rather than let the dirt surface."

Sharon had it summed up. Everyone else was pissed and angry, frustrated at having been used, but there was a soft, subtle vibe of satisfaction in the air, too. And it was coming from Venec. I looked at him, my eyes narrowing in suspicion.

"Boss? You have something up your sleeve. What?"

Everyone looked at him then, and Venec smiled, that small, barely there smile that always made me think of a wolf contemplating the lamb.

"It was a very clever scam. Very clever, yeah. It almost worked. But the key word is *almost*."

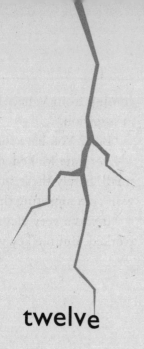

twelve

"What's going on in that brain of yours?" I asked, but his wall was up and I couldn't get even a hint of a flicker.

"This needs to wait for Ian to get back," he said. "You all should go get some lunch. Take your time, I think he's going to be a while."

There, I caught just a hint of something…and then it was gone, and I couldn't tell if it was related to his scheme—and it was definitely a scheme, with that smile—or worry for whatever Stosser was up to.

We grumbled but obeyed—beside the fact that we couldn't exactly force the boss to spill, our stomachs were all starting to rumble. There was a unanimous vote for pizza, and Venec told us to eat at the restaurant. I think he was afraid that if we stayed in the office, we'd wheedle it out of him or something. Both of us had our walls up, but I swear even as I left the building, I could still feel the tendrils of smug anticipation drifting from him. He *wanted* to tell us, but wouldn't.

By the time we came back, filled with Vinnie's Original and a couple of liters of soda, Stosser had returned, and we were back in business.

"We all good with the public?" Nifty asked.

Boss man looked dead-beat tired, like he'd been running on empty for twenty-four hours, so I was guessing that he'd used a heavy dose of current with his snake oil. One of his more useful—to us, anyway—skills was glamour. Just like in the old fairy tales, yeah, except Stosser used it to enhance his already considerable competence and sincerity, not his looks. He'd cast it on us once or twice, to make a client feel more confident. Like a lot of the old magics, it didn't *create* competence, just enhanced it so an observer would get a stronger sense of trust and belief. The glamour-casting elves of legend? Stosser was to them like a lightning bolt is to a lightning bug.

From the look of him, apparently glamour burned calories at a seriously high rate, same as current-hacking. No wonder all the old witches in fairy tales and woodcuttings were skinny—I can't imagine they were getting enough food on a regular basis to make a house move around on chicken-feet legs, or make it look like it was made out of gingerbread, or whatever it was they did to keep the business going.

He also had a wrinkle between his eyes that hadn't been there that morning. Something was niggling at him, something he didn't want to think about, maybe, or didn't know what to do about. I wasn't sure if that knowledge came from Venec or my own observation, but I knew it for a fact, and if I knew, so did Ben. Whatever his meeting had been, it hadn't gone as well as he'd wanted.

"We're good," the boss agreed, apparently unaware that at least two of us were on to him. "Just so long as nobody blows anything up or accuses the mayor of sodomizing chickens, at least for a month."

"No chickens with the mayor, right," Nick said, making a mock-note of that.

That was about as much levity as we were capable of right now, apparently.

"All right." Ian stood and walked over to the chalkboard, although he was watching us, not it. "I looked over your diagram. Looks nasty but logical…and there's no way we can bring this to the Null courts. Yes?"

"Pretty much, yeah," Venec said, and where he should have been annoyed there was still that shimmer of evil delight coming from him. "We don't have any standing to bring it ourselves, and they've muddied the waters with their games enough that nobody else would be willing to waste the time or energy. We can't connect the lines legally, not without the ki-rin's involvement, and the ki-rin's presence is enough to make the entire thing seem too fantastical to be true—and even if by some miracle or maneuvering they got a *Cosa*-friendly judge and jury, they'd probably side with the ki-rin's story, and ignore all the other evidence, on sheer tradition."

"We need the ki-rin to actually testify," Sharon said. "Put it to direct question. If it can't lie, truly, then a direct question, the right question, would break it all apart."

"Forget about it," Ian said sharply. "It has stated clearly

that it will not speak on the matter, not in the court and not to the Council, and certainly not to us. It has the equivalent of diplomatic immunity—there's nothing we can do or say that will force it to change its mind."

"And it's not like brute force is an option, either," Pietr said, almost regretfully. "None of us could do more than tickle it."

"What about Bonnie's bodyguard?" Nick asked. "I bet Bobo could dent its hide."

I let out a heavy sigh, only partially feigned. "Let it go, Nick." Bobo would do it, if he thought J would consider it part of his job to keep me safe, but there was no way I was going to be the one to set it up. "I don't think that would do much for the agency's reputation, having a fatae enforcer to beat up suspects," I added dryly.

"I don't know, some corners, it might enhance it," Venec said, just as dryly. I started to laugh, and then realized that he wasn't kidding.

"Even if it did speak up, what good would it do?" Trust Sharon to get us back on track. "Ki-rin don't lie. Its companion *was* attacked with intent to do serious injury, and it *did* kill the assailant who did it. By those narrow standards, approved by pretty much the entire Cosa, it did nothing wrong."

"Hell, by the standards of most of the *Cosa* and half the Null population, murdering the guy wasn't wrong, no matter who did it," Nifty said. "I mean, this wasn't some upright citizen who got railroaded into a bad gig. He attacked the girl with full willingness to force her. Nobody's sorry to see this guy leave the planet."

Put that way, it was tempting to kick back and let it go, yeah. There hadn't been any innocent victims here. Except that there were, or there might be. If Venec was right, this could spread beyond the four people directly involved, and blow up the entire city, boom.

Plus, us. We had to break the damn case, or risk losing all the cred we'd managed to accumulate so far.

And I couldn't quite get rid of the look on Mercy's face, the smeared lipstick and the broken-down insides...

Venec took control back at that point. "It would be nice to keep that bastard from collecting on his friend's murder, but that's got to be our bonus, not the main goal, not anymore."

The satisfied shimmer around him intensified, so much that I was amazed everyone else couldn't see it.

"The rise in antifatae sentiment in the past few months muddied the waters even more, but that may be to our advantage, not theirs. That movement wasn't a direct part of the original scam, but their little games have added fuel to the fire, to use my earlier metaphor—and given us the exact tool to put it out. We can make an example of the humans involved...and expose the ki-rin as an accomplice, whatever its reasons, so the fatae will have to back down from their anti-Talent stance."

There were nods of agreement all around the table, waiting to hear what rabbit he was about to pull out.

"The important thing is to make sure everyone knows what the real motive was, that there wasn't anything other than greed motivating all this, and force the various factions to back down."

"And you have a way for us to do that?" Ian made an "impress me" sort of gesture with his hands in a way that made me wonder if they'd orchestrated this between them, while we were at lunch. Then I shook myself, mentally. Of course they had. Neither of them left anything they could control to chance.

"I do. If we handle it right. This was a very clever scam, as I said, but our conspirators made one very important mistake. They didn't predict the future."

"Huh?" Okay, from my packmates' expressions he'd lost everyone there. That made me feel better. There was an urge to let my wall down and try to figure out what he was thinking, but I squelched the desire under the rock labeled Bad Ideas, and waited with everyone else.

"This scam was planned...what? Eight months ago?" Venec asked rhetorically. "More than that, if that's where the payments started. So call it at least ten months ago... before we opened for business. They didn't count on us being here—or the fact that we've built up credibility. I'm less enamored of Fate than Ian, but there's a delicious sort of inevitability to our involvement."

He looked at us individually, and the weight of his gaze on me, however brief, was like a static charge along my skin. I kept my attention on what he was saying, but it was more of an effort than it should have been.

"Four players—villain, villain's dupe, the victim, and the knight errant who dispatches the villain. All they had to know was their own role, to believe in it wholeheartedly, and let whatever happened...happen."

Oooooooh. I thought I saw where he was going now. From the way Nifty was nodding, he did, too.

"Truth, and truth," Sharon said. "That's what stumped me, the fact that everyone was telling the truth—within a very narrow definition. They had no doubt because they didn't let themselves think outside their role. The spell they came up with enhanced it, but what they did was true, somehow. That's how they were able to use the ki-rin—the residue of the spell merely guaranteed that nobody would doubt what it claimed, because they believed it, too. Once it wore off, the perp could claim contrary, and raise the doubt...but who would believe him over a ki-rin?"

A ki-rin who would no longer speak to anyone on the subject.

Ian's eyes squinted shut, and I swear I saw virtual whiskers curl forward like a cat's when it sees something intriguing. "What are you thinking, Ben?"

"I'm thinking that this plot rests on the trio's need to look like they were caught up in circumstances beyond their control, that they each had equal and valid claim to being innocent. The girl, who should not be blamed, the male who might have been not guilty, the ki-rin who cannot be questioned. They're relying on the confusion of conflicting reports, the Council's desire to have as little fuss as possible, and the ki-rin's impeccable reputation for honesty, to keep everyone off-balance...so we have to throw *them* off-balance."

"And we do that by...what?" Pietr asked.

"By spreading a fact that's worse than the truth," I said, thinking out loud, knowing the way Venec's mind worked.

"Something that would be so reprehensible that they would have no choice but to counteract it."

"What the hell could be worse than what happened?" Pietr asked.

"A lie," Ben said quietly. "The lie that the ki-rin was lying."

Ian sat back in his chair and let out an explosive "whooof" of air. "Twenty years I've known you, Benjamin, and suddenly I discover you're evil."

Venec laid out the details, and I was impressed. Ian was right: it was evil. In a really, beautifully, evil-to-do-good way. And, like all the best plans, it was really simple.

"Simple, yeah, but it's not going to be easy," Pietr warned, when I commented on that. "The rumors will have to be inserted carefully, allowed to spread naturally, so nobody will doubt them. The slightest hint of a trap, and it all falls apart."

"Done this before, have you?" Nick joked.

"Maybe."

Everyone except Sharon looked quietly gleeful at the idea. Our straight shooter sat there with a wrinkle between her perfectly plucked blond brows, and looked like she wanted to say something but wasn't sure opening her mouth would be smart, right then.

"What?" I asked her quietly.

She started, and shook her head. "It's nothing."

"Bullshit."

"I just...doesn't this bother you? Lying, spreading lies?"

"Nope."

That surprised her; she'd obviously expected me to have moral qualms, to be part of the Staunch Truth Brigade.

"Look…" I paused, trying to explain it properly. "I'm blunt to a fault, and I don't have much patience with prevarications or runarounds. But I was raised to consider intent, not pretty words. And the intent of these four…it was to kill someone. I feel sorry for Mercy—I don't think she really understood what she was getting into. But if she took part willingly…if the ki-rin agreed to this…then we need to know, however we get that confirmation. And if she didn't, if the ki-rin used her, or if the ki-rin itself was used…then they'll be exonerated once and for all."

"The ends justify the means?"

"This isn't the easy case we all thought it was, at first. It's way more complicated, and there are way more players involved. So yeah, we use whatever tools we have. Including, yes, saying not-quite-true things, which will disappear as soon as the ki-rin takes the bait and refutes them."

"And what if it doesn't?"

"It has to. That's our job now, to make sure it does."

"Exactly," Venec said, making us both jump. Our new weird connectivity apparently still didn't keep him from being able to sneak up on me, damn it. "I trust that you will all handle this with delicacy and subtlety," he said, speaking to everyone, now. "Remember, not more than three targets each, to keep too many from being traced back to us too obviously, so pick your shots carefully. Not you, Nick. I saw that wobble there. Sit your backside down, you're not going anywhere."

Nick looked put out at being left out of the fun, but Venec

was right; he still looked shaky as hell, and based on observation, it would take him a day or two to really recover from his current-hacking.

Venec's plan depended on street-team tactics: starting a person-to-person buzz that would, hopefully, take on a life of its own. Viral marketing, except what we were pushing was bait to bring the ki-rin back to us. We were supposed to pick our three targets from where our contacts were the strongest: Sharon would hit her legal ties, starting with the ones who already knew about this case, while Nifty and Venec worked the lonejack population, Ian did his thing on their Council counterparts, and Pietr and I went back out to the fatae community.

"So. Any idea where we can find a handful of fatae to whisper into their tufted ears? I doubt they're still hanging out in the park...."

My first thought had been to call Danny back, but something held me back. Danny had been helpful to us already, had ties, if indirectly, to the case. He had a bias toward our side of things. Ideally, the rumor should spread from someone who had no horse in the race; someone other fatae would not doubt. Plus, Danny was half-human—he might be doubted, for that reason.

Bobo? Maybe. I didn't know how to find him, though—I'd have to wait until he came on the job tonight.

But I wasn't without connections, in the meanwhile.

"Come on. Time to visit an old family friend."

From the street, it just looked like an old brownstone, the same as all the other brownstones lining the side street off Fifth Avenue. In other words, it looked like you needed a personal worth of at least a million just to be allowed inside.

"Miss Bonnie!" The maid who met us at the door was all smiles, and gave me a good, rough hug. "You finally come to visit! You are well?"

"I'm fine, thanks, Li. Is Herself in?"

"In the sunroom, as always." Li took our coats, and stepped back, letting me find my own way to our hostess.

"I take it you know these people," Pietr said dryly, at this show of familiarity.

"Herself was friends with my mentor's mentor," I said, and that was all the warning he got.

"Oh, my god."

I didn't turn to look at Pietr, but allowed myself just the slightest smile of one-upmanship.

"Bonnnnita. You are playing gamessss with your friennnnndsssss againnnn?"

I made a low bow, but couldn't keep from laughing, which probably ruined the effect. "My apologies, Madame. I am a very bad worm."

Madame was curled in her usual place, directly under the glass roof-panes that gave the room its name. She didn't need the sunlight; her body chemistry kept her warm in any weather, but dragons, like cats, loved nothing better than to nap in a sunbeam.

"You have lived here for nearly a year, and only now you come to visit? Tssssssssk."

You haven't been scolded until you've been scolded by a Great Worm. I kept my bow, and waited.

"Bah. Innnntroduce me to your friennnnnd, Bonn-nnita."

"Madame, this is my friend and companion, Pietr Cholis. He, like I, is an unworthy worm."

Pietr got over his shock long enough to step forward and make a better-than-passable bow.

Madame ducked her great head down to inspect him, the foot-long silver whiskers on either side of her triangular head twitching forward to test the air around him. Greater Dragons were blind as bats, in more ways than one—their eyes were gorgeous, faceted things, completely useless in daylight, but their whiskers were like sonar, telling them everything they needed to know and maybe some things you'd rather they didn't.

"Greetingsssss, Pietr. You are welcome to my home."

"The honor is mine, Great Lady." He shot me a look that promised retribution, but he was grinning like an idiot. Madame had that effect on humans.

"I regret that we cannot stay long, Madame. You are correct, I have been tardy in paying my respects, and I desired to remedy that, and yet my responsibilities carry me elsewhere."

"Ohhhhhh?" Madame's long length coiled down from her divan, her movements somehow conveying an eager leaning forward, the way a human might to hear something better. Pietr shifted, but held his ground without fear. I'd known he would; having sex with a guy doesn't tell you everything about him, but you get a sense for how they'll react under pressure, and Pietr was as much a rock as his name suggested. I wouldn't have blamed him if he'd flinched, though.

I'd thought I'd been prepared when J first brought me here: I'd already encountered a rock dragon; how much more could Madame be?

I had been, as I said, an unworthy worm. To compare an Ancient with a common rock dragon? Useless. No matter how many times I saw her, Madame never failed to enthrall: the paintings artists had done for millennia failed to capture how iridescent her tiny feathers were, or how delicate her breath felt when it touched your skin, carrying the faintest hint of jasmine and warm tea.

It was only after you got past the magnificence of her form that you realized that she had the soul of a gossipy old grandmother.

"Yes," I said solemnly. "We are on an errand of great significance for our teachers." A teacher, to Madame, would carry much greater weight than "boss." My association with J meant that, to her, I was no menial worker to be employed; a student obeying her teacher's command was something she could respect, however. "There has been a terrible scandal, and we need to right it, before any more are harmed."

"A ssscannndal? You are teassssing me, Bonnnnnita." Those whiskers twitched in interest.

"Never, Madame." I would have placed my hand to my heart, but she would suspect me of mockery, then. "It is merely a matter of delicacy...." I paused, as though suddenly struck by a new thought. "Indeed, perhaps you might advise us, you who have seen so much, if such a thing has happened before?"

Madame leaned forward even closer, the ears set at the back of her head now twitching forward like a cat's.

"A ki-rin," I said into those ears, "has failed the truth."

The story we were spreading was that the ki-rin, rather than defending his companion, had killed the human for putting the moves on her, after she had encouraged his attentions. Two birds with one stone: we insulted both the ki-rin's honor, and that of his companion, to say that she would solicit sexual attention without formally ending her relationship with the ki-rin and retiring with respect. Nasty, but effective, and within the bounds of what we believe happened. The ki-rin had not lied…but was refusing to tell the truth not lying by omission?

"It is impossible." Madame's response was natural, but she was sniffing the bait with interest. I played the thread out carefully, willing Pietr to follow my lead and look saddened and yet resolute. I didn't dare look to see how he was doing, though.

"All that we have been taught tells us so. And yet…on my own honor and that of my mentor, and my mentor's mentor whom you knew, Madame, it is so. You have heard the story, of how a ki-rin took justice for the despoiling of his noble companion, as only proper."

Madame nodded, but did not speak, waiting for me to continue.

"The facts do not agree with the ki-rin's story, Madame. The facts, in fact, contradict its story, and tell a different one. It is distressing, and worrisome to my teachers, who value truth and tradition above all things."

Well, truth, anyway. I'm not sure Stosser ever met a tradition he didn't screw with, somehow.

"Annnd what will you do with thesssssse facts?"

"Madame, we would speak with the ki-rin, but it refuses to return to speak with us. Is that not odd?"

"Asssss though it were guilty connnnscience?"

She said it, not me. I felt the hook settle in Madame's cheek; all I had to do was make sure it stayed there. "I would not believe it so," I said, willing my confusion and, yes, my hurt, my sense of betrayal to show through. A ki-rin had to be better than the rest of us. If it wasn't... "And yet... what else are we to think? It is a terrible thing, and not to be spoken lightly of."

"Innnndeeeeeed nnnnot," Madame agreed, her expression looking far more feline than serpentine. Bingo.

We excused ourselves soon after, regretfully declining the offer of afternoon tea. Li met us at the door with our coats, and once we were back out on the street, I let myself breathe normally again.

"That was...you just manipulated a dragon!"

"Yeah." I felt a bubbly sort of giddiness hit me. "I did, didn't I?"

"I fear you," Pietr said solemnly, and lifted my hand to his lips and planted a dry, tickly kiss on my fingers. "Where next?"

"Downtown. There are a couple of bars that cater to the fatae.... And I hear they've got damn good beer on tap."

It took us four bars and more beer than I was comfortable drinking that early in the day, but we finally found a little pub where at least half the clientele were nonhuman. The rest looked to be Nulls, surprisingly. Or maybe not surprising at all: people who were half in the bag before noon probably didn't blink if their drinking buddy, in better light, might possibly have horns, or wings, or iridescent skin. The bartender was Talent, but he seemed more intent on the racing pages on the bar in front of him than anything we might say or do.

"You're wrong," I said to Pietr, as though we were continuing a conversation we'd started just before we came in.

"I'm not. You're a sentimental fool who clings too hard to tradition, without any basis in fact. Hell, I don't see why it matters, anyway. The guy deserved to die. So what if maybe the ki-rin lied about the details—the world's a cleaner place for it."

Even in the dim bar interior I could see Pietr's eyes widen slightly, indicating that he'd seen someone within earshot show interest in our conversation. Excellent. Inevitably, one of the roots we had planted today would reach the ki-rin. All we had to do was wait, and be ready.

A human, or any other fatae, might ignore the rumor, or deny it, or even become violent in his or her defense. A ki-rin, accused even by whisper of lying, would be so deeply and personally insulted that there would be no other option but to respond to that accusation. Once it did that, we would be in the position to ask questions it either could not answer, or would expose the entire plot.

We might not be able to put any of them in jail, but everyone involved would be exposed for what they were—not victims, not noble creatures, but killers for hire. We were doing good work.

So why did it leave such a nasty taste in my mouth? I took another sip of my beer, hoping to wash the taste of ashes away. We were almost done.

"Seriously," Pietr went on, readying the hook the same way I'd done with Madame, "it's so obvious the ki-rin was covering for whatever the girl did, but—"

"You lie!"

Maybe we'd set the hook a little too hard, as Pietr's target got physical. I barely had time to duck before a fist about the size of a Virginia ham came slamming down on the bar next to me, knocking over my beer and sending the liquid in a foamy rush down the bar.

I noted, almost absently, that the bar had a definite slant in the middle, making all the beer run into the channel. I wondered if that was planned, to make sure customers didn't wet themselves after a few taps too many, and then I was heading for the floor, looking for cover.

"You lie, you stinking human gutter-trash!"

Pietr, of course, had disappeared. I swore once, but my heart wasn't in it. It was instinct for him, he didn't mean to run out on the fight, really. Not that his intentions, or lack thereof, helped me a bit.

"You shouldn't eavesdrop if you don't want to hear unpleasant things," I told the fatae. A particularly normal-looking specimen, if you ignored the fact that it had a beak like a squid's instead of a nose. I had absolutely no idea what breed it was, and didn't particularly care.

"Take it back!"

"The hell I will. The ki-rin lied!"

Oops. I had been the one arguing against the ki-rin lying. Pietr had been the one saying it had. Oh, well. I didn't think my pugilistic dance buddy cared who had been saying what, anyway. All us be-nosed humans probably looked alike to it, anyway.

It took another swing at me, and missed, the attempted roundhouse almost coming back and clocking it in the face. Long arms and poor depth perception did not a good brawler make. Also, I suspected it had been there drinking for a while before we arrived.

"You break it, you pay for it," the bartender said, barely looking up from his papers. I ducked under another wild swing, and tried to see if anyone else was going to come join the dance. There were three fatae sitting at a nearby table, watching, but they didn't seem inclined to do anything, and the human in the corner was carefully not seeing a thing. If I wanted to, I could just head for the door; Pietr would get out on his own. No part of the deal had involved getting a concussion; our medical plan sucked. I judged the dash I'd have to make past my dance buddy to get to the door, then abandoned the idea. The hook wasn't set yet. It was more than just making sure the suggestion took, there was a "tag" on it, a sort of sticky-note made of current. A Talent might notice it, if they were the suspicious type, but only if they were looking. Nulls and fatae should be oblivious, heeding the urge to pass it on to whomever they mentioned the rumor to, passing it along like a cold virus.

"Stinkin' lyin' humans, tryin' to drive us out of town…"

326 Laura Anne Gilman

Sounded like our unfriendly neighborhood bigots had been priming the pump for us. Good. Or: not good, but useful. The fatae took another swing, and I ducked inside rather than away, getting right up in his face.

The smell of fish and stale beer almost knocked me over, but I leaned in anyway, and whispered, "The ki-rin lied."

Tag.

The fatae snarled, even as I tried to duck back away, and those overlong arms clobbered me good. The room spun, and I swayed, just as a bottle came down on the back of squid-nose's head. He fell forward onto the barstool and crumpled to the ground. Pietr stood there, blinking at me and grinning lopsidedly. "I think we're done here."

Two down, four to go.

thirteen

Ben had seen his partner exalted, exhausted, despondent and in the grips of a terrifying and dangerous euphoria. He had never seen Ian look quite the way he did right now. It wasn't sadness, it wasn't exhaustion, or resignation, but some terrible blend of them all, on a base of fury.

The moment the pups had left on their various missions, his partner had let his facade slip, making Ben leap to the only possible conclusion.

"Aden."

His partner nodded curtly. Only his beloved little sister could so tangle Ian up that he didn't know what to do.

"She really doesn't learn, does she." Ian wanted to remember the little girl she had been, once upon a time, who adored her big brother and would do anything for him. Ben knew better. That little girl had grown into a woman who still adored her brother—and would do anything to stop him.

Although Aden probably called it "bringing him back to his senses." "She was behind the most recent rumors, too? I'd have thought she could do better than that."

"Oh, she did. She went several steps better." A strand of Ian's hair lifted, staticky with current, and he smoothed it down, focusing until his core settled again. "Our Pusher was there, in the meeting."

"I assume you had him taken out and beaten." Ben wasn't joking.

"After he told me who hired him, yes. The meeting was adjourned rather quickly after that. Nobody wanted to admit that they had been manipulated by a Null. Oh, yes. Aden only gave the man his doorway into me. The rumors were the work of someone else—Aden's partner. A Null." His mouth twisted like he'd bitten into something rotten.

"She brought an outsider in?" The only thing Aden Stosser hated more than her brother's pet project was mixing Nulls with what she saw as Council business.

"I suspect they brought her in," Ian said. "Which means that her obsession has become a commonly known thing beyond the Council. She needs to be warned."

Ben had his own opinions about that—namely, that it would do her a world of good to be taken down by a Null; teach her some humility—but this was his best friend's sister they were talking about. So he merely nodded, and twenty minutes later, without permission of or warning to their target, Ian Translocated them directly into the house Aden had been renting, down on the Carolina shoreline.

It took a minute to recover, and by then Ian was already striding forward.

She was sitting in an oversize living room, a glass of tea resting on the table beside her, a book open on her lap, and soft music playing from speakers in another room. Behind her, the shoreline ebbed and flowed under overcast skies.

"You're being used." Ian's voice was like molten lava, cutting through Aden's protestations at their unannounced entrance, and practically making the air sizzle in reaction.

Aden didn't even bother to deny his implicit accusation by asking what he meant. "Maybe I'm using them?"

Ben bit the inside of his lip, knowing any comment he made right now would only make things worse. Aden thought she was far more of a player than she was. She was formidable, yes—she was a Stosser, after all—but she still wasn't as good as she thought she was.

Ian and Aden stared at each other, the family resemblance striking in both the physical and the feel of the current rising in both of them. They had been born of the same family, trained by the same mentor...they were so very similar, and yet completely opposed in this matter.

"Pick better tools," Ian said, finally. "This one will cut you, too. And I'm tired of bandaging up your damned boo-boos, especially when you get them working against my people."

His sister stood up and stalked forward to face him. She was a foot shorter, but carried herself with the same arrogance that made her seem taller. "Your people? Your puppies. Your little lapdogs, sniffing and peeing everywhere." She pulled back her words, and tried again. "My Pusher was only supposed to make you both reconsider. But something went wrong with your partner. He—" her voice dripped venom; she had never liked Ben much "—was warded somehow, the Push kept getting misdirected."

Ben checked himself slightly at that—misdi...oh. Damn. Bonnie, the connection between them, had she gotten hit with it? But there was no time to worry about it now.

"Ian, stop this." Aden sounded sincerely worried. "Stop this before someone gets hurt."

"And by someone you mean...what?" Ian had his temper on but good now. "A Council member who did something they shouldn't have, and gets called on it? Or a Null teenager killed because current got out of control? Which is the greater sin, Aden?"

Her temper flared again to match his own. "Don't you blame that on me! It was your fault for starting this. The Council has been taking care of their own for generations, and doing a good job of it, and lonejacks are lonejacks, they deal with their own people. That's the way it's always been, and it's a good system."

"It's a crap system. You of all people should know that."

Ben tensed. Any mention of Chicago was thin ice, even in the best of situations. This...wasn't that.

"Is there a problem, Aden?"

Two men in the hallway, suddenly, and a large dog next to them. Ben felt his skin prickle. If they were Talent, they were holding back, hiding themselves. But Nulls could be just as deadly. And dogs...

For all that he joked about the puppies, Benjamin Venec was afraid of dogs. And Aden, that bitch, knew it.

"Is there a problem?" one of the men repeated.

"There's no problem," Ian said, his voice practically oozing the confidence and sincerity that got them out of—and into—trouble on a regular basis. But the speaker had his eyes on Aden, and gave no sign of having heard him.

"Bill. This is my brother, Ian. He stopped by to see if we couldn't work our little differences out." Aden's voice was high and brittle, filled with…anger, Ben decided. He didn't know her well, not as well as he did her brother, but he could tell that much. She was angry, and a little bit afraid—but of Ian? Or this Bill? Was this their mysterious businessman?

"Ian Stosser. What an…unexpected pleasure."

Ben, thus ignored, felt free to step back from the scene, even as the man with Bill did the same, taking the dog with him. They were not the players in this little playlet, just understudies.

Or stagehands.

"So. You're the scum trying to use my sister's delusions for your own purposes."

Ben groaned. Ian had gone from Player to Big Brother. Damn it, this was no time to protect the crazy little bitch….

"Ian. Be polite to my partner." Aden's voice was sharp… the fear was rising. Why? Ben reconsidered Bill. Tall and well-dressed, with a face that could pass as comfortably handsome…but there was something about him that set Ben's hackles on alert. This was a nasty bastard. A sadist, possibly. Mean, definitely.

"Why?" Ian stalked forward, circling the man. "I know

you," he said flatly. "Bill West. You were involved in the Sagara incident, back last autumn. Eight people died."

"Hardly involved. We employed one of the consultants who worked for the company in question. The Sagara field was completely out of—"

"Eight people died because your consultant said it was all right to drill. Right into an unquiet ley line."

Venec hadn't heard about that. The Council must have hushed it up. That meant this man had his hooks into at least one Council member, somewhere.

West made an elegant gesture with his hands. "Sometimes, people die. That is the price of risk. You know that, certainly, of all people. Or have I heard the story of the Chicago incident incorrectly?"

Ian turned on his sister, his teeth bared in a snarl. Ben stepped forward, realizing as he did so that he was intending to protect Aden, not Ian. Both Stossers had tempers that could combust in an instant, and regrets would only come later. The dog snarled, and Ben stopped cold.

"You told him?" Ian's hair lifted with static. "Private Council matters—*that* Council matter—you told to an outsider? Have you totally taken leave of your senses, Aden? And they say that I'm a loose cannon? You are the one who endangers us!"

Infuriated, she raised her hand, wreathed in dark blue current like a neon torch. Ben swore, pulling current from his own core to form a shield. Ian would do anything for a cause...but he would not believe his sister could willingly kill.

The current in her hand said differently.

"I told him nothing." Her voice was tight: she was afraid of her partner. That made him the priority.

Getting between two Stossers was not something he would recommend, but he would have done it if the first man, Bill, hadn't raised his hand as well, summoning not current, but his companion. Ben hesitated, feeling the current rising in him, waiting for direction.

"If they die now," West said, almost conversationally, "our problems are solved. Such a shame, the siblings driven to this…"

Even as Ian and Aden turned at that comment, the second man moved forward, and Ben saw that he was holding a nasty-looking handgun.

"Idiot Null," Ben muttered, and shifted his aim, the lash of current he had planned for Aden instead flickering out and wrapping itself around the gunman's hand. The man yelped as it burned the skin, jerking his hand upward even as he pulled the trigger.

The bullet escaped the muzzle, smashing into something that broke with a hard crash. The current wove around the metal, fusing the internal workings. If that bastard tried to fire again, it would explode in his hand.

"Don't bring a goddamn gun to a goddamn current fight," he snarled. Guns worked against Talent if they were unprepared, not expecting the blow, but Venec was never unprepared.

"You dare?" Aden asked West, her voice a perfect match for Ian's: hard and hot and outraged. Despite the seriousness of the situation, Ben felt the urge to roll his eyes. There were days he sympathized with people who wanted to kill this family.

"I dare whatever I please," West said, somehow refraining from showing the sneer that was in his voice, as though his gunman hadn't just been unarmed and rendered useless. "I told you I wanted to stop him…. And you've just given me the perfect scenario. Nobody will doubt that you two let your tempers get the better of you, his loyal partner tried to intervene, and tragedy ensued…."

He let his other hand dip into his pocket, and came out with a long black tube. "One of my associates came up with this," he said, lifting it so that they could see it clearly. "It's a prototype, but I am assured that it works quite well. Try to use current against me, and you will regret it, I assure you."

"There are many things in life I regret," Aden said flatly. "Killing you won't be one of them."

Current flashed, a hot orange neon that filled the room and made Ben blink, but before he could recover there was a backlash like he'd never seen before, the current some-how twisted on itself and sent back toward the caster. Aden absorbed most of it, the shock dancing across her skin like the static globes they sold in novelty stores that mimicked lightning storms. Ian recovered first, slapping a dark blue bolt at their attacker's torso, aimed directly at the heart. This time, Ben saw the wand lift, and the current redirect itself to the mouth of the tube, regurgitating at only slightly less power, heading directly back at Ian.

In the afterflash, Ben also saw the second man pulling a long, narrow knife from somewhere and lunging at Aden.

Personally, he'd let her take a blade, if he thought it would get her out of their hair. But explaining that to Ian could get dicey. So he lunged in turn, going low under the current streams, and knocked the guy's feet out from under him, bringing them both onto the hardwood flooring. He was tired, and annoyed, and worried about that tube-thing, so he didn't use any finesse, shoving his hand down on the man's chest and stopping his heart with one swift blow of current.

The body ran on electricity. Current ran alongside electricity. Killing someone with current was easy, if you had the stomach for it.

He rolled, as soon as the job was done, and came up behind West, crouching. The tube, he assessed quickly, was enough to hold off one Talent, but not two: the combined brother-and-sister attack was making West stagger. All it would take to finish him off would be one distraction.

Ben shoved forward, grabbing West's arm and tearing it downward, so the current he was redirecting went down into the floor. He felt a sharp tingle run through him, but a Talent was grounded to prevent that sort of thing from doing damage.

Bill West wasn't that fortunate. He let out a scream, even as the current surged through him like ground-to-cloud lightning, frying his entire system.

He fell to his knees, his nice suit barely mussed, and dropped forward.

Silence, and the scent of burnt flesh, filled the room.

"I hope you didn't put too much of a security deposit down on this place," Ian said, stepping forward to pick up the tube. It had melted under the current rush; the plastic was fused into a solid, misshapen rod. There was no way to determine what it had been or how it had worked.

"Damn you, Ian." Aden sounded more tired than angry, however. "West was...out of line. I want to stop you, not kill you. I don't want to kill anyone."

"And yet," Ben said, unable to stop himself, "people keep dying every time you get involved. Maybe that should be something that you consider?"

"Ben," Ian said, cautioning him. Then he turned to face his sister. "We did good work together here. Teamwork, even."

She almost smiled, and for an instant Ben could see the little girl she had been, the one his partner still saw when he looked at her. Then it was gone. "Don't get used to it."

"You have to stop this. Ben is right. If you're going to ally yourself with people who don't have the same scruples you maintain...either yours will get bent, or they will get you dead. Is that what you want?"

"I can't stop, Ian."

Ian sighed, the sound of an old man, too tired to go on fighting. "And neither can I."

Ben really, really wanted to tell them both off, but Ian's expression stopped him. Of all the things he had gone through with Ian, this one thing he could not follow. Ben didn't have family. He didn't understand, he could not share the pain...or whatever odd joy his friend got from having her around, even when they were fighting. He could only be there when the pieces fell apart. And with Aden, inevitably, they would. But it could not be tonight.

They still had a job to finish.

* * *

It was nearly midnight when Pietr and I ended up back at my apartment, our last target tagged and bagged. It wasn't anything planned…we just ended up there, without discussion. Without expectation, either; the entire evening had been companionable but totally…packlike, I guess. No vibes, uncomfortable or otherwise. Part of my ego, I think, was a little bruised—what, I wasn't so irresistible that he was dying for another taste?—but mostly it was just…comfortable.

Thinking of sex made me think of Venec, and even in my exhaustion I knew with him it would never be comfortable. Comforting, maybe. But never comfortable.

Pietr went facedown on the sofa when we staggered in, not even bothering to take off his shoes, and didn't move. Poor thing. I thought about getting a blanket and draping it over him, but it was too much energy to move. I slumped in the chair, and stared at the mosaic.

We had figured that it would take about twenty-four hours for the seeds we'd planted to grow into anything useful. That meant we were in waiting mode until tomorrow, maybe even longer. In the meanwhile, I decided, it was time to deal with other things.

Current could purge booze from your system, but it wasn't fun or pretty. After I'd rinsed my mouth out a couple of times, I took a long hot shower and took a long, slow and steady hit off the building next door's electrical system. I wasn't taking enough to raise their costs, but it was starting to become a regular habit, and that was rude. Maybe I should send their super a bouquet of flowers? I really was going to have to find some kind of regular refueling station, something that wouldn't impact other people. I'd have to ask the pack, see what they were doing. It wasn't the kind of thing you discussed casually, usually, but I figured we'd pretty much gone beyond normal *Cosa* manners our first case, and not looked back.

Out of the shower, I styled my hair into its spiked, sparkly best, then did myself up in what J used to refer to as my out-of-gum clothes. I wasn't quite sure what he meant by that, but when I finished lacing up the corset and lining my eyes until I looked like an Egyptian queen, I felt like I could kick ass from one end of the city to the other without breaking a single purple-tinted nail. I stopped to consider myself in the mirror. The scarlet brocade corset and black skirt could run the gamut from SCA glam to urban goth, but the kitten-heeled boots whispered "slinky."

Benjamin Venec wasn't going to know what hit him.

I stalked out of the bathroom, my heels making a satisfying clatter on the hardwood, and Pietr let out a low whistle. He was still sprawled on the sofa, but he'd turned onto his back, and was flipping through a bunch of magazines. The hour it had taken me to get ready seemed to have revived him somewhat, and I suspected I was going to have to make that bouquet of flowers for the next-door super larger than planned.

"You planning to go break hearts or crush gonads?" he asked, once I'd curtsied in response to the whistle. Thankfully, there was only admiration in his voice, and no jealousy.

"Maybe both, maybe neither. Depends on what I find when I get there," I said. He didn't ask any more questions, just shook his head and went back to the magazine. I swooped over to drop a kiss on his forehead, staining his skin with mochaberry gloss. "You crashing here tonight?"

"I'm still too drunk to move," he said without apology. "Try not to step on me when you stagger home."

"If I come home, dear boy. If I come home."

He laughed, and waved me out the door.

I wasn't just heading out to club, despite what Pietr thought. No, I had a specific goal in mind; or rather, a specific quarry. I just didn't know where he was. But I knew how to find him.

That damned connection could be useful, as well as annoying.

The spring night air was cool on my bare arms, and a faint breeze moved the fabric of my skirt against my legs as I stood on the sidewalk outside my building and slowly, carefully, let down my wall.

Like water flowing over a dike, the awareness of Venec entered me, an ordered rush of sensations and current-hum. Not signature, not quite, but something more raw, more... disordered. I'd never thought anything to do with Venec would be disordered. The thought amused me.

He was downtown, all the way downtown. Somewhere noisy and crowded and loud. Good. I took a hit off the streetlamps, the shot of current curling like a swirl of static in my core, and headed toward him.

"Well, well, Big Dog. I wouldn't have thought it of you." The trail led me to Mei-Chan's, one of the bars Mercy had been at the night of the attack. Was Venec working, or had he been intrigued enough to go take a look-see? Or was this how he blew off steam, and I never knew? Whatever reason, he was on my ground now, not his. I liked that.

There was a line at the door, even at 1:00 a.m., but the bouncer took one look and let me through. I wasn't a goth chick, not really, but that wasn't what the bouncers looked for. Their checklist was simple: does he have money? Is she hot? Will they look good on the dance floor or in the gossip rags?

Inside, the club was pretty much as I remembered it: loud, crowded, and high-end trying to be dangerous. I was probably in the upper end of age for the girls on the floor, and rather than depressing me, the thought made me want to laugh. I could outdance most of them, and still get up in the morning to go to work, if I wanted to. Right now, though, I had a different kind of dancing in mind.

I bypassed the bar, three deep and doing a rousing business, and headed into the crowd on the dance floor, following my instincts and the deep-tingle that said "Venec."

He was dancing with a girl. Actually, as I watched, I changed my initial impression. She was dancing with him. His body was there with her, but he wasn't.

"Honey, you're missing the best part," I told her. She was too far away to hear, even if the music hadn't been pumping, but Venec looked up, pinpointing me without hesitation. Wherever his thoughts had been before, they were present and accounted for now.

I stalked across the floor, sliding one hand between them before the girl even knew I was there. "Sorry, darling," I told her in my best dangerous purr. "I'm not in the mood for cute and cuddly tonight, and I'm really not up for sharing."

She was cute, in a Barbie-goth way that never did much for me, but she was also smart enough to know when to back off. I slid my arms around Ben's neck, and stared up into dark, very annoyed eyes. Not annoyed with me, though; I could tell that, even through both of our walls. No wonder Barbie hadn't been able to engage him; he was totally inside his own head.

Good. That's where I needed to be, too.

"You and I, we have to talk," I told him. Even with the noise, he heard me perfectly.

"Talk?"

"Talk," I repeated, not without a little reluctance. In office gear, Venec was quietly hot. In black leather pants and a soft blue-black shirt showing just the right amount of neck, he was unfairly hot. If you liked the mussed, cranky, deep-thinking type, anyway.

I liked.

There was no way you could talk in Mei-Chan's, not even in the allegedly "quiet" rooms. I got my hand stamped in case I decided to come back later and blow off some steam, and led Ben out to the sidewalk. The usual pack of smokers was gathered by a lamppost, talking quietly as they filled their lungs and rested their ears.

"What the hell is going on?" I asked him.

Ben had the decency not to look surprised, or to try and pretend that we were still in work mode, with the generally accepted boss-to-worker protocols. This was a straight guy-girl thing.

"I don't know. I really don't."

Oh. Well. I hadn't expected that.

He sighed, and went over to one of the smokers to bum a cig. I also hadn't expected that. What else was I going to learn about Benjamin Venec tonight?

"Walk with me," he said.

If I'd known we were going to be strolling, I'd have worn a top with a little more top to it. I unfurled a little current to warm up my exposed skin, and used the remnant to light his cigarette with a flicker of fire coming out of my fingertip, a trick I'd picked up back in high school.

"Cute," he said, leaning in until the cig caught, and then pulling back to study me with those dark eyes. "Two hundred years ago you'd have been stoned as a witch."

"Two hundred years ago I'd have been stoned as a witch for a lot more than that."

He didn't smile. "You and Pietr have something going on?"

"Who's asking?" Boss or not-boss, I meant. Was this office-concern, or personal?

He didn't respond for the length of half a block. I realized suddenly that we were following the same path that Mercy and the ki-rin had taken, that night a week before.

"Have you ever heard of a current merge?" He didn't wait for me to answer, taking a hit off his cigarette as though he hated the taste of it. "I hadn't, not until I did some research.

"Most of us use the same current but on different, call it wavelengths. That's part of what makes up a signature. Merge is a kind of shared wavelength. Rare, but not unheard of.

You could go your entire life without ever finding someone who is a match, even if you're riding the same subway every morning, but once you interact..."

The shiver of sparks flickering from my core out into his skin, the sensation of his current sparking mine, then coming back to me. I shivered again, despite the fact that I was comfortably warm.

"Is that what happened? We've got a merge?"

"I think so."

"Huh." I considered that. I'd been prepared for...I don't know what, something more tangled, complicated, maybe even mystical. Knowing it could be quantified, that there was a way to understand what was going on, made it manageable. Maybe.

"And that means...?"

"I don't know. My sources are from the Old Days, so they're couched in...annoying phraseology."

"Oh, god. They don't say soul mates or anything, do they?"

He laughed, but it wasn't an amused sound. "They do."

I was chewing over that when I realized suddenly that at some point, we'd started walking hand-in-hand. And neither of us had noticed. And it felt...familiar. Right. I had never, ever been a hand-in-hand girl. Ever.

"What else did your research turn up?" I decided not to mention the hand thing, if he wasn't noticing.

"On the useful side? The ability to find each other, pretty much anywhere. You seem to have already discovered that. Useful but annoying? You may not be able to shut out a ping from me, now. And vice versa."

"So far, nothing I can't live with. Um. You can't actually hear my thoughts through my wall, can you?"

"Thank god, no."

It was tempting to be annoyed at the relief in his tone, but I was too busy trying to untangle the specifics of this merge-thing. I dismantled my wall halfway. "How about now?"

He cocked his head, as though listening. "No."

The wall came down all the way. "And now?"

He dropped the cigarette, half-unsmoked, on the ground, and used the tip of his shoe to grind it out. "I can hear... white noise. Like someone murmuring in another room. But nothing specific, and I can only tell it's you because I know it's you."

Huh. "Does it bother you?"

I don't know if he was aware of the fact that he had crooked his arm so that I was pulled in closer, but I'd noticed it. "It should," he replied. "It should piss me the hell off, and annoy me, and distract me. It doesn't. I think that bothers me more than if it did distract me."

As he was talking, I felt a pressure building up. No, not pressure; more like the weight of a cat pushing against your leg, asking to be noticed, only against my core. Ben was taking down his wall, too, letting me sense him.

"Like a waterfall," I said. "Steady, quiet...yeah. It's not disturbing at all, now that I know what the hell it is."

and this?

I jumped, literally, straight into the air.

"Damn." I'd never had a ping come through like that, clear and solid as an actual voice. No, it *was* an actual voice, silent but audible inside my head. And all he'd done—I knew, but I didn't know how I knew—was think the words.

Telepathy wasn't possible. People had been trying forever and ever amen to manage it, but all we'd gotten were strong pings and—if you knew the person really well, or had a butt-load of power behind it—a stream of emotions or visuals. Ben's Push probably helped, but this…

Wow. And also, uh-oh. As intriguing as it might be to have this whole new area to dig around in, and the possibilities for what this could mean for stuff we could manage on the job—no wonder I'd been able to send him the stuff from Mercy's apartment!—it still meant something else entirely when we were off the clock.

I realized I'd been watching him as we walked, just soaking in the view, and forced myself to look away. "Um. Did you walk this way intentionally?" Because we'd followed Mercy's path all the way to the waterfront.

"No. I was wondering if you had."

It was subtle, like the waterfall backdrop in my awareness, but I felt the slide sideways, as Ben went back to being Venec, and we were on the job again. And, like the awareness of him, it didn't bother me at all.

We had walked all the way to the edge of the city. New York may never sleep, but it does occasionally doze, and other than the siren of an emergency vehicle racing uptown, the night was quiet. There weren't even any cars on the street in front of us, making the flashing traffic light and walk signs seem somehow surreal.

We crossed the street against the light, our heels echoing oddly.

"They would have come this way. She was ahead of the ki-rin. It was all choreographed. She had to look like she was alone...."

"The hug she gave the ki-rin, before the attack." The knowledge came to me, as I retraced her steps one final time. "It wasn't a sudden burst of affection. She was saying goodbye."

Venec nodded. He had let go of my hand as we crossed the street, and I moved ahead, finding myself bouncing a little as I did so, exactly the way Mercy had, in my gleaning.

I stopped before I reached the site of the attack, though. Venec caught up with me, standing at my shoulder, looking at the path.

"There are fewer offerings," he noted. "On both sides."

I nodded. "People are starting to reconsider their initial flush of outrage?"

"Or maybe they've just found new things to be outraged over. All it will take is one burst of news and they'll be back here, so don't relax. Where was the dark current you felt?"

Okay, time to see if this merge was good for anything useful. I thought about how to direct him to what I "saw," and a thin thread of current dipped into the awareness of the waterfall, coming out with droplets of water clinging to it, like a sheathing of liquid ice, if that made any sense at all. I turned and looked at the offerings, and Venec's current followed mine.

Unlike sharing the view with Pietr, I couldn't tell what Venec was thinking, or if he was even seeing the same thing—we weren't seeing it together, just side-by-side. Some of my worries about this thing we had faded. I wasn't the most private of people, okay, yeah, but Venec was. I didn't want him to feel imposed on or anything. At least, not when I didn't intend to impose.

thank you But the thought, although dry, was gentle, almost affectionate, not cutting.

On the verbal surface, we were all business. "I see it. It's not fresh, though. Whoever left it, they haven't been back."

"Is that good, or bad?"

"They're still out there," he said, responding to what I hadn't asked. "But right now, it's not our problem. Nothing we can do tonight. Come on. There's a diner around the corner that's still twenty-four-hour. I need coffee."

How he knew about this diner I don't know—it was about the size of a phone booth, covered in shiny aluminum siding, and had room for six tables along its length, and a cracked Formica countertop that had probably been there since they installed it in 1951.

The waitress had probably been there that long, too.

We slid into the table farthest at the back, and ordered coffee.

"This thing…I called my mentor earlier, asked her about the merge, in a purely hypothetical formation," Ben said. "Most of my books came from her, anyway—she's an archivist at Founder Ben's."

Okay, I was impressed. Back in the 1800s some smart rabbit got the idea to collect every bit of historical data he could on verified magic—the stuff we know for true, not the legends or myths—and store it somewhere safe, so no matter if there was another Burning, or we suddenly lost all sense of ourselves, there would be a place our history was safe. Naming it for Franklin—the founder of modern Talent in America—had been a no-brainer. Venec having an archivist as a mentor…it didn't really match the picture I had of him, but it didn't *not* match, either.

He seemed oblivious to me switching around my mental picture of him, playing with the spoon in his coffee. "She's used to me asking about odd bits of spells, especially once I started back with Ian. All she could turn up was that it was something that was celebrated, and yes, it usually had a sexual component to it, too."

Not that I had asked, or anything.

"That's a problem. Sex would be a very bad idea." He stopped stirring his coffee, and stared at the murky brown liquid. "I mean…" He sighed, and I knew—the link—that the sigh was as much at himself as me or the situation. "I mean because of the situation. Not…" He stopped and raised his head to glare at me, like I'd been the one to trap him in that sentence.

I thought about letting him dangle a little longer, but the glare had as much confusion as annoyance in it. "Ben. It's okay. I get it. I agree. Sex between boss and employee, not good for office politics." His shoulders lowered a little in relief, and he lifted the coffee to his lips.

"Although Nick totally thinks we should get it on."

I timed that just right, and coffee sprayed everywhere. The waitress glared at us, like a snarf was declaration of war, or something.

"He does, does he?" There was that lamb nom-nomming

look in Venec's eyes again, the one that made me feel a little
nervous and a lot intrigued, before it was shuttered behind
the usual distanced amusement.

"For the good of the rest of the office, yeah." This conversation felt a little surreal, even for me, but he was rolling
with it....

"And how does Pietr fit into this?"

Big Dog had a bone, and didn't want to let go of it. This
had to be settled now, while we were still being civil to each
other.

"Does the merge give you any say over what I do with
my life?"

"No. It doesn't. I apologize." He looked annoyed again,
but same as before I could tell it wasn't me he was annoyed
with, but himself for being annoyed. That could come in
handy, yeah, when he was reaming us out in the office. Or
maybe not. I didn't want to know *everything* he was feeling,
and I sure as hell didn't want him to know what I was feeling.
Unless I wanted him to, that was. Damn it, this was all getting way too complicated. Complicated made me cranky.

"You feel it, too. Sparks. Serious sparks. And you're the
kind of guy who wants to—" I almost said "control" and
switched it out at the last instant to "—know what's happening every step of the way. I get that. But if we're going
to be smart and civilized about this, you've got to accept the
fact that I haven't been celibate since I was fourteen, and I'm
not going to start now."

"Fourteen?" Those dark eyes mock-widened, even as he
accepted my slap-down.

"Don't start on me, I was a smart girl, I knew my sex ed,

and I have a pretty good radar for partners. There's only one I'm embarrassed about, and that's...not a story I really want to tell you."

Two people walked into the diner behind me, and Venec stopped laughing. I craned my neck as discreetly as I could in order to see what had changed his mood.

"Oh. Wow."

The guy on the left looked totally normal. Human, or close to it. His companion... Not so much. I'd never even seen a picture of anything like that. About half my height, wearing a leather trench coat and slouch hat that didn't do a thing to hide the fact that its body was covered with thick, coarse white fur. It was gesturing with one arm, showing a padded paw with thick black claws that looked deadly.

"Don't stare," Venec murmured. "It's bad manners, and you don't want to piss him off."

I dropped my gaze down into the dregs of my coffee, and picked up the spoon to stir it, to give myself something to do. I was pretty sure I was blushing, which I never did. "What is it?"

"Demon."

I swear I strained something, resisting the urge to swivel in my seat and gawk openly. Demon were rare. Not ki-rin rare, but unusual enough to merit gawking. "Do they all look like that?"

"No. Each one looks different."

"Then how do you know...?"

"Red eyes. Dark red eyes, the only fatae who have 'em. Also, bad-tempered. Although not as nasty as the angeli.

You can talk to a demon, even work with one. Angeli? Not so much."

That I knew—the fatae breed known as angels took their name way too seriously, looking down at any species that wasn't them, especially humans.

"How'd you know it was a demon, then?"

"You live in New York long enough, you know P.B. He's a courier, carries messages that are too important to be trusted to the post office or a standard messenger. Rumor has it the last person who tried to steal something he was carrying ended up looking like dog food."

"I'm telling you, Jock, it's bad news. The entire city's twitching over it." The demon's—P.B.'s—voice carried in the sudden stillness. "And the last thing we need right now, people wondering if any of us can be trusted, after all, feeding into those damned..." He suddenly seemed to realize his voice was too loud for secrecy, and dropped to a lower murmur as they took a table as far away from us as they could get.

"The gossip's spreading," I said. "You think this is going to work?"

"It has to. I can't think of any other way to get the ki-rin to talk to us, and if it doesn't... Right now the scales are balanced—the fatae don't trust humans and humans aren't trusting the fatae. The assault pushed everything to breaking point. We have to be able to take the tension back down again. Everyone has to have equal liability in the events for there to be equal trust."

"And if we can't bring it back down? If we can't prove the ki-rin and Talent were equally involved?" I knew the answer, but I was hoping he'd be able to tell me something different.

"You said it already. Then we could have a very nasty intra-*Cosa* showdown. And nobody will win."

Yeah. But there was more in his words, or the tone, or something, that caught my attention. "There's something you aren't telling me."

He was surprised, then tried to pull but...but I was already on the scent. "It's Aden, isn't it? She was...doing something. Feeding someone information? Causing trouble?"

"What do you..." His expression changed, his jaw hardening and then relaxing as he realized I hadn't intentionally gone digging, and he gave up trying to hide anything. "It's taken care of."

"You tie her up and toss her overboard?"

That got a quick rueful smile that made my toes curl a little inside my shoes. "I wish. No. But it's dealt with."

"That was where Ian was, the oil he had to pour. To calm the trouble she was stirring up, as usual."

I wanted to be angry, but what good would it do? Ben knew Aden was trouble. Hell, Ian knew Aden was trouble. But we'd figured out already that he would never act against little sister, so we just had to deal with it. And it sounded like they had, at least for now.

"Is it going to come back and bite us on the ass?"

"Probably. Aden... She's doing what she believes is right. She just...lacks the ability to get perspective."

I had no idea what he meant by that, but it didn't feel like the right time or place to dig. So we sat there drinking our coffee and talking about nothing—first pets and school memories—until the old-fashioned white-faced clock on the wall informed us that it was 3:00 a.m., and the waitress came around to close out our tab, since she was going off-shift.

"We're going to feel like hell in the morning," Venec observed.

"So why are we still sitting here?" Not that I minded, exactly, but he was the one who'd told me, months ago, that he expected us all to get a full night's sleep.

He shrugged. On him it didn't look quite so annoying, more like a complete sentence than an incoherent exasperation. "I haven't been sleeping much, lately."

My hand found his across the table, and I curled my fingers around his palm. His skin was weirdly chilled, despite the coffee. "Ben... We didn't start this, the violence or the prejudice. It's always been there, in one form or another. We didn't cause it, and we can't solve it, not all of it." I was beginning to see why Stosser was so exasperated with his partner, sometimes.

"We're just people, boss. We can only do a little bit, here and there. Even all of us together can only do a little bit."

"I want everything," he admitted, ruefully, like he was admitting something shameful.

"Yeah, I'm getting that." Who knew the Big Dog had the heart of a Knight Errant? "But sometimes, all you get is some of it."

We weren't talking about the case, not entirely. Not anymore. But I'd already given him my speech on that; it was up to him to decide if he could handle it. Better to keep us focused right now.

354   Laura Anne Gilman

"You were the one who told me...what did you tell me, Venec?"

He knew what I was talking about. "Carry it on the skin, not the spine."

"Right. So now I'm going back home to get a few hours of sleep, and I suggest that you do the same. Normal people need sleep before they try to save the world...or even one big-ass city."

I left him sitting there with the check—he was the boss, he could damn well afford to pick up the cost of two cups of coffee—and went home. Pietr was passed out on the sofa, facedown and snoring. I threw a blanket over him, shucked out of my gear, and crawled up into my loft bed, pretty sure I was going to be asleep before I hit the pillow.

I woke up groggy and my head filled with dreams of other people's voices. Venec hadn't gone to bed, after all; he'd been arguing with Stosser—and been annoyed enough that he hadn't kept his walls up. Gah. Thankfully, it was just voices, and not words. As much as having an inside track might be useful, it would probably get me into more trouble than it was worth.

"Hey."

Unlike me, Pietr stuck around in the morning. I glared at him, well-aware that I'd forgotten to take my eye makeup off last night, and my eyes were a gummy mess.

He didn't flinch, but just waved in the direction of my kitchenette. "I got some coffee."

That was the smell that had woken me up. "Thanks."

Pietr had also gotten the newspaper from my front door—I

was probably the only person in the entire building who still took an actual newspaper, but the delivery guy still placed it, folded neatly, against my door every morning, Monday through Saturday.

"What time is it?"

"A little after seven. We still have time."

He'd managed to take a shower, too, I noticed; his hair was still wet, and his face had a scrubbed look, clean and fresh-shaved.

"You didn't use my razor, did you?" Because, friend or no, if he had…

"Hell no. And I didn't touch your shampoo, either. I didn't want to go in smelling like…what the hell do you use, anyway?"

"Tea tree. My scalp's sensitive."

"Yeah, well, you dye your hair that many times, it's a wonder it hasn't gotten pissed and left."

"That line works better coming from Nick," I said, recognizing the pattern of comebacks. "You can do nastier."

He grinned, and snapped the paper back into its proper folds. "So. Have good hunting last night?"

I had to think about it for a minute. "Yeah. I think so."

"Good. Go wash your face. You look like a raccoon after a week-long bender."

After that crack, I didn't talk to him the entire way into the office. Venec was already there, wearing the same shirt he'd had on that night—and I was right, it was hand-tailored; under the office lights I could tell—but he'd changed into a pair of black jeans, and taken a shower somewhere along the line. The waterfall noise came forward out of the background, and I realized it had never left, just faded to not-noticeable status. I gave it a mental shove back, and my awareness of him faded. Good. Maybe familiarity—and knowing what it was—would be enough to keep it contained.

Then he looked at me, and every hope of that went out the window. My breath caught somewhere between my chest and my throat, and there was an ache in my thighs that the tumble with Pietr should have put down for a few more days at least, damn it. I'd thought knowing what was going on would make it easier, not harder, but based on the oomph we just gave each other with a single look, keeping sex out of this thing was going to be trickier than we'd hoped.

Fortunately, we were both stubborn as sin.

Nick tossed me a glazed donut, and I caught it with one hand, even distracted. Nifty held up six fingers, rating my catch. I gave him one in return.

We had apparently walked into an ongoing discussion of the way the rumor-net was spreading. Nifty was the only pup who didn't seem worried.

"Relax, people," he was saying. "We primped the pump, but good. It will come forward—or someone will make it come forward. Like Venec said, the word on the street is that they're afraid this will make them look even worse, feed the antifatae feelings. It's a *shonda* for the *goyim.*"

I couldn't help it, I laughed. Nifty had a way of coming up with Yiddishism that a good ol' black kid from Philly really shouldn't be using. "Let me guess. Your coach again?"

"Ex-girlfriend, actually."

Venec held his hand up, and I could feel the tension in

him, a different sort from last night's, like a crack of thunder
through the waterfall. "Hush," he said, listening intently.
The current strands around him were almost visible, and I
got a sense of our rumor-net vibrating like a spider's web
with a juicy fly caught somewhere in the sticky mess.

stosser a whisper of thought told me, identifying the
ping Ben was listening to. I couldn't hear it myself, but I
knew.

Somewhere out there, our lures had gotten a bite. But was
it enough?

We waited, polishing off what was left of the box of donuts
on the table, while Venec held a silent debate with Stosser,
wherever he was.

"Heads up, puppies," he said suddenly. "Ian wants to bring
you in on this."

"Bring us in?" Sharon asked, and I could see the others
bracing themselves for a Translocation.

"Like a conference call," Venec said. "The way you
share mage-sight, only in a group. Ian will be lead, I'm the
conduit."

"Have you guys ever done a group like this before?" Nifty
asked, which was the exact same thing I'd been wondering.
Sharing the bubble with Pietr had been stressful enough.
Holding seven of us? Over a distance? Stosser was damn
good, but...

"No time like right now to learn something new," Venec
said. "Get ready. In ten."

I started counting back, sliding into fugue-state, but somebody was off a beat because I was still at three when I felt a

tug somewhere around my midsection and midbrain, and fell into a group-fugue.

Wow. This was weird. I was pretty sure that thought was mine, but I couldn't swear to it. A bunch of different flavors melting into each other, like too many scoops in a sundae. Then a coating of something heavy on top...Venec as hot fudge? Yeah, that was about right. Bittersweet fudge. Yum.

I managed not to share that thought with the group, and then we were all in the same pipeline, looking through Stosser's eyes. I knew that immediately, because the point of view was too damn high, and there was the shadow of a long narrow nose just at the edge of my awareness.

focus a cranky reminder came.

Heh. I wasn't the only one noticing the nose.

We were in a large room...no, a warehouse of some sort, or a repair bay. Concrete floors, metal walls, lighting far overhead, glaringly white. And, in front of us, the ki-rin.

The first and last time I'd seen a ki-rin, other than through my projected gleanings, was at the scene of the crime, when it was at a distance and covered in someone else's blood. I hadn't looked too closely then. Now, I—through Stosser's awareness—stared.

The fatae was about the size of a large pony, like I'd already noted, but its body was more like an elk's than a horse's. Dun scales sparkled at throat and belly, but a plush golden coat covered its legs and torso, leading to the long neck with the white-gold lion's mane, and scaled dragon's head. It was looking directly at us, and I noticed with a sense of shock that it had whiskers similar to Madame's. Well, I suppose that made sense. Ironically, the horn in the middle of its forehead—the murder weapon—was the last thing you noticed. It was smaller than I'd thought it would be, barely a foot long, and not ivory the way a unicorn's was, but dun brown and slightly curved, more like an antler than a horn. Under the horn, looking directly at us, two large, deep-set eyes the color of coal and filled with an impossible sadness.

He killed a man, I reminded myself. He let his companion sell herself, and conspired to cover up murder.

I did only what was within my right to do.

I flinched, thinking that it was responding to me. But no, that musical voice was echoing in the warehouse; we were hearing it through Stosser's ears, via the current-link.

"We know, Si-Ja. We know." Ian's voice, as filled with sadness and regret as I had ever heard. How could you not feel regret, confronting such a magnificent being? And how could there not be sadness, seeing the sadness in the ki-rin's gaze?

Sadness would not bring back the dead. Regret would not undo the harm.

You spread lies. It attacked my companion.

"Yes, he did," Stosser agreed. "But did we lie? Or merely misrepresent the truth? Nobody is denying that the guy was scum. You were within your rights, by the standards of the fatae, to claim retribution, and defend her honor. But the truth is not truth when only part of the story is told, noble one."

The ki-rin snorted, and I swear flames came from its

black-rimmed nostrils. Stosser stood his ground, despite the angry response.

You accuse me of lying?

"Ki-rin do not lie. And yet, I know that you do not tell all that you know."

The ki-rin raised its head and stared directly at him/us. *It attacked my companion. She was in dishonor.*

"You took money to be in that place at that time. She took money to approach those men, and to accept the consequences of what happened. I do not condone nor do I dismiss that man's actions—they were of his own volition and deserved punishment. But you knew what would happen. You were complicit in the attack, and premeditated the murder."

Her honor...

"Her honor was sold. As was yours." The sadness was still there, but it was delivered on a cold steel blade. Ian Stosser did not like being used, played, or made a fool.

There was a long pause, and those great coal-black eyes shone with tears.

The action was his. He could have walked away. He could have listened to her saying no.

"It's called entrapment. There is no honor in it."

The ki-rin's head dropped, and something inside me crumbled. No Ancient should ever be cast down so, not even by its own actions. It was...it was painful to watch. Like Mercy's agony, this was private. We should not be here, we should avert our eyes....

Our job was to see what others would not, could not. We were there to make sure all the pieces fit together, that the entire story was told, not just one side of it. Stosser did not turn away, and so neither did we.

"Why, Si-Ja? What reason…?"

I could refuse her nothing, my beloved child, my companion. She had such talent…and dreams, dreams I had fed, to grow and to see, but such things took money. I am old, human. Old even for my kind, and when I die she will be alone…and my wealth, what little remains, will not pass on to her.

The missing artwork on the wall. Not knickknacks—her own work. Destroyed, in a fit of rage, of shame, of despair. I knew it, kenned it, the way I knew Mercy's own signature. The information flowed from me into the rest of the pack… and Stosser, our point man.

"You wanted to send her overseas to study?"

There were people I knew, connections I had made over time—she would have had the best of teachers…but she would not be able to find work there to support herself, and such a life is not inexpensive. I had miscalculated the market, lost too much to recover in time. A man knew a man who knew my broker: we were approached, an offer was made. Mercy was not to be damaged—her virtue maintained. The price…

It sighed, and the tears fell. *We did not understand. The price was too great.*

She was not to have been raped…but the price was paid nonetheless. Traditions were a bitch like that. Sometimes the magic cared about the literal interpretation, and sometimes it went for the heart, the soul of the agreement.

Mercy wasn't innocent any longer. Her purity had been destroyed the moment the deal was carried out. The ki-rin had no choice but to reject her. And it had broken both their hearts.

Ian turned to his left, finally looking away, and we saw that the two of them were not alone. Three figures waited as witness. Two were human, a burly man in a leather jacket who looked more like a biker than a Talent, and a young woman in an elegant suit and expensively styled hair. They both nodded at him, indicating that they had heard the kirin's confession. Next to them, a tall, slender female with dark green hair and skin the color of birch bark closed her eyes once, and nodded as well, her hair falling in front of her face like the limbs of a willow tree.

The *Cosa Nostradamus,* Talent and fatae, had their proof.

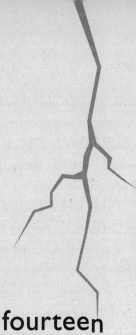

fourteen

I don't know what everyone else did, the next two days. I went home to my apartment, closed the door, and crawled into bed. And stayed there. J's birthday party came and went with only my ping of apology. My mentor was kind enough to let it go, for now. There would be a reckoning, and explanation, later, although I was sure he already knew what had gone down. He had too many contacts within the Council not to know.

When I finally got hungry, I ordered out for Indian food, and let the scent of curry stink up my clothes and my skin, and then crawled back into bed. The shades were drawn against the light, and half the time I didn't even bother to turn on the lights, moving around comfortably in the darkness.

I was beat. Not just physically, but emotionally. The last time I was this drained…it had been when I was in college,

364 Laura Anne Gilman

still, and I'd just discovered that Zaki, my dad, had been murdered because he admired a married woman too obviously. That had been a painful kind of exhaustion. This wasn't. I didn't feel pain, or sorrow, or anything. That was just it. I felt hollow.

Lying on my back, I summoned enough current to project colored lights on the ceiling, my own personal laser show. It was frivolous, and wasteful, and exactly the kind of thing that, if you screwed up and did it in front of Nulls, could cause trouble you couldn't explain away. But here, in my own little cocooned world, it was a distraction and a comfort. If I'd gotten around to buying a stereo, I could have added some of J's beloved Pink Floyd, and the mood would have been complete. Although I was tending more toward Werewolf Church, right now. Something grim and melancholy; hoping that their emotions would jump-start my own.

Current was a science. Hard magic. You knew what you got when you did *A* versus what you got from *B*. In theory, anyway.

Old magic, the wild power, the stuff the fatae lived on… It was messy and inconsistent and couldn't ever be trusted. But it was part of us, too. Passion. Art. Hate. Need. It was the power base of current, the spirit of the law, and would not be denied. I'd forgotten that, for a little while.

I wouldn't ever forget it again.

On the third morning, there was a knock on my door. I seriously considered ignoring it, but it was morning, and I did still have a job—hopefully—and eventually I was going to have to rejoin the rest of the human race.

Besides, my scalp was starting to itch, and I was tired of leftover curry.

I climbed down from my loft, and went to open the door.

"I brought coffee."

Venec. Of course. I took the thermos from him, and stepped back to let him come inside. If I'd been aware of my unwashed hair and curry-scented skin before, I was three times as aware of it now, plus the fact that I'd answered the door in a pair of shorts that shouldn't be worn outside, and a tank top with rude anime on it, neither of which did much to actually cover my body.

"Drink the coffee. Go shower. We have a nine o'clock appointment."

"With who?" Clients met with Ian, not us. So what…

"Council."

Right. Shit. I gulped the coffee, already heading for the bathroom.

I wondered, as the hot water was returning me to a people-appropriate stage, why Venec had come to get me personally. It would have been easier to send a ping. Had he knocked up the others, too? Was Ian collecting them?

The answer came easily, the moment I wondered. He was worried about me. My mood had been reaching him, and he wanted to make sure I was okay, before I had to go face everyone else.

It was sweet, that concern. Kind of annoying, too—both the worry and the fact that I'd been leaking, despite my walls—but it was sweet.

Benjamin Venec was not a man who did sweet easily. Or well, for that matter. I was proud of myself for being mature enough both to recognize that, and to prize it.

By the time I got out of the shower, he was gone. The thermos, and a note scrawled and left on my table were all that reassured me I hadn't hallucinated the entire thing.

177 Union Street, 13th flr

I couldn't remember ever seeing Ben's handwriting before. It was thick and slanted, and I'm sure a specialist could find all sorts of fascinating nibblets about him by studying it. I left the paper on the table and went off to get dressed. No funk this time: Council meant Council clothing. A knee-length navy blue pencil skirt and a cream V-neck sweater that showed just a ladylike hint of cleavage, a gold chain at the collarbone and subtle diamond studs in my ears, one to a lobe, and navy blue shoes with a demure two-inch heel, stockings, and I was ready to go.

The morning sunshine was a little shocking, and the world seemed to have taken a giant leap toward actual spring while I was hibernating. The trees were budding madly, and my eyes started to itch. The pollen count must be skyrocketing. Even so, and even knowing where I was going, and why, it was difficult to keep my mood low. Spring in New York City could be dreary...or magnificent. It was giving us magnificence today.

177 Union Street was a tall stone building, built at the turn of the last century. Ben hadn't needed to leave the address: I knew the building.

The home of the Eastern Council, New York City.

As usual, the Council was insisting on putting their thumbprint on things—once all the work was done. No, be fair, Bonnie: some of the players had been theirs, they had the right.

There was no receptionist in the front lobby, just a large marble desk with an old-fashioned register. I signed in, and noted that the Big Dogs were already there, and Sharon, but not the others. There was a steam-powered elevator that took a lifetime to reach the 13th floor, and it was with considerable relief that I got out intact. I might not be entirely comfortable with elevators, even now, but hydro-electronics just gave me serious heebie-jeebies. I don't care how many decades it had been running without incident in a building filled with Talent, it still wasn't my idea of safe.

"Hi." Like me, Sharon was dressed in subdued colors and classic style—the difference was, that was normal for her. Her blond hair was back in a chignon, and she'd dragged a two-strand pearl set out from somewhere. She so totally channeled the 1940s cool screen-goddess look, I'd be envious if I didn't know it would be a total flop on me.

"The Guys already in?"

"Yes. They said to wait until we were called."

Her hands were laced together, as though to keep them from twitching, and I reached out, on impulse, and covered them with my own. Her skin was cold, too cold for just the air conditioning.

"Hey. It's okay." I left my hands there, trying to give her back some warmth, not even thinking that she might take it the wrong way. She didn't.

"I've never appeared before the Council before," she admitted. "What are we supposed to do, or say?"

I'd forgotten, again, that Ian and I were the only Council-raised members of the pack.

"It's the sentencing phase," I told her, tugging her hands so that she'd follow me over to the row of seats against the wall, and made her sit down next to me, letting go of her hands only because mine were starting to pick up her chill. "We present the evidence against the accused, and the Council members determine punishment."

"You've done this before?"

"Not me, no. My mentor sat on the Council for a while, and used to consult for them, after. I've heard stories."

Before she could ask about those stories—thankfully, because I didn't think they'd calm her nerves much—Ben appeared at the doorway. He didn't bother to look around for us, just pointed a finger, and then crooked it to indicate we both should come with him.

"Once more, dear friends…"

Sharon almost giggled, then she caught herself, and we marched into the Council chamber with suitably solemn and professional expressions.

What I hadn't told Sharon was that we shouldn't have been there. Council didn't hear testimony from peons, and we were assuredly peons. Ian should have been handling this. So why had they called on us?

I didn't bother to ask: we'd find out soon enough.

Despite lonejack assumptions, the Seated Council isn't a formal body. At any given time there are about twenty members, and only half of them are considered active, although everyone tends to stick their thumb in the pie. When we walked in, the long board table had fourteen people seated behind it, so they had called out a considerable number for this. I tried not to let my uncertainty reach Sharon; the last thing she needed to know was that the Council was on high alert.

The Big Dogs knew, though. Venec's suit should have been my warning sign: he was a good dresser—and occasionally a hot one, as his club gear had shown—but today's outfit would have done a senior VP investment banker proud, with just the right hang to announce that it was bespoke, and just enough style to show he was alert and comfortable with himself. Stosser was...Stosser. His suit was a traditional navy that could have come from the same store as Sharon's gray pinstripe, this year's fashion with a timeless dress boot underneath that he'd probably owned since he was my age, and had resoled every few years. And topping it all off, he had slicked back his long red hair into a ponytail, and tied it with a matching navy cord. I wondered, for the first time, how many times his family had gotten on his case to cut it short, and blend in.

Like Ian Stosser was ever going to blend.

"And who are these children?" the woman in the middle asked. Sharon got her chin up at that, but I bit back a grin. Luce Jackson could call just about anyone in the city a child. J had once hazarded a guess that she was at least 93, and maybe older. Still sharper than the proverbial tack, the terror of her entire family, and the iron hand behind half a dozen liberal charities up and down the eastern seaboard.

"Madame, may I present Sharon Mendelssohn, one of our

top field operatives, and Bonita Torres, who is our finest lab technician."

Technically speaking, we didn't have a lab, much less technicians, but I merely stepped forward and presented myself with a formal head-and-shoulder bob. Sharon did the same, about half a second behind me.

"And you have brought them here to testify?"

"If the Council wishes confirmation of details, they are the ones best to answer," Ian said, smooth as cream.

"All right. Let them be seated until called."

Our relief was probably visible as we retreated to the cushioned chairs along the back wall of this room, as several of the Council members chuckled softly. But it was a sympathetic sound, not a harsh one, so my anxiety level went down a bit, and I could practically feel Sharon unclenching her jaw and loosening her shoulders.

"The Council is here this morning to consider the instance of an attack against a sovereign fatae, the Honorable Si-Ja and his companion, the Talent Mercy Trin, and the resulting death of the Talent Roger Mack and injury given to the Talent Aren Geb. All parties have stated their rendition of the events, and there is a clear conflict between all versions. We have therefore requested that the situation be investigated, to determine where the truth lays. Ian Stosser has already presented to us their findings, with a rather... complicated explanation of the events."

Just the people named. Not the man who had started all this: he was not their concern, he was not Council. But word was out: his community would pass judgment. It wasn't our job. Our job was to find the truth. No matter what it took. The sour feeling in my stomach? That was just part of the job.

The members started arguing with each other over interpreting the testimony that Ian and Ben had already given, and I listened with one ear in case we were called on, and let the rest of my attention rest on the Big Dogs. Stosser was restless, tapping his finger against the knee that was crossed over his other leg, staring fixedly at something. Ben, on the other hand, looked like he had all the time in the world, and nowhere he'd rather be than sitting right there. I let down my wall just a bit, and was splashed with a wave of tension, agitation, annoyance, and, deep into the core of all that, a sense of anger that the Council had to even discuss the matter.

Poor Venec. He really was such a lonejack.

Thinking of that made me think of the men who had attacked Mercy, trying to scare her into silence. Lonejacks, probably. Fatae-haters. There was no justice there, except the beat-down we had given them: but they were still out there. Lurking. Building hatred, and there was nothing we could do to stop them. Not until, unless, someone hired us...and then it would be too late.

"Ms. Torres."

I almost jumped when they called my name, only that part of my attention I'd given over to the Council murmur keeping me from being totally startled. I swallowed, stood up, and walked slowly forward. Better me than Sharon, was all I could think; she had audibly yelped when they called my name, what would she have done if they'd called her?

"Ms. Torres. You were the investigator on the scene, who collected the primary evidence, is that correct?"

"Yes, ma'am."

"And as part of that evidence, you, ah…gleaned the emotions from the scene of the attack?"

I hesitated, not sure how to proceed. Was this a trick question?

Into my hesitation came a gentle wave of reassurance. *answer the question* Ben told me.

Right then. I took a deep breath, and pushed my shoulders into a comfortable "at attention" posture. "Ma'am, no. I did not garner emotions from the scene because there were no strong emotions attached to the signatures we were collecting."

"Are you sure that you simply were not able to sense those emotions? Empathy is a very rare skill, and you were no doubt overwhelmed by the scene itself."

That came from another member, a—comparatively—younger male. He was trying not to be patronizing, but I still wanted to bare my teeth and snap at him. I resisted the urge.

"No, sir. We are not reading emotions themselves." And anyway, J was of the opinion that most so-called empaths were frauds. "We collect signature, and often if the caster was strongly…motivated, we will find that within the signature itself, like…like an inclusion in a diamond. There were no such inclusions at the time." And because I couldn't let the implied slap go by, I added, "We are trained professionals, sir. The scene is processed carefully, and our own feelings do not enter into our notes or our evaluations."

"But you were disturbed by the scene?" he insisted.

"Sir. A woman had been assaulted, a man was dead. Another man was injured and a ki-rin had been distressed. It was our duty to determine the cause. Any personal feelings were secondary and not to be allowed to intervene." Oh, god, I could have been one of J's hoitier toitier Council contacts, with that response. It did the job, though.

They let me sit down, and started arguing together. I settled in for a long haul, but it took them about ten minutes to come to some consensus.

"We have heard the arguments. We have heard the evidence. We are in agreement."

My breath caught, and I swallowed hard. Mercy...what price would they impose on Mercy for her foolish greed?

"For the attack on the ki-rin's companion, no matter the reason, Aren Geb shall pay to the ki-rin a blood-price of one gold coin."

That was the price they placed on Mercy's... I bit down my anger. Mercy had been a participant, however traumatized. A single gold coin was a traditional sum, and nothing more than saving face with the fatae, so that none could say the Council did not address the damage done.

"For the use of the solemn bond between ki-rin and companion for foul purpose, and for arranging the death of Roger Mack for another's gain, we charge Aren Geb with murder."

There was a release of air in the room, as though a dozen invisible people had let out a sigh, all at once. It creeped me out; bad enough that Pietr could disappear—there was an entire room of them? But nobody else seemed to notice.

"For the betrayal of the solemn bond between ki-rin and companion, the girl Mercy Trin has already been punished more than any might mete out. For her part in arranging the death of Roger Mack for another's gain, we change her with murder."

Sharon sighed, and even Ian looked saddened, although his expression never changed. Stupid, foolish, greedy girl. The Council decrees were not law, as such, but they had the force of tradition behind them, and even lonejacks and Gypsies followed a murder conviction. By the end of the week every Talent in the country would know what they had done.

The punishment was shunning. Not to speak, not to touch, not to acknowledge in any way that the shunned was Talent. They were no longer a part of the *Cosa Nostradamus*.

Mercy...as damaged as she already was by this, by what she had done...

Hopefully Mash would still take care of her, despite the shunning. Alone, she wouldn't last a year, not in that state.

I didn't give a damn about Aren Geb.

"And what of the ki-rin?"

Ben. Standing up straight and angry in his expensive suit, his voice calm, but his gaze met each of the Council members in turn, and I was insanely proud of him, an emotion that surprised me.

"What of the ki-rin's involvement, Council members?"

Luce stood, matching him gaze for gaze. Her face seemed even more seamed and wrinkled than it had when I arrived, but her back was straight and her voice didn't waver or crack.

"The ki-rin is out of our concern." The words were soft, but firm. Ben waited, then bowed his head to the truth of that, and stood down.

And then it was over, and we were leaving the Council chambers, solemn and silent. Stosser waved us on, stopping to talk to someone who had not been in the chamber.

Nobody said anything until we were in the elevator, and the doors slid shut in front of us, the sound of water rushing behind us.

"The ki-rin was just as guilty as the others," Sharon said, stabbing at the control panel as though it were a Council member.

"I know." Venec, standing next to me, sounded really, really tired. I didn't dare look at him, afraid it would be too much and I'd crack.

"The fatae won't punish it though, will they?" Sharon went on, as the elevator slid down thirteen floors. "They'll call it a human affair, and brush it under the rug, because the ki-rin is too precious, too rare to be involved with anything so base as murder for hire. Because it had to be the human's fault, not their precious ki-rin."

I wanted to say something to counter her bitterness, but there was nothing to say. She was right.

"There are rules, Sharon," Venec said, and his sorrow and anger rasped against me like a physical thing. He repeated more softly, as though to himself, about something entirely different, "There are rules. The fatae are not ours to discipline."

Without looking down I couldn't say whose hand found

the other, his or mine, but the touch of skin to skin, brushing fingertips, calmed us both, not erasing the anger, but making it a smoother, quieter thing.

By the time we got back to the office, Ian having joined us en route, that calm was shattered.

The rest of the pack was gathered in the main room, but the coffee carafe was full, the newspapers untouched, and Pietr was a blurry outline of gray misery. Even Nick looked like someone had poured a bucket of soggy onto him.

"What happened?" Ian asked, even as Ben gave a quick once-around the room, looking for clues, anything that was out of place or threatening.

"The ki-rin." Pietr answered for all of them. "Bonnie, Danny called this morning, looking for you. He thought we'd want to know. The ki-rin..."

"It killed itself, didn't it?" I said softly, and at his jerky nod a sense of dread I'd been carrying without even knowing it slipped down my spine and crashed to the floor.

There are rules.

I'd known. Mercy's misery, the ki-rin's stony silence... the refusal of the Council to say or do anything against the ki-rin... It was a noble beast that had done something terrible for love. There was no way it could go on pretending it hadn't happened...and no way it could live with the fact that it had.

"A ritual slaying," Nick said, picking up the story, as I went to sit down next to Pietr, letting my head rest against his shoulder. I wasn't sure, but I thought that his outline solidified a little, and he came more clearly into view, when

I touched him. Venec stayed where he was, in the doorway, still as though he were carved from stone.

"It had a sword, or got a sword, and fell on it, right through the breastbone. I can't imagine too many people other than a ki-rin know exactly where their breastbone is, much less how to puncture it…so it's a suicide. Case closed. Nothing for us to investigate."

"No," Ian said quietly, his voice more terrible than any lamentations. "Nothing for you to investigate." He paused, then turned and went into the inner office, closing the door behind him, leaving us there. We were finished. Case closed.

Normally after a case, we'd go drinking to celebrate. This time…nobody seemed in the mood.

"This job sucks," Nick said, and someone let out a ragged laugh of agreement.

I looked up, and met Venec's gaze. His eyes were hooded, his skin tired-looking, but there was a stillness to him that wasn't sadness, or anger, or frustration but a sense of something else I couldn't quite grasp.

"They chose their own paths," he said, talking to all of us, but looking right at me. *Into* me. "The job sucks, but you all did it well, with honor, and with respect." He paused. "I'm proud of you. And so is Ian, even if he's too much of an ass to remember to say it. Now go home. Get some rest. Drink yourselves into oblivion, if that's what it takes. I don't want to see any of you here until next Monday."

The others didn't wait for him to change his mind, and nobody seemed to notice that I stayed on the sofa, not moving as they all grabbed their stuff and disappeared out the door.

And then it was just the two of us, staring at each other from across the room.

"Bonnie…"

He sounded so tired, I didn't have the heart to say whatever it was I thought I needed to say. I just got up, and walked across the room, and put my arms up around his shoulders, bringing him forward so I could whisper in his ear. "We're proud of you, too, boss."

And then I kissed him on the cheek, and went home.

★ ★ ★ ★ ★

Don't miss the next investigation in
TRICKS OF THE TRADE

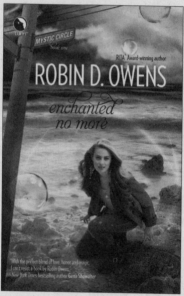

PRESENTING...THE SEVENTH ANNUAL
MORE THAN WORDS™ ANTHOLOGY

Five bestselling authors
Five real-life heroines

This year's Harlequin
More Than Words award
recipients have changed lives,
one good deed at a time. To
celebrate these real-life heroines,
some of Harlequin's most
acclaimed authors have honored
the winners by writing stories
inspired by these dedicated
women. Within the pages
of *More Than Words Volume 7*,
you will find novellas written
by Carly Phillips, Donna Hill
and Jill Shalvis—and online at
www.HarlequinMoreThanWords.com
you can also access stories by
Pamela Morsi and Meryl Sawyer.

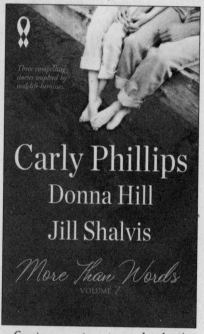

Coming soon in print and online!

Visit
www.HarlequinMoreThanWords.com
to access your FREE ebooks and to nominate
a real-life heroine in your community.

MTWV7763CSTR